A R E V I V E D

M O D E R N

C L A S S I C

EFRAIM'S BOOK

ALSO BY ALFRED ANDERSCH

The Father of a Murderer

ALFRED ANDERSCH
EFRAIM'S BOOK

TRANSLATED FROM THE GERMAN
BY RALPH MANHEIM

A NEW DIRECTIONS BOOK

Copyright © 1967 by Diogenes Verlag AG Zurich
Translation Copyright © 1970 by Doubleday, a division of Bantam Doubleday Dell
Publishing Group, Inc.
Published by arrangement with Doubleday, a division of Bantam Doubleday Dell
Publishing Group, Inc.

Manufactured in the United States of America
New Directions Books are printed on acid-free paper
First published clothbound by Doubleday in 1970
First published as New Directions Paperbook 779 in 1994
Published simultaneously in Canada by Penguin Books Limited
Design by Raymond Davidson

Library of Congress Cataloging-in-Publication Data

Andersch, Alfred.
   [Ephraim.   English]
   Efraim's book / Alfred Andersch ; translated by Ralph Manheim.
       p.   cm. — (Revived modern classic)
   Originally published: Garden City, N.Y. : Doubleday, 1970. With new introd.
   ISBN 0-8112-1262-9
   I. Title.   II. Series.
PT2601.N353E313   1994
833'.914—dc20   93-38230
                                                         CIP

New Directions Books are published for James Laughlin
by New Directions Publishing Corporation,
80 Eighth Avenue, New York 10011

For G.

Note

The passage in italics on pages 41–42, *somewhere very far away* etc., is taken from Chris Marker's novel *Le coeur net*. The sentence on page 150, beginning *On at least one occasion*, is a quotation from the testimony of Henryk Poswolski at the Treblinka trial (*Frankfurter Allgemeine Zeitung*, April 13, 1965). The passage *We saw an enormous fire* etc., on pages 150, and 304, is taken from the testimony of the witness Dr. Ella Lingens at the Auschwitz trial (Bernd Naumann, *Auschwitz*, Frankkfurt a/M, 1965).

Efraim's Book

One

On towards four in the morning it starts to rain. Awakened by the sound, I switch on the bedside lamp and raise my wristwatch to my short-sighted eyes. Then I grope for my glasses, put out the light, get up and go to the window. When I went to bed, at two, I did not draw the curtains. My hotel room looks out on empty space. The rain whishes through the cold beam of the floodlights on top of the concrete posts around the loading yard. I see two lorries and a black Mercedes, the rain splattering against their black roofs. Beyond the vacant lot the curve of the Stadtbahn, lighted by lamps with yellow globes, forms a dull-gold arc ending at the point where the tracks vanish under the dome of the Zoological Gardens station. The tracks are deserted and silent, but won't be for long; soon the Stadtbahn will be starting up again. Later, a little after seven, it will be light and the Interzone train from Frankfurt will come along. I have watched it on each of the two days I have spent in Berlin, and decided to take it for my return journey. The outbound train leaves Berlin at 19:39. You have to book a berth well in advance. I didn't care for that landing in Tempelhof on Thursday afternoon. For a moment it looked as if the wings were going to graze the rooftops. That was unpleasant. But then I was in the Berlin autumn, cool, colour against a white backdrop. Now Berlin is getting a bath. Perhaps autumn will be over tomorrow, this autumn whose translucence I hadn't really remembered. The rainy night outside makes me think of an unlighted shop window; the objects seem to reflect the street lights and I try to recognize them, but all I can make out is the loading yard, the Stadtbahn tracks, the Zoological Gardens station, and on the left the row of lamps on Fasenenstrasse vanishing behind the squat dark mass of the Jewish Community

Centre. It occupies the site of the old synagogue that was burned down. I passed it yesterday. A few fragments of the old synagogue, picked out of the ruins, have been fitted very skilfully into the façade of the new building: a door frame, for instance, and a column. Until half-past eight yesterday evening I was determined to leave Berlin as soon as possible. But at half-past eight I met Anna Krystek. We wandered about until two. The feelings she inspired were not exactly new to me; but on the strength of similar experience I can expect our relationship to keep me busy for a while. Perhaps it will make me prolong my stay in Berlin. I go back to the bed, take off my glasses and lie down again. I feel wretched. The evening has been tiring. At forty-two I don't take drink as well as I used to. Without my glasses the window is only a grey spot with the rain whishing behind it. The worst of it is that I can't get drunk any more, no matter how much I drink. I just feel wretched afterwards, especially if I've smoked a good deal. Consequently I seldom drink these days. Anna drank very little. I felt obliged to drink in her company. She is twenty-three and I didn't want her to see that my body is already giving me problems. In the end my body falls asleep but my mind continues to wander. I am pursued by a nightmare in which I keep packing a suitcase. Meg is prodding me because we have to catch a train, but the packing doesn't get ahead. My arms and legs move very very slowly and I am unable to speed them up. I wake up in torment shortly after seven; I seldom sleep any later. Although like all newspapermen I often have to stay up late at night, I am an early riser. I usually make up for it by napping for an hour after lunch.

I get up and look out the window again. The same weather as yesterday and the day before, middling bordering on fair, with a dash of sun; it's still too early to tell whether what I see overhead is a perfectly clear sky or a thin, white, homogeneous layer of clouds. In any case the rain during the night has brought no change in the weather. The Interzone train passes. I've made a date with Anna for five in the afternoon. The thought of it is upsetting to me now, embarrassing. True, I consider myself in love with Anna, but the thought that when we meet I shall have to exert myself courting her, as they call it, strikes me as absurd. I'm past that age; whenever I become involved in this process, I hear the mechanism creaking at the joints. But few women are willing to forgo the ancient rites. I have no idea what Anna actually expects of me. The phone rings. London calling. The phone is beside my bed. I sit on the bed with my legs crossed, waiting for Keir's words of reproach. A cavernous silence, the silence of Keir's flat in Holborn, those messy grimy rooms in Chichester Rents, the sleeping quarters of an aged animal. My room here is modern with all the comforts of a first-class hotel, grey wall-to-wall carpeting and Danish furniture. I hear Keir clearing his throat and then, as he waits for the connection, sing a verse from the "Ballad of Mary Hamilton": "Arise, arise, Mary Hamilton," he sings, "arise and come with me, there is a wedding in Glasgow Town, this night we'll go and see." This "wedding" means gallows, the gallows-wedding that awaits Mary Hamilton because she has set her illegitimate child adrift in a frail bark on the ocean. My only thought, as I listen, is that there is a quarter in Berlin called Wedding. Keir Horne sings in an undertone; the walls of the small room in which he is phoning—everything in it is covered with dust—absorb the rumble of his drinker's voice. Then he falls silent, coughs, and finally says my name in its English form, George, which suddenly strikes me as odd because last night Anna kept calling me Georg. I answer and Keir asks with annoyance whether I've been listening the whole time. When I say that I like to hear him sing, he tells me in a roar not to change the subject and starts finding fault with my dispatches, which, he declares, can't even be used as human interest stories. For a while we discuss the Island. This is the big day, he says; today the Russians will make it known whether or not they intend to dismantle their offensive bases off the American coast. I try to conceal the fact that I am not up on the developments. Last night Anna knew more about it than I did. She gave me an analysis of the situation from her point of view. Comrade K., she said, is a traitor. I pass on her words to

Keir as my opinion: K. would knuckle under, nothing would happen. That, says Keir, is quite possible, but no reason for me to be
roaming around in Berlin. I tell him that nothing is going on here
(which is true) and that no one is in the least bit excited (which
is an out-and-out lie). Last night at Lampe's they were all talking
about the arrest of the editors of *Die Revue* and marginally
about the Island. *Marginally* is a new cliché in Germany that I
hadn't heard before. All sorts of new expressions have come up.
Speaking of his new film, Lampe said he was just beginning *to
tune into* it. When Keir says there's plenty of material in Berlin,
his turn of phrase strikes me as feeble compared to that of a German newspaperman who told me that here I was "on the wire."
I slip into German and explain some of the new expressions to
Keir. As he listens with apparent interest and assures me that I
have never been so close to the "wire" as now, I lie back on the
bed and look up at the ceiling, framed in a plaster frieze. That
makes it an old-style Berlin hotel room after all; they've just
modernized it, and very cleverly too. Keir is speaking English
again: he asks me, since I've just come from Rome, what could be
meant by *a proposition to view the ruins of Rome*. I catch on at
once: he's been doing *The Times* crossword the whole time. I
should have known it; it comes out in the Saturday edition and
Keir sits over it until Tuesday or Wednesday. He can dictate a
political column and be working out solutions at the same time.
The difficulty of these puzzles is that you first have to analyze
the clues. The formulation of the clues is a puzzle in itself. I am a
total failure at it. I speak and write English fluently but seldom
succeed in understanding a single clue in *The Times* crossword,
a clear indication of my relation to the country of which I have
become a citizen. I haven't the faintest idea what *a proposition
to view the ruins of Rome* is supposed to make me think of. Keir
asks me insidiously if at least I know who is *the lowest of
women we hear*. Surely *The Times* isn't interested in a term for
a certain professional group. I break off the game, which is one of
Keir's ways of reminding me now and then that I don't belong,

that I'm not one of *them*. He's been doing this kind of thing for years, almost unintentionally; if I were to point out his intention, he would feel ashamed. Suddenly I am interested in knowing whether Keir is sitting in his old rocking chair, whether he is shaved or unshaven, how much he drank last night, whether he is tired or feeling rested. He patiently provides the information, he knows my mania for such investigation. He is sitting in the rocking chair, he is unshaven, he drank no more than his usual quantity of beer—enormous—and he's feeling fine at the moment. I feel tempted to transform my simple inquiries into a delving for reasons. I might ask for instance: "Why do you drink? Why do you do crosswords? Why do you live alone?" And I imagine him answering: "I'm an old man. It's my right." "You're only sixty-three," I say, "most men don't give up until they're older." "The poor fools," he answers with a laugh. It goes without saying that my questioning degenerated into no such dialogue. Such conversations take place on the stage, not in real life. Besides, he would have given me very different answers from those I have just imagined. Keir is indeed an old man and he does live alone, but he has not by any means given up, and he would not speak of old men who do not give up as poor fools. This whole imaginary dialogue stems from my wishful thinking; it is only because I have certain reasons for wanting Keir to give up that in my imagination I make him express opinions that are not his. I suspend the inquisition. My simple questions—those I have really asked—have told me all I want to know. In return I tell him about my activities last night, about my visit to Lampe's, and about Anna whom I met there. I make it sound as if I were very much interested in Anna; I don't want Keir to think that I'm still bogged down in my relationship with Meg. He listens attentively, asks no questions. When I've finished, I go back to the beginning of our conversation. I ask Keir if he wants me to believe that we would be willing to die for Berlin. That's "nowhere," I say, lapsing again into the German jargon. Keir explains that he believes in the sacred number three. There would be three world wars revolving around Germany; two were too few. Keir believes in fate. He believes in reason as well; but reason has taught him that time spins destinies. Reason is a small clockwork mechanism that ticks in the great machine of time. As for me, I believe neither in fate nor in reason. There is nothing but a vast confusion. Things happen or do not happen, men come and go, do this or that, after which something happens or does not happen. Everything is always possible or impossible. There are no laws and there is no freedom. For instance, it is utterly without significance that at this moment, on Sunday, 28 October 1962, shortly after seven A.M., I should be lying in a Berlin hotel room talking on the phone to Keir Horne in London, in other words forming words and sentences which are conveyed over a system of thin wires, while in the same way other words and sentences are slipping as though drawn by a bodkin into the acoustic duct of my left ear.

I shall try to reconstruct the exact wording of the next part of our telephone conversation, because I literally writhe when I think of the *gaffe* I committed. The only way in which I can appease the disagreeable feeling that comes over me when I remember how deeply I hurt Keir is to set down my blunder in writing. By way of proving my contention that nothing would happen, I say that the people of Berlin are peaceful, law-abiding folk. Some few years ago they killed a few hundred thousand children with poison gas, and since then they have known that it didn't matter much what became of them. At first there was no response from Keir. The pause should have been a warning to me. Then he managed to answer.

"George, it was only a very few Germans who did that to the children."

"I know," I say, "the rest only looked on or fought for the very few, or knew nothing about it."

"I didn't know anything about it either. Anyway, not right away."

His answer has come quickly. I can't help seeing his face, fat, bloated with drink under a mop of white hair, bushy white brows over dust-grey eyes. And now I hear him weeping; the tears from his dusty eyes must be dripping down over his drinker's face. All at once the rumpled bed I am lying on is a trap; I feel caught in it. I cry out to Keir: he mustn't be angry, I really hadn't been thinking of anything in particular. He pulls himself together and asks if I've found anything out about Esther. I tell him I'm working on it. I don't want to tell him now, over the phone, what I heard on Friday afternoon from a certain Frau Schlesinger who is living in the Jewish Old People's Home. Or that last night Anna Krystek had hit on a new idea of how Esther might be traced. Even if my acquaintance with Anna should turn out to be unimportant, it looks as though the investigating I promised to do for Keir would keep me in Berlin. That doesn't suit me at all.

I hear Keir saying he won't be able to keep me much longer. It doesn't come as a surprise. He told me as much in his last phone calls to Rome. I repeat my request that he should fire me soon, I don't want him to hold it up to me again that he by-passed our Bonn bureau in ordering me directly from Rome to Berlin. I wasn't keen on this assignment. I like Rome, I'd rather have stayed there. I think I must have been thinking out loud, or perhaps Keir reads my thoughts; he says that in sending me to Berlin he had wanted to give me a last chance.

"I thought it would shake you up. The trouble started in Rome. All of a sudden you started writing literature."

"Literature?"

"That's right, bloody literature! Instead of news!"

He shouts. Because he wept before, he has to shout now. I hold the receiver at a distance. Actually he's losing his grip on the job just as much as I am, but for different reasons. But unlike me he doesn't know it yet. At a suitable distance from my ear his telephonic bellowing becomes a high monotonous scream. Keir is always in top form so early in the morning. He regularly drinks until two A.M., then he dozes off in his rocker. At seven he wakes up stone-cold sober and calls up his foreign correspondents or one of his department heads. You never know whose turn it will be to be ruthlessly jolted out of a sound sleep. Then he goes to bed and sleeps peacefully until noon. From one o'clock on he works hard at the office, often until midnight, especially on Friday when our magazine goes to press. When the screaming stops I bring back the receiver to my ear and ask Keir if he has seen Meg. She was in the office yesterday, he tells me. Keir overflows with sarcastic admiration for her photographs of industrial England. I haven't seen my wife in a year; all I know is that she has spent the summer in the Midlands, which is just like her. She has dropped me postcards from Birmingham, Nottingham and Stoke-on-Trent. I invited her to visit me in Rome but she didn't come.

"You can't imagine what she's done with the wall of an old marmalade factory in Liverpool! Meg is first-rate, George!"

The admiration in Keir's tone is genuine, the sarcasm false and superimposed. In Keir's attitude towards Meg there has never been room for criticism. He tells me that Cameron has engaged her as artistic adviser on his new film. Yes, Meg is an outstanding photographer. I ask Keir to give her my regards. He says he will. Then he wishes me good luck and abruptly hangs up. I hear the click.

For a moment I listen to the void. The hum, which I should like to interpret as the humming of space between London and Berlin, but is simply static, has stopped. Then I press down the cradle and order breakfast. I go into the bathroom and start shaving. I lather my face and adjust my razor blade. I shave methodically, beginning with the cheeks, then passing over the chin to the neck, and last the upper lip. It goes quickly and pleasantly because I haven't a tough beard. In the mirror I see, in the usual shaving grimaces, the face of a small thin man: the forehead and cheek bones not too pronounced but still clearly delineated; the nose slender, somewhat pendulous; dark-blue, slightly staring eyes behind rimless glasses; the long line of the mouth between thin lips; smooth black hair cut short. All in all, a typical newspaperman's face; not what people expect of a reporter, not the face of a panting dog but, as Meg once said while studying me in the viewfinder of her Leica, a dry, parched landscape waiting for water, for salvation, for redemption. She's right; for me news chemistry is a branch of the science of salvation; I have got into the habit of analyzing the rain of news items for the promises of salvation they may contain, though of course I have no idea what manner of salvation I expect. Keir warned me long ago. During the war, as we were listening to one of Hitler's speeches in the canteen of our radio station, he suddenly said: "When you come down to it, the whole idea of redemption is immoral—anybody who shouts 'Heil' is suspect."

I've almost finished shaving when the waiter brings in my breakfast. From the pile of books and magazines I collected on Friday and yesterday, I pick out the latest number of *Die Revue*. As I leaf through it, it seems hopelessly out of date because it appeared before the editors were arrested and the editorial offices occupied by the police. I make a habit of eating breakfast alone and reading the paper over it. Even when I am in London staying with Meg, I avoid having breakfast with her. I get up as early as possible, make my own coffee, and devour the morning papers. Today, while chewing my bread and jam, I concentrate on a photograph of the cabinet minister who had the editors arrested. A soulless, intelligent face. The features are not unpleasant, but so encased in solid flesh that they can hardly be seen. The fat flesh in which his eyes and mouth are buried gives him an expression of good-natured brutality. A shrewd bar-fly, who does his business over drinks—you might even be able to win him over to a good cause if you knew how to flatter his ambition. The man has humour, he's base but genial. At present everyone is trying to puncture his humour, the innocent enjoyment he derives from putting his detractors in jail. If the humour is ever driven out of him, he may be dangerous. He's already malignant. But he's not a new Hitler. Everyone I've discussed him with since my arrival in Berlin thinks he has the makings of a Hitler. That's nonsense. He hasn't got Hitler's narrow, rigid, abysmally gloomy murderer's

face, that face which changed only when the mouth opened wide
to eject its knife-like scream. Hate as the orgasm of an impotent
murderer. This man isn't impotent. He's not a water drinker, non-
smoker or vegetarian. He's just a jailer who likes to drink with the
prisoners. Still, it's something that they're putting up with min-
isters with such faces again. That would appeal to Keir. Though
our *Weekly Review* isn't leftwing, though it's not even as half
as liberal as *The Guardian*, Keir wouldn't hesitate to publish a
critical portrait of the minister. Odd that I should have landed on
a conservative paper. Actually all this could be said more amiably
in English. The manner would be amiable, well-behaved, com-
monsensical, glacially aloof to be sure, but not inhuman. I sit
down at the desk, move up the typewriter and put in paper. I let
my fingers roam over the keys, push away the mound of agency
releases that I can do nothing with. Having smoked too much last
night, I force myself not to reach for a cigarette. Instead of writing about the minister I write: "The autumn in Berlin is clear,
dry and still. The people who were out walking yesterday in the
Berlin Municipal Forest were disturbed only by the occasional
rat-tat-tat of an extra-heavy machine gun which, practising on the
far shore of the Havel, brings to mind the news reports about the
Island. The water conveyed the sound from Sakrow, which belongs
to the Russians, over here to the 'West.' When I was a boy, the
Berlin Municipal Forest was called the Potsdam Forest. We used
to play cops and robbers there. When I left it yesterday, I crossed
the bridge between Stölpchensee and Pohlesee. I did not turn
into Bismarckstrasse, but went on in the direction of Kohlhasen-
bruck until I found a cab to take me back to the city." Keir would
shake his head if he read that. For the first time in many years I
have written something in German. I'm still sitting around in my
pyjamas. I take the paper out of the typewriter, crumple it and
throw it in the wastepaper basket, go back to the bathroom and
turn on the shower. I remove my wrist-watch, undress and shower.
My body is as thin as my face, no longer young and not yet old,
covered with pale but not pasty skin. Copious dark hair on my

chest and sexual parts. My legs are firm and powerful; with these legs I can walk far and fast. I dry myself. Before leaving the bathroom I arrange my toilet articles pedantically on the glass shelf over the wash basin. In the room I put on fresh underwear and my grey flannel suit—I brought only this one suit from Rome because I had planned to spend no more than three days in Berlin. Standing at the wardrobe mirror I put on a dark-green knitted tie. Black shoes, not pointed, with well-worn soles; I tie my shoe laces at the window, resting first one foot then the other on the radiator; the two lorries and the black Mercedes, from whose roofs the rain splashed back in little fountains last night, are still down below: because it is Sunday nothing has changed in the loading yard. I have made up my mind not to postpone my visit to Bismarckstrasse any longer. Late Sunday morning is a good time for it. I remember my watch, take it from the bathroom and wind it before putting it on. It's only a little past eight, still too early. With a glance at the books and magazines lying around I think of reading to kill time, but I feel closed in, restless. I slip on my raincoat.

There are not many people in the lobby downstairs, the breakfast room is deserted. The night clerk hasn't been relieved yet; busy over the register, he gives me a cold greeting. The morning papers are lying on the reception desk, I buy a few and, standing in the entrance hall, leaf through them. In reading the articles and advertisements I am struck by the unfamiliar words and word conglomerates. I have the impression that the tone has changed since the old days. While living outside Germany I have had considerable contact with the German language. I worked with it during the war after Keir took me on at his propaganda radio station, but that's not the same as being inside. Just recently I spoke German for half an hour every morning with Baron Collaudi, an Austrian film broker and an operator of the melancholy type, in the small windowless lounge, lighted day and night by frosted light bulbs, of the Albergo Byron where we both lived. The clientele of the Byron consisted of small film producers, publishers, politicians,

journalists, and relatively successful writers and actors in symbio-
sis with parasites who are useful to them: impoverished gamblers
and confidence men, who know who is connected with whom and
what, remember obscure affairs, and provide tips. By and large the
denizens of the Byron are connoisseurs, drawn by the moderate
prices and the atmosphere of the Spanish Steps–Via Veneto
quarter. The lift in the Byron is not as ancient as the old Roman
hotel itself, but it too is as old as the hills, and in its creaking cage
I made the acquaintance of the baron and of Lorenza, his young
Italian fiancée, a buxom and beautiful girl, very much concerned with her virtue. Like myself, Collaudi had one of those
rooms on the sixth floor that cost only two thousand lire. Low-
ceilinged rooms that hold the heat, but from their windows one
can look out over the roofs of Rome and listen to the melodious
cries that rise up from the chasm of Via Borgognona. I had got
into the habit of chatting with the baron for half an hour every
morning in the lounge. Like all the visitors to this dreary place,
who occupied the ornate uncomfortable chairs along the walls, we
spoke in a whisper because the room was so small that conversation in a normal tone of voice would have intruded on the others.
The baron knows just about everyone who frequents this place of
spurious discretion and was always introducing me to people I
had no desire to meet. I don't really know why I took up with him,
perhaps because he has the so-called sixth sense, as he has several
times intimated; it has not escaped him that my relations with
journalism are not as they should be. But perhaps he is simply a
close observer, who saw that I usually had time on my hands and
judged accordingly. In asking me to go into business with him
he wanted to help me. He expounded his theory that the business
world was dominated by the principle of disloyalty and that this
was the basis of freedom. A good businessman should not be dis-
honest, that was a vulgar delusion stemming from total ignorance,
but he must feel free to change his partners when necessary. In
his ingratiating Austrian German, the aristocratic version of the
popular dialect, the baron held forth: Liberalism, after all, was a

product of the merchant class and its sole foundation was the right to change business connections. For instance, when a man was on the downgrade, you had to drop him; not only was this the secret of success in business, it was also an act of freedom. "You seem," I broke in, "to define tolerance as understanding for the struggle for existence and freedom as the rejection of human sympathy." But Collaudi easily disposed of my objections.

"Take yourself, Herr Efraim. As a journalist you seem to be on the downgrade, or am I wrong?"

"Yes, probably," I admitted, without so much as a pang.

"Well, then, would it strike you as unjust if I said I wouldn't bet two cents on your future—as a newspaperman, that is?"

Despite his theories the baron does not give the impression of a cold realist but rather of an easy-going eccentric, which may be one reason why I have almost made friends with him. Heavily seated in one of the Albergo Byron's gilded chairs, he let his cigarette ash fall on his suit. I have never found out whether he should be reckoned among the rich or the poor inhabitants of the hotel. Sometimes the big business deals he spoke of struck me as quite credible, and then a moment later I suspected him of wanting to borrow money from me. His idea of my turning businessman is not so bad; I consider it seriously. Arranging for the financing of films, organizing co-productions, dreaming up projects is a pleasantly unprincipled and anonymous occupation which occasionally brings in a lot of money. I have some of the requirements: I know the film industry and I've had experience in public relations; I speak several languages; the baron wasn't crazy. We sat smoking in the dreary lounge. On the wall facing us a heliogravure dating from around 1900 in a heavy black frame showed two lovers walking in the woods, so intent on themselves that they fail to notice the young monk who is looking after them, envious of their happiness. The title is finely engraved below: *Painful Memories.* A very odd picture for the sitting room of a Roman hotel. At ten o'clock Lorenza called for us; bejewelled and fresh, she had already been to the hairdresser's. Together we went out through the glaring sun and shadow to the dark Caffè Greco round the corner, where we drank *espresso* at the bar. On my last morning in Rome, just before I drove out to Fiumicino (my car is still in the airport car park, my bags at the Byron), the baron asked me again to go into partnership with him on my return from Berlin. I push the revolving door and step out on Kurfürstendamm, which is almost deserted this early Sunday morning. Here and there a car, mostly headed westward in the direction of Grunewald—people wanting to walk in the country of a Sunday morning. A well-dressed couple crosses over from the traffic island on the corner of Joachimsthalerstrasse; he tall and well-built, with the air of a man about town, English-type beard; she considerably younger, skinny, the gamine type, holding his arm. With his left hand he is leading two Afghan hounds on a double lead. Nice-looking people, strikingly so. I've seen a lot of nice-looking people in Berlin. They pass close to me; standing in front of the hotel, I've lighted a cigarette after all, the first puffs on a cool morning on an almost deserted boulevard; the man with the cropped English beard gives me a brazen but not unfriendly glance, he's taller than I, he looks condescendingly down on me, then he turns to the girl, they're talking about me, or maybe that's just my imagination; I look after them, they have no children, they have dogs. What have they done with their children? They disappear around the corner into Fasanenstrasse. Ordinarily when I see somebody in Berlin I don't ask myself whether he might be a murderer; if I do now, those exotic animals with their morphine eyes and the relative emptiness of the Kurfürstendamm are probably to blame. Now I've lost interest in the couple, for a moment I took a liking to them, now I forget them. I didn't come here to look for murderers. I don't hate anybody.

I decide to go to the AP bureau which is only a few doors down the street; maybe there will be some interesting dispatches. The editors have gone home to bed; two German girls, busy over the teletype machines, are holding the fort. Some of the machines are making their usual ticking sounds. The girls look sleepy. They barely nod in response to my greeting. They tear off the tapes as they come out of the machines and cut them into strips which they sort out on the desk. I go over to the machine connected with the Moscow Bureau; it's running, but only testing. The test letters come out clean, the electrical impulses are right. One of the girls points to the desk where the latest messages are lying. I look through them, they've come in late that night, and now for the first time I read what Keir must have known when he called me: that K. will speak on TV this evening and announce his answer to the American President's demand that the missile bases be dismantled. Which means he's going to dismantle them. The sentence I borrowed from Anna—*K. is a traitor*—must have given Keir the impression that I was on the ball, or at least up on the news. That's a relief. Bud Collins, who suddenly turns up, draws the same conclusion from the dispatch: if K. were going to shoot, he says, he would shoot and not arrange to make a speech. Collins, whom I last met in Hanoi while covering the Indochina war, is up early because our troops here are being alerted and he's doing a story about them; he has an authorization from Major General Yates. Collins invites me to come along. Like Keir and Baron Collaudi, he wants to give me a chance, but I decline. The whole newspaper world seems to know that, as Collaudi put it, I'm on the downgrade. I hang around the bureau a little longer, looking through the dispatches, then one of the girls gets up from her work, comes over to me, and hands me a tape that has just come in. "two berlin schoolgirls aged fifteen," I read, "have just committed suicide together stop alarmed by the smell of gas the mother of one of the girls entered the kitchen and found her daughter sylvia and her school friend evelin dead end." It must have happened yesterday afternoon; the police were late in getting out the report to the press. I ask the AP girl why she thought this would interest me; she shrugs her shoulders and turns away, disappointed. To please her I ask for details; she gets busy very competently on the phone, and shows me the address on the map, Hähnelstrasse 6, that's near Innsbruckplatz, half an hour's walk,

I reckon. The bureau is dusty and run-down, it's on the sunny side of Kurfürstendamm, but you'd never know the sun was shining outside; the girls have grey faces, Bud Collins, who left long ago, has grey hair now, I was shocked to see him looking so old; the machines click. I decide not to take a taxi and walk south on Uhlandstrasse through Wilmersdorf. I come to an area of prosperous looking blocks of flats, some of them new. There are still gaps where bombed buildings have not been replaced. Beyond the Stadtbahn underpass, on Bundesplatz, I have to turn left. Hähnelstrasse is a short, very quiet street; though it branches off from a main thoroughfare, there is little traffic. Late autumn, a Sunday morning in Berlin. Hähnelstrasse 6 dates from before the First World War, a building without a face. The flat is on the fourth floor. I ring the bell and an oldish man in shirtsleeves opens it. I show him my press card and he introduces himself as Inspector von Cantz. The parents, he tells me, have been shipped off to some relatives and, taking advantage of the peace and quiet, he's trying to dig into the motives. In other words, I'm in the way, but after some hesitation he lets me in, leads me to the kitchen, shows me the gas taps which were all open when the children were found and their schoolbooks lying open on the kitchen table. In the midst of their homework, Sylvia and Evelin had decided to kill themselves. "I've been looking at their notebooks," says the inspector. "They weren't bad students."

"Where were they found?" I ask.

"Lying on the floor. Naturally in each other's arms."

From the kitchen window I look out on the back gardens which in this area are not ugly, not even gloomy, but desperately boring.

"They killed themselves out of boredom," I say.

The inspector looks up. He too is a grey man, like Collins. I try to explain.

"I've been working in Rome lately. There people kill themselves because they can't understand why happiness hasn't come to them. They cut their wrists and in the end they die screaming with rage at their unhappiness. A kind of revolt, you see."

He listens attentively.

"In most cases of suicide in Rome there are knives, flashing weapons. Here there's a smell of gas, something grey and creeping to which they resign themselves. Sylvia and Evelin thought there was nothing more in life for them but this house, this homework, this kitchen. And they capitulated. Children have a tendency to melancholia."

He goes on looking through the few papers the parents had collected for him. "Interesting," he says, "but you know, I don't believe in national characteristics. There must be some specific reasons why these children died."

"Have you questioned their parents? Their teachers? Their school friends?"

He shrugs his shoulders.

"I'll ask around tomorrow. There's not much we can do. It's hard to investigate suicide because we can't incriminate the guilty parties."

I leave him to his search for specific reasons. Here in Berlin the case will be featured for two days in the local news columns; in Frankfurt there will be a story of some length in the "News from Germany" section. For London the case won't exist. Newspapers ought to be entirely different. The Island on page four, the facts in twenty lines; on the front page long stories about Sylvia and Evelin, detailed accounts of the investigation, careful analyses until the case is cleared up. As if anything could ever be cleared up. These children died by pure chance. A slight shift in their mood yesterday, brought on by an infinitesimal change in the light or by a memory of something, a cranky teacher, for instance, or a swim last summer; if they had suddenly got the giggles, Evelin and Sylvia would still be alive, they would grow up to be women, they themselves would have children who might commit suicide or might not. Everything is chance. It's chance that Inspector von Cantz should be sitting in his shirtsleeves in the kitchen of a flat in Friedenau, bending his grey head over the belongings of two dead children. On Innsbrucker Platz I observe that most of the

people are moving in the direction of the two churches on Schöne-
berger Hauptallee, one Protestant, one Catholic, both resplend-
ently new. It's ten o'clock. The main services must begin at this
time. Pure chance if it's ten o'clock. And chance that I'm here on
Innsbrucker Platz looking for a cab to take me, after an interval
of twenty-seven years, to Bismarckstrasse in Wannsee. I could just
as well be in London, Rome or Hanoi, or dead, or still living in
Bismarckstrasse.

Now there are through traffic arteries, straight as a die, that
didn't exist in Berlin in my day. I begin to get my bearings only
when the cab turns off to the right from Potsdamerstrasse and
cuts through Zehlendorf. The Schlachtensee Stadtsbahn station,
Spanische Allee. Yesterday the cab driver brought me out here
by way of the Avus. I stop the cab at the Wannsee station, get
out and pay the fare. Beside the station, the Dutch brick semi-
circle, consisting of a few shops, a coffee shop and a bar. In the
days when I shuttled back and forth between Wannsee and Lichterfelde West—I was going to school in Dahlem and took the bus
to Thielplatz from the Lichterfelde West Stadtbahn station—
this row of shops wasn't here. But at the boat landing down below
there was a restaurant, a wooden structure, which is still there;
some of my school friends lived in the area and we used
to meet there occasionally, especially on winter afternoons; in the
summer we were too busy with boating and swimming. The
restaurant was out of bounds to schoolboys but we went there
just the same and drank grog. When the Nazis came in, none of
those boys cut me or tried to have me expelled from their group,
or even stayed away because I was there. The teachers too treated
me decently. But from 1934 on I didn't visit my friends in their
homes. My father said I would have to be realistic; we must put
restrictions on ourselves before they were imposed on us by
others. Esther, who stayed on after we had left, must have had a
harder time of it towards the end. Yesterday I had a cup of coffee
in the new coffee shop, then I looked at the shop windows, bought
cigarettes, and stood there for a while, undecided, listening to

the breeze in the autumn trees; then I turned off to the right from
Bismarckstrasse. First I skirted Königstrasse, which has been made
into a throughway, then turned right into the woods towards
Pfaueninsel. For a long time I stood looking across the Havel at
the gardens on the island, but I didn't take the ferry across. The
little wooden pavilion by the landing is worn and weatherbeaten
now. On the shore under the trees, now as then, the grey sand
is interspersed with rotting rushes. The bay between Pfaueninsel
and the woods is shaded, the ice lasted longer than elsewhere. I
often came here to skate with my friends, occasionally with Esther,
because her mother asked me to teach her to skate. I did it reluctantly; no boy wants to run around with a girl who's just a kid.
I remembered such things yesterday. Today I don't hesitate for
long but turn right into Bismarckstrasse. Nothing has changed:
to the left the Stadtbahn embankment, to the right the Berlin
Rowing Club. First the low yellowish wall, which hugs the slight
right curve at the beginning of the street. Then the entrance to
the narrow strip of park where Kleist is buried. The grave is only
a few steps away and seems changed. If I'm not mistaken, there
used to be a flat stone slab surrounded by a low fence under an
old tree. Instead I see an upright granite tablet; fence and tree
have vanished. Strange! But who cares? Kleist and Frau Vogel
committing suicide here—old stuff. It doesn't strike me as any
more or less tragic than the suicide of Sylvia and Evelin yesterday
afternoon. Too many suicides are trying to impress me this Sunday morning. In those days I used to think a good deal about
Kleist's violent end, which took place so close to our home; for
that reason I read his plays when I was only nine or ten, and so
intensively that I still know a few passages from *The Broken Jug*
or *The Prince of Homburg* by heart.

The buildings of the two rowing clubs to the right and left of
the park came through the war undamaged and have been renovated; but no life stirs in them. On the shore stands a black long-
legged bird with a white bill and grey feet. I have forgotten what
these birds are called. The autumn passes from the park to the

Kleiner Wannsee; brown, golden and red, it fades into the water of this little arm of the Havel, which lies still and nacreous-blue in the feeble sunlight. I had a kayak, which I usually kept on our lawn right beside the lake; I used to paddle past here, under the bridge and into the Grosser Wannsee. Today the little river looks as though it were never traversed by boats, as though it always lay thus deserted in a faint Sunday light. The brown beech leaves and red maple leaves that have fallen into the water glitter for a time, then sink to the bottom, disproving the law which claims that no energy is ever lost. All sorts of energy are lost. For the first time I begin to suspect that this whole area, these villas in their gardens, these built-up lake shores, Kleist's grave and even the Stadtbahn, which from time to time I hear faintly in the distance—that all these things have outlived themselves. They are still here, they lie soundless under an empty autumn sky, but they are no longer alive. Only the tall trunks of the pine trees here and there, bright red under their dark-green crowns, have something timeless about them. I leave the park and continue up Bismarckstrasse. Iron fences with hedges behind them. I can't see much of the houses and gardens, that too is unchanged. No. 7 was the house of Rose the sculptor, I sometimes watched him work; he didn't work directly in stone, but made clay models which he baked. He was too frail for stonework. He explained to me the difference between hewing and modelling while kneading his animals, which he sold for good prices. A few, which he did not sell, were left standing in the garden behind the house and gradually disappeared under the vegetation. In most of the gardens in Bismarckstrasse the trees and shrubs grew rank and crowded in on the houses; my mother was one of the few who did something about it. She took care of her garden. No. 12. I almost pass it by. There has been hardly any change but in the first moment I don't recognize the house, anyway not with the kind of recognition that hits you between the eyes. I merely stop at the garden gate and look in. The front path is still paved with the flagstones that I passed over for fifteen years. The jasmine bushes to the right of the house are scarcely taller than in my childhood, somebody must have clipped them now and then. Their foliage is thin and yellowish. The lawn beside them is not as well kept as it used to be and there are no roses round it, but asters have been put in wherever possible. Their flowers, pinkish-white and golden-brown, are fading; wilted by the first cold rains, they droop from the raffia strings binding the stalks to the stakes. My mother also grew asters, not here, but in the back garden sloping down to the water. A good piece of land. My father had the house built in 1912 by a conservative architect who crowned it with a high gable. My father was only thirty then, his business—importing leather—was doing very well and he tended to invest his money in real estate. In 1914 he volunteered, was wounded several times, the last time so seriously that they gave him the Iron Cross First Class and assigned him to rear echelon duty. After the war he made less money than before, but was able to keep the house to which he was very much attached. Our successors seem to have let the apple trees on the other side of the lawn grow wild; they evidently didn't know how to take care of fruit trees, for the trunks and branches are gnarled and overgrown with green lichen, the bark is split in places. In my time the trees bore big red country apples. I always remember my father as a melancholy clown, though he was short and solidly built. Because my father was a businessman, I have always had a certain affection for businessmen, I feel sorry for them, even the successful ones breathe a kind of sadness, they drift this way and that, coming from nowhere and going nowhere, they buy something and sell it, the money and merchandise pile up or slip through their fingers, I like to watch them in their aimlessness. The light that creeps round the house seems old. The house used to be orange but has now paled to a nondescript freckled brown; apparently it has never been repainted.

A plastic sign bearing the name of the new occupants is fastened to the garden gate. The name is Heiss. I already know who lives here, I looked it up in the directory yesterday: a Professor Hugo Heiss. The gate is ajar, I don't use the bell—still our old bell—but go right in and follow the walk to the house. At our house door I stop. Inside I hear a girl's voice singing—some popular song. I ring. The singing breaks off and the girl's voice calls out: "Mamma, the doorbell." A woman who, to judge by her voice, is nearer the door, probably in our old kitchen, answers: "I heard it." Her steps approach, but there are other steps too, lighter and more rapid, that make a scurrying sound. The door is opened. I state my name, explain that I once lived here and that I . . . The woman doesn't let me finish. "You'd like to visit the house," she says. "Do come in."

The source of the lighter, scurrying steps comes in sight: a child of five or six, a little girl with large blue eyes, a snub nose, and smooth brown hair hanging down to her shoulders. As I enter the hall the songstress comes down the stairs from the upper floor, she has one hand on our old carved-oak banister; she is about sixteen and is wearing slacks; she looks exactly like her younger sister except that she has apple-sized breasts under her dark-blue sweater. The woman introduces her daughters as people introduce children: the younger is Elga, the elder Marianne. "I'm sorry my husband's not here," she explains, "he's in South America." Her daughters look very much like her, but she is simpler, more transparent, with bright eyes and the face of a kindly country woman; it is tanned and firm. The girls seem more citified and refined, less open. Very nice people; they seem generous and warmhearted. I am rather surprised at my reception; it's as if I had been expected. Frau Heiss leads me into the living room and asks me if I'd like to sit down.

"No, thank you," I say. "I won't take up your time. Just a quick turn through the house."

One glance tells me that at least these people are not living with our furniture. That makes it easier for me to speak to them. I remain standing at the window.

"I lived here until 1935 with my parents. Then they sent me to England, to stay with an uncle."

"Your parents were put out of the house in 1943," the woman

continues my story, while her daughters listen. "Do you know what became of your parents?" She doesn't wait for my answer. "I've always known someone would come," she said. "My husband always said: 'they're all dead,' but I didn't believe it."

I don't doubt her words; this woman looks like a simple soul, but she has fine antennae. There would surely be advantages in living with such a woman. For a moment I envy Professor Heiss. I'm curious to know what the husband of such a woman looks like, what kind of man he is.

We go upstairs—at a sign from their mother the two girls remain below—where my parents' bedroom and my own used to be. Here again no traces of our furniture, thank God. My room is now Marianne's. A chest of drawers with sea-shells spread out on top. A good many books, schoolbooks and others, a violin. It looks almost the same as when it was mine. I look out the window over the garden and down at the Kleiner Wannsee. The grove at the end of the old garden makes an impression of darkness. It always did. I suppose I've seen all there is to see.

"We've been living here since 1948," says Frau Heiss.

Not noticing my surprise, she continues: "The people who moved in after your parents were thrown out in 1945. Then came refugees. Later on they were relocated and the Senate assigned the house to us when my husband was called to Berlin. I've kept urging him to find something else, but he's not very good at such things."

She looks up, sees my face and says: "Oh, you thought we came right after your parents!"

I don't know if she realizes that I'm not only surprised but disappointed as well. In any case I'm embarrassed. "I'm sorry I thought that," I say quickly. "It was stupid of me, of course. I quite forgot that it's been almost twenty years. That's a long time."

Suddenly she takes my hand and holds it fast for a time. Her gesture doesn't strike me as melodramatic; perhaps a bit too emotional, but I enjoy the pressure of her hand. Still, we'd have been a very unequal couple, she and I.

"Don't take it to heart," I say in an attempt to smooth things over. I almost manage to laugh. "It's always been that way, in every period of history, people losing their homes, their property being divided up as spoils, other people moving in as victors, and so on."

She drops my hand.

"No, it never happened before," she says in a cold angry voice, suddenly grown hostile. "If this didn't concern your parents, I'd describe what never happened before. Never!"

There is no need, and of course she knows there is no need, for her to describe anything. She knows I've seen the films and photographs. We turn to go.

The wall along the stairs is lined with pictures of volcanoes and other mountains. I stop and look at them, wishing to take my leave on a neutral topic.

"My husband is a geologist," she says. "He's off on an expedition to the Andes."

That's something else I failed to do: pick a profession that would have left me independent, independent of political systems and ideologies. Baron Collaudi probably has something of the sort in mind when he suggests that I go into business. But it would have been best if I had studied science. That was Uncle Basil's advice when I was at Public School in England, preparing for my final examinations. But then came the war and some devil must have driven me to journalism. (No, not a devil, it was Keir Horne.) While descending the stairs of our old house with Frau Heiss to the hall where the daughters are waiting, I quite forget that geology wouldn't have helped Professor Heiss if he had been a Jew. Frau Heiss is well aware of that, she knows that certain things had never happened before.

"My husband has been offered a post in America," she says very clearly for the benefit of her children, "but so far he's been unable to make up his mind. He'll accept it now, though."

Her tone had become almost hysterical. Marianne looks at her mother in alarm, and even little Elga notices a menace in the air; she presses close to her mother. I try desperately to steer the conversation into quieter waters.

"Don't overestimate the scientific opportunities that will be open to your husband in America. Maybe he'll be homesick for the European universities."

"I know my husband very well," she answers obstinately. "He may be incapable of looking for another house, but he will understand at once what it means that you should have paid us a visit." And she adds, half turned towards her almost grown-up daughter: "To think there are people we can't ask to see us because it would be tactless to say: 'Won't you visit us in our home!'"

I had no intention of playing the role of fate in this family, especially as I don't believe in fate. For the Heiss family my visit that Sunday morning was an utterly unforeseen episode. They accompany me to the garden gate, we are almost friends, but for some reason that escapes me, for the moment at least, I have rather lost interest in them. Elga is nothing more than an exceptionally charming little girl, Marianne is a teenager with apple breasts and long silky hair, and Frau Heiss is a pleasant woman with a countrified air. The daughters bid me a pleasant good-bye. Frau Heiss finds no proper way of winding things up.

"You're disappointed, aren't you, Herr Efraim?" She doesn't wait for an answer. "You expected to find the people who took the house from your parents. Deep down you even hoped you would."

She has the sixth sense. It displeases me that this motherly woman should see through me so clearly. It makes me feel like a child.

"And it wasn't for revenge that you hoped to find them," she thinks out loud in a voice tinged with hysteria, "not to make trouble for them. But in the hope of discovering that they were perfectly nice people, that the people who drove your parents out weren't really so bad. . . ." She breaks off, emits a hoarse whispered "*ach!*" connoting profound dissatisfaction with my person, and goes back into the house. Marianne and Elga look after her in perplexity. A moment later the little one runs after her. But a change comes over Marianne: with an amused though not disparaging shrug of her shoulders, she tries to explain to me about her mother. Which shows that Marianne doesn't understand what has happened. It would be bad if she already understood. At her age I didn't even understand the trouble in my own house. If I had stayed in this house, I shouldn't be standing at the garden gate with her now, I'd have been gassed with my parents. Of course I should have been a victim of pure chance. It's pure chance that twenty years ago Jewish families were exterminated, and not other families twenty years before that, or later, now, for example. I have never found a really conclusive explanation for my parents' death, and people who have explanations to offer strike me as highly suspect. In half an hour Frau Heiss and her daughters will be sitting down to lunch. They could just as well be dragged out of their house and murdered, if fate willed it so. Consequently I am in perfect agreement with the pretty teenager's shrug of the shoulders—the disrespectful shrug of a daughter at her mother's melodramatic, and in her opinion pointless, agitation. I side with her against her mother. A flirtation starts up. We exchange significant and confused smiles. We have no desire to know why we may be murdered tomorrow.

I'm back on Bismarckstrasse, now walking in the opposite direction. I had wanted to see whether the house where Esther and Frau Bloch lived is still there, so as to be able to report to Keir, but I abandon the idea. Why wouldn't it be there? Obviously no bombs landed on Bismarckstrasse. I'm through with Bismarckstrasse. It's been just as much of a failure as that village in Sicily where I first came under fire early in 1942, and which I visited from Rome to revive the memory. The place left me completely cold. Our house at Bismarckstrasse 12 hadn't left me as cold as the hills along a certain stretch of road near Caltanisetta, which I hardly remembered in their uniform and never-ending limestone-grey and olive-green, or as the low stone walls behind which we lay, and which provided no cover at all when we came under mortar

fire, so that blind with fear we clung to those Sicilian stones with
our hands and our eyes, and in the half-darkness between the edge
of my helmet and the hollow in the rock my glasses clouded over
because I was sweating with fear. I couldn't manage to draw the
slightest trace of fear from the crumbling masonry where I had
buried it. In our house at Wannsee at least I was able to refresh
a memory or two, but not able to recall my parents more keenly
than anywhere else in the world. If the house belongs to me
some day—despite my indifference in these matters, Uncle Basil's
solicitor has initiated restitution proceedings—I shall sell it at
once. I won't come out here again. For one thing I should find it
painful to meet Frau Heiss again.

I take the Stadtbahn back to town. I have been attracted by the
harsh bareness of the Stadtbahn stations since my trip from Zoo
to Friedrichstrasse on Friday morning. On Thursday evening,
immediately after my arrival, some fellow newspapermen at the
hotel bar acquainted me with the mechanism of the border crossing, and on Friday morning I did what every foreign newspaperman does when he gets to Berlin. I hadn't known that you're
already in the *other country* as soon as you set foot on the Stadtbahn platforms of West Berlin. That smell of poverty and disinfectant, of fine grey dust and puritanism. When I spoke of my
trip to Anna last night, she listened attentively with a touch of
envy in her eyes. In view of what Sandberg had told me about
her, I was careful not to tell her I had bought a ticket for the
Berliner Ensemble tomorrow night; they are doing Brecht's *Days
of the Commune.* I had bought the ticket on the unanimous advice of half a dozen English newspapermen who had gathered
at the bar for their six o'clock whiskey; they were almost frantic in
their peculiarly British way when it came out that I wasn't in the
know and had my doubts. I buy the pathetic Communist rag
which is on sale even here at the Wannsee station. Here there
are no kiosks, no advertisements urging me to buy anything
whatsoever, only a poster recruiting workers for the German Railways. I have a weakness for puritanical countries. The train pulls

in. There are only two other passengers. During the trip I feel
hungry; it's lunch time. I get off at the Zoo station, buy the latest
edition of one of the big papers and repair to the Schultheiss
Restaurant on Kurfürstendamm, across from my hotel. I had
lunch there yesterday and ascertained from my study of the menu
that pig's trotters are obtainable. At the next table a man was
devouring a helping of pig's trotters and since then the thought
has assailed me at every stirring of hunger. I sit down at a table at
the back, order my pig's trotters and a glass of beer, and open
the newspaper. I read the news about the Island; it's not news to
me but as a member of the profession I'm interested in seeing
how the people here handle it. The rewriting technique is pretty
much the same as ours. You'd have to look through the whole
mass of agency releases in order to determine whether they've
really got the facts straight. But I can see one thing at a glance:
the headlines are politically slanted. *Elimination of bases—Re-
moval of threat to world peace.* I can't help thinking of our German teacher at the Dahlem High School, who always gave us bad
marks for making substantives of verbs. Around me people are
eating and drinking with close attention. The "Letters from Our
Readers" section has a number of communications about a political murder trial which has been reported in the Italian press
because it happened to be Italians whom a German officer—in
civilian life a reputed architect, professor and authority on city
planning—had caused to be executed, perhaps in order to fore-
stall a possible mutiny. Undoubtedly a man possessed by the idea
of planning. I immerse myself in the letters. The waiter interrupts
my reading to serve me my pig's trotters—with sauerkraut and
purée of peas. The purée is topped with a little brown butter with
bits of fried bacon in it. The pink pickled meat is encased in a
fatty rind cooked soft; I barely taste it, then cut it off and lay it
to one side. Better not. The meat is excellent, salty and tender,
but I regret that the work of cutting it cannot be combined with
newspaper reading into a single unbroken pleasure. I manage,
however, while raising the bites to my mouth, to read short para-

graphs from the epistles. They are concerned not so much with the professor, the planner of cities and murders, as with the verdict that has just been handed down; because the knife with which he liquidated twenty persons was perhaps not held by him alone, he was acquitted. Divided responsibility. *In dubio pro reo.* So now he can go back to his—probably well-planned—cities. Only a few cranks will refuse to sit at the same table with him. Frau Heiss, perhaps, if she were put into this unpleasant situation. I am pleased to see that all the letter writers are indignant at the verdict. My own moral indignation over the butcher in question is spoiled by the fact that while observing twenty members of an Italian labor battalion lined up in a night landscape near Avignon —cypresses, vineyards, summer—observing them through the sights of a hidden machine gun as they talk and curse in an undertone and stand about sleepy and unsuspecting, that while sitting behind the machine gun of my imagination in the Schultheiss Restaurant I am able with great enjoyment to feel pieces of pickled pork on my tongue, to chew them and swallow them. Of course I could stop eating, but what for? My inclination to puritanism and antisepsis is not as highly developed as I should like. The pig's trotters taste good, and I happen to have this habit of reading the paper as I eat. After my meal I feel heavy and sleepy. I drink another few sips of beer, pay the bill and go over to my hotel. I lie down on the couch into which my bed is transformed during the day and in a few minutes fall asleep. I dream a conversation with Ho Chi Minh, whom I once interviewed in a village near Hanoi during the war in Indochina. If I should decide at the last minute to stay in the newspaper game, I'd ask Keir for the job of Far Eastern correspondent. He'd surely let me have it, first out of joy at the return of the Prodigal Son, and second because if he didn't give it to me some competitor would. It's in Asia that all the decisions will be made, and I don't mean the political decisions, or at least not exclusively. But it wasn't in Tonkin—*somewhere very far away, above the fever jungles, above the silent cities, above the mouths of the streams, above the humid coasts*, that I met the dream-Ho; I met him in the house in the rue de Nevers in Paris where long ago I was issued the *laissez-passer* which later admitted me to his headquarters. As I remember it, that house in the rue de Nevers consists solely of iron doors which close with a crash when you leave the rooms crowded with whispering little Indochinese. Iron doors opening out on long cement corridors; the conversations in the rooms cannot be heard in the corridors, but they are heard in the tropical rain forest covering the Chau-Tai Hills. In one of these rooms lay Ho on a kind of divan, a slight man wearing his Chinese *litevka*. I implored him to leave Paris where he might be discovered and arrested any minute, but he only smiled. And the more he smiled, the more desperate I became. I wake up about three o'clock. I phone down for coffee. After drinking two cups of the fluid they call coffee in Berlin—I feel a violent longing for an *espresso* at the Rosati—I sit down at the desk, pull up the machine and put in paper. I am exactly in the mood in which I have written my best newspaper stories, a state of mingled thoughtfulness and tension. My fingers fiddle with the keys. The cigarette I've been smoking burns itself out in the ash tray. Then I start typing. I can only type with two fingers. I write: On towards four in the morning it starts to rain. Awakened by the sound, I switch on the bedside lamp and raise my wrist-watch to my short-sighted eyes. Then I grope for my glasses, put out the light, get up and go to the window. When I went to bed, at two, I did not draw the curtains. My hotel room looks out on empty space. The rain whishes through the cold beam of the floodlights on top of the concrete posts around the loading yard. I see two lorries and a black Mercedes, the rain splattering against their black roofs.

I break off, go to the window and look out. The Mercedes has meanwhile been driven away, otherwise everything is the same as this morning. Only the light has changed; now it's a dismal-Sunday-afternoon-in-the-city light. I sit down at the typewriter and continue. But I'd better admit right now that I did not begin my report, or whatever you want to call it, exactly in the form here cited, which is its final form. In my first draft I used the third person of the imperfect; in other words, I proceeded as though writing about someone else. I wrote: On towards four in the morning it started to rain. Awakened by the sound of the rain, George (formerly: Georg) Efraim switched on the bedside lamp and raised his wrist-watch to his short-sighted eyes. Then he groped for his glasses, put out the light, got up and went to the window. When he went to bed at two, he had not drawn the curtains. His hotel room looked out on empty space. The rain whished through the cold beam of the floodlights on top of the concrete posts around the loading yard. He saw two lorries and a black Mercedes, the rain splattering against their black roofs. That Sunday and later I wrote more than twenty pages in this way. It was not until many weeks later that I felt the need of writing in the first person and in the present. *Feeling* is the right word for the phenomenon which led to many changes in my text, until at length I formally consecrated the presence of my person; I can't exactly explain it, because after all there are all sorts of books whose so-called heroes make the most subjective impression although the books are written *about* them and not *by* them. In writing this sentence—much later and in an entirely different place—I am acknowledging my intention of writing a book and not just a sheaf of private notes intended only for myself. One journalistic attitude that will always stay with me, whether I give up newspaper work or not is that I can't conceive of writing for myself. (That is, if I go on writing at all.) If I were going to write for myself, I could spare myself the trouble; if all I wanted were to be one with myself, or two, to come to terms, or quarrel, with myself, thinking would be adequate. On the other hand I share Keir Horne's distaste for literature; his suspicion that I was trying to write literature (*bloody* literature) instead of reporting the news, is one of the reasons why I am trying to give my bit of literature (a book, it can't be denied, is literature) the form of a news story. Actually of many news stories, for I can't belie the school in which I have been moulded. Its basic principle is that every sentence must contain a fact, or at least say something.

That Sunday I'm up to the fourth or fifth page of my story, still written in the third person singular imperfect, roughly at the place where Meg is prodding me to pack the bags, when the chambermaid interrupts me; she has to get the bed ready for the night. I turned on the desk lamp long ago; it has meanwhile grown dark. I go out into the corridor to stretch my legs and because the sight of menial service is distasteful to me. Finally it occurs to me that I've stood Anna up. It's seven and we were to meet at five at the Café Bristol. At first I am overcome by a violently disagreeable feeling, then I am almost relieved. I didn't avoid this meeting deliberately, no, I really forgot Anna for a few hours. I'm sorry I forgot her but console myself with the thought that a meeting in the dismal, empty atmosphere of a Sunday afternoon on Kurfürstendamm would have brought nothing but embarrassment and forced conversation. Of course I can't be sure; Anna might have pulled me out of my *cafard*. I shrug my shoulders. Tomorrow I'll ring her up and go and see her; a journalist can always think up plausible excuses. The chambermaid has finished. I close the door behind me and sit back down to my machine. I'm not hungry; I'll have some biscuits and a glass of water later on. In the course of the evening I get to the end of my conversation with Keir, which comes out so wretchedly in this first draft that I'm quite depressed when I go to bed at midnight. You see, I wouldn't want it thought that I wrote this first chapter as it stands here—up to the point where I pull up the typewriter and decide to write—all in one breath that afternoon and evening. No, I'm not that prolific.

Two

Even as a journalist I'm a slow worker. I wrote my reports from Asia, which put me in the top bracket of the English newspaper world, as slowly and painstakingly as if they had been long narrative poems. I owed my success to a very simple observation: one day it struck me that even in our England the art of reporting has died out. The papers have their correspondents all over the world, who send in not direct reports but articles, which at best provide astute analysis, whereas the great reporters of former days wrote nothing but what they had seen and heard, neither more nor less. They were plain, honest men. What enabled me, who am not a plain honest man, to adopt their working methods was my belief in chance. Because I do not believe in the laws of history and still less in political ideologies, I am able to watch the play of chance with a cold eye, to observe its chaotic workings without drawing conclusions. Which factions win or lose the struggle for the world will depend on whether chance gives them outstanding or mediocre leaders and on the fluctuations in the mood of the masses, which in turn are determined by developments in chaos. The course of world events will be determined, for example, by the progress of K.'s diabetes, by the good or bad aim of various marksmen, and by the insouciance of a president in Dallas, Texas. Aided by this conviction—just about the only one I possess—I was able to portray a French colonel after the battle of Dien Ben Phu, the Dalai Lama, or a sheikh of the Arab desert tribes whom I met near Kubarah, in such a way that the circulation of our conservative paper gradually increased. Of course it was Keir who gave me my chance to write as I wanted to, not only because he has an enormous journalistic flair but also because of our special relationship. If not for the ties between us, through Meg as well as Esther, I'd never have got *on the wire*. Connections are every-thing.

It is in the Albergo Byron, on another Sunday, but this time in the morning, that I block out this reflection which, I imagine, will only make my book unwieldy and have to be deleted (I've decided to keep it after all!) in a thick black notebook with an oilcloth cover. (I did not insert the reference to the assassination of President Kennedy until much later; I had never expected to find so compelling a proof of my theory.) It is about ten o'clock on Sunday, 11 November 1962. I returned from Berlin to Rome on Thursday, 1 November. Fine warm autumn weather, the sky over this city of compact brownish red is a dense blue. On receipt of a suitable tip, the receptionist of the Byron has given me back my old room. I have put the large drawing board I work on—I had left it in the hotel—back on its two trestles, put my typewriter in place and spread out my papers. Whenever I arrive in a city where I mean to settle for any time, I go to a large dealer in draftsman's equipment and buy the biggest drawing board available and a couple of trestles, because you can never find a decent work table in a hotel. I have found that these simple contrivances can be sold at small loss when one leaves town. The octagonal red tiles of my attic room at the Byron are well worn and have settled in places. It was hard to find the right spot for my table. Now it is in the right-hand corner, the light from the window, which faces south, falls on it from the left. A comfortable chair, covered with faded red velvet, was on hand. Next to the window a high double door opens out on a very narrow balcony with a rusty wrought-iron railing; it runs round the whole upper story of the Albergo and offers access to any of the rooms. I often go out on it to look down into the deep chasm of Via Borgognona, or over the rooftops at the various church steeples, the Quirinal Palace, or the dome of St. Peter's. One would expect this balcony to favour sociability and secret trysts; but strange to say, no one but myself ever seems to set foot on it, for I have never, though I come out here at all hours, glimpsed another human being. This I find most surprising. The emptiness of this airy passageway, which to be sure is hardly wider than a balustrade and makes for dizziness, sometimes gives me the feeling of being all alone in an enormous old palace. The room has running water but no bath; it is small, old and shabby, but uncommonly cheap. With my expense account from the paper I could afford to stay at a much better hotel, but by the end of May when I started my job in Rome I had half decided to give up journalism and the saving would enable me to live for a time without income. It's time I made up my mind.

To my surprise Collaudi and Lorenza were no longer at the hotel. They left town together, so Mario tells me. This surprises me; I always regarded the baron as a permanent fixture of the Albergo Byron. He has left me a letter in which he speaks of urgent business in London, Anglo-American-Italian co-productions. He mentions staggering sums of money and projects that sound fantastic, but in this line everything is fantastic, at once possible and impossible. In his letter Collaudi renews his offer to take me into partnership. He even asks a favour of me: he wants me to speak to Cella on his behalf and persuade him to make certain changes in his new film. Since *Il Coltello*, Cella has been the rising young man of the Italian cinema; the producers know they will have to work with him but they are making a last attempt to impose conditions. The baron gives me the details of Cella's idea for his second picture, indicating the points which the industry finds unacceptable. These of course are the very points where Cella *must* abide by his plan; if they are falsified, the picture and Cella himself will be ruined. Collaudi with his easy-going intelligence knows that too; he likes well-made films, but the only thing in which he takes a passionate interest is the art of putting through a business deal, and here he devises the subtlest tactical moves: such as sending a well-known English journalist to see an ambitious young director. What an operator! He even offers me money, a by no means negligible sum.

I suppose I haven't the makings of a businessman after all. I

easily let myself be talked into all sorts of things, and if the baron
were here . . . Incidentally, the plot of the picture seems familiar
—now where could I have read this idea, a murder foreshadowed in
a dream? But who cares? The one thing that matters is that I
must screw myself up to a decision with regard to my profession.
I set aside this Sunday morning to write to Keir. In the ten days
since my return to Rome I've completed the first chapter of my
book—provisionally, of course, I'm well aware that what I've written can be no more than a rough draft. If I stick to the actual
order of events, I should have to start now with an account of the
evening at Lampe's when I met Anna. On her account I left Berlin not on the Interzone train as originally intended, but by
plane. I had pressed her to go to Rome with me and she had finally given in. The train is repeatedly checked by the East German
police and would not have been quite safe for her. In the plane
to Frankfurt I explained to Anna that in Rome I would occasionally have to leave her alone because I would be very busy. I
had the impression though that she wasn't listening very attentively. That should have been a warning to me, but she had never
flown before and I thought that accounted for her far-away air;
we had good flying weather and she seemed absorbed in looking
down at the earth. Well, I've completed my stint in Rome. Knowing that my job was drawing to a close, I even began to work
rather conscientiously for the paper. Keir must have been surprised,
undoubtedly it has given him new hope and it's high time that I
shatter his illusion. I feel as though I were postponing a parting
when I ring the office in Fleet Street from the Foreign Press Club
on Piazza San Silvestro, usually in the late afternoon between six
and seven, when the twilight is breaking in on Rome and it's already dark in England. I ask to be put through to the news telephones and instantly recognize the voice of Baker or Wright or
O'Connor or whoever happens to be there. I chat with him for a
moment about the weather in London or his family before saying:
five hundred words, and giving him the slug: *Mafia,* or *The Pope's
Illness,* or *Government Resigns* (because they do the headlines

in London). Then I begin to dictate, while visualizing O'Connor's thin serene face or Baker's bored beefy face, wedged between mouthpiece and receiver; I have often watched them as they turn off their eyes, which seem to go blind as they establish contact between their hearing and their hands and take down the story in shorthand, while at the same time it is being recorded on tape. In ten years I have learned to dictate in such a way that I am seldom interrupted by their monotone "will you repeat please"; we have the feel of each other. When I've finished I know that O'Connor, or whoever it is, leaves the open booth for a minute and goes over to the big square table, which almost fills the windowless, artificially lighted room, for a cup of tea. The black table top is marked with a thousand tea spots that no scrubbing brush will ever remove. O'Connor sits down at the table and drinks tea, or he goes over to his grey overcoat that's hanging on a hook beside the door, fishes out a packet of cigarettes and starts to smoke. Now his eyes are a little more alive than before, but not much. He's probably thinking of his private affairs. Occasionally he exchanges a word or two with one of the others. He has been working in this room for twenty-three years. He takes down an average of eight stories an hour; in a six-day week that comes (the news telephone room is operated on three six-hour shifts; it is closed only from midnight to six in the morning) to 288 items. Since 1939 O'Connor has taken down all the news of the world. A leg injury kept him out of the war. He devotes a good part of his free time to union work. He lives with his wife and two almost grown-up children in a terrace house in Tooting and takes the Northern Line to work. His face is serene and thin, I can't think of anything else to say about his face, except that he can turn off his cool light-blue eyes at will. When he is on the early shift, he alone of all the passengers in the coach does not read the paper; he just sits there in his grey overcoat with the package of sandwiches in its left-hand pocket and stares into space; I don't believe he hears the rustling of the newspaper pages. When I think of men like

O'Connor, it's hard for me to say good-bye to newspaper work; I feel like a deserter.

After the sentence "Connections are everything," I set aside my notebook and didn't pick it up again until after trying to write Keir a letter. I stand up and go out on the balcony; I lean on the rail and peer down into the Sunday stillness of Via Borgognona. I follow the street eastward, attracted by the morning sunlight cutting across the shadows of the Spanish Embassy building. The strollers on Piazza Mignanelli traverse the tall rectangle of golden light admitted by the open street, small bleak figures moving quickly or hesitantly across the stage; I watch them as though from the wings. One drawback of Rome is the overpowering temptation to rush from one's room and down into the street. Couldn't I write Keir another time? No, I stand fast. I come back into the room and sit down at the typewriter. Dear Keir, I write, I owe you news of my search for Esther. That's what you sent me to Berlin for. Don't lie, don't tell me it was the situation on the Island; you know as well as I do that you could just as well have sent Peel of the Bonn bureau, you know there was no news of the Island in Berlin, that the best you could hope for was a human interest story, which Peel could have handled a good deal better than I because he has been covering Berlin for years and can judge at a glance whether morale is *high* or *low*. (One of the duties of every English or American newspaperman assigned to Berlin is to find out whether morale is *high* or *low*. It is not possible to translate these words literally, to speak of *hohe* or *niedrige Moral*; that would give the matter undue weight; on the other hand, this thing we are supposed to look into is something more than the good or bad *Stimmung* (mood) of the Berlin population. The meaning actually is *Moral*, but the *Moral* of a military unit. Those poor besieged soldiers!) So, I continue, let's forget about that. In any case, you made me visit a country which I had erased from my map. Never mind! It was just as I feared: it didn't even excite me. Before landing in Berlin I still had the vague feeling that I had some sort of past: parents, grandparents, great-grandparents, and a tradition, like you, you with your clan of Scottish parsons, your parish registers, your tombs in Argyll, in a word, that I too had a heritage, cursed perhaps, but still a heritage. But I found nothing, there was nothing left, not for a moment did I experience the least excitement, the kind of excitement you feel when you've hit on a trace. There are no more traces, I have no trace of a past. I'm exaggerating. They are giving me back my father's house. But they can't show me my father's grave. And that didn't upset me, it didn't make me angry, I felt nothing, nothing, nothing. You could have spared me this experience, Keir.

The smoke of my cigarette hovers in midair, suffused with Italian sunlight and the sound of Roman church bells. Keir, I write, you blackmailed me, you knew I'd refuse to go to Berlin if you hadn't made it an assignment. I would have thrown up the job three weeks ago as I do now. But to your official order you added a private request: you asked me to make a last attempt to find out what became of Esther. I don't know why you hit on this idea now of all times, when any number of people have done all they could for you in this matter and all come to the same conclusion: that it is not possible to trace Esther. You yourself never dared to go to Berlin; you were always afraid that in the course of your search you would meet old friends of Marion Bloch, that as they listened to you a glimmer of recollection would dawn in their eyes—a recollection not very flattering to yourself. Incidentally, your fear is groundless. In the Jewish Old People's Home on Iranische Strasse I spoke with an old woman who was on the train that took Marion Bloch to Auschwitz, and though she remembered your friend and described her to me exactly as I remember Esther's mother, your name meant nothing to her. One could always rely on Frau Bloch's discretion.

These sentences are as tactless as the words spoken over the phone two weeks ago, with which I brought Keir to tears. But while in my telephonic ramblings I had merely been momentarily careless, with no intention of wounding Keir, now, as I am dimly aware, a hateful undertone has crept into my writing. I cannot

wholly eliminate hatred from my feeling of friendship for Keir.
I'd better *get straight* or this letter is *under the floor.* (That
slipped right out of my machine. Can it be that I have a weakness
for my old compatriots' new idiomatic turns?) Out of sheer ani-
mosity towards Keir I falsify certain colours so as to put everything into a light unfavourable to him. As though his sense of
guilt were not already great enough! For instance, I was idealiz-
ing Frau Bloch just now. It's true that she was the soul of discretion, a perfect lady, probably the most distinguished resident of
Bismarckstrasse, and respected accordingly. I often observed how
when she stopped to talk with neighbours, they would involuntarily abandon their usual easy manners for a respectful bearing;
I remember how they stood stiff and unnatural in her presence,
evidently feeling that she had conferred an honour on them by
addressing them. Later, when she had to wear the yellow star,
that must have changed; then, no doubt, the same people scur-
ried nervously past if they had the bad luck to meet her. I myself
thought Frau Bloch enormously distinguished; and even in my
twelve-year-old ignorance I sensed, when occasionally at my parents' urging I went to the house to take Esther out to play, how
Frau Bloch had shut herself up in the tastefully furnished villa
where she lived with her illegitimate daughter—she had much
better taste than my parents and was probably a good deal richer
too—as in a shell of suffering. Yet, though I was impressed by the
atmosphere of cultivation, by Frau Bloch's distinction and even
by her unhappiness, I have to admit that I also found them rather
dull. And it was probably this bit of dullness that made Keir behave towards her as he did. After a visit from Frau Bloch—the
Efraims and the Blochs were the only Jewish families in the street,
and we paid occasional courtesy calls—I once heard my father
say to my mother—a remark surely not intended for my ears—
that elegance and beauty alone didn't exactly fill out an evening.
These were rather strong words for my father who was usually
careful to avoid malicious, not to say cynical, remarks. I remember
my mother's answer well. She said that dull people—if Frau

Bloch were dull, which was not at all certain—had a very hard time of it because their dullness, for which after all they could not be blamed, prevented them from making friends, that there was something peculiarly tragic about them, an air of being cut off from life. And then she spoke of Frau Bloch's individual difficulties, of how hard it was for a lady of excellent family to be left with an illegitimate child to bring up. To be sure, my mother went on, the Bloch clan didn't take a tragic view of the matter—some of its younger members went so far as to speak openly of Aunt Marion's hard luck and to make light of it—but it was just this liberal attitude, this sympathy and understanding on the part of her people that had led Frau Bloch to part company with them, to leave the large house on the Tiergarten and bury herself in Wannsee. She's just hoity-toity, my father said, but he knew what my mother meant, for he was not a liberal-minded man but a conservative who voted, under the Weimar Republic, for Stresemann's German People's Party.

I don't have to tell Keir what he already knows, that Marion Bloch's name is on the list of persons deported to Auschwitz—but not Esther's. Keir had someone check on that shortly after the war, but I myself consulted the lists on Friday morning, the day after my arrival in Berlin. A friendly little man, one of the 7000 survivors among Berlin's 160,000 Jews, gave them to me in an office in Iranische Strasse. The man was handsome, small, with a face like a hazelnut under white hair, large dark-brown eyes and black eyebrows; he seemed a little out of place in this dismal office, there was something Oriental about him. I asked him why he stayed in Berlin. He said it made no difference where one lived. We recognized each other at once: independently of one another, we had come to the same conclusions. It makes no difference where one lives, what one does, who one is. He was very helpful. They have the names in a card file, there's no need to plow through all the lists. And so I found Marion Bloch's name rather quickly on a list of 1862 persons sent to Auschwitz on 1 March 1943. Of these, 1676 went to the gas chambers immediately on their arrival. The clerk mentioned the woman with whom I later spoke at the Old People's Home as one of the survivors, and in her I was fortunate to find someone who remembered Frau Bloch, who had even conversed with her on the trip, in so far as such an exchange of faded snippets of news that moulder on the lips can be called conversation. One of the snippets of news that Frau Bloch had left behind in the memory of this Frau Schlesinger concerned Esther, and it was surprising, to Keir it will be sensational. The Old People's Home of the Jewish Community is right next door to the administration building and I was able to visit Frau Schlesinger at once. But before going, I asked to be shown the list on which the names of my parents are inscribed. On 2 February 1943, a month before Frau Bloch's life was deliberately snuffed out by synthetic gas in a room specially constructed for this purpose, they were sent to Theresienstadt. There my father died a few months later. My mother was sent to Auschwitz in 1944. There her trace is lost. My father was sixty-six, my mother sixty-one when they were killed.

These recollections—which, as I have said, I merely jot down; I shall rewrite my notes later on—have carried me well into the afternoon; it's been a long time since I pushed away the typewriter with the beginning of my letter to Keir to make room for my notebook; an hour ago I drew the curtains because the sun in its westward path had reached that segment of its arc from which it shines glaringly into my room. The Sunday is passing. If Anna had come straight to Rome with me, I'd have gone out long ago, lowered the top of my little convertible, and taken her for a ride to the Praenestine Hills or to Sant' Oreste. Seen from my room, the light suggests a hot day in Rome, but I know it's rather cool out; after all, this is 11 November. But it's not cold, the open car would have been all right for this clear, cool autumn day. Of course I don't know whether Anna would have enjoyed it. Oh, the driving perhaps, the speed; but would Rome and the Latin hills appeal to her? Well, if she gets here, we'll find out. If her second attempt to leave Berlin doesn't come to grief in Frankfurt like the first. If she accepts my invitation I won't be able to dispose of my time as freely as I do now, I won't be able to waste it as aimlessly as I'm doing today on an unfinished letter and memories. I shall have to look out for Anna; you can't just bring a girl from Berlin to Rome and leave her to her own resources. I'll find it hard to change my habits. If it were Meg coming instead of Anna, no such thought would even enter my head. Never have I felt that time shared with Meg was wasted. But Meg won't be coming because I don't accept the conditions on which she would come. Anna has been a surprise to me though. For the first time since I left Meg—because I decided one day to stop accepting her conditions—the prospect of living with a woman gives me a certain pleasure. Gave me, I should say. It gives me no particular emotion to think of this girl, while the thought that Meg might step through the door of my room at this moment throws me into a state of excitement—hell, I've got to stop making comparisons! Still, there's something pleasant about the thought of Anna, it has the quality of a clear, cool, well-organized idea. Anna would come out with one of her rare, but for that very reason shattering, Berlinisms if she knew she was playing the role of an ideal being in my meditations. She is young, spontaneous, and probably sensual; her skin radiated a strange dry heat when I touched it. I have never been able to think of Meg in this way, carefully sorting out her qualities. I enjoy it. It's a new experience for me, being able to think of a woman without losing interest in her. I'm growing older. In another relationship, the kind you plunge into head over heels, so much objectivity would not be possible. Towards Meg it would be a kind of disloyalty. But it's no offence to Anna because I don't think she has fallen in love with me. I assume that she likes me as I like her, and besides I offer her a possibility that must tempt her. Almost any woman, who like Anna lives in straitened circumstances and is not tied to another man, would accept such an offer. That Anna should have stopped short in mid-temptation shows strength of character; she knows of course that she belongs in Berlin, that for her Rome would be an exotic excursion, nothing more.

It is also conceivable that Werner Hornbostel tried to hold her back, though it seems unlikely. He's not the type that starts running in circles when he sees that a woman is breaking away; not that he's complacent, or that he doesn't love Anna enough—I believe he loves her a good deal in his own way—but because this hulking, easy-going blond youngster has too much sense to imagine that he could make Anna stay with him if she no longer feels like it. Besides, he is much too wrapped up in his musical manipulations; he wouldn't let even the greatest sorrow interfere with his work. In this respect I could well take a leaf from the young man's book—I who used to break off my occupations at every whim of Meg's. True, they were always journalistic occupations. It's possible that not even Meg would be able to breach the wall I'm building around myself with these notes begun in Berlin. Hidden behind them, I don't know whether I really ought to hope for Anna Krystek to come. I feel the same as I did that Sunday afternoon in Berlin when I was so relieved to find that I had forgotten my date with her, that it had slipped my mind because I had started on this journal which has plunged me again today into a passive daydreaming over notes, into a sea of memories and meditations on the surface of which float fragments of formulations with the help of which perhaps I shall be able to build a raft—a crude wooden structure that will save me from shipwreck.

My usual afternoon weariness overcomes me. I lie down on the bed, eat two apples, read *Il Messaggero*, let it droop, and doze off for fifteen minutes. When I wake up I decide definitely not to go on with my letter to Keir. I take the paper out of my typewriter, put it in with my notes and write Keir a few lines saying only what Frau Schlesinger told me about Marion Bloch, to wit, that Esther left her mother's home in November 1938, and was never heard from again. Frau Bloch did not forget to mention that Esther took her dog with her when she left home. I clearly remember Devil, Esther's black-and-grey cocker spaniel. I make no mention for the present of my conversation with Mother Ludmilla, who confirmed Frau Schlesinger's statements, but on a sudden impulse merely add that I shall be going to London in the next few days and will then give him further details. It was Anna who gave me the idea of making inquiries at Esther's school, where I had my strange conversation with Mother Ludmilla. My first reaction to what Frau Schlesinger told me had been doubt; I said to myself that Frau Bloch had hidden Esther and spread the story of her flight to prevent the authorities from looking for her. The fact that my parents had said nothing of Esther's disappearance in their letters—until the outbreak of the war I received letters from Bismarckstrasse regularly—favoured the idea of a conspiracy to save the child who had not, like myself, had a chance to emigrate. But Mother Ludmilla's words dispelled my doubt; she accounted for my parents' silence by pointing out that they had not wished to endanger the success of Esther's flight. What finally convinced me was the detail that Devil had gone too; Frau Bloch would surely have been incapable of lying so cleverly. I knew how Esther felt about her merry dark-haired dog; sometimes the three of us would go racing through the woods by the Havel; I remember a sand-coloured sweater that was much too big for Esther, I remember her pale, flushed, stubborn face under her stiffly set hair and, as we sat in the grass, the dog lying with his head in her lap and looking up at me when I called him "mutt" or "mongrel" to tease Esther, in which I succeeded so well that she howled with rage. Devil and Esther were inseparable. Not until several years later, when I had long been living in England, did I realize that I had developed a feeling of affection for my childhood friend, an affection I can call to mind at any time, as one recalls all very early experience, a certain kind of wind one heard blowing round the house and through the trees at night, the smell of summer holidays or the tinkling of a bicycle bell.

At about three I leave the hotel. At the desk I ask—forgetting that it's Sunday—if there are any letters for me, but there is no post on Sunday; no news of Anna can reach me before tomorrow

morning unless she wires; but she seems to be in no hurry. Last
Friday, incidentally, I finally rang Cella and arranged to meet him
at six today at the Rosati, not because I was so eager to oblige
Collaudi but because I thought there might be a story in it for
our *Weekly Review*. The man's fame has spread to England, and
I can't get out of the habit of thinking about the paper. While
strolling down Via Borgognona and turning left into Via del
Gambero, I reflect that the sentence "It makes no difference
where one lives, what one does, who one is," which came to me in
my room just now—I didn't write it down until later—is exaggerated and sentimental. In fact it's probably untrue. Of course,
a man has no say in determining who he is, the decision has been
made before he has let out his first cry, but it's not a matter of
indifference to him, he never ceases to mull over the riddle of his
existence, or else he tries "to make the best of it," to quote an
American newspaperman with whom I once had to kill a night
somewhere west of Hanoi and who was quite bewildered when
I said that one might just as well try to make the worst of it. That,
he said, was a typically German idea, as though, once I had told
him I was born in Germany, I had ceased as far as he was concerned to be an English journalist. Actually, when I said that, I
was thinking not of myself but of Keir Horne who had always
been a genius at making the worst of his life and feeling fine in
the process. (I'm letting my resentment against him get the better
of me again. How do I know that he really felt fine in certain
situations?)

In Via del Gambero I stop for a while to look at a film poster.
Then I cross Piazza San Silvestro and continue along the façade
of the post office. It's not true either that it doesn't matter to me
where I live. At present I'm living in Rome—brought here by the
hazards of journalism; Keir suddenly had the idea of putting me
on Italian politics—and I've discovered that for a man in my situation Rome is a good place to live. The city has something easy-
going and cynical about it, which to me means that it is thoroughly adult; I don't care for men who cultivate their puberty in

some corner of their soul. It's only in a very cynical man that I can accept flights of enthusiasm, in Captain Evans for example who led us through Sicily; he was cold and businesslike the whole way, exposing us as little as possible, but then when we moved into Enna on the hilltop he suddenly left cover and, reeling drunk, took a few steps out onto the piazza; high over the rolling sea of olive groves and travertine villages, he flung his outstretched arms into the cone of fire of a machine gun as though plunging into a hurricane composed of all the scents of Magna Graecia and Arabia. The cynicism of Rome is like that. Piazza San Silvestro, for example, is not remarkable as architecture, the Rinascente department store and the Central Post Office are not noble edifices, the center of the square is full of waiting buses, but the baroque façade and cupolas of San Silvestro in Capite give off that red Roman light surmounted, as it is on this relatively quiet Sunday afternoon, by a cool cobalt-blue sky. Somehow this light enables one to bear the fact that unlike Captain Evans, other people, my parents and Esther's mother for example, were mechanically killed and burned; not that one is reconciled to it, the beauty of Rome is not as false as all that, but it gives an intimation that in the end even the keenest, most senseless suffering will fuse into a sum of grief, into a red twilight. Especially after Berlin, Rome is a tolerable place.

At the government shop in the hall of the post office I buy stamps and Nazionali cigarettes, stamp my letter to Keir and throw it in the air-mail box. It will be in London tomorrow afternoon. Then I leave the post office, go over to the newspaper stand, glance at the papers, but do not buy any; I am inclined to stinginess in certain respects. No, that's misleading: it was not my stinginess in small matters that prevented me from buying L'Espresso that Sunday afternoon. I stroll on and sit down on one of the benches that have been put here for people waiting for the bus. To dispel my nervousness I open the packet of Nazionali, carefully tearing off a little piece in one corner so that the first cigarette comes out smoothly when I tap the packet. Pedantic as I am by nature, I can't bear to see the slovenly way some people rip the whole top off a packet of cigarettes, so that after three or four have been smoked the rest wobble about since the top of the packet is no longer there to hold them, get crushed and sprinkle pockets with tobacco; but no more than it was my stinginess which deterred me just now from buying a paper, is it pedantry which now makes me immerse myself in my technique of opening a packet of cigarettes. My behaviour is determined by very different feelings (or rather qualities). I read the signs indicating the bus routes and wonder if I should take a ride somewhere, but abandon the idea. There is little traffic on the square; only in two or three hours, after the big football games in the outlying districts, will buses spew the homecoming masses out on the square. By way of distraction, I watch the woman with the evil eye who is always walking back and forth on the east side of the square, between the church and the next street corner. She is rather tall and wears a coat that falls down to her feet; there is something splendidly ravaged about her face. Her gaze really is evil, it appraises the passers-by coldly and seems to come from a desert; besides, she has a cast in her right eye. When you've known her for years as I have, you know that she's not evil at all but only poor and pervaded by a profoundly tragic mood. People either avoid looking at her and pass her by, or redeem themselves by putting a few *soldi* into her silently opened palm, which is not even explicitly held out. Occasionally I stop to chat with her after giving her my offering; we say a few words about the weather or about the traffic getting worse, never any more, and she never tries to draw me into her private life. Castellani of *La Stampa* literally fled when I once exchanged a few words with her in his presence; he was frightfully agitated when I caught up with him in the arcade and asked me if I had taken leave of my senses; you don't joke with the *mal'occhio*, he said. Castellani is one of the most enlightened newspapermen in Italy. I didn't tell him that this woman had not only brought me no misfortune, but that once many years ago—if you were going to be superstitious—she had actually brought me luck, for eighteen years ago, in the summer of 1944, when I was twenty-four, I had been sitting on this same bench waiting for eleven o'clock to strike from the belfry of San Silvestro; at that hour I was to report to Keir Horne who had set up his office in the rooms now occupied by the Circolo della Stampa Estera. Keir had been travelling from one theatre of operations to another, setting up a team to work on a new type of radio broadcasts beamed to Germany, a kind of propaganda which, as Keir explained to me that morning, would be absolutely unprecedented in one respect, to wit, its news and commentaries would be free from lies; it would be permissible to mention Allied defeats and German victories. Later I realized that such scrupulous fairness was typical of a man who, while working in Germany, had committed certain sins of omission. It had taken years of pleading, no end of maneuvering and the fullest use of his inborn charisma before Keir succeeded, much too late, as he remarked with bitterness, in winning the support of the military and civilian blockheads for his original and, I have to admit, highly effective contribution to the British war effort. Not until the summer of the second to last year of the war was he given the green light. He had picked out my name on some list or heard it from friends in London, and I was called back from the front, south of Florence, to report to him. Yes, it was here on this bench, on a hot summer day about two months after the liberation of Rome, that my journalistic career began. I remember well that I was keeping my fingers crossed in my eagerness to get away from combat duty. I had twice been slightly wounded, I had a vague feeling that the third time would be it, and, having no desire to die at the age of twenty-four, I wanted very much to get away from the front. It was then that I saw this beggar-woman for the first time; she was walking back and forth on the same shaded portion of the square, between the church and the street corner, and she looked exactly as she does today, not a bit younger, just as today she looks not a bit older. I believe she is as old as the Wandering Jew. I was struck by her ravaged face, and though I

knew nothing of the *mal'occhio* then, I sensed the evil and the
tragedy in her gaze as I crossed the square towards her. On that
occasion she accosted me—she never accosts anyone any more—
she must have been very hungry, and I gave her what was left of
a C-ration I had in the breast pocket of my tunic. I still believe
that the blessing the *iettatora* gave me in return had something to
do with the outcome of my interview with Keir. Superstition is a
degraded form of the belief in fate, I am superstitious though I
don't believe in fate—or rather, *because* I don't believe in fate.
The sight of Captain Evans' extraordinarily beautiful death made
me think for a time that words such as *destiny* or *lot* had some
sort of meaning; later, when I found out how my parents died, I
abandoned that ridiculous notion along with the last vestiges
of my belief in a higher being. In the light of Auschwitz I prefer
to vindicate God's honour by presuming that he does not exist,
and the honour of those gods who surely existed at one time and
are perhaps still vegetating in some forgotten corner of space and
time, by presuming that there is nothing left in their lap. The life
of man is a chaotic jumble of biological functions and chance, and
only the effect of the Roman light upon me, the way in which it
manages to change my mood, can occasionally shake me in this
conviction.

Here I must interrupt myself to state, after the fact, that once
I started looking at the old beggar-woman that Sunday in Rome
I really did succeed in diverting my thoughts. I really did sit there
thinking about my first meeting with Keir Horne, I really did forget the impulse that had sent me in the direction of the Circolo
della Stampa Estera and immerse myself in my memories. In so
doing, of course, I merely postponed the eruption of my feelings;
but my written account follows the curve of my emotion very
closely.

It must have been about eleven o'clock when—after the intermezzo with the beggar-woman—I went up to see Keir, whom I
found alone at the far end of a string of empty rooms, sitting behind a desk, smoking a pipe and apparently suffering from an acute

absence of anything to do. (At that time I was still unaware that most journalists are at great pains to give the impression that they never work. Keir, who is in reality a work horse, also observes this rule.) In the first ten minutes of our acquaintance he gave himself an air of military briskness. I was struck from the start by his filthy fingernails. They revolted me and I found the whole man rather preposterous: a civilian between forty and fifty—which seemed pretty old to me at the time—a typical base wallah with military pretensions, who had procured from some headquarters supply room an officer's tunic without insignia, which because of the heat in Rome he wore unbuttoned. Naturally his apparent lack of self-assurance was a deliberate act, as I realized later when I got to know him better: partly the fun of playing a role, partly an attempt to test me, because he could not have used me in the work he was recruiting for if my reaction had been that of a strict military man. I ignored the clipped tone from the first, sat down without asking permission, and lighted a cigarette. At that he dropped the army mask, but immediately put on another: that of a Cambridge don. He was the brilliant snob, inquiring about my studies in the characteristic tone of a college fellow, with an occasional allusion to his own academic career. I had to disappoint him by informing him that I had barely managed in 1938 to complete public school and that immediately afterwards, in 1939, I had offered no opposition to being drafted, though I was not even a British subject. (I finally acquired citizenship in 1940 on a drill ground in Wales, immediately after being appointed corporal.) My story moved him and from then on he was Keir, an unpretentious man who asked intelligent questions and in a few minutes formed a fairly accurate picture of me. Probably in order to find out whether I still had sufficient command of my mother tongue (whether I had it *im Griff*, "in my grip," as they say so aggressively today in the land where it is spoken, a formulation betraying the tendency of the males among my former compatriots—women seldom use such turns of phrase—to dispose of problems once and for all. To get a problem in your grip is to

seize it by the neck, which you twist abruptly, whereupon the
problem is laid out flat, disposed of once and for all. That's the
way to deal with problems. Never leave them in suspense. I'm being unfair, at any rate exaggerating. What was it Inspector von
Cantz said to me in Berlin? "You know, I don't believe in national characteristics.")—where was I? Oh yes, with Keir, who
suddenly started talking German to find out if I was one of those
refugees who couldn't talk their native language without an English accent and occasionally had to cast about for a word. He himself spoke German with next to no accent, though sometimes his
German seemed slightly artificial because his vocabulary was almost too large. He asked me if I wished to study after the war,
and I said no. What then did I intend to do? "Write," I said. Had
I already written anything? I saw no need to tell him about my
literary efforts in the attic of Uncle Basil's house in Clanricarde
Gardens. Occasionally, when I couldn't endure the color-scheme
of Clanricarde Gardens for another minute, I went out, settled
myself in a tea shop in Notting Hill Gate, and wrote. It goes
without saying that Keir didn't believe me and guessed everything.

"When you first started writing," he asked me, "I don't mean
your school papers of course, did you write in English or in
German?"

I answered evasively. When could I have written, I lied, I had
been in the army for five years. And I pointed to my corporal's
stripes, which stamped me as a soldier. My camouflage was almost
complete: in reality I made repeated attempts at writing in the
barracks; only in November 1943 when we embarked for Africa
did I throw all the stuff away.

If I disregard my stirring and mixing of news dispatches in
Keir's truth-loving psychological war kitchen, I have written German in two periods of my life: from my matriculation in London—
I am vain enough to recall that I passed the Higher School Cer-
tificate with distinction—up to my departure for Africa, and now

again since Sunday, 28 October 1962. In the intervening period I was an English journalist.

Receiving no answer to his question, Keir catechized me along different lines: "But if you had a chance to write, what would you write? Novels?"

At that time I regarded the novel as obsolete and communicated this opinion to Keir. He seemed disappointed.

"What then? Biography? Travel books? Essays? Poetry?"

"Something in between," I said. "Perhaps a mixture of all that or perhaps something entirely different."

"If it has anything to do with people," he said, "I mean relations between people, it's going to be a novel regardless of the modernistic trimmings. To tell you the truth, I have old-fashioned tastes. Do you know Trollope?"

I shook my head. I had little inclination to make literary conversation. I hadn't come here to talk about literature but to save my neck. I had been pretty lucky all through the war, Sicily had been my first taste of fire; after the first few battles I had got used to it and soon regarded myself as a hardened soldier. But in the last few weeks the old fits of terror had come back whenever the shooting started. Keir seemed to sense my lack of enthusiasm about this conversation; he changed the subject and spoke of his days in Berlin. He did it so skilfully that I didn't even notice how he had finally maneuvered the conversation to where he wanted it, to the subject that was important to him. I won't say I suspect him of having called me to Rome for that reason; he certainly had every intention of finding out whether he could use me to work with him, but something in my file or something that had come up in conversations with the German refugees he frequented in London for professional reasons—strange that we've never discussed how he came across my name!—some accident, surely nothing more than an accident, must have given him the idea that perhaps I could provide him with information about certain persons in whom he was very much interested. He began to question me about all sorts of people in Berlin. I was amazed at how many

acquaintances we had in common. He seemed to have known an
astonishing number of Jews in Berlin. He asked me if I was one of
the Efraims who owned the fine baroque palace in Stresemann-
strasse. I had to disappoint him. I told him they spelled their
name with "ph," and that the Efraims with an "f" were not such a
wealthy old family. He mentioned more names, found out little
by little what people I knew, and finally, apparently at random,
dropped the name of Bloch. Bloch being a rather common name,
we explored various possibilities, then I remembered Frau Marion
Bloch and mentioned her; my impression that I had given him
the key word that he had been after the whole time is still firm in
my memory. He asked question after question in a tone that was
no longer casual, and when I spoke of Esther, he stood up, went
to the window for a long while and looked out at Piazza San Silvestro to hide his agitation. He drew violently on his pipe, but
soon seemed to forget it. At that time he hadn't started taking
snuff yet, but stuck to his pipes, some ten of which were lying on
his desk grouped picturesquely round a half-empty chianti bottle; but I could see no glass; either he had hidden it before I
came or he drank out of the bottle. Even then he was fat but not
excessively so, though already his blond flesh had begun to over-
flow. Later he became heavy and slow-moving, at that time he was
still the nimble type of fat man. His behaviour had aroused my
curiosity and when he turned back from his contemplation of
the piazza, I studied his face. The nose was large and rather
broad, yet well-shaped, there was sensuality and a note of contempt in his strong arched lips. His eyes—behind the not very
thick lenses of his horn-rimmed glasses—were grey, a grey not of
cold stone but of blown dust, and suffused with a keen, sympathetic intelligence. Under heavy brows and behind round
lenses, they were attentive; un-English eyes in so far as they
seemed prepared to weep or to laugh at any moment. In later
years they often had an absent look. It was by his eyes, I believe,
that one most readily guessed him to be a lady's man. His soft
blond hair has gone prematurely grey; it was wavy then and he

wore it parted; it gave an impression of incompleteness, for that face enlarged by fat, framed in wide cheeks and a double chin, that face with its sensitive features, carefully hidden secrets and critical acumen, ought to have had a baroque wig as its crown and culmination—an idea that came to me much later when I knew of Keir's predilection for Dr. Johnson and his times. I should have liked to get Meg to do a montage showing Keir's head in a full-bottomed wig, in order to prove to him that he was living in the wrong century, but I never did because at a certain moment in our lives innocent games between Keir, Meg and myself became impossible. His wig would probably have been full of fleas, just as his fingernails were grimy, and his desk covered with pipe ashes and wine spots; it was probably because of the grime which surrounded him then as now that I did not immediately guess his relations with Marion Bloch, although his agitation aroused my suspicions; I simply could not imagine that anyone so meticulous about her appearance, a true lady, who was too hoity-toity even for my conservative father, could have taken up with a man who left a sediment of sheer filth wherever he went. To be sure, I have no idea what Keir may have been like as a young man of twenty-three in Berlin; at that time, in 1925, he may have been more fastidious, he may even have cleaned his fingernails.

I have no idea, it surpasses my imagination, and it surpassed my imagination then; I could only stare in speechless incredulity when he told me he was Esther Bloch's father. He didn't hesitate very long but gave me this information at lunch that same day after he had taken me on and promised to make all necessary arrangements with the army. We had gone to a restaurant on a side street off the Corso and were sitting at a table on the pavement, eating spaghetti. I stopped eating and watched him as he continued to eat; I tried to connect this man with my memories of Esther but did not succeed; I could not conceive of this powerfully built, fat, intelligent and slovenly man as the father of a little girl with a pale, flushed, stubborn face framed in stiffly set hair. To me Esther had always been a half orphan; I never gave much thought to the fact that she had no father, not even when for the first time I heard the word "illegitimate" in my parents' conversation about Frau Bloch. The way in which they said it did not suggest that there might be a problem in it, let alone a jack-in-the-box father who would jump out when the word was opened and who now had indeed jumped out, though not with a grinning but with a very sad mask. For what finally persuaded me to believe Keir was the look of fear that came into his eyes when he spoke of Esther, though he went right on eating (as I too have accustomed myself to go on eating while reading or listening to the ghastliest news): this was a father's fear for his child. And I also perceived a shadow of Keir's sense of guilt in his manner of telling me, with a shrug of the shoulders, that he had last corresponded with Marion Bloch in 1936.

It was during lunch that I first heard certain well-documented facts about the technique of persecution in Germany; as a specialist in psychological warfare, Keir Horne was one of those few members of the Political Intelligence Department of the Foreign Office having access to authentic intelligence. As he communicated these facts, fear for my parents thrust itself in among the images of a street in Roma Vecchia, between the conical, almost black stones of a palace wall across from the restaurant, into the rock-yellow light of the Castelli wine in the glasses from which we were drinking, onto the green sun shades of the trattoria, stamped with an advertisement for Cynar, and in between the snatches of Italian sound around us—an *allora*, a *si, ma certo,* a *comunque*, which dissolved in Keir's eyes, horror-stricken at the thought of Esther's possible fate, while his gaze along with mine involuntarily followed a group of nuns whose white trapezoid coifs suddenly entered into a segment of glaring light. I had known that my parents were having a bad time, that they had probably been deported, that they would not survive the life in the camps, but I had been unaware of what Keir now told me. He said:

"They don't kill you people as one kills enemies. They exterminate you like vermin."

Then he asked me whether, under these conditions, I really wanted to work on broadcasts beamed to Germany. But the word "vermin" had struck me like a lightning flash. In the second Keir needed to pronounce it, which may have coincided with the unbearable whiteness of the nuns' coifs which were just sailing through a puddle of sun in a shady Roman street—a particle of the Gregorian calendar and a colour, a fragment of time and a tatter of space came suddenly together and passed away—the word entered into me like an ancient signal, like a trophy and a fervent prayer. In one moment and without hesitation I entered into the secret order of vermin.

That was long ago. How pompous I was in those days! "Secret order of vermin"—what a poetic metaphor for a simple reaction of defiance! Actually the whole previous paragraph is a fairly accurate reconstruction of my sixth-form and barracks style, which, as I note with surprise in writing these lines, I still have at my command, especially when calling to mind the times it went with. For today I very seldom *call* anything *to mind*; at the most I remember, I think of something in the past, or some old story occurs to me; barely a third of the phrases that I find in Dornseiff, Wehrle-Eggers or Küpper under the relevant key words, are of any use to me. (Immediately after starting to write these notes, I acquired the leading German dictionaries of synonyms in Berlin; and as a matter of fact they have helped me to rediscover my old language.)

What has happened to me between then and now—I wonder as I leave the bench on Piazza San Silvestro and cross over to the press club—that I can no longer abide certain metaphors which I once used with intense pleasure? The answer is simple: the same as happens to everyone whose language has suffered. Because when people start destroying human beings like vermin, when they set out not to destroy enemies but to eradicate a seed, then they destroy not only six million souls but also, just in passing, the language of the survivors. I observe how the survivors—with the exception of a few politicians—are always biting their tongues and how literature tries to get along without metaphors. The language has got the evil eye, whereas the beggar-woman, whom I am passing again, has lost it; she is merely a woman who can be defined with a few adjectives: miserable, tragic, old. We exchange a friendly look and I slip a hundred *lire* piece into her hand, because she probably takes in very little this Sunday afternoon on the almost deserted square. Come to think of it, I owe nothing to the magic words she said when I was on my way to see Keir; I abandon my superstitious belief that her magic played a part in Keir's decision to have me transferred from the front. It was not that beggar-woman but Esther who may have saved my life, because what impelled Keir to assign me to his staff was his desire to have near him a childhood friend of his daughter's, someone with whom he could talk about Esther. Nothing else. I had next to no qualifications for such a job. My high-flown literary endeavours—which, moreover, I did not mention—were just about the last thing that might have justified a claim to so extraordinary a soft option. It was not that I had written those things, but the fact that one evening I had tossed them into the stove of a barracks in Wales, which enabled me secretly to register a slight advantage in this respect. No, I crossed the border into the land of journalism without papers and exclusively by pull. An influential man didn't want to be utterly alone in the attacks of terror he suffered for his child—that is what brought me to my so-called profession.

The rooms of the press club have been deserted by my colleagues in the profession which at the moment is still mine. The fine autumn Sunday and the momentary lull in the news—a new cabinet has been in office for a few weeks, there is still no sign of the next government crisis—gives us an opportunity for private life—excursions into the environs, visits to museums, quiet studies, and love affairs. I have the press club all to myself. Even the staff is nowhere in sight. The bartender is absent; the bottles are all neatly lined up behind the bar. The armchairs of the most varied shapes and colours, the little tables with their magazines and empty ash trays, lie silent in the reddish afternoon light which pours in from the piazza. Silent lies the lake. What have I come here for? I have no news story, no feature for the news telephones. Then what am I doing here? Actually, I know exactly what I should like to do now, at this moment and in this place. Immediately after leaving the hotel I sensed what was wrong with me, no, not right away, at first I merely noticed some of the women coming towards me, but I didn't give the matter much thought, and then that big film poster on Via del Gambero hit me in the pit of my stomach. To gain a little time I light a cigarette. Rooms like this have always had the power to drive me crazy, large forsaken rooms where ordinarily long artificial conversations are carried on, where a fabric of supposedly utilitarian, but in reality totally abstract, relationships is woven; sitting in comfortable chairs, people appraise each other across little tables, put out feelers—and then suddenly you find one of these rooms empty; sitting in one of these chairs in the reddish light, in the silence, observed by no one's and by a hundred eyes, you can penetrate your innermost secret, shatter your taboo. After all the pretentious bombast which ordinarily prevails here and in which you have participated, you can finally debase the room and yourself. I spent so much time on the square down below because I already knew what was in store for me if I found the club empty, and when at last this Sunday afternoon I climbed the stairs unswervingly, it was because of course I was dead sure the place would be empty. For after the film poster came the newspaper stand, where I bought none of the displayed papers, not because, as I have written, I am stingy in certain respects, but because the covers of certain illustrated magazines were once again of such a nature that during the seconds in which they reached my retina nothing else existed in the world. Yes, I am often stingy in the most ludicrous situations, but if I failed to buy L'Espresso just now, though I had not yet read it, it was not out of stinginess but because to buy any-

thing other than one of those pictures would have made me feel
like a cowardly hypocrite. Instead I went my way, sat down on a
bench, wallowed in memories, and postponed the moment of
going to the club, but I did not take any of the waiting buses to
go somewhere, because the thought of the probably empty club
rooms, where moreover I should find the pictures I had at first rejected, was stronger than anything else. Now I dig them out
from the piles of magazines on the tables, set them in front of me
and look at them; as I do so, my inner tension subsides a little.
And besides, I am disturbed; suddenly I hear someone speaking,
I'm not alone any more, the sound of the voice—only one voice—
is so soft that I can't understand a word or even tell what language is being spoken. I have the impression that it is rising up
from deep water, vaguely bell-like and muffled. Its presence em-
bitters me. I quickly spread the Sunday edition of *The New York
Herald Tribune* over the cover of *Le Ore*, and go out to see who is
speaking. In the lobby of the club I see John, a German newspaperman whom I know superficially and have spoken with now and
then; he is talking on the phone in one of the booths, hence the
underwater voice. (I have never heard anyone talking under
water, or from under water to the surface, but I can think of no
other comparison; recollections of German fairy tales probably
have something to do with this image.) John must have come in
right after me and gone straight to the phone booth. He sees me
and nods; I leave the lobby, sit down again in my leather chair,
and wait impatiently to see if he will come in or disappear after
his phone call. Naturally he comes in and asks leave to sit down
just a moment; I have no choice but to assent politely, the word
moment gives me little hope of being alone again very soon. John
is excited—he too! but of course on supposedly professional
grounds—he seems to be thinking about his telephone conversation. The usual opening flourishes; he speaks excellent English,
though with a strong German or rather Rhenish accent. I decide
to speak to him in his language. When I tell him in German that
I have just come from Berlin, he looks at me with surprise, where-

upon I add, as if I owed him an apology for using German words, that my trip to Berlin has enabled me to brush up on my German. He is too tactful to say that my German is still tinged with the intonation of my Berlin childhood; he probably knows that I am a native of Germany, after all I'm as well known in the newspaper world as a speckled dog, everyone knows my story. John adjusts quickly; though obviously he has something entirely different on his mind, he politely takes the cue and remarks that if I've been in Berlin I've had a chance to see the shit with my own eyes. To these words I do not react, first because I don't want to start a political discussion which, as I know from experience, would go on and on, delaying indefinitely the moment when I should at last be able to uncover *Le Ore*, and second because what he terms "the shit"—the Wall, the cutting of a big city in two, the isolation of West Berlin—does not strike me as so intolerable as to warrant such a choice of words. It is not so long ago that there were ghettos of a very different kind and how do I know whether or not this John, who is now so indignant over conditions in Berlin, helped to create them? Actually he didn't, he has been living in Rome since 1937; a German journalist to be sure, but he managed to come through the political winter in relative decency and wrote nothing disgraceful, I've looked into it. When the controlled press finally got too much on his nerves, he temporarily retired from journalism and wrote a book—which is said to be remarkable—on stylistic trends in Roman baroque. Yes, weird things happened in those days. We smoke. I give no indication of wishing he were somewhere else. He is half a head shorter than I. Since I am far from tall, that makes him decidedly short, but you don't notice it when he's sitting down; he's an imposing sitter, a very self-possessed little man, grey-haired, wiry, with quick brisk movements, cold, ageless, and a Rhinelander; he pronounces his vowels full and round like Goebbels, his long stay in Italy has taught him to take a dignified pose, what they call *signorile*. What strange people often deflect us from the most essential undertakings! I am unable to repress a laugh; that helps me to bear the situation, but completely flusters this busybody. He gives me a look of annoyance, I readjust the corners of my mouth and manage to listen to his tale of woe. It doesn't amount to much. John, as he informs me, has written a perfectly amiable piece about a Thomas Mann exhibition which the West German propaganda office has just put on in Rome. Only at the end of his article did he indulge in a bit of impertinence, which was promptly deleted as he discovered when he received the paper this morning. On that account he had just disturbed his editor-in-chief's Sunday rest. Seething with fury, I see John taking a manuscript from the inside pocket of his lightweight silk jacket, but there's nothing I can do to prevent him from reading me the passage his paper has censored. The gist of the passage is that it caused quite a stir when Conte B. turned up at the West German ambassador's reception ("the Thomas Mann vogue has assumed such proportions that His Excellency actually gave a reception"—that, of course, is malicious). For Count B. is not only the foremost Italian authority on Tuscan culture, but also a member of the Central Committee of the Communist Party. Who on earth could have invited him, John asks blandly in his article, and why did he come? The guests began to whisper, and certain acute observers expressed the opinion that the Germans were trying to keep up with the Americans and that certain contacts had become timely. In general, those present had expressed surprise at the influence of Thomas Mann in the present day. And John concludes his article with the predicateless and pregnant sentence: In present-day Rome. Feeling grateful to him for confining himself to a short quotation, I compliment him on his charming style, and he laps it up. My flattery enables him to get back to the subject—which improves my chances of getting rid of him soon—and relay to me, with indignation, what his boss has just told him over the phone: that the editors had cautiously consulted certain persons close to the ambassador about this passage and these persons had intimated that it might be preferable, etc., etc. "And it was nothing," said John. "Just an interesting little sidelight on cultural policy." And adds: "Do you know, it doesn't really amuse me any more. Always afraid of stepping on somebody's toes." But having unburdened himself, he is no longer as excited as at the start of our conversation, and moreover his boss, who must be a shrewd customer, has already taken John's mind off his grievance by showing that he himself was better informed on the subject: this whole business about Count B., the boss had declared, didn't amount to much; the count had been close to every German government and hadn't turned Communist until after the war; Mussolini had assigned him to guide Hitler around Florence, and the count had a store of delightful Hitler anecdotes. John wants to tell me one of them, which he has obviously just heard from his boss, but at this point I interrupt him and tell him very rudely that I have no desire to hear a delightful Hitler anecdote. This creates an embarrassing situation which John tactfully glosses over; shortly thereafter he takes his leave. He even turns his departure into a victory on points by apologizing quite openly for his blunder. A self-assured little man—though one who must occasionally put up with the suppression of his journalistic efforts—he makes his way to the door with great dignity. Has he really forgiven my rudeness?

That creep has really succeeded in disturbing me. I find something irresistibly comical in John's mixture of baroque stylistic trends and suppressed news. I had to grin inwardly and this obstinate compulsion to laugh decomposed the desire which the Sunday afternoon quiet of the Circolo had aroused in me. The jocular undermines the erotic. All that remained was my desire to attain my goal. I try to approach it indirectly, by way of a practical reflection which may dispel my merriment. I might ask myself, for example, whether John's statement: "It doesn't really amuse me any more," goes for me as well. Do I want to get out of newspaper work because it has ceased to amuse me? I'm not sure; no, not really; and there I sit in utter dismay, because all at once I've ceased to know why I don't want to be a journalist any more. Did I ever know? It suddenly dawns on me that I have not made the slightest attempt to clarify the reasons for my decision. The decision is made, and that's that! That's the easiest way. One thing I know: my reasons are not those that might impel John to give up his profession. No news item of mine is ever suppressed, and I don't have to avoid stepping on anyone's toes. I am an English newspaperman. The conclusions to which my stories lead —whether I state them explicitly or not (and I practically never state them) have often jarred with the ideas of my conservative paper. For instance, since I've been back in Rome, I've been describing the new Italian policy as an expression of this intelligent people's instinct of self-preservation. Keir has protested several times; once he asked me over the phone if I thought I was writing for *The New Statesman*; but then, with telephonic winks of connivance, we agreed on minor stylistic changes. In England the conservative reader is especially eager for information. A journalist who substitutes wishful thinking for facts doesn't last long. (That is why the English reconcile themselves so easily to facts. How long it took them to realize that it wouldn't do to reconcile themselves to Hitler!) No, offended professional honour is not my reason for wishing to give up my present profession. And it doesn't really seem to have ceased amusing me. When I consider what a passionate, almost maniacal newspaper reader I am, how avidly I wait for my paper every day, how I pounce on my own articles and scrutinize Keir's layouts, looking forward to being annoyed or delighted at my findings. Why then do I want to leave the paper? Really, as Keir supposes, for the sake of literature? He guessed right, though he couldn't have suspected the existence of these notes. I hadn't even started on them when he accused me of "writing literature." But it's true that I want these notes which I've been working on since my trip to Berlin and which are definitely literary in intention, to add up to a book, or at least something coherent that will make me free or drain me dry—it's true, I believe, that they are gradually undermining my taste for the uncomplicated amusement I have hitherto derived from journalism. Instead of amusing me, they have flung me into something I can only describe as a tormenting pleasure. But I made the deci-

sion to give up my job and do something other than newspaper
work long before starting on my notes. Can it be that I had some
intimation of the sad joy of literature, which demolishes everything else? To such questions I find no answer.

At any rate not now, and not here in London, an hour after
landing at Heathrow, three days after abandoning myself, when
John had gone, to a tormenting pleasure, a sad joy of a very different kind at the Circolo della Stampa Estera. The weather in
London is rainy but not cold, although this is already the 14th
of November. In my remaining days in Rome I scribbled one
thing and another, mostly reflections (which I should beware of),
until I realized that in everything I was writing I was avoiding
what I really ought to be writing: a record of my most intimate
life. Then on Tuesday I booked a flight to England for the next
day and here I am. In response to some voice or inhibition, I
did not drive straight to the flat which I refuse to refer to as *ours*
although it still belongs to me and Meg; Meg has given me no
reason not to continue regarding this flat in Malet Street, Bloomsbury, as mine, for since our separation she hasn't had an affair
with any other man, nothing very long-lived in any case. I must
still have a key to the flat, though I don't know where it is. Besides,
Meg and I are still married. But instead of driving to Malet Street,
I put my bag in the left luggage at the Air Terminal and, seduced
perhaps by the situation of the Terminal in Kensington, not
far from Uncle Basil's flat where I spent my first years in London,
I sauntered through the streets. At Barker's in Kensington High
Street I bought a thick writing pad of lined paper, octavo format,
with a light-blue cover; then I strolled along Palace Gardens in a
light drizzle that made the enormous white mansions look like
wet towels on a line. Stopping from time to time under the black
roof of my umbrella, I looked at them as one looks at old acquaintances. I hadn't been in London for over a year, and not in this area
for ages. In this way I put off my meeting with Meg. Actually she
may not even be in London, I didn't wire to say I was coming. If
she's not here, I'll stay at a hotel. I once wrote a poem about the

plane trees in Kensington Palace Gardens. Those trees are hoary
monsters. Much later I pointed them out to Meg, and she called
my attention to the yellow that shines through the watercolour sur-
faces of their trunks; to tell the truth, I have never again seen such
a yellow in plane trees; in the midst of grey almond-green fish
pools, it shone with a Mongolian gleam when Meg projected it
for me in the darkroom in Malet Street. In the glow of the projector over which she was bending, I discerned a look of triumph
in her face; she had forgotten me. From this area with its white-
painted embassies, its black-lacquered doors, its withdrawn gardens, grey under the rain, from this area where I had spent the
lyrical hours of my young manhood, she had managed to distil a
Hunnish colour, an emblem of the steppes, a colour she had surely
dreamed of as a child, at night in a little terrace house somewhere
deep in the Potteries where she came from, the daughter of a
family of potters. Compared to these photographs, my schoolboy's
poem, which I no longer remember, must have been pallid. Passing by the gate-keeper of Palace Gardens, a big man in a long
black coat, with a top hat over his dignified red Beefeater's face,
who seems to have changed no more than the beggar-woman
with the evil eye on Piazza San Silvestro, I suddenly emerge into
the flat, flowing roar of the Bayswater Road, a brown rapids of
motor cars of every shape and size, between banks of low houses,
none of them over three stories. I do not cross the road. I have no
desire to lose myself in the contemplation of Clanricarde Gardens, I am satisfied to note at a glance as I make my way leftward
towards the tea shop of my schooldays, that the street still exists
and that its colours have not changed. However, I fail to find the
tea shop; it has vanished without a trace, replaced by an Italian
espresso bar with a wide glass front which in no way recalls the
windows, covered with gathered curtains, of an old tea shop in
Kensington. Here I sit at a table directly behind the glass panel
with an empty coffee cup in front of me, and leave the writing
pad with the blue cover, which I have just bought at Barker's, un-
touched. Have I taken this walk for the pleasure of walking, or in

order to put off my meeting with Meg? Somehow, as I left the
Air Terminal, I felt that before meeting Meg I had to clarify
my attitude towards her in my own mind and that I would do so
by writing; at the last minute, so to speak, I wanted to secure my
defenses, so as not to succumb to my passion for her. The truth
is that I hate her. . . . Of course this was an absurd project,
doomed from the start to failure. Not until much later, during
the long cool winter I spent in Rome, was I finally able to write
a memorandum from which I quote: That day at the press club
I succeeded in breaking off the tormenting pleasure I had prepared for myself. I don't remember how I managed it, but in any
case I suddenly stopped; I pushed away the pictures I had un-
covered after John's departure, stood up and left the club. I was
desperately afraid of relapsing into the vice that had taken hold
of me in the years following my separation from Meg. I attempted
relations with other women, but failed every time. This was the
only possible substitute for my frantic desire to remain in contact
with Meg. I was over thirty when I met Meg, she was the first
woman with whom I abandoned myself to joy. Actually I don't
care for sexual intercourse. Meg freed me from this distaste. Her
warm, always suntanned body with its dry fragrance! When I
was forced to leave her—of course she will reject this definition of
the reasons for our separation, she will always insist that she would
have liked me to stay with her—I was unprepared for the fact
that certain memories would haunt me. Of course it was stupid of
me not to realize that the mechanism of sexual bondage would
continue to function as though nothing had happened. Time and
time again I set it in motion, I couldn't restrain myself. It was so
easy, quite without Meg, to wind up the clockwork of my feeling for her; I sank into an automatic, artificial relationship with
her; like a madman I so drained my body that in the hours between
orgasms I was numb and utterly empty, utterly incapable of work.
Luckily I hadn't much to do; as soon as Keir heard I had left Meg
—she herself must have told him—he transferred me to a soft
job in Stockholm, where there was next to nothing to report,

anyway nothing of interest to our paper. In the end I fell ill, a
mild case of flu, but it laid me low; by the time I recovered, it
was winter and the Swedish doctor who had taken care of me
sent me to the woods for a few weeks. Busy with ski bindings,
waxing techniques and exaggerated cross-country runs, I adjusted
myself to the season of bitter boredom and worked out a system
for forestalling attacks of sexuality, which by and large worked.
That December at Dalarne made me older. So much for the memo,
the text of which I inserted in my manuscript later. I am still
sitting in the Italian café in Notting Hill Gate, a little perplexed
because in an hour I shall see Meg. I last saw her a year ago and
we flew straight into each other's arms. For Meg that presents no
problem, but for me it does. I don't want my feeling, or whatever you choose to call it, to get the better of me again. I don't
want disorder. I ought to be able to do what I did last Sunday in
Rome: to stop short. The world must be something more than a
chaos composed of accidents. The cigarette butts pile up in the
ash tray, the table top discloses a composition consisting of an
empty coffee cup, an ash tray, a sugar shaker, a bakelite beaker
with paper napkins in it, and a writing pad. Looking across
Notting Hill Gate, I register the row of shops I can see from where
I am sitting: a branch of Barclay's Bank, Venngard & Son, Jewel-
ers, Established 1874, David The Cleaners, Seward Bros., a wine
shop, Reven St. John O'Brady (what a pompous name for a
licensed bookmaker's!), and finally Frank Swan, Estate Agent.
The river of cars flows past the signs, the red double-decker
buses, and now a large dark-green delivery van with gold letters:
Mann's. What is Mann's? No matter. The dark-green and gold
slide gently through the amorphous afternoon. This on the one
hand; on the other hand, a few hours ago the Tiber estuary down
to the sea, olive-grey to steel-blue, the island of Elba, as sharply
delineated as a map, the storm over Finale Ligure, the Po Valley,
a meandering trumpet theme, the high peaks of the Valais above
the cumulus glaciers. Almost to the Channel we had wonderful
flying weather. When I left the press club, I decided to say noth-

ing about my most private affairs in these notes. I regret my inability to hold to this decision. As I was walking down Via del Babuino—it was not yet time for the evening *corso* and there were relatively few passers-by—it seemed to me that it would be easy to be a discreet writer. I felt that I had triumphed over a lust. The silenus in front of Sant' Atanasio, beside the closed newspaper stand, smiled at me. He is nude, but his body is mottled with grey and green spots, and his smile is impenetrable. The old palaces of Via del Babuino were bathed in the Roman evening light. The silenus played smilingly with the thought of sex. But here a hungry and distinguished-looking gentleman is passing by the glass panel behind where I am sitting; he has on a long grey double-breasted coat that has seen better days and is walking with a cane because he has a clubfoot; his narrow face would go nicely with a Rolls Royce, but he looks starved and down-at-heel. Then come two Indian women, one wearing a dark-red sari under her shabby Selfridge's coat. On the plane I was thinking that the world could bear looking at from above. Even then, to be sure, a chaos, but a chaos held fast as in a relief map and easy to survey at a glance. In this café it is very different: a confusion of English and Italian sounds, the smell of coffee, inferior fat and toasters, and from outside the rising and falling roar of the motor-car river. Opposite me sits the typical elderly Englishman reading his paper, a kindly looking man, grey hair, grey beard, grey woollen waistcoat, four carefully sharpened pencils in the breast pocket of his jacket. A very pretty girl comes in, slender and petite, but not too small, silk rain-coat, kerchief over brown hair, attractive legs, eyes alight with curiosity, faint smile, followed by an Indian of about thirty-five, thick black hair, dark-brown uncommunicative face, altogether he makes an impression of uncommunicativeness. To the left of me sits a spinster, a semi-intellectual in a dark-blue coat. To which, as I have said, add the empty coffee cup, the ash tray with the remnants of my cigarettes, the sugar shaker, the bakelite beaker with the paper napkin in it, the writing pad. I rise discouraged in a world composed of clubfeet and Tiber estuary, Selfridge's Indians and green-and-gold delivery vans. I shall arrive at Meg's confused and utterly unprepared. As unprepared as I came to certain passages in these notes. It's easy to say, "I want no disorder." But neither four kindly sharpened pencils nor an Etruscan smile can help me. If all sorts of things exist, I have to say they exist.

On leaving the café, I cross Notting Hill Gate after all, for I should be reluctant to leave the area without refreshing my memory of Clanricarde Gardens. It seems certain that I won't see this northern part of Kensington again for years, the merest chance has brought me here today, perhaps for the last time; but, as though wishing to settle here, I stop outside the showcase of an estate agent and read the notices. It's a habit with me; in cities to which I am a total stranger I can stand for minutes on end outside such showcases, imagining that I am going to settle here and slip into a strange existence, a new life. This agent is advertising a flat in Clanricarde Gardens: *First Floor, Unfurnished Flat, Accom. 1 Bedroom, 1 Rec. Room, Kitchen and Bathroom, Small Dining room, Const. Hot Water, Central Heating, Balcony, Rent £ 400 Per Annum.* This is exactly the same flat as Uncle Basil's, only the number is different: number eight; we lived at seventeen, and Uncle Basil had in addition two rooms on the top floor, the manservant occupied one, I was given the other when he took me in. He himself lived on the first floor, which had a balcony, at that time the only one on our street; it was supported by the pillars above the porch. It must have been a great sacrifice for Uncle Basil to take me in, not for financial reasons, he was a successful physician, head surgeon at St. Bartholomew's Hospital, but because I must have seriously interfered with his solitary way of life. Actually he was not my father's brother, but a cousin, he came of a Dutch branch of the family, but had come to England to study medicine and stayed on. His flat was full of Dutch paintings and furniture. He left all this to me; his will had been carefully drawn up and duly registered when he was fatally injured in an air raid not far from the hospital; he died a few days later, a very inappro-

priate death for so gentle and quiet a man. At his funeral I was
already in uniform. I didn't sell the Dutch heirlooms but put them
in storage on the advice of Mr. Spender, Uncle Basil's solicitor,
the same who later attended to the restitution of our house in
Berlin. They are still in the warehouse of a London shipping firm.
When I set up house with Meg, I could never make up my mind
to move those things to our place; they just wouldn't have fitted
in with Meg. Uncle Basil had no relations of any kind with women
and I never detected the slightest sign of homosexual leanings in
him. William, his manservant, whom I obstinately persisted in
addressing as Mr. Collingwood, at which he just as obstinately
took offence, was an elderly gentleman. He inherited one-quarter
of Uncle Basil's money and retired to the country, somewhere in
Dorset where he came from and where he is still living, surely as
old as the hills. Uncle Basil bequeathed the remaining three-
quarters of his fortune to the Jewish Community of London, for
he was an orthodox Jew. No—"orthodox" calls for a restriction;
actually he was a pantheistic Jew, but he occasionally attended
services at the synagogue in Portland Place and did not operate
on the Sabbath. He often spoke to me of Spinoza, Menasseh ben
Israel and Rembrandt, and told me stories from the history of
the Jews in Spain and the Netherlands. He definitely made a virtue
of the necessity of having to look after me, for he gave me a past
of which I had hitherto known nothing and which fascinated me.
My father paid his taxes to the Jewish Community with meticulous
regularity, but he went to synagogue only on the Day of Atone-
ment and the so-called *Jahrzeit*, the anniversaries of his parents'
deaths. Politically conservative, he regarded himself in religious
matters as an enlightened liberal. My rare visits to the synagogue
as a child have left me with nothing but a vague memory of the
candles on the *menorah*. Uncle Basil disapproved of such indifference, but he did not speak disparagingly of my parents and
made no attempt to win me back to Judaism. I don't believe it
was in his nature to try to convince anyone of anything, and he
contented himself, after dinner when Mr. Collingwood had cleared

the table, with telling me stories which fascinated me because he told them very naturally, in a high, thin voice, his face hovering like a yellow lamp amidst the dark Dutch interior. After that he would busy himself until midnight with his studies on the Sephardic Jews. His only recreation was an hour's walk in Kensington Gardens, in every season and every kind of weather, after leaving his surgery in the afternoon. His favourite writer was Henry James. In his papers Mr. Spender and I found a large, though unfortunately unfinished, manuscript on the appearance of the Wandering Jew among the Marranos of Cordoba in 1644 under the name Juan Espera en Dios, as well as a number of poems, all addressed to an ancestor of our family, one Balthazar Efraim, who had been a student of Grotius and had never come back from a trip to Java. His portrait by an unknown Amsterdam painter hung in Uncle Basil's bedroom. One of these poems, in my imperfect translation, runs as follows:

undoubtedly balthazar those thoughts are enclosed
in peeled red brick a man in middle life who has ceased to speak
or when he does then only yellow words substrates of mirrorings
mirrors are not free mirrors duplicate the anomaly of alkmaar
facing mirrors give an intimation of the law of unending series
of the origin of cora's blondness in grey polished depths
balthazar you will yet test the possibility of constructing
vertical canals which can be set up facing one another for your sole
    desire
is to make a certain blondness vanish in a mirror to look on as cora
negates the law of unending series and sinks into a mirror
it must be possible to solve the problem of unfalling water
but you will have to face the fact that the opposite wall of water
assuming its surface to be clear enough
to have mirrored cora before her vanishing
must also mirror her vanishing a blowing blondness in a blowing
    blondness
resign yourself balthazar behind red bricks
mumble still fewer yellow words not until far down in the series
will the mirrors efface the anomaly of alkmaar.

I wish I knew who this Cora of whom my uncle spoke in several of his poems was or is. So there must at some time have been a woman, a blond, who touched his heartstrings. But he did nothing about her except to play esoteric mirror games. I now believe that he had the same distaste for sexual intercourse as I did before meeting Meg and as I have had since giving her up, but in his case his profession may have had something to do with it, this daily cutting of flesh and sawing of bones, the pervasive smell of blood in which the sensitive little gentleman lived.

Lord, what digressions I've indulged in! Memories are overgrowing the present and will stifle it if I don't watch out. Naturally, if I have set up a souvenir shop in this section of my notes, it is because under the souvenirs I hoped to hide what I really ought to be showing. In spite of the life I have led, which has been anything but bourgeois, the bourgeois sense of shame acquired from my parents is still strong in me. Even to hint at certain things costs me quite a struggle. (The sentences and the involuntary use of words like "hide," "show" and "hint" convince me that my writing has finally lost its private character. It is intended for others.)

Just a word about Clanricarde Gardens, the Victorian hell into which I turn at the next corner. Today I am not frightened as I was that afternoon in 1935 when I first entered the street, accompanied by Mr. Collingwood who had met me at the station because at that time of day Uncle Basil was busy in the operating theatre. The name of course had led me to expect something connected with gardens, at least a remote resemblance to the Bismarckstrasse I had left thirty hours before (not suspecting that I wouldn't see it again for twenty-seven years). Instead I saw two solid rows of three-story houses, all with the same pillars at the entrance, the same stucco borders round the windows set in grey walls, the same basement grilles behind which stairs led down into cellars whose dusty desolation suggested the ashes of crime novels. Still, it was not these houses—though I felt an instinctive revulsion towards them—that made me feel I was entering an abode of ghosts. Perhaps it was the high, pitch-black wall that blocked off the street, for Clanricarde Gardens is a blind alley. No, what really filled me with horror was the smouldering colours. For up to the first story the brick walls, the pillars, cornices and window frames of the houses in Clanricarde Gardens were painted. During the war and in the postwar period the colours faded, but as I now observe they were carefully restored more recently and pains were taken to reproduce the late-Victorian colour scheme. Today I can smile at the satanism of this palette, my reason tells me that a snobbish taste selected these colours, but at that time I was afraid of them. The white suggests bluish mould, the green, absinthe or vitriol, the red, abscesses, the edges of ulcers or clotted blood, the yellow, bile or decomposed henna, and the only possible explanation of the morbid blacks and blues is that before mixing them that artist made a study of cobras' pupils or the shadows of vampires' wings. From this cold sea of colours the grey brick towers then rose into the London afternoon fog—just as today they stand smoky and blurred in the November drizzle, and I can still remember how, when the manservant had left me alone in the sitting room, I stood dispirited behind the window panes, peering out at the street until at last Uncle Basil arrived. He was as embarrassed as I was and our first dinner together was monosyllabic. It was only later, by much thought and effort, that he made it possible for me to love him. Mr. Collingwood led me to the attic room, which I occupied until the war broke out and from which, every night before I went to bed, I looked out into this street that had made itself up to look like an artificial inferno. Or an artificial paradise. For at night it phosphoresced like a diabolical whore under its make-up, under the fog dust and the St. Elmo's fire of its street lamps, occasionally causing me to creep out of the house late at night and wander about London. But I did not find what I was looking for, or if I found it my revulsion was stronger than the desire that had driven me into the streets.

The night is falling fast. I leave Clanricarde Gardens and go down the Bayswater Road to the Queensway Underground station. Nowhere do I feel so at home as on the escalators of the

London Underground. Various sections of London have been
home to me: Bayswater, Kensington, Holborn, Bloomsbury. I
lived in Bayswater as a boy and again later on; I went to school
in Kensington, I learned my trade in Holborn, and lived with Meg
in Bloomsbury. I systematically explored the streets of enormous
areas in London and most of the bus and tube connections come
to me without thinking. I have the feel of London. In Berlin I
sometimes had to reconstruct, and not only because the city has
changed, because large parts of it have been obliterated. Even the
house on Bismarckstrasse struck me as strange, I looked at it as I
might have looked at a photograph in an album, but here on the
escalator of Queensway station I glide down into the depths of
the tube as into a familiar element.

With a sense of relief I light a cigarette. The little posters advertising theatres and cinemas, stockings and cigarettes glide past
me. Or I past them. The other escalator, bearing homecomers from
the city, is overcrowded; this is rush hour. Down below, the warm
wind of the ventilators blows over the platforms. Tottenham
Court Road station is jammed with people standing head to head,
I have difficulty in clearing a path to the exit. Quiet: those who
speak speak softly. Outside, the traffic noise of St. Giles Circus. I
twine my way across the broad intersection and hurry into the
silence of Bloomsbury. The trees on Bedford Square are bare,
their crowns are lost in the night, but the street lamps illumine
the house doors. The back of the British Museum is a dark mass.
I remember how one summer night as we were coming home
rather late, Meg stopped and pointed at the museum. "Look,"
she said, "there it lies like a sacred cow, chewing the Elgin marbles!" Meg detests sights and sightseeing. In the university buildings on Malet Street only a few windows are lit up. At the end of
the street the windows of Dillon's bookshop form a spot of light
which is reflected in the wet pavement; I decide to rummage
through their books tomorrow or the next day. There's light in
our flat on the second floor of 31 Malet Street, Meg is at home,
I hope she won't mind my descending on her like this. I'm looking

forward to seeing her, but I'm not excited; at the café in Notting
Hill Gate I was still excited and most of all anxious. Meg is
aghast when she sees me, she says I'm impossible, why hadn't I
wired? If she had known she would have been able to call off
Cameron, who will be coming in half an hour to take her to dinner, they have to discuss Meg's ideas about a film, he has taken her
on as artistic adviser; she turns up her nose at the words "artistic
adviser." Meg and I know each other well, and I know the word
"artistic" gives her the creeps. She hasn't even dressed yet, she
tells me; then she stops, thinks it over and says she'll phone
Cameron, maybe she can still reach him and explain why she can't
make it this evening; she'll tell him her husband hasn't heard
about the invention of wireless telegraphy. And she scolds me in
a soft friendly voice, falling back, as she sometimes does when excited, into her native dialect, the language of the Potteries. "You
slop," she says for example, a mild insult deriving from the
vocabulary of the pot-banks; slop is the crude red clay that is transformed into slip, or fine clay. Meg once took me to Stoke-on-
Trent; we went to the factory where her father is employed and
watched him working at the potter's wheel, making a vase. His
father and grandfather before him had been potters, and Meg's
brother worked in the same factory. "Now you're thinking this
looks easy, aren't you, sir?" he challenged me while pressing the
half-liquid clay. Though I was his son-in-law, he always addressed
me as sir, but without servility. When I asked Meg to make him
stop, she only shrugged and said her father belonged to the class
of sir-sayers, that she came of a working-class family and I should
never forget it. Meg is basically apolitical but her class-
consciousness is highly developed, whereas Anna, though far to
the left, has none at all. Strange! After our return from Stafford-
shire Meg took the sir into her erotic vocabulary; she would sometimes call me sir in bed, and laugh at my irritation over her
ironical reversal of our relationship.

"You're not to put him off," I say, "or I'll turn right around
and leave."

We haven't kissed, touched each other or even shaken hands since she opened the door. On my last return from a long absence abroad, about a year ago, I hugged her passionately and she offered no resistance. A week later I moved to a hotel in Kensington, where I spent the whole winter and spring until Keir sent me to Rome. But this time we keep a hold on ourselves.

"Maybe I'd better go to the Stanhope," I suggest. "My bag is at the Air Terminal anyway."

"I'll ask Cameron to drive by and pick it up," she replies; "I'll bring it here on the way back."

She understood my question and I her answer. So I'm not in the way. Even if she is having an affair with Cameron, it isn't important enough for her to ask me to stay at a hotel. Meg wouldn't hesitate to send me to a hotel if she wanted to come back to our flat with Cameron. Maybe they have another place where they can be alone; maybe Cameron is a bachelor.

"Give me your receipt," says Meg. I take it out of my passport and give it to her.

"But it's miles from here," I object. "Where are you going to eat?"

"At the King's Head," she says. "It's not much out of our way."

That is a blow. The King's Head was "our" pub, especially in the early days. I met Meg in 1950 and married her in 1951. Two years later we separated. In the summers of our years together we often drove to the King's Head on fine evenings; we bought beer which we drank in the park overlooking the road, and watched the Thames as it flowed yellow through the smoky twilight. London was beginning to recover from the war. At that time I had an old Morgan convertible which I had picked up in a god-forsaken hole in Wales, where I had been sent on a story; it was a joy to drive along the river with Meg, past the bridges, round Westminster and back again to the river, until the blunt grey tower of Chelsea Church emerged, or rather its ruins, for it had taken a direct hit and had not yet been rebuilt. I hide my displeasure, but Meg understands.

"We never ate at the King's Head," she says simply, "the restaurant was too expensive for us in those days, don't you remember?"

We exchange a smile. We've come up in the world. Now we can go to any restaurant we please; Meg had no need to be taken out by Cameron. Our conversation so far has taken place in the hall; I finally take off my coat and we go into the living room which looks out on the street. I notice no change and sit down on our old couch which is still covered with the same brown-black material as when we first furnished the flat. Meg sits down beside me, gives no sign of being in a hurry, and kisses me in a way that is neither peremptory nor sensual, but friendly, almost loving. For a moment, though, I sense the closeness of her skin, of her perfume. A year ago it was entirely different, then I took her in my arms in the hall and she lay right down with me on the couch. This time, as I've just written, we keep a hold on ourselves, no, that isn't quite right; in this moment at least there is no tension between us.

"You must dress," I say, for she is wearing a grey sweater and black slacks. She nods and disappears into the bedroom. When she has gone, I ask myself whether she has changed and decide that she looks the same as ever. When I met her in 1950, she was twenty, even younger than Anna Krystek now. Anna, I reflect, is nineteen years younger than myself, one more reason to steer clear of her. Meg was born in 1930, she is thirty-two now, and in the twelve years I have known her she has not aged. True, she was never young the way Anna is young, or if so, then much earlier. When I met Meg she was a fully developed woman, sure of her movements and thoughts. I hear her opening a cupboard door, then the sound of the shower in the bathroom. I walk round the room in which there is not much to see. Only the couch, the table at which we eat when there is company—I still think "we"!—(when we were alone we ate in the kitchen), on the hall-side wall shelves containing books, records, the record player and loudspeaker. No pictures, Meg hates pictures. None of her photographs in evidence either. The general effect is one of bareness; many of our friends found our flat cold and forbidding. Uncle Basil's heavy old furniture and pictures would not have fallen in with Meg's taste, which is why I never even attempted to introduce them into our home. Our thick old goatskin rug.

Suddenly Meg is back again, it never takes her more than fifteen minutes to dress. She is not wearing evening dress or a miniskirt, but a dark tweed sports suit that is very becoming to her. She hasn't the right figure for evening dresses, whose décolleté presupposes softness and fragility. Though she is small and slender, there is something athletic about her. (I, on the other hand, though not sickly, am all skin and bone, the asthenic type.) The usual women's clothes don't suit Meg; though there is nothing mannish or even boyish about her figure, they make her look awkwardly disguised; she looks best in slacks and sweaters, as she was just now, in her lab coat, or in sports dress on an athletic field. Nor is Meg the type for elegant lingerie, it bunches up on her. Meg looks most beautiful, most alluring, stark naked.

"Are you playing hockey this season?" I ask.

"Of course," she says. "We're playing Coventry on Saturday. Want to come?"

This is Wednesday. "I don't think I'll be in London that long," I say. "I'd like to fly back to Rome on Friday."

"Too bad," she says, visibly disappointed. "And it's so silly that we've lost this evening."

"I've only come to give Keir a report on Esther. I've been in Berlin."

"Yes, of course," which shows that she has been seeing Keir and that they talk about me. "Did you find out anything?"

I nod. She looks at me expectantly, but at that moment we hear the sound of a car drawing up in front of the house. Malet Street is quiet at this hour, one can distinguish the sound of one car from another. Meg goes quickly to the window.

"It's Cameron," she says. "I'll hurry down so he won't have to come up."

She takes her bag from the table and asks: "Will you wait for me?"

"If you don't come home too late. If you do, I may be asleep."

She leaves as usual without saying good-bye. So she doesn't want Cameron to meet me. Or me Cameron. I go to the window and watch as she steps out of the house and approaches a large silver-grey car, a Bentley. A street lamp throws its light on the rainy pavement. Cameron hasn't got out, he opens the door from inside. I see only his hand, his wrist, a white cuff and a bit of his jacket sleeve. When Meg has sat down beside him and the door closes, the hand, withdrawing from the door handle, grazes Meg's thighs for a moment. I can't make out whether it has actually touched Meg's body, but it looks that way from here. Cameron does not start up at once but lingers only for a few seconds, probably because Meg has said: "Let's get going." The car drives off in the direction of Bedford Square. I stand at the window for a while after it has gone.

This chapter is drawing to a close and it's time for me to lay my cards on the table. It's absurd to pretend to be writing this in the late autumn of 1962 immediately after starting to write in Berlin. Actually more than a year has elapsed since then. It has taken me a whole year to write these two chapters and a part of the next. A time-consuming occupation—but I've hinted as much in two or three passages: when I referred to my hurried account of how I came to start writing in Berlin as a rough draft, when I spoke of "entries in a notebook," of "random jottings," and finally when I related how during the winter I spent in Rome I managed to write a "memorandum" about my feelings towards Meg, something my bourgeois sense of shame had long prevented me from doing. It is true that I am still at the Hotel Byron, sitting at my drawing board in the small attic room, but the autumn of 1962 is far behind, it is now early winter 1963–64. The Island crisis is long past. Three days ago the President of the United States was shot. The news overwhelmed me and I went back to the press club after a long absence. My old colleagues were sitting there as

though paralyzed. I listened to their conversations, then I went
back home to the Byron to work on my manuscript. The hotel
is beginning to get on my nerves. My room has become too small
for me; there are times when I should like to go from one room to
another. I have started looking round for a flat, though I'm not
entirely sure that I shouldn't be looking in London or somewhere
else. Apart from the political news this autumn is hardly different
from last year's. In the course of a walk the other day I saw that
they are already putting up the Christmas Market on Piazza
Navona. I shall be able to watch the confectioners pulling, kneading and rolling their blobs of pink or arsenic-green sugar mixture
into sticks. As I write this, I hear two bagpipers from the Abruzzi
playing as they make their way down Via Borgognona. The
pifferari, who always come to Rome at Christmas-time, play well,
but I prefer London street musicians. Once when Meg and I
were queueing up outside a cinema in Regent Street, we heard
a fiddler and two flautists playing an old motet. By changing the
time, they turned the old air into a slow march, which descended
on the street crowds with the darkness. I should stop here; apart
from my visit to Meg this chapter has become one long digression; instead of briskly telling the story of those days last autumn
when so much was decided for me, I have lost myself in recollections. Oh well. I shall get back to my experiences in Berlin very
soon, after Christmas perhaps. I have started already; I covered
quite a few pages with an account of my acquaintance with
Anna Krystek, then I dropped it because all at once my past
seemed more important, but most of all because for a time the
episode at the Circolo della Stampa Estera obliterated everything
else. My narrow escape from a relapse.

With the bagpipe *canzone* still sounding, I turn away from the
window in Malet Street and start waiting for Meg. I go to the
bedroom which is really no bedroom at all, but just a room with
a big bed in it. I used it to work in, Meg has left it as unchanged
as the living room. The large table at which I wrote my articles
is still in its place beside the window; my old Remington is even

there on top of it. Meg has merely put on its oilcloth cover to keep
out the dust. I open the table drawer, it is full of writing paper.
I was always able to work at this table; Meg's presence in the flat
did not bother me. Her darkroom is right next door, I could
hear the faint sounds she made at her work: her adjusting of the
enlarger, the dripping of water as she took negatives out of the
developer to examine them under the red light. I open the darkroom door and switch on the light, not the red darkroom lights
but the bright ceiling lamp. Meg does all her work in this small
room; she needs no studio because she refuses to do studio photography. The darkroom is always shipshape. The two enlargers,
the shelf with the cameras on it, the file of negatives and diapositives, the projector, the cupboard in which she keeps her working
materials, the baths for developing and printing, the shining drum
dryer and the lamps form a well-organized unit. Beside one of
the enlargers I see a pile of pictures; I look through them, they are
school pictures, children in class and in recreation period; full of
life for all their polish and precision. Meg has only contempt for
the modern photographers who turn out blurred, coarse-grained
pictures in order to communicate life and movement. Meg's work
is famous for its sharpness and brilliance; she is thought to have
a secret method, to have devised an original combination of film-
ing and developing techniques. I put the pictures back carefully
in their place. Of course I haven't come into this room to admire
Meg's neatness; I wanted to remember how she was always willing
to put aside her professional pedantry for my sake. True, she always called out, "Quick, close the door," when, drawn by the
thought that Meg had practically nothing on under her smock, I
went into the darkroom—sometimes her presence in the flat
disturbed me after all—and she managed, while I was undoing her
smock, to finish developing the enlargement she was working on
and toss it into the fixing bath, but after that she was all mine.
I believe the ruby-red darkness of this room used to excite us. I
put out the light and return to the living room. How shall I pass
the time until Meg gets back? I look to see whether there are any

new records and find that she has acquired a few Beethoven piano sonatas. I put on a record but remove the player arm almost immediately when I notice that I am hardly listening; I'm not in the mood this evening, the empty flat makes me restless. Should I go to some pub until Meg gets back?

Finally I killed time by making myself some coffee and sitting down at my old typewriter to describe my meeting with Cella. If Meg has to go out with a film director, all right, I can match her. The part those studio gods played in my life last autumn is comical—first Lampe in Berlin, then Cella in Rome, and now this Cameron, though all I ever saw of him was a hand, a wrist, a white cuff and a bit of sleeve. Collaudi would be pleased with me if he knew. Should I ring him up tomorrow and tell him about my conversation with Cella? I have his address in London. And maybe he knows what's being said in film circles about the relations between Cameron and Meg—he's sure to know, a knowledge of people's private affairs is part of the business.

I knew Cella at once by the pictures I'd seen of him, I wrote then, and now a year later I fit this note written in Malet Street into my book. I recognized him at a distance amidst the cars that had parked on Piazza del Popolo or were driving through it; the tables outside the Rosati were not very crowded in the cool dusk; Cella was sitting right next to the entrance, hatless, in a black wool coat; a man was talking to him and he was listening. I went up and introduced myself, he rose, forced a smile and sat down again. The man with whom he had been talking went into the café. I sat down, ordered a vermouth, and began immediately to talk about his new picture. He showed no surprise at my knowing all about his project. To be sure, he was wearing dark glasses though it was almost night, and I couldn't see the look of his eyes. But he asked no questions about the source of my knowledge; he talked to me and I talked to him as though we had been having business conferences for years. He was a small man of thirty-five at the most, and had something owl-like about him. He probably wore dark glasses as a protection against the lights on the piazza, the tall lamps around the obelisk and the projectors that lit up the fountain below the Pincio terrace, although those lights were not very glaring but merely cut sharp or soft circles of general brightness out of the blue-black of the November night. I came to the point so quickly because I was afraid Cella might know by looking at me what I had been doing two hours before at the Circolo della Stampa Estera. Like all men who indulge in self-abuse I have strong guilt feelings. I am almost certain that Cella actually did know. He is just as much of an introvert as I. Still, I had controlled myself at the last moment. The core of Cella's picture is the following story which he took from Hebbel's diary: An apprentice in Hamburg dreams he is murdered on the way to Bergedorf, and tells his master the dream. "Strange," says the master, "that just today you must take some money to Bergedorf." Though terrified, the young man is obliged to go. When he comes to a lonely and ill-famed stretch of the road to Bergedorf, he turns back, goes to the nearest village and asks the mayor to send someone with him on this stretch of road. The mayor sends his servant. The moment the servant has left him, the young man is again gripped by fear; he returns to the same village and asks the same mayor to send someone with him all the way to Bergedorf. Again the servant has to go. On the way the young man tells him his dream and the servant murders him. Cella himself informed me of the source; a friend of his, a German scholar at the Villa Sciarra, had called his attention to the story years before. Regarding me as an Englishman (and according to my passport I am one), he assumed that I had never heard of Hebbel.

I did not tell him I was a native of Germany. But now I knew why the plot of the picture had seemed so familiar to me when I read Collaudi's letter: in the first form of secondary school at Dahlem I had had to learn Hebbel's ballad *Der Haideknabe* by heart. Still, it was new to me that Hebbel had drawn on his diary for the ballad; in fact I had never heard of the diary until Cella called my attention to it. (Yesterday, to check Cella's source, I went to the Villa Sciarra; the park in which it is situated, on the slope of the Gianicolo, seems sunk in sleep at this time of year. The old villa contains an excellent collection of German books. While an uncommonly melancholy librarian—there is a kind of Italian melancholy that verges on sheer hopelessness—was finding the book for me, I looked out of a window in the dark-panelled room across the Tiber at the palaces and churches of the Aventine and at the Tiburtine mountains in the distance. A library like this will be a great help to me if I should finally decide to stay in Rome. Returning to the Byron I immersed myself in the diaries of this remarkable North German. The Jews are too modest to become Christians, he writes. That's Uncle Basil in a nutshell. Or: Who can find fault with a machine if it comes to life by crushing human beings? We have come into contact with such machines; they really have become living beings while the men who serve them have seemed more and more dead. Charlotte Corday's head, Hebbel notes, blushed visibly when the executioner stroked its cheek after the decapitation. If I ever see Cella again, I shall advise him to make a colour film and find out whether this is true. Of course the actress playing Charlotte Corday would have to let herself be guillotined at the end, so demonstrating total identification with her role. Ultimately I came across the story of the Hamburg apprentice and inserted it in my account of my conversation with Cella, because in Malet Street I didn't have the passage and hadn't even read it. Meanwhile Cella's film has appeared, I went to see it a few weeks ago; I regret to say that it's not as powerful as his first, *Il coltello*.) He told me the anecdote recorded by Hebbel in order to draw my attention to the main theme of the picture which, as I already knew from Collaudi's letter, was projected against a modern background. Cella turned the Hamburg apprentice into a Sicilian who had made money in Turin and who sets out, with a valuable jewel in his pocket, to visit a girl in his native Sicily. He dreams his dream in Turin (flashback of the Turin surroundings in which the Sicilian, now a capitalist, had made his fortune, plus dream sequence showing the murder). The actual story was to take place at an inn in southwest Sicily, where the "hero," whose car has broken down, is obliged to spend the night. Cella's brilliant idea, which he described to me in detail, was that the dream-murder sequence should run through the entire picture, gradually transforming itself into the real murder with which the film ends. At this point I broke in, saying: "But mightn't it be a good idea if this murder he had been dreaming and thinking about the whole time *didn't* take place?" I didn't tell him that I was passing on the suggestion of Collaudi and the producers, who found the project too gloomy and thought a happy ending would result in a better box office. God knows I had no intention of acting as those people's mouthpiece, but on the spur of the moment the idea of letting the poor devil off alive struck me as perfectly plausible, though of course I knew this would ruin Cella's whole conception. He turned his dark glasses with the strangely black and excised mirror-image of the Piazza del Popolo towards me, and I felt that I had fallen in his esteem: "He's got to die," he said tersely. "He has dreamed his fate." Another believer in fate. Like Keir. Or like Hebbel. The smartest people—when they believe in nothing else—believed in *that*. For a while we discussed the mythical, psychoanalytical and sociological aspects of Hebbel's story in high-flown terms. (If Cella's picture did not turn out as well as I had hoped, it is because he did not succeed in fully unifying these different aspects.) I gathered enough material for an article for our *Weekly Review*, which I actually wrote. At about seven he excused himself and left, instantly surrounded by a group of men who, taking our handshake as their cue, rushed out of the Rosati. I looked after him as he crossed the square in their midst, small, owl-like and unruffled at the centre of a gesticulating knot of fashionably dressed figures. It must be hard for an artist to please everybody. They vanished under the arch of the Porta del Popolo.

The writing of this recollection actually did distract me for a few hours. Once or twice I sank into contemplation at the machine. Once I went to the kitchen and made myself a bite to eat; I found butter and cheese in the refrigerator and bread in the bread bin. Meg hasn't changed anything in her kitchen arrangements either; even the whiskey bottle is in its old place. It's past eleven but I'm not tired, the whiskey keeps me awake. Even so I decide to make up my bed on the living room couch, so as to have created a *fait accompli* before Meg comes home. I know her too well not to realize that before going out she did not forget to ask me where I wanted to sleep. Her failure to ask was intentional. In this connection it was always her tactic to leave me the initiative—I write this a year later in Rome and wonder whether I shouldn't go on with it, but then I decide after all to spin out my notes about Anna first, because, come to think of it, what made me curtail my stay in London was my fear that Anna might meanwhile have arrived in Rome. So I shall keep myself waiting for Meg, though it's hard for me. I shall probably pretend to be asleep when she comes home.

Three

Before I left her on Saturday night, Anna gave me her address and phone number. Monday morning I fish out the slip of paper from the pile of scraps beside my typewriter on the table of my Berlin hotel room. She lives in Neukölln, Treptower Strasse 21, fourth floor. Was I ever in Neukölln as a boy? I don't remember. At that time Neukölln was known as a Red neighbourhood, a Communist stronghold; that, if I remember right, did not repel me, but you simply never went there if you lived, as I did, in the West of Berlin. It would never have occurred to my parents to show me that part of Berlin, which is way out to the southeast beyond the Tempelhof airport, and is said to be ugly; I don't even think my father was ever there. Towards the end a number of well-to-do Jews were lodged there after they had been put out of their houses and flats in the old West; my parents and Frau Bloch were fortunate in Wannsee; they were able to live in Bismarckstrasse to the very end. Jews, I reminisce for a moment, German Jews, Jewish Germans, Germans; but the problem involved in this combination of words no longer interests me; it's obsolete.

This morning the loading yard down below is teeming with weekday activity. Standing at the window in my pyjamas, I count a dozen vans unloading crates which disappear into the back doors of buildings facing onto Kurfürstendamm, and some fifty parked private cars. Rain. Not a downpour like the one in which I woke up on Saturday night, but a fine steady rain seeping out of a foggy mass that veils everything, including the Interzone train which turns up punctually from the left, rounds the curve and disappears into the Zoological Gardens station. My favourite weather— slight low pressure, cool but not cold, and a drizzle, which doesn't bounce back from the roofs of the cars, but merely coats them with a skin of tarnished silver. I still have the slip with Anna's address in my hand. For the moment I put it aside and go into the bathroom, brush my teeth, shave and shower, looking at my face and body until they vanish in the steam that clouds the mirror and my glasses—these fifteen minutes every morning are the only time in the day when I feel the need of mirrors—put my pyjamas back on again and sit down irresolutely on the bed. After yesterday's writing binge I feel very much sobered, almost depressed. It's ridiculous to want to write a book. Some simple bit of journalism—that's what would appeal to me. I should like to write a piece of clear newspaper prose, none of this subjective stuff I was doing yesterday. The worst of it is that I keep thinking about a book, though all I've done so far is write a few personal notes. My jottings must have a dreadful squint, because from the very first I was looking both at myself and at someone else who was watching me with a sneer. Disgusting! To make sure that it would be better to abandon the attempt, I go over to the table and pick up the written pages; but the words suck me in, some of it doesn't seem so bad, I remember my mood when writing, the feeling of being moved over a galvanic field, something I have never before experienced, not even while working on successful newspaper stories. I look up from the pages, irritated because I refuse to believe that my hangover has left me; perhaps it's the congenial weather that has put me in a better humour, as well as the fact that I am now able to think of Anna again and that the memory of her gives me a sense of falling in love, whereas yesterday afternoon I forgot her. This morning the falling-in-love process suddenly starts up again as though nothing had happened. Along with these delightful stirrings—the weather, Anna!—I feel that my depression has not left me; the fact is that what appeals to me this morning is this interchange of light and dark colours in my head. (Here I first wrote "within me," in order to avoid formulations such as "in my heart" or "in my soul"; in the end I decided to make my head the seat not only of my thoughts but of my feelings as well.) I ring the hotel switchboard and ask for

Anna's number; my phoning at this impossible hour, 7:30 A.M., is not uncalculated; a phone call at an outrageous hour is always amusing and flattering to a woman; and so, though at heart I dislike the mechanism of courtship, I set it in motion. At the same time I give her an opportunity—in case she finds my failure to turn up yesterday afternoon unforgivable and has lost interest in me—to suggest coldly that I call later in the day; then I'd know where I'm at. I must actually have roused her out of a deep sleep, for after picking up the receiver she is mute, unable even to say hello; only after I have stated my name does she sleepily summon up a little bundle of monosyllables: "Oh, oh yes, it's you," and finally arrive at a dissyllabic word over which she bends for a moment before picking it up: "Georg." Once again the German form of my name startles me; so many years have passed since it was transformed into a single palatal vowel embedded between two lingual consonants to produce a soft, cloudy, lyrical sound, whereas from Anna's mouth it suddenly hits me with two sharply separate vowels and three precisely defined consonants. Since Anna has addressed me by my first name, as she did at the end of Saturday evening—she began when we came to her friend Werner Hornbostel's flat; all at once she stopped calling me Herr Efraim and I, availing myself of the tacitly given license, called her Anna; it was almost like England, but Anna has never been in England, and, besides, our change in the form of address was not as free-and-easy as it would have been in England—since, as I was saying, she still says Georg to me this morning, I see that I haven't spoiled everything by standing her up yesterday. In a few moments she seems to be wide-awake, for when I begin to apologize she interrupts me after the first few words.

"It's just as well you didn't come," she says. "I was in a bad humour. I'm sure everything would have gone wrong. I only waited ten minutes, then I pushed off. I skedaddled around the corner into Schüterstrasse, so you wouldn't run into me in case you were just late." She stops short and asks: "You don't mind my being so frank?"

"No," I say. "Of course not."

I wonder what she means by saying everything would have gone wrong. But I know I mustn't ask her such a question—it's too soon. Incidentally, though Anna is a Berliner and uses expressions like "push off" and "skedaddle," she doesn't speak the Berlin dialect but a perfectly pure German. When I questioned her about this, she told me it had cost her years of hard work at dramatic school to get rid of her Neukölln intonation. This makes it easier to get on with her because, though a Berliner myself, I was allergic even as a boy to *Berlinisch*, which is not really a dialect but a jargon. My parents made only moderate use of it, though in company my father liked to tell Liebermann anecdotes. He admired Fontane, saying that, though very *Berlinisch*, he was, thank God, not bumptious. And my mother was incapable of what in Berlin is termed "native wit"; even with regard to language, she was of a frail constitution. I'm not even very fond of the "pithiness" that is imputed to the Berlin jargon; pithy remarks always cut one off sharp. In any case I can't conceive of Anna Krystek being endowed with the rough and ready wit that is known in Berlin as *Schnauze*, although she claims that she once spoke the most unadulterated Neukölln slang and still does in critical situations. Maybe I'm mistaken, but that's what I like to think in my present stage of in-loveness. In any case, Anna is not bumptious. Or maybe she is. Those remarks of hers at Lampe's party, which created such a sense of amused complicity between us—weren't they an indication of bumptiousness converted into a subtle art of characterization? Could she be a bitch? She doesn't look like it. She is medium height, skinny, pale and ash-blond. That of course means nothing. Women who look like that can perfectly well be snobs, gossips, and cocktail party bitches. But in Anna's case words like medium height, skinny, pale and ash-blond mean that she really is what these words connote: medium height, skinny, pale and ash-blond. For instance her face, which seems almost flat because her cheek bones are very high, close under her eyes, is clothed in smooth, anemic-looking skin. When I first

saw Anna, I wondered whether deep-black hair might not be better suited to that pallor, but soon decided against any such
hypothetical contrast and in favour of her blondness, which is undoubtedly natural, a colour suggestive of weak tea. Her hair, like
her skin, was smooth; she wore it combed back in a loose wave
and gathered at the neck into a knot which looked as if it would
come undone at any moment. Now, as she speaks into the phone,
her hair must be lying loose on her pillow, if she uses a pillow. I
assume that the phone is beside her bed. Do we speak of ash-
blond because we think of ashes, which are actually light-grey, or
because this is a blondness with the fire gone out of it? The
colourlessness of Anna's skin and hair actually does give her face
a spent quality that contrasts charmingly with her mouth and
eyes. Her mouth is not very small, but medium-sized like her body;
Anna is just a bit taller than I, about five feet six, which makes her
seem ever more slender than she actually is. I have always been
attracted by women taller than myself, yet Meg is almost an inch
shorter, five feet four. Anna's mouth then is medium-sized and
slender and, as I have said, speaks willingly and abundantly in the
pure German of the stage, but entirely without affectation. I like
that. Women who are lively in conversation appeal to me more
than the silent sphinxes who are thought by the inexperienced to
have some secret which they jealously guard at the vertical but
reveal in a horizontal position. Whether a woman has tempera-
ment or not can be seen from her conversation, and women who
have nothing to say in company are boring also in bed. I am anything but a connoisseur of women. In all my life, which has now
been going on for forty-three years, I have gone to bed with a
dozen women at the most. That, I may add, is enough for me; I
don't feel that I've missed much. Anna's eyes are light brown and
wonderfully changeable; they can observe coolly or take on a dark
warmth; slightly sunken behind the high cheek bones, they are
also very large, which is important for an actress: Anna's eyes
make her face photogenic. (Meg once described to me how a
photogenic face must be constructed.) They produce a very un-

usual effect: although they have a definite colour, a brown which, though light, is objectively darker than the colours of her hair and skin, they appear, because of their luminous transparency, to be lighter than the hair and skin. The contrast which the almost anemic quality of her skin and the neutral tone of her hair require —if Anna is not to vanish into shadowy insignificance—is produced not by night-black but by morning-bright irises. In short: Anna is a pale girl with light eyes and a slender, mobile mouth. She gives an impression of something undeveloped, of something still hidden, a sense of intimation.

These weapons which Anna has at her disposal are to be sure so inconspicuous, so unspectacular, that she will have a hard time of it in her profession. During the evening at Lampe's, for instance, she was unable to steal the show from two celebrated film beauties. Only Lampe himself—he still gets ideas now and then —began circling round her and finally abducted her from me by coming up to her and saying: "You *are* rather tall, Fräulein Krystek! It must be rather hard for you to find a suitable partner." Naturally a young actress is defenceless against an oily advance like that. Accordingly, when about an hour later I had to leave because of an embarrassing incident which I myself had brought about, it was really sweet of her to turn up at my side and thrust her arm in mine. We went quickly into the hall, picked out our coats from the heap on the table, and left Lampe's flat like conspirators.

Back to my telephone call! While Anna is still reacting with such charming frankness to my apologies, taking all the embarrassment out of them by assuming a share of the guilt, by playing the role of a girl who had been glad to come but then preferred to push off and skedaddle, I start wondering whether she is so politely indulgent because I am a Jew. A beastly idea, I know, but it does pass through my head. My old compatriots always take a different tone once they find out who I am; they suddenly switch, like John only recently, who after disturbing me in my solitary occupation at the Circolo della Stampa Estera, reacted with exquisite tact to my deliberate rudeness. I shouldn't complain about it, but it bothers me. To dispel this thought in relation to Anna, I express it. Her answer surprises me.

"That's funny," she said. "I was just wondering the same thing, whether I act differently with you because you're a Jew. Well, I do. Even if you didn't interest me in the least, I'd be a little nicer to you than to somebody who's not a Jew."

That's being frank, at least. What really delights me is that Anna says the word Jew in a perfectly natural way. I have discovered that most Germans say it very strangely, with a slight catch in their voice as though speaking of something indecent. As though they had to give themselves a little push in order to get it out. It's very much the same when a prude pronounces the word "naked." There really is something obscene in those people's attitude towards us. I decide to accept the premises of Anna's last sentence but to look into the reasons behind them.

"Can it be," I ask her, "that I interest you only because I'm a Jew?"

"Possibly," she admits. "It certainly has something to do with it. But the main thing after all is that you do interest me and that I like you. Don't you agree that that's the main thing?" She doesn't wait for an answer—and what could I have answered—but adds at once, "Anyway, Georg, there's nothing more in it."

To say that there is or isn't something *in* a thing, a situation, an idea, is one of the most common locutions of the new German slang. At Lampe's party most of the people thought there was nothing in the Island crisis, but a great deal in the affair of *Die Revue*. Everyone understood what this meant. I myself find the phrase expressive, I certainly like it better than to hear someone claiming to have got something in his grip. (When I phoned Keir yesterday morning, and later in my draft of a letter to him, I used the phrase as a matter of course.) What bothers me about Anna's sentence is that the phrase, as she has used it, has lost its special quality, the quality of offering a clear hint, and taken on something definitive. If she had said, "I don't think there's

anything more in it," or simply, "there's nothing more in it," she
would have preserved the point of the sentence and given me
the opportunity, which it and I need, to take pleasure in it. Instead, by her apparently so incidental use of "anyway," she gave it
an expression of absolute certainty, which contradicts its essential
nature. Her naïve remark about the main thing being that I do
interest her and that she likes me is merely a token of the splendid
self-assurance typical of girls of her age—which is why I had nothing to say in reply—but her "Anyway, Georg, there's nothing more
in it" is an expression of her convictions. Even without Sandberg's
help I should soon have found out that Anna thinks she knows
all there is to know about certain matters, especially politics. This
already led to a quarrel between us on Saturday, during the half
hour we spent looking for a cab in Grunewald after leaving
Lampe's house. We quarrelled about her way of making apodictic
statements such as "K. is a traitor." Her saying that there is nothing more in our relationship—and, to make matters worse, "anyway"!—than sympathy and interest, also strikes me as extremely
apodictic. It also contradicts her remark at the beginning of our
telephone conversation that "everything would certainly have gone
wrong" if I had kept our date yesterday afternoon. How can "everything" go wrong if there is "no more" in it? When I call her attention to the contradiction, she asks in all seriousness whether
interest and sympathy aren't quite a lot.

"Even they can go to smash," she says in a voice suggesting that
she held someone to blame, "when it's dreary on a dreary Sunday
afternoon in a dreary café."

With that of course she won me over completely. Besides, those
words prove to me that no one is lying in bed with her. All through
our phone call I have been listening for a sound, if only of breathing, which would tell me that she's not alone. I've heard nothing,
but the intimate lament of this sentence proves to me more than
the silence surrounding it that there is no witness to our conversation. Even Werner Hornbostel, whose mind is almost always
far away, busy with some musical speculation or other, and who

moreover doesn't care in the least whether Anna has an affair with me or not, would have been affected by the tone in which Anna expressed her concern that something might go to smash between her and myself. Precisely because he seldom listens, he wakes up at the crucial moments of a conversation; on Saturday night, for instance, he suddenly broke off the sonorous puzzle he was working on when I began to speak of Esther and my mission in Berlin. No, Anna couldn't say such words in his presence. So it merely remains for us to decide where, if we want to see each other again, we can meet without running the risk of something going to smash, but all I can think of is another café, this afternoon perhaps?

I sense Anna's reluctance. Wondering why I haven't asked her out to dinner, I remember that I've bought a ticket for the theatre in East Berlin tonight. On Saturday, after everything Sandberg had told me about Anna and she had told me about herself, I didn't want to mention it, but now I do, and thoughtlessly ask her if she wouldn't like to go with me.

"Do you think I can get hold of another ticket?" I ask.

"No," she says quickly.

"Never mind," I say, "then I'll let it go. I'm not so mad about the theatre. Let's have dinner together and roam around afterwards."

There is indignation in her voice when she says: "See here, Georg. You're going to that theatre tonight!"

That's an order. "But why," I ask in surprise, "won't you let me try at least to get another ticket? We foreign correspondents have all sorts of dodges. . . ."

She interrupts me. "You have no dodge," she says brusquely, "that will take a German resident of West Berlin through the Wall to East Berlin."

How stupid of me not to have thought of that! Of course I knew all about the strange conditions prevailing in the city where I was born, but in four days those things don't really become a part of you. A newcomer like myself tends to forget about these absurdities. Still, it was unforgivable of me not to have thought at least of Anna's very special situation in the midst of those strange conditions. "Stop, stop, it doesn't matter," says Anna when I apologize. Now I see the reason for her sudden breathless anger; it was because she couldn't cross over to East Berlin. On the other hand, in view of all I know about her, it's obvious why she insists that I at least should cross the Wall to see that play. I try once more to tell her that I'm really not keen on seeing it and would much rather spend the evening with her, but nothing I can say makes any impression.

"You'll go, and then you'll tell me all about it," she says. "I never did get to see *The Days of the Commune*. They didn't put it on until after the Wall. Do you know the play?" I had to say no. Anna waxed enthusiastic and in her enthusiasm a wee bit *Berlinisch*. "*Na, Mensch!*" she says—*Mensch*, not Georg! "You've got a treat ahead of you! There's a new young actor in it, Thate, they say he's terrific. And Flörchinger plays Thiers and Bismarck —you'll swoon!"

She's amazingly well-informed, it must be because she's an actress.

"You know what," she says, "come and have lunch with me tomorrow if you've nothing better to do. First I'll take you round our market and then I'll make you something to eat while you tell me how it was and how you liked the play."

We arrange to meet at half-past eleven next morning at the Neukölln Underground station. Anna has hit on something much better than any of my cafés. A gay, friendly invitation, as innocent as the early hour she has picked, the continuation of a friendship. There's nothing more in it. Suits me. Much better than an invitation to tea, which has become the classical threshold of intimacy. "Fine," I say. "See you tomorrow, Anna"—throughout the conversation I have avoided calling her by her first name, though she has several times called me by mine—but quickly before hanging up, she says: "Don't forget to ask at Esther's school." "No," I say, "I wouldn't have forgotten."

When she hangs up I absently hold on to the receiver, and

after a while the switchboard answers. I pull myself together and order breakfast. Then I dress. At breakfast I am annoyed with myself for not having sent for the morning paper. I pick it up in the lobby on my way out. *Moscow withdraws missiles from Cuba.* Good, now Keir has no more reason for keeping me here. *Action against Spiegel causes stir.* That's not for me; our Bonn bureau attends to German internal affairs. With a sense of relief I step out into the street. Just my inquiries at Esther's school, then goodbye Berlin, unless Anna Krystek succeeds in detaining me a little longer. I've taken my umbrella and put it up although it's barely drizzling; I detest the feeling of rain on my head. Today Kurfürstendamm isn't as quiet as yesterday, Sunday morning; the usual weekday traffic. The AP bureau is bustling with activity, they're all there. Bud Collins, always in the know, confirms that the Island crisis is over. My German colleagues are all talking about the prosecution of *Die Revue;* its Berlin man shows me a picture of the editor-in-chief being arrested. He seems to be about my own age and build. He too is rather short and thin with smooth short hair that clings to his head and a hooked nose. He is wearing dark horn-rimmed glasses. He doesn't look Jewish to me. He looks like a young prig who wasn't allowed to be a Jew. Bewildered and contemptuous, he peers into the camera—an impeccably dressed young citizen who thinks he is dealing with a cabinet minister, not with a system. But even that's pretty bad when you're too nervous and sensitive to bear that minister's face. I inwardly wish him luck and go back out onto the street. My early morning enthusiasm for newspaper work has left me in there. For a time I roam about Kurfürstendamm and the side streets in search of something that might interest me as much as the young couple yesterday with their two Afghans, but I find nothing. Then as I approach my hotel my eye lights on a stocky middle-aged man outside a men's clothing shop. He is wearing an English tweed coat of the latest cut, too short for his bull-like figure; from it protrude grey-checked trouser legs draped gracefully over pointed Italian shoes. From under black matted brows he is staring at the shop window as avidly as I stared yesterday at my plate of pig's trotters, a muscular aggressive little glutton lost in thoughts of elegance. I watch him for quite some time, fascinated by the sight of this defenceless lust, but then I have to turn away when he gives a distrustful look round him before disappearing into the shop. His week is off to a good start.

Back in my room, I decide to work a bit more on my notes, though I am not as I was yesterday afternoon in that state of cool tension in which writing comes easily to me. On the contrary, I observe that I've sat down at the typewriter as though facing a chore. If that's how it is, ought I to go on? It's not yet too late to break off. The few pages I've written don't mean a thing; I can tear them up, throw them into the wastepaper basket, and go back to journalism or take up something else, some job to see me through my life. No, I go on writing, start touching up my telephone conversation with Keir. I feel that something is wrong but fail to suspect that what troubles me is my use of the third person. I started my record as though writing a novel; it didn't dawn on me until some weeks later that the stratagems of the novelist must be subordinated to the veracity of the reporter, in my case, at least. Still, despite my vague uneasiness, I go on writing, get back into the mood, probably because of the quiet rain outside the window, which spins a cocoon around me. And I've stuck to it, for I am writing this recollection of that first morning when I approached my "book"—as I have called it in my mind ever since —as a chore, at the Albergo Byron a few days after my return from London, a few days after that night in Malet Street; sitting again at my drawing board (as I am now, a year later, as I insert this parenthetical note—yes, a year later I am still sticking to my manuscript, though I have become impatient and eager to get out of this cramped hotel room that isn't much more than a garret), casting an occasional glance at the roof gardens across the way, whose vines and wisterias have shed nearly all their leaves. Bare vines run back and forth between the clay or wooden tubs in which the plants are rooted. The sky overhead, in contrast to the

sky of the Berlin drizzle, is as blue as it was on the day I flew to
London, but I don't let the fine weather interfere with my work,
I sit over my manuscript every day from early morning to noon.
Even Anna Krystek couldn't take me away from it if she had come.
But she hasn't come. In the afternoon I attend to my most urgent
work for the paper and occasionally make a phone call to our news
service; to oblige Keir, I am continuing for the moment, despite
the uproar in London over my piece about the Pope, to go through
the motions of being a newspaperman. Keir fumed over the phone
when he'd read it. He was going to fire me on the spot, then he
changed his mind. I can't very well leave him in the lurch at this
point, especially as the work right now is pure routine, which I
can handle in two hours in the afternoon. Politics are still in
the doldrums and the rumors that the Pope is dying have again
subsided; our excellent contact at the Vatican assures me that
the old gentleman's stomach cancer has been temporarily arrested.
So there is nothing to prevent me from spending my mornings
in Berlin. At about half-past twelve I am overcome by fatigue,
hunger and a feeling that I can't grind out any more today. With
the help of the two telephone operators who sit in a glass cage
down in the lobby I manage to locate Esther's old school. All
I remember is that she went to a school operated by nuns at
Steglitz. Frau Bloch was not a Catholic but at the end of 1933
she transferred her daughter from state school to a Catholic private school where she thought the child would suffer less from
anti-Semitism. I seem to remember that there was some difficulty,
but the school took non-Catholics and in the end the child was
accepted. Here Esther, born in 1925 and like myself not baptized,
completed primary school and the following year, the year in which
I left Berlin, started secondary school. I don't remember the name
of that religious order, but one of the telephone operators calls
the Berlin Board of Education and finds out that the Carmelites
have for many years been running a school in Steglitz. Yes, I believe Esther did speak of Carmelites. I ask the operator to put
through a call and take it in one of the booths beside the glass

cage. The school answers and I ask to speak to the principal. "You can't speak to Mother Ludmilla now," says a feminine voice. "She will be in seclusion until two o'clock." Good Lord, I think, but of course I can't say that. I thought it would be considerate not to call during school hours, but apparently a nun can be called out of the classroom more readily than out of seclusion. I suppose she is alone in her cell—and they tell me that quite openly. Incredible. I ask at what time I can reach her; the voice tells me there are no fixed hours but that four o'clock is the most likely time. The voice sounds as if it came from a large forsaken room paved with stone. I say I shall call again at four and thank the voice, but before I've finished hanging up I decide to ride out to Steglitz that afternoon and speak to Mother Ludmilla in person. In case she did know Esther, she certainly wouldn't tell me anything over the phone; I want to get this thing over with, and leave Berlin as soon as possible. If I were sure my visit to Anna Krystek tomorrow would amount to no more than the prolonging of a passing acquaintance, I could arrange to take the Interzone train tomorrow night. I think of asking the hotel receptionist to get me a berth but postpone the decision. I cross the street to the Schultheiss Restaurant, as I did yesterday; this time, however, I order not pig's trotters but Königsberg meat balls. To renew old experience. I try to work out what I really mean when I wonder whether my relationship with Anna will become something more than a passing acquaintance. I was in love with her when I woke up this morning, but now I'm not, and I have no idea whether I will be in an hour, this evening or tomorrow morning. But even this morning when I was in love with her, especially during our telephone conversation, I had no notion of what might happen next. I break off my speculations and bury myself in the newspaper.

The proprietor in person brings me the *cannelloni*, which after my morning stint of writing, often bring me to the Trattoria da Corrado. Since Anna Krystek has not come and perhaps won't come at all, I might, if I felt the need of having an affair, try to make friends with the American girl who with her mother has

ventured into this little *trattoria* in Via Bocca di Leone where I
usually have lunch because it's not expensive, because it's near the
Byron, and because the cook makes *cannelloni* the way I like
them. I sprinkle—a breach of all the rules governing *cannelloni*
—a little more parmesan on the subtly calculated mixture of heat
and gentle warmth, and over *Il Messaggero* observe mother and
daughter who are sitting at the next table studying the menu
in bewilderment. It would be very easy to get acquainted. The
daughter is in her mid-twenties and ash-blond like Anna but in a
very different way: there is something radiant about her. She is a
tall, pretty American girl. The mother seems to be about fifty and
is not one of those scarecrows in floral hat and veil, who are so
basic an American contribution to the civilization of the twentieth
century, but the progressive rich woman type; no make-up, very
simple, very expensive suit; her sole concession to the taste of
Providence, Rhode Island, is the obligatory string of pearls. As
their reaction to the menu and manner with the waiter show, the
ladies are new to Rome and to Italy. I really ought to step in and
see to it that they get something proper to eat and that the young
lady doesn't come to any harm in the course of her stay in Rome.
She is definitely too intelligent, too full of happy mockery to fall
for any *papparazzo* from Porta Marancia or Pietralata, but if some
beau from Parioli sidles up to her at the Excelsior or at Doney's,
she might, out of sheer curiosity, let him maneuver her into bed.
I am presumptuous enough to believe that she would be better
off with me, but expunge this corny notion from my mind by
telling myself that I could not possibly compete with the charm,
the concentration, the smooth exotic courtship that a good
cicisbeo would offer this girl. No, let her have her Roman flirtation and her Roman nausea as well, when lying abed one morning in a flat in Via Archimede she sees before her a lover who is
suddenly bored, unabashedly bored, no sentimental boyfriend
tortured by guilt, but an Italian man who despises her and wants
to be alone. Thus feeding on *cannelloni* and clichés, I am able
to relapse into newspaper reading and inactivity. Even in connec-

tion with the ladies' lunch my help is not needed, for meanwhile
the proprietor has made his way to their table and is giving them
excellent advice, though in very broken English. Yet it would have
been easy for me to strike up an acquaintance, surely a pleasant
one, for the girl seems attractive and, even unusual, she radiates
freshness and intelligence. I should probably have been able to
talk to her. My acquaintance with her would have been just as
fortuitous as my meeting with Anna at Lampe's party, for just as
that Saturday night in Berlin I might equally well have met an
entirely different girl at an entirely different party, so now I might
be sitting in an entirely different restaurant in Rome, across from
an entirely different woman who might interest me just as much
as this American girl. Or as Anna. I recapitulate a few situations
in which I have struck up an acquaintance with women and find
none that was not accidental. My meeting with Meg is no exception, it was pure chance that I happened to be in London when
Keir, quite contrary to his habit, summoned me to his office where
I met Meg, who had come to discuss some of her photographs
they were using in the next number of our *Die Revue*. He
seldom saw her at the office, but usually met her at his flat or for
lunch at The Three Tuns; in fact he did his best to hide Meg from
us, so that if I had not by chance been in London and gone to
Keir's office during that precise half hour, I may perhaps never
have met Meg. Keir, of course, would not agree to this; in his opinion there is no such thing as chance—even the most random episode is a reflection of *destiny*, though not really of *fate* as I
inaccurately maintained at the beginning of these notes. But even
to this mild form of belief in predestination I cannot subscribe. I
don't believe we are predestined to anything whatsoever. When I
consider how absurd it is that I was a German and became an
Englishman but am still a Jew, it seems to me that I might just as
well be a Russian or a Masai or a wolf or a motor car. My humble
respects to all finders of meaning. Those idiots—Keir isn't really
one of them because, though he believes in destiny, he does not
believe in salvation—have never troubled their heads over the

thought that if my life has a meaning, my mother's death in a gas chamber at Auschwitz must also be meaningful. As for me, I refuse to believe in the meaning of Zyklon B. No, we're accidents and nothing more. Nobody even cast us, unless the hand from which we rolled for better or worse was the hand of a cheat. There is no such hand. We have no cause and no aim. We exist and that's that. There's nothing more in it.

The accident to which I owe having met Anna began then on Saturday night at Lampe's party, or rather at seven o'clock that evening when I ran into Sandberg at the hotel bar. I hadn't seen Sandberg in years. We were alone at the bar because the other newspapermen, who all work for dailies, were still being kept busy by the Island crisis. Chaps like Sandberg and myself who write for weeklies have an easier time of it. Sandberg told me he had begun to write for the German papers now and then. Two years ago he did a political somersault that caused quite a stir. Up until then he had been one of our most fanatical anti-Communists and Cold Warriors, then one day he came out for peaceful co-existence and East-West rapprochement. Like myself he emigrated from Germany before the war and became an English journalist, but in 1950 he went back and stayed on in Berlin, at first as a correspondent for our conservative paper. I saw him now and then at editorial conferences in London where, to Keir's silent displeasure, he obstinately but brilliantly spouted anti-Communism. Since his swing he has been writing for our left-liberal competitor. Keir doesn't like Sandberg and says he's not to be trusted; I myself have always been rather fond of him. He has changed a bit; he's a few years older than I, a short, broad-shouldered man with blue eyes in a sensitive face, intelligent eyes which are at once friendly and stubborn. Finding ourselves alone, we spoke German. Sandberg looked up and said softly: "Well, Efraim, it seems you're on the downgrade?" Without waiting for an answer, he asked: "How's Horne? He doesn't seem to have his heart in it any more either." I couldn't tell him anything about Keir; I hadn't seen him since last spring and had only spoken to him on the phone a few times, on which occasions my main concern had been to find out whether he was sitting in his rocking chair, why he did the *Times* crossword, how much he had had to drink, and whether he had seen Meg—all matters that could hardly be of interest to Sandberg, who is a political animal. Still, though seldom on Fleet Street these days, he had noticed that something was wrong with Keir. That I was on the downgrade, as he put it, was not hard to see, one had only to read my feeble articles, and Sandberg still read his old rag assiduously. But Keir's loss of heart was not yet noticeable in his work for the paper. Did Sandberg know something I didn't know? Could something be wrong between Keir and Meg? I couldn't ask Sandberg. If that was it, he wouldn't tell me. I was sure my colleagues knew whatever there was to know, but naturally none of them had mentioned it to me. I probably ought to fly over to London one of these days, and not only to report to Keir on my search for Esther. I resigned myself to the fact that Sandberg always hears the grass grow, and not just the political grass. He changed the subject spontaneously.

"Wouldn't it amuse you," he asked, "to work for the German press for a change?"

I must have given him a look of utter consternation, because he added as though apologetically: "Just an idea. Maybe it would get you out of the rut."

"What amazes me," I said, "is how you can do it."

"A lot of people say that." Plainly it cost him an effort to come out with an explanation. But in the end he did.

"I simply wanted to spend a few months in Berlin," he said. "I was curious, that's all. But one night I woke up thinking: England doesn't need you, Germany does." He gave an embarrassed laugh. "Forgive me, Efraim, for putting it so pompously."

"You really are overdoing it," I said. "Nobody needs anything."

"Isn't that even more pompous," he asked in his gentle way, "though it sounds so modest?"

He was right. I could have kicked myself for that sentence. I, for instance, had once needed Meg. Now I no longer need her—

though that's not so sure—but there certainly was a time when I thought I couldn't live without her.

"I understand, except that it's the other way round: you need Germany."

"Possibly," he said. "Probably."

"But wouldn't you rather dispense with it even so?" I asked. "After all, it dispensed with us."

At first he didn't understand. "Oh," he said finally, after grasping the meaning of my question. "You think I'm a Jew. But I'm a goy, Efraim, didn't you know?"

For some reason, which escaped me at the moment, I had always believed him to be a Jew. I tried to get off with a joke. "But you look so Jewish," I said. "I know," he answered with a smile, though his way of smiling suggested that he was rather dismayed, not only at looking Jewish, but also at the fact that despite his appearance a slight barrier had now risen between us. There was no help for it: all at once he had become a German goy who needed Germany, whereas I was still a Jew whom Germany had dispensed with.

I felt sorry for him; my only reason for letting him drag me to Lampe's party was that I didn't want him to think I had anything against him; he said I'd meet some interesting people. One thing that doesn't interest me in the least is interesting people, but I went for Sandberg's sake. I like him, he's sensitive and bright and a great journalist, he hears the grass growing, I wouldn't want him to think I hold it against him that he loves Germany. Though I am a Jew, I have nothing against people who love Germany as long as they don't expect me to share their feelings. I am utterly indifferent towards the love some people bear countries or peoples; when I reflect that their whole attitude towards what they call their country results from a chain of accidents—they might just as well be Frenchmen or Americans, or even Negroes or Jews, as Germans—I can only laugh. Or yawn. Am I supposed to love the Jews merely because I happen to be a Jew? I love my parents because they were good parents, not because they were Jewish parents. If they had died a natural death, I should slowly, imperceptibly, forget them. Because they were murdered, I can't forget them. I love the Jews because they are persecuted. We took a cab and drove down Kurfürstendamm; the lights of the broad avenue sparkled in the dry blackness of the autumn night. After Halensee station there was less illumination and soon there was no other light than the street lamps of Königsallee. An area of villas and then Grunewald with its lighted windows in between segments of pine trees emerging reddish from the darkness. In a side street we stopped outside a new house, which was flat and white. Lampe's gathering, which had begun at six, turned out to be a cocktail party given by the producer of Lampe's new picture to celebrate the signing of the contract with Lampe and with the author of the novel on which the film was to be based. Cold buffet. Since I didn't know anyone, I clung to Sandberg for a while. Then I appropriated Anna. She was in the group, consisting chiefly of German newspapermen, for which Sandberg headed when we came in. No sooner had he introduced me to them and to Anna than they pounced on him rather brutally. The Island crisis finally gave them an opportunity to attack his swing to the camp of the appeasers. A prominent English correspondent and resolutely anti-Soviet—this unusual combination had won him general sympathy when he first came to Berlin; the disappointment when he turned coat had been all the greater. Patiently Sandberg turned aside their attempts to pump him. "We'll get together," I heard him say. "You'll see." And a little later, in response to their jibes: "You forget there's a general trend towards reason." He added in English: "We're on the winning side." I wondered whom he meant by "we," and then suddenly I saw the depth of Sandberg's opportunism. He was on the side of reason because he expected it to win out, just as he had formerly bet on stupidity because it seemed to have the better hand. I wasn't shocked. I'm not a moralist. If I were, I should not have been able to work all these years for a newspaper whose policy I have just serenely characterized as stupidity. How was I able to put up with it for so long? At the moment of writing this, I still feel a sentimental attachment for my good old stupid conservative paper. True, my reasons for sticking it out are entirely different from Sandberg's motives for his shift. What makes Sandberg so outstanding a political journalist is his cold concentration on questions of power. His reporting reflects the situation at the momentary centre of power, nothing else. Nevertheless his attitude roused me to opposition. "You are an optimist," I said, "and I've come to regard optimism as a form of stupidity." I uttered these words as politely as possible, hesitantly, almost apologetically, but of course they were insulting. I had doubted Sandberg's intelligence, wounded his pride in it. He hid his irritation behind a smile that seemed not embarrassed but thoughtful; I don't even think he was really angry, he is too sensitive a man not to be able to control such a feeling as anger; he had probably begun to examine my argument objectively when Anna remarked: "Sandberg is right. There won't be a war. K. is a traitor." This wasn't exactly the kind of help Sandberg could have wished for; all eyes turned to Anna in amazement, and I too looked at her attentively, though I won't claim not to have noticed her before she spoke. Anna's remark created general embarrassment. Her manner of speaking made it clear that she was not, with satirical intent, impersonating someone who regarded a retreat on K.'s part as an act of betrayal, she was not doing a parody; if there was any irony in her words, it was directed against her listeners. Don't worry, was her meaning, he's a traitor, you people can rely on him. Having no desire to come to grips with such an attitude, the members of the group drifted away. Sandberg went off to say hello to Lampe, who, as he told me at the bar, was a friend of his, and the others joined other groups. This gave me the opportunity to talk with Anna, who, I might add, didn't seem to mind the desertion. I told her that in Rome a good many bright people shared her opinion, but she seemed in no need of consolation. We went on to talk about the political situation which Anna analyzed from her point of view; she had kept up with the news, which I had neglected all day; thanks to what she told me, I was able, when Keir phoned me the next morning, to pretend that I knew what was going on.

This morning again there's no letter from her, but one has come from a Berlin estate agent I consulted about selling the house in Bismarckstrasse. He has meanwhile looked it over and offers me a sum that I find amazing. I do a little calculating; barring devaluation, it's enough for me to live on for several years without having to take a job. I shudder at the thought that I have made Frau Heiss show this man through the house; I hope she doesn't think I want to force her out. I shall write and tell her she can have all the time she wants, in fact that I won't sell the house as long as she is living in it. Not out of magnanimity but because I won't be needing the money in the foreseeable future and because I shall be much better off with the money invested in the house than lying in a bank account from which I withdraw a certain sum each month. I haven't fully made up my mind to embark on the life of a so-called independent writer, for which to be sure a little capital would come in handy. As I do every morning, I step out onto the narrow balcony that runs round the Albergo Byron. The weather is cold but clear. In the last few weeks they have been drastically renovating the building across the way; I watch four construction workers who are placing a travertine beam forming part of a window casing. The stone must be enormously heavy. They have built a plank runway over which they move it to the window on rollers. They work slowly and methodically. The economy of their movements follows a rite that was established a thousand, perhaps two thousand years ago. Since this is the upper beam—the base and the sides are already in place—they lengthen the runway by adding a plank at the upper end. From there four workers lift the beam and set it down on the lateral *travi*, first on the right, then on the left. They lift it only very slightly. It looks easy. I realize that the process I am observing argues against my theory of chance. These men are not Roman masons by chance, they have been Roman masons for a thousand years. Now they mix some cement in a sheet-iron trough and spread small quan-

tities of the mortar so carefully that the joints between the travertine blocks are invisible. This is how the builders of the baths of
Caracalla must have handled their mortar. The masons across the
street light cigarettes and one starts reading *l'Unità*. This the
builders of the baths of Caracalla did not do. Presumably they
spent their morning break talking about the latest chariot races
at the Circus Maximus, about women and the price of bread. The
stone window casing across from me is beautiful. Only now that
they have been set in place are the travertine blocks entrusted
to the workings of chance. Once the work is done, they will be
bought and sold, expropriated and returned to their owner, worn
down and again renovated. One day they will be recovered intact
from the ruins of the building and used in a new building. Like
an indestructible ornament, work runs through chaos. I go back,
set a cup of coffee beside the typewriter and start to work. I
have decided that I must finally face up to the problem raised by
my method of alluding to political events in these notes. I feel
that before going on with my manuscript I must decide whether
to retain this method or not. Why, for instance, do I keep talking
about the Island crisis, when every, even moderately, well-informed
reader must know that I'm talking about Cuba? Why do I speak
of *Die Revue* when the real name is being bandied about all
over the world? The name of the minister who had the editors
arrested is also, sad to say, world-famous. What is the point in referring to a certain K. in code, as though there were something
to decipher? Naturally Anna didn't speak of K., she said: "Khru-
shchev is a traitor." It looks as if I were trying, with such tricks, to
give my book a quality of eternity, to keep it from aging too
quickly—on the supposition that the Cuban crisis or the *Spiegel*
affair will have been forgotten by the time it appears, if it ever
does. After all, neither the conflict over the Cuban missile bases
nor the clash between the *Spiegel* and the "minister" is exactly a
world-shattering event. Both are infinitesimal, short-lived movements in cosmic matter. I admit that for a moment I had some
notion about lending a paradigmatic significance to ephemeral

happenings, but I quickly dropped this intention: I make no attempt to interpret these events; they merely form a kind of background; they are in the air. Nor do I believe in the eternity of literature; not even the greatest works attain the age of travertine blocks, and my literary efforts will long have been forgotten when the window I have been watching them set in place on the building on Via Borgognona is recovered from the ruins. And when I furthermore reflect that all of us, we words and stones, will one day be a gas cloud drifting through some solar system . . . no, there is no reason for me to lend anything a quality of eternity by spreading an imaginary cloak over it.

Nevertheless, I shall stick to my method. Sandberg is to blame. My picking a false name for him yesterday—for Sandberg is not his real name—is what prompted these reflections. Everyone in German or English press circles knows whom I mean. The man I call Sandberg is a concrete figure, his real name is known to all. Of course no one will object to my substituting another name, people will simply say that I'm writing a novel, and without stopping to think will speak of a *roman à clef*, which implies certain methods of coding. To ensure myself against this misunderstanding, I have, just briefly, lifted the veils over the names, which were perfectly transparent to begin with. The reader will search the title page in vain for words to the effect that none of the characters in the book is identical with any living person. I wish to give no occasion for the knowing smile that such a note would provoke. But now, having said this, I want to make it clear that none of the characters in this book is identical with any living person and that none of the political events to which I allude is identical with the actual events as they actually occurred. As I have said, Sandberg is to blame for my making this statement. When I began to describe him yesterday, because I wished to give as complete account as possible of my experience since starting on these notes, because the conversation I had with him was in fact roughly as I recorded it, and because I need him as a transition to my meeting with Anna, I thought it would suffice to sketch in this widely known journalist and, for the usual reasons of discretion, hide him behind a false name. But the more I thought about this man, the more I concentrated on recalling him to my mind, the more he evaded me. Suddenly I realized that I knew nothing about him. I have met him perhaps ten times in my life, I have talked shop with him a few times, have learned a few things about his private life, and have read almost everything he has written. In other words: I know nothing about him. Once I had come to this conclusion, I knew why I had called him Sandberg: because he was a stranger. For the same reason, it suddenly came to me, I had spoken of an Island crisis, of an affair of *Die Revue*, of a cabinet minister, and of K. I know nothing of the people, events and things concealed behind the people, events and things designated by certain names. It would have been presumptuous of me to speak as if I knew what they meant. (Am I beginning to understand why I no longer want to be a journalist? Have I become an incompetent journalist because reflections, reservations and inhibitions of this kind have thrust themselves between the facts and myself?) I don't know and I'm afraid I shall never know who the man is that offered me the possibility of a character named Sandberg. Any more than I know what is concealed behind the name of that minister or of a certain K., or what has gone on beneath the surface of the episodes referred to as the Cuban crisis or the *Spiegel* affair. On the other hand, I hasten to add, I know the figure I call Sandberg very well, I know very well who the man I refer to as the minister or that ominous K. is, and what I think of the events that I have termed the Island crisis and the affair of *Die Revue*. I can't recognize the real persons. But I know the figures and events I have invented very well.

That is why I haven't coded the words Hitler and Auschwitz. I could not have invented them and I refuse to consider for a single moment the possibility of not being able to recognize them. Their meaning is established once and for all.

I ought to be getting on with my account of Lampe's party, but suddenly I have lost all desire to. Up to this moment an account of that evening has played an important part in my plans; I intended—a typical novelist's idea—to make it a kind of show-piece. I confess that one evening in Rome after my return from Berlin I drew up a plan for my book, as if I had been a real novel-ist. But actually I have not yet made up my mind whether the book is to be a novel. I sometimes speak of a draft or a record, and then again—because I don't really know what to call it—of a book; I have only twice ventured to use the word novel: when I wrote that in my case the ruse of the novel must give way to the truth of the record, and then again when I mentioned the danger that these papers might be taken for a *roman à clef*; in both instances I rejected the term. Still, I cannot entirely dismiss Keir's belief that a book is a novel if it deals with people and the relationships between people. I decided at the outset to write something that would be published; I have said that I was writing for readers, and quite possibly readers don't care a fig whether the thing they are reading is a novel or not. Finally, if a pun can serve as an argument, my notes may, simply because I am writing them in Rome, turn out to be a *roman*. Enough of these speculations! What is far more important is that just now, as I wrote the words "one evening in Rome," it suddenly dawned on me that I have totally forgotten up until now to say what I do with my evenings in Rome. I have related in detail how I spend my mornings; I have also recorded a certain Sunday afternoon, and my conversation with Cella took place during the quick Roman shift from dusk to night; but I have said nothing about my evenings. There isn't much to say; I spend them like everyone else. I have dinner, I occasionally go to the cinema or a concert, I read; before going to bed I spend half an hour at a *café*—it's too cold by now to sit in the open—then I return to the Byron and go to bed, usually rather early. I am al-most always alone; true, I still go through the motions of being a newspaperman but I confine my relations with my colleagues to the most indispensable contacts. I wonder whether I should try to make friends, and if so in what circles; it is very easy to make pleasant acquaintances, you only have to strike up a conversation,

almost everybody is interesting in some way, but for the present I
defer the problem. Even at Lampe's party most of the people were
certainly interesting, but the party itself was not interesting,
and for that reason I won't describe it. Anna, however, though
she had no need of my political consolation, wanted to be nice
to me and told me about some of the people. This enabled me to
contemplate a man who will be my colleague if I ever succeed in
being a novelist.

"He's the one whose book is going to be filmed," said Anna,
nodding her head in the direction of a big man too fat for his
age—my own. At that time I didn't know what I know now: that
the man's weight was an occupational disorder. This profession is
definitely unwholesome: you sit too much, you smoke more than
you ought to, you're always drinking coffee or tea. Perhaps my
constitution, my small size and natural skinniness will preserve me
from overweight. For a few moments we, Anna and I, gazed together at the German novelist, who had no idea that he was serving as a catalyst for our first rapprochement, for as we silently
came to an agreement about him, Anna and I discovered for the
first time that we were able to understand one another. It was not
important to us that Herr M. was wearing a decent but uninspired-
looking suit that couldn't bear comparison with the elegance of
Lampe's suit, nor did it matter that he gazed with smug arrogance
over people's heads, obviously not hearing what this one or that
one might be saying to him, but merely making a show of understanding by putting on an idiotic, absent smile while his eyes
behind his glasses shifted from impression to impression, from
an unknown face to a detail of Lampe's interior, that incredible
chichi compounded of cut-glass, of a frieze copied from Schinkel,
of mediocre paintings and sculptures of various periods, Italian
majolica vases, cast-iron "objects" with various things hanging from
them, and large photographs of dolls with spotlights turned on
them; he didn't know what to look at first, at some beautiful lady
with whom he would have liked to engage in subtle conversation
—failing to suspect that small talk was needed, he was dreaming of

an enormously witty dialogue that might if all went well land him in the lady's bed—while his eyes grazed over a "Flight into Egypt," of whose Dutch origin his host had been assured and which indeed displayed an alien saturated red even in the turban of a stable boy, so that for one moment the novelist, though retaining his blasé smile, doubted the remark with which he was planning to introduce his report when he went home to his wife and friends—that stereotype of critical bewilderment, to wit, that Lampe's place looked exactly as Little Orphan Annie would have imagined it—all this, I say, was much less important to Anna and to me than the fact that we saw it together and saw it in the same way, so that I instantly understood what Anna meant when she concluded our swift observations with the words: "He doesn't know what he's in for."

By this she meant that the author was basking in the idiotic hope that he would recognize his book after Lampe had filmed it, although even I, a total outsider, knew that the films made in the land of my birth were at best in the taste exemplified by the chichi of Lampe's villa in Grunewald. Because this party was attended by people who produced inferior articles, who did poor work for much money, the evening was so uninteresting that I shall not describe it. Apart from the incident I provoked, I can scarcely remember anything about it.

At length Lampe came up to us and addressed those two sentences to Anna which enabled him without difficulty to abduct her from me. I looked after her and caught sight of her now and then, immersed in her conversation with Lampe. Her silver-green changeable-silk dress went beautifully with the spent blond of her hair. It didn't cling to her but, when she moved in certain ways under a certain light, its narrow flow suggested some detail of her thin, rather too tall, probably pale body, whose long slenderness was openly visible only in the bare arms.

Sandberg happened by and I asked him who she was. He followed my eyes. "Anna Krystek," he said, when he saw whom I meant, and added with a smile: "A Communist." I must have made a face, for he sprang almost eagerly to her defence. "No, not a drawing-room Communist, as you might suppose from seeing her here." He broke off. Then after a time: "Anna Krystek would be a story for you. She was an actress in East Berlin . . . well, actress is saying too much, she went to dramatic school over there" —he made a vague gesture in the direction of over there. "Just as she was about to start in, getting her first small parts, at the Theater am Schiffbauerdamm I think, the Wall wrecked everything. You see, she was living with her parents in West Berlin. She couldn't make up her mind to move. Because if she'd moved to East Berlin, she'd have had to stay there."

"Was it only because of her parents she stayed?" I asked. "Or did she have political reasons as well? Maybe the Wall made her see the light?"

"I don't know," said Sandberg. "She talks very left. Almost Chinese. You heard her just now. It makes people keep away from her, though she's a remarkable girl. She's said to be talented. Lampe has offered her a couple of parts, but she turned them down."

"Why?"

"Because Lampe's a damn fool. He wants to cast her as a socialite, and she wants to do kitchen-sink parts. But Lampe doesn't go for Pinter or Osborne."

"What about the other directors?"

"How should I know?" Sandberg shook his head smilingly. "You know, Efraim, I've passed the age of helping young actresses with their careers. Besides, la Krystek is a fanatic. Not my type." He grew serious again. "But I really think you could do a story about her. I remember some of your interviews in Hanoi, shortly before the French moved out. Something along those lines."

I don't like people to give me suggestions. In that respect I'm like Meg who, if anybody suggests a "subject," resolutely shuts up her camera with a remark such as: "You and your shitty subjects." True, I accept assignments; when Keir sends me out on a job, I deliver the goods (not always, but usually), but I take a dark view of colleagues' tips even when they are well meant. If I had ever planned to do an interview with Anna Krystek, the idea would have gone up in smoke the moment Sandberg suggested it to me. Neither then nor later did I regard Anna as an object of journalistic exploitation. As she momentarily reappeared, looking cool and unconcerned with Lampe beside her bending her ear—was she turning down another part?—I wondered if Sandberg had been right in calling her a fanatic. Nowadays anyone with any kind of conviction passes for a fanatic. One or two definite opinions are enough to discredit you. But your credit is restored if it becomes evident that you have expressed your opinions out of calculation. Sandberg's view of Anna's fanaticism was quite benign; most of these people surely thought that if Anna turned down a part she was merely angling for a higher price. And this was far from lowering Anna in their esteem.

For a time I went from group to group, listened in on the conversations, and watched for the silver-green dress when a gap opened up in the milling crowd. Just as I decided to leave, not to wait any longer for another chance to talk with Anna, the incident occurred with which I almost disrupted the party. I was standing near some men who were arranging to bring their evening to a meaningful close with a tour of the Berlin night spots. One of their number, as could be gathered from the conversation, had devoted the previous night to the same sort of thing. The others were pulling his leg, asking if he had sufficient staying power for another such night. He answered with a smile: "I'll go on till I'm gassed."

I went up to him and asked: "What did you say?" Then, without waiting for an answer, I came in with an uppercut. Though a head taller than I, he was not exactly the athletic type, and I had learned the rudiments of boxing in the army. He staggered back, but one of Lampe's little tables prevented him from falling. Ash trays and magazines fell to the floor. He clutched at his chin as though he didn't know what had struck him; then he wanted to fight but two of his friends held him back; it amazes me now, how quickly they had grasped the motive for my assault. For a moment it was almost still in the large reception room, the décor seemed to vibrate, the guests crowded to the scene and informed each other in whispers; then from the stillness there arose the loud, menacing exclamation which summed up the general opinion: "Outrageous!" I looked round contemptuously, prepared to stop the mouth of the exclaimer, whose voice, it seemed to me, expressed the arrogance of the whole world's respectable riffraff. At this point Sandberg took me by the arm and said gently: "Come along, Efraim, you'd better leave." I came to my senses and when I reached the door Anna was beside me. She put her arm in mine, but when she spoke her words were more mocking than sympathetic. She looked at me and said: "You don't seem to have all your marbles." Then we went out and rummaged for our coats.

Outside, in the silence and dim light of Grunewaldstrasse, I asked Anna if the word "gassed" was really and truly used in that sense in Germany today. "In West Germany," she said, but then added as though to offer an excuse for "the people over here": "It's because they have no political consciousness." I observed that it took no complicated political consciousness but only a simple moral consciousness to make people avoid the use of certain words, but she dismissed my argument. "There is a dialectical relationship between morality and politics," she said in a professorial tone. Anna uses terms like "political consciousness" and "dialectical relationship" quite naturally, one doesn't get the impression that they were drummed into her, though of course they must have been drummed into her at some time. I understood why Sandberg, in suggesting an interview with Anna Krystek, had thought of my conversations with those young Asian Marxists in Indochina, who emerged from the jungle like pale steel ghosts and vanished into it again. In a French whose sounds seemed to originate in the space between their teeth and lips, they said approximately the same things as Anna Krystek said in her careful

stage German with its distant memories of Neukölln. We argued
intensely about politics and morality for quite a distance, as we
made our way through the darkness of Grunewald and down
Königsallee where there was more light and some traffic.

"Anyway," I said, wishing to wind up the argument because we
were entering the Halensee Stadtbahn station, "the man I
punched will think about the meaning of a word for the first time
in his life."

"Nonsense!" Anna's face seemed hard in the cold light of the
station. "There'll just be one more anti-Semite in the world."

"Oh well," I said. "One more or one less." I could feel that
Anna didn't like me at that moment. I had struck somebody,
but now I was feeling sorry for myself. Not because I was really
interested but more to conciliate her, I asked: "What do you
suggest?"

"Enlightenment," she said, still angrily, and then in a more
dogmatic tone: "Enlightenment and laws."

"Maybe you ought to be a teacher," I said. "Not an actress
but a teacher."

She did not take my remark amiss but seemed for a moment
to be thinking it over. One thing that distinguished her from the
young Asian Marxists was that she had no objection to our conversation taking on a personal tone. Besides, it suddenly dawned
on us that our situation needed clarifying: we had walked together through an area of cool darkness, past lighted or sleeping
villas beneath rustling pine trees, and now we had come to a
station.

I introduced myself: "My name is Georg Efraim," I said.
Women always find it hard to introduce themselves. Some ancient rule prevents them from simply stating their names. It has
to be done indirectly. I spared her the embarrassment by telling
her that I had questioned Sandberg about her. "I know all about
you, Fräulein Krystek," I said, half jokingly, half in earnest. I
wanted her to know that I knew what people said about her. The
silver-green dress had vanished beneath a grey woollen coat with

two rows of buttons and a wide pointed collar. The coat made her pale face under the ash-blond hair, a few wisps of which had come loose, still thinner; it turned Anna into a schoolgirl who was looking at me attentively as though to read something from my lips. Wishing her to know as much about me as I did about her, I told her I was from Berlin, and so on. The whole exchange took no longer than the clamour of a train which pulled into the station underneath us, stopped, and pulled out again.

"I'm going to see my boyfriend," said Anna. "Would you like to come along? He plays the piano in a jazz cellar in Moabit."

I nodded. It was about ten o'clock, I didn't want to go back to my hotel just yet and Anna made her offer in such a way that it didn't strike me as odd for us to be seeing her boyfriend together. I had to think back to remember where Moabit was. Somewhere north of the Tiergarten. Anna bought the tickets. When we were on the platform, a train pulled in with a sign saying Wannsee, reminding me that I had not yet been to my old home though I had walked in Potsdam Forest that same afternoon and gone as far as Pfaueninsel. But I had avoided Bismarckstrasse and had gone instead to Kohlhasenbrück, where I had found a cab that had driven me back to town. I decided to go to Bismarckstrasse next day. Now I rode with Anna in the opposite direction, northwards. At Westkreuz we had to change. We spoke little. I caught sight of the synagogue in Fasanenstrasse, then from the curve in the Stadtbahn tracks of the back of my hotel, where the window must have been from which next morning I watched the trains rounding the curve and disappearing into the Zoological Gardens station. We didn't have to change at the Zoo; our train continued on to Friedrichstrasse. I remembered trips on this stretch of Stadtbahn as a boy. Before the train crossed the Landwehr Canal there was still a dromedary standing in the light of a street lamp, there was still a red boat beside the locks. The dark expanse of the Tiergarten, beyond which the lights of the city cast a restless glow. To the right, skyscrapers, enormous dwelling boxes with hundreds of lighted windows. I had already noticed them on Friday morning when I took the same line to East Berlin to buy my theatre ticket, but at night they had dematerialized into serried rows of lights. Anna gave me no explanation for the emergence of this statistical grid of lights from the metaphysic of the Tiergarten; I assume that the sight of this spacious new city with its Western prosperity, its churches and cinemas, was distasteful to her. Is she indeed a fanatic, as Sandberg claims? We got off at Bellevue. I saw the flood-lighted Castle in its garden, and right beside the station two of those beautiful blocks of skyscraper flats rose gleaming into the blue-black night. But Anna didn't look at them or at the Castle; she stopped still and looked after the train in which we had been riding.

"At the next station it'll be on the other side," she said.

I told her I had gone over to Friedrichstrasse the previous morning and strolled about near the station and on Unter den Linden. She listened attentively and—as I've mentioned before—looked at me with an almost envious expression; clearly she expected me to express an opinion about the events, and was disappointed when I didn't. Though I can scarcely claim to be a journalist any more, I still tend to confine myself to *facts*. I make a sharp distinction between news and opinion. I have always been a reporter, never a commentator or editorialist like Keir. It worries me that I am always slipping into reflections and analyses in these notes. It's a flaw; as a former journalist, I am sensitive to matters of craft. In view of what Sandberg had told me about Anna, I avoided telling her I had bought a ticket for Brecht's *Days of the Commune*. I didn't tell her until Sunday morning, and then out of thoughtlessness, because I had stood her up on Saturday afternoon, was undecided about my intentions towards her, and had lost sight of her problems. But here on the platform of Bellevue station, where we stood chatting for a few minutes, stimulated by the fact that our train was continuing on into the East Zone, I was delighted with Anna. This tall, bright-eyed bird-girl in the grey plumage of her coat fitted in perfectly with what I saw here: the wooden shed of the Stadtbahn workers, the notice board on which the wretchedly made-up Communist paper was displayed, the "Men Wanted" posters of the German Railways, and the smell of poverty and disinfectant, the fine grey dust of puritanism that assails one in these stations. At Lampe's party, I had admired Anna in her silver-green dress, but here she appealed to me still more. If, as I have written, the hard bleakness of the Berlin Stadtbahn stations still attracts me, the reason may be that it has merged in my memory with the image of Anna Krystek that night on the Bellevue station platform.

(The use of words like "delighted," "admire," "appeal," the statement that Anna "fitted in with" certain surroundings, are typical of the reaction of a forty-two-year-old man to a girl nineteen years younger than himself. When I first met Meg, I did not react with aesthetic pleasure, not consciously at least. To this day it's a matter of indifference to me whether Meg is objectively beautiful or ugly.)

Leaving the station, we walked along a street bordered by old blocks of flats. "Did Lampe offer you another part?" I asked, for want of anything better to say. Anna had not headed for the new quarter with its blaze of lights, but for the dark area on the other side of the Stadtbahn tracks.

"You really do know a great deal about me," she said. In Grunewald I had already noticed that she took long swift steps. I didn't mind, I'm quite capable of walking fast, but like all short thin men I take short steps. Short, quick steps as befits a newspaperman. But I can walk very quietly when I want to; "You creep up like a cat," Meg used to say. Now I did not walk quietly; my pace was loud, quick and short. Though poorly synchronized, Anna and I kept together as we raced down the street, past houses that were already asleep and bare trees. A man stepped out of a doorway with a dog. The shops were in basements with steps leading down to them. Dairy, hardware, stationery. Their windows were dark, only a furniture shop had its lights on; I saw a sofa upholstered in burgundy and an ornate cabinet with a dismal glitter. By day these houses undoubtedly presented a scale of dirty greys and windows with ancient, many times laundered curtains. I'd like to live there. At the corner I read the street sign: Kirchstrasse. A good neutral name. Anna said that this time she was going to accept Lampe's offer.

"It's stupid to keep turning him down," she said. Lampe was making a television film of Shaw's *Androcles and the Lion* and he had offered her the role of Lavinia. "Nice of him, wasn't it?" she asked. "A small part, but something can be made of it."

"If he lets you make something of it," I said. I didn't know the play and wanted to say something that made sense. Meanwhile I've looked into it and found out that the role isn't so small and that Anna is to play the part of a "charming Christian girl," as Shaw says in a stage direction. Sometimes Lampe has a good idea after all.

"Oh, he lets his actors do as they please," said Anna. "Everybody says so."

"Maybe you ought to come to Rome," I said. "I could introduce you to a few Italian film directors. . . ." I broke off, as startled at what I had said as Anna, who—how could she have helped it?—misunderstood. She stopped still, her face illumined by the Moabit Furniture Paradise, and in her eyes I saw the same look of mockery as when, on our way out of Lampe's villa, she had alluded to my missing marbles.

"Man," she said, "you're certainly a fast worker."

I had to laugh. "Nonsense," I said. "I wasn't even thinking of that." But I was glad my face was in the shadow because I could feel that I was blushing. I really believed that I had only been thinking of the film industry, of Collaudi's suggestion that I should go into it, and certain press conferences I had attended in Rome, at which producers had presented their star directors. I hadn't met Cella yet; if I had known that evening in Berlin that I should be sitting with him at the Rosati a fortnight later, I might in my embarrassment have boasted of knowing him. I made a clumsy attempt to justify my bright idea by speaking of the qualities of the Italian film directors.

"I suppose they're just waiting for me to come along," she said dryly. Undoubtedly she was right. What had got into me, making her such a proposition? Anna did nothing to relieve my embarrassment.

"How do you even know I have any talent?" she asked in the inquisitorial tone that is only possible at her age.

"I'm told that you have."

"They'll say anything. None of those people ever saw me act. Don't you realize that over there we learn an entirely different style of acting? And I can't change. I certainly won't fit into any of Lampe's crap. But even a good director wouldn't know what to do with me."

I remembered my colleagues' British enthusiasm that had led me to take the train to East Berlin the day before and buy a theatre ticket. "You must be mistaken," I said. "The people here are wild about the way you people act over there."

I said "you people" without thinking. From the very start Anna Krystek had made me regard her as someone from the other side.

"They go to see our productions," she said, "finished productions in which everything fits together. But if you take one of us out and put him into something entirely different, he'll just be a foreign body." She turned away and we walked on. "That's why I turned down Lampe's offers. Now I'll give it a try, but it's bound to be a flop."

I didn't press the matter. I could have questioned her about her dramatic school and her first small parts in East Berlin, but I was still too amazed at my asking her to go to Rome to be able to concentrate on her problems. Had I fallen in love with her so quickly and so hard? I certainly found her attractive. But I was almost beginning to regret having let myself be inveigled into this expedition through an unknown quarter to an uncertain goal, a meeting with a man who did not interest me in any way. Did Anna herself interest me? It was a matter of relative indifference to me whether she succeeded as an actress or not. A few minutes

before, on the station platform, she had seemed very attractive.
Now I should have preferred to be alone. I wanted very much to
leave her. Then I could spend a quiet half an hour in some corner
bar, having a beer before going to bed.

Last night before retiring at the Albergo Byron, I finally—over
a glass of white wine; there's nothing I like better to drink here
in Rome than this common *castelli*—found the key to why I went
along with Anna that night: without my wanderings with her,
without my date with her next day, and most of all without my
failure to keep it, I should not next day, which was a Sunday,
have started on my notes. Of course I can't prove this assertion,
but I'm sure it's true. In some way that evades my understanding,
my meeting with Anna that evening was the spark which set off
my book. By this I don't mean to say that I shouldn't have begun
it if I hadn't met Anna. Then some other event would have
sparked it off, but it pleases me to think that it was this tall shadowy girl who disposed me to embark on a certain arrangement of
signs with the help of which I hope to chart my position.

But yesterday evening—one of those Roman November evenings after my return from London—I once again failed to work
out why I so quickly, so abruptly, suggested her coming to Rome.
All the way from Piazza Navona, where I had taken a last glass
of wine, to the hotel, I pondered the question in vain. I passed
Sant' Agostino; the façade hovered grey-violet over the stairs and
over the narrow little square, and I knew that inside the closed
church the innumerable candles and votive lamps round the Madonna del Parto were slowly burning down. I once spent some
time at the Biblioteca Angelica next door looking for manuscripts
of an Italian sixteenth-century author who wrote about the Wandering Jew. The monks have a collection of three thousand Renais-
sance and baroque manuscripts.

Behind the Palazzo Galitzin I discovered a fountain I hadn't
known; then I went to the Tiber and stood for a while gazing at
the ugly Palace of Justice and the beautiful Castel Sant'Angelo a
little further downstream, before slipping back into the labyrinth

of narrow streets. The orange-red and altar-cloth-yellow houses
moved in the light of lamps dangling on strings. The day had
been clear and I knew that high above the houses the November
night lost itself in the pure depths of the sky. On the porch of
San Lorenzo in Lucina I stopped to look at some medieval marble
fragments covered with inscriptions and symbols; beside the door
crouched two lions dating from the year 1000. I wondered what
it would be like to take such walks through the old quarters of
Rome by night with Anna: would she derive the same satisfaction
as I did from the façade of a church, a fountain, a stone fragment,
a segment of red wall so often replastered that its surface moved
like a living body, from glancing into a bar filled with cold-blue
light, where twenty men were standing, talking quietly? I don't
think so. At best she would admire Rome politely. I'm not even
sure of that. She might still turn up; she hadn't written to me yet,
and after all not quite four weeks had passed since we met. A
few people came out of the cinema on Piazza di Lucina and I
joined them in crossing the already quiet Corso to Via Frattina, where I stopped outside the pet shop. A dim light was burning within. In the dark window puppies lay in a knot, sleeping.
Only a little spaniel was awake; he kept tapping on the window
glass with his paws. This shop brings me now and then to Via
Frattina. For some time now I've been thinking of buying a dog.
But I can't keep one at the hotel. The little spaniel reminds me
of Devil and Esther. Even if Esther is still alive—Devil must have
died years ago.

I lost my desire to take my leave of Anna when Kirchstrasse
stopped at the Spree. Yes, it was the Spree, as I recognized as
soon as we stepped onto the bridge; I had seen it often enough,
in many different places, as a child. Anna seemed to find it perfectly normal that I should lean on the iron rail and look down at
the river, though there was nothing to be seen but black water, an
old factory and a barge tied up at the bank beside it. They formed
a shadow play of drifting clouds, low tarred flanks, spars and a
few spots of brick-red. On the other side, a road with a grass em-

bankment ran along the shore; in the light of the street lamps birds
could be seen on the embankment, a good many of them, a hundred I estimated, big swans and all sorts of ducks and gulls. They
were asleep, some sitting, some standing; from time to time a
swan spread its wings and sent a white message out into the night.
When I think of Berlin, what I always remember first is that moment on the bridge at Moabit, on my third night in Berlin after
an absence of twenty-seven years.

Someone had had the idea of transforming an abandoned pub
in Turmstrasse into a jazz cellar, but hadn't bothered to redecorate
or put in new furniture; the only innovation consisted of a few
photographs of well-known musicians, pinned to the walls. The
place gave an impression of chill and poverty and was half empty
though it was Saturday night. The venture can hardly have been
profitable. Wherever I go, I observe a loss of interest in jazz, ex-
tending even to myself, an indication that I am living in a slow,
tedious period, a period without *drive*. The few people sitting
there in hard chairs were specialists, the typical scholastics of jazz,
whose poker faces noted every change of colour in the sound produced by the combo on the low platform. From time to time a
mediocre saxophonist broke into the excellent performance of the
rhythm section. The bass player and the pianist—Anna's boyfriend
—were especially good. Anna hesitated to accept the whiskey I
ordered for her; I noticed that there were Coca-Cola bottles on
most of the tables. She had taken her coat off but had thrown it
over her shoulders, only for a brief moment had the silver-green
dress cast its glitter into the dingy surroundings. Her boyfriend
had nodded to her. I observed that he was tall and blond, undoubtedly somewhat younger than Anna. He had light tortoise-
shell glasses—everything about him was light in colour—and he
gave the impression of being not Anna's boyfriend but a younger
brother. He played cool but mostly blues, and he somehow managed to draw melodic lines through his brittle playing. I watched
Anna. She seemed bored. I don't believe a woman can really
take an interest in cool jazz. In an interval Werner Hornbostel

came over to our table. He was very young and unsuspectingly friendly; the one thing that made him seem older than he was was his way of losing himself in his thoughts. When he started playing again, I asked Anna what else he did. She told me he was studying composition at the Academy of Music, that he came from Hamburg but lived here to avoid being drafted into the West-German Army. That aroused my journalistic curiosity; I questioned her and learned that a good many young men from West Germany studied in Berlin and established residence there because residents of West Berlin were not subject to the draft.

"We'll go up to your place for a minute," said Anna to Hornbostel when at midnight he was relieved by another pianist. He showed no surprise or indication that he might have preferred to be alone with Anna. Even the "we" in Anna's sentence, which made a unit of her and me, opposed to another unit consisting only of himself, didn't seem to trouble him.

"He stays up all night working anyway," said Anna by way of explaining the situation.

"Then I'll be disturbing you," I objected. But the young man said: "Not at all." "No one can disturb him when he works," said Anna. Their relations seemed pleasantly free and easy.

Hornbostel lived nearby; we walked a short distance in the direction of the Spree. On the way Anna decided to explain my presence after all, and told him about my uppercut at Lampe's party. He understood what she was trying to tell him, and for a moment put his arm over her shoulder.

A little later he asked me: "Why did you hit him?"

"I saw red, that's all," I answered rather brusquely. "Is that so hard to understand?"

"No, of course not," he said. "But tell me this: did you feel better after hitting him?"

He saw his question had touched a raw spot. "Forgive my curiosity," he said. "I'm only asking because I myself sometimes feel like hitting out. If I don't, it's because I'm afraid of feeling embarrassed afterwards. Not sorry, no, it's not that, just embarrassed, as if I'd started bellowing or crying . . . is that it?"

I don't know why I admitted that that was just how I had felt afterwards, not immediately, but while walking through the cool night air of Grunewald with Fräulein Krystek. He was one of those big gangling blonds who even when very young seem all hesitation and detachment, so that one doesn't mind confiding in them.

"All right," he said, "let's drop it." There was something in that sentence, in the tone, which restored the dignity of an enigma to my aggression. Hornbostel had made no attempt to solve it, but had only alluded to the enigmatic nature of my action and let it go at that. I don't know if he shares my opinion that secrets, provided they are real secrets and not merely apparent ones, are not made to be cleared up, but he behaved as if he did. Only towards the end of my visit to his place did it turn out that he was after all a solver of riddles—like Keir—a man who looked for explanations.

Hornbostel came to a halt outside a large iron gate and unlocked a smaller door inserted in it. Crossing a courtyard paved with bricks, we entered a large room which, when Hornbostel turned on the light, proved to be empty except for some scraps of wood and cement piled up in one corner. "You live here?" I asked in amazement. "No," he said. "Downstairs." At the end of the room a stairway led to the cellar. Anna told me the factory belonged to Hornbostel's father who made corrugated paper in Hamburg; it had lain idle for many years. In the long cellar corridor I saw strange things: an unbaked clay foot at least five times life-size; it reminded me of the so-called foot of Constantine on the Capitoline, except that it was not so brutally naturalistic, but more elegant and stylized; the toes seemed less obscene than Constantine's. And there were other parts of the body—a man's body—some lying on the floor like the foot, others in crates. These objects were the heritage of a monumental sculptor of the Hitler period, to whom Hornbostel's father, an "enthusiastic fellow traveller" as his son put it, had given his already idle factory as a studio; while explaining the presence of these articles, he passed his long thin fingers over the nipples of a torso and reached into the navel, that is, the bevelled hole which the sculptor had sunk between the taut manneristic flanks of the belly. There lies the artist, the young man said contemptuously, pointing to the dispersed plaster moulds of nipples and navels in the dingy cellar light. Perhaps I should have struck up a conversation with him about the difference between hewing and modelling, such as I had carried on as a child with Herr Rose, the sculptor in Bismarckstrasse, but I was silent and overwhelmed because I realized that I had here before me, dissected into his parts and carefully preserved, one of the murderers of my parents. Then I heard the iron sound of a shovel. Anna pricked up her ears too. "It's only Frau Wendt," said Hornbostel. "She's stoking the fire." He went ahead and we followed him down the corridor to the furnace room where an old woman was shovelling coal. She was wearing a grey overall and her hair fell over her face in strands; she scarcely looked at us. Hornbostel exchanged a few words with her. Retracing our steps past the parts of the murderer's body, we turned into a side corridor where the musician had his room. He had transformed a large whitewashed storeroom into living quarters; the furnishings consisted of a piano, a bed, a table, a bookcase and a few chairs. His clothes were hung up on hooks. The manuscript paper spread out on the table was covered with symbols unknown to me. When we had removed our coats, Anna put water on an electric hot plate and laid coffee cups on the table. I went to the large factory window and saw to my surprise that the Spree was flowing six feet below it. On the far side I again saw a road and, illumined by the street lamps, birds sleeping on the grass embankment. In the still water I could see the bright rectangle of the window. I envied Hornbostel his lodgings. After a while he said to me: "Forgive me. I should have smashed that stuff out there long ago. I was going to once, but Frau Wendt came at me with a poker. She said she'd kill me if I dared to lay hands on it. I wouldn't put it past her. She was his"—he gave the sculptor's name—"house-keeper and I suppose that was the biggest thing in her life." A car passed on the opposite bank but provoked no movement among the birds. "My father kept her on as caretaker," I heard my host saying. "Somebody had to keep an eye on the factory. But her only reason for staying was to guard that shit." The guardian of the treasure. I remembered her formidable coal shovel.

"I don't mind so much any more," said Hornbostel. "I'll be leaving soon. I can't live in West Germany. But I can't stick it out much longer in Berlin either. Too much like a national park."

Anna had stopped fiddling with the cups. I turned round, and as I had expected, she was watching her friend closely.

"Where can a man go?" Hornbostel asked me. "Can you suggest anything?"

"Italy," I said. "Even if you're poor they won't deport you from Italy."

"Isn't Italy insufferably beautiful?" he asked.

"It's beautiful," I said, "but not insufferably beautiful."

He listened attentively. Anna said: "Why don't you go to East Berlin? That's no national park."

But he seemed not to have heard her. He turned away and was soon busy with a tape recorder that was on a stand beside the piano, at the same time producing sounds with a tambourine and various other objects that he fished out of a wooden box. From time to time he stopped the tape, cut it and pasted the ends together. He said Anna and I could talk, it wouldn't disturb him. Anna stretched out silver-green on his bed, I pulled up a chair, we drank coffee, smoked and talked. For the first time she addressed me as Georg; no one had called me that since I left my parents. I felt grateful to her for bringing me here. We spoke of one thing and another. When I began telling her about Esther, she sat up and listened eagerly. Hornbostel interrupted his work and looked at me.

"Then she might be alive," said Anna. "When did you say she went away?"

"1938."

"The war hadn't started yet in 1938 and they hadn't started shipping people to the east. Her mother would probably have been notified if Esther had been picked up."

"You talk as if you knew all about it," said Hornbostel. "You weren't even born until the year after. They must have killed the child. They killed everybody."

"No," I said. "Fräulein Krystek is right. In 1938 there were still ways of leaving the country."

"How old would Esther be now if she were still alive?" Anna asked.

"She's five years younger than I," I said. "That would make her thirty-seven."

Anna did not conceal her surprise. "You're forty-two? You look younger."

I don't look younger than I am, I look ageless. Meg says it's hard to guess my age because I'm the short thin type with smooth black hair.

"But if she escaped, she'd have sent news," said Hornbostel.

"Does anyone know exactly why she ran away?" Anna asked.

I told them what Frau Schlesinger had heard from Marion Bloch in the cattle car on the way to Auschwitz. On 16 November 1938, the last Jewish children had been removed from the German schools in Berlin. On the morning of the second day after that, Marion Bloch told her travelling companion, she hadn't found Esther in her bed.

"Did Esther's mother go to the police?" Anna asked after a time.

"Esther had taken her little dog," I said. "That convinced Frau Bloch that she had run away in earnest. Besides, the child left a letter to her mother. Frau Bloch finally decided it was best to let things take their course."

"What was in the letter?" Anna asked.

"Frau Schlesinger didn't know." We could all imagine what was in it: a child's tear-stained plea for forgiveness, because by then—

she was thirteen—she must have known she was leaving her mother in the lurch.

"She's still alive," said Anna. And for a moment even Hornbostel envisaged the possibility, saying how wonderful it would be if Esther were still alive. We fell silent, overwhelmed at the thought that a child might have outwitted the murderer who was lying out there in the corridor, waiting to be put together again. But the thought was too beautiful to be true, and besides it hardly mattered whether Esther had evaded her so-called fate, for thousands of children had not evaded their so-called fates. I dislike the word fate, I refuse to see predestination in the gas chambers—no, they were the outcome of various accidents. As I have already written in my account of my visit to Frau Heiss, it was pure chance that Jews were exterminated twenty years ago and not entirely different people twenty years earlier or later, now, for instance. I didn't say that to Frau Heiss, because I knew she would fly at me just as Werner Hornbostel did when I expressed this view.

"You must be mad," he shouted at me. "First you hit a man because he thoughtlessly talks about getting gassed, and then you come up with a theory that helps you to affect lofty indifference. Don't you realize that such a thing could only happen in Germany, nowhere else, and that it had to happen exactly when it did? It was willed, do you understand: willed!"

That of course was a third possibility: if it was neither fate nor chance, then this unspeakable thing was the product of a will, and then one might discover an explanation for it. But there was no explanation for Auschwitz. *On at least one occasion SS-Man Küttner, known as Kiewe, flung a baby into the air and Franz killed it with two shots.* No one has ever been able to explain Auschwitz. *We saw an enormous fire and men were throwing things into it. I saw a man who was holding something that moved its head. I said: "For the love of God, Marusha, he's throwing a live dog into it." But my companion said: "That's not a dog, it's a baby."* I am suspicious of anyone who tries to explain Auschwitz. I wasn't suspicious of Werner Hornbostel; I saw that he was still a child whose explanations were childish cries of protest against the inexplicable.

Anna diverted us from our quarrel by asking: "Do you know what school Esther attended last?"

I thought back and remembered that Frau Bloch had sent her to a Catholic private school in Steglitz.

"You ought to ask about her there," Anna suggested. "Perhaps she confided in one of her teachers, and perhaps the teacher is still there."

That was good practical advice, not very promising, but once it had been given I had to follow it. Hornbostel was enthusiastic. I let myself be mildly infected by the hope that I detected in Anna and her friend, by their hopeful interest in Esther's story; it seemed to mean a good deal to them that this one child might return to the land of the living. And so I promised to inquire at Esther's school; it is thanks to Anna that I took a step which was not wholly useless, that I made the acquaintance of Mother Ludmilla, and—foolishly—believed I could bring Keir a straw of hope, something he could cling to.

I stood up to go, but the young musician asked me to stay a little longer; he wanted to play a tape for me.

"Something I've just finished," he said. He ran the tape—the machine was hooked up with a radio—and at first I heard nothing but what I had been listening to the whole time: a few piano chords, a tambourine, a rattle, the tapping of fingers on a pot, whistling. Then a pause, then the sounds started in again, but now I was able to distinguish a pattern; with his cutting and pasting Hornbostel had produced a tone fabric which here and there condensed into rhythmic figures. He looked at his watch and when the tape had ended he said: "Exactly two minutes." He ran it back and played it again; this time it became clear to me that the various sounds had been exactly timed, that there was not only a rhythm but a theme as well. He had even composed a ripieno part, for under the sonata of sounds one could hear the conversation I had been carrying on with Anna, so soft that I could not understand it, yet recognizable as a dialogue of two human voices, one low, the other higher. I couldn't have said whether the whole was tonal or atonal—a musicologist whom I told about it explained to me that it was "ecmelic," a Greek word for the extramelodic tones of the natural scale that do not fit into our tonal system. But I found Werner Hornbostel's piece quite melodic; the theme of this music was undoubtedly a rhythmic screen enclosing a conversation. I cannot dispel the thought that this principle of composition must be applicable to literature. If I should ever complete my notes and decide once and for all to lead the life of a writer, to "dedicate myself to literature," as they used to say, I shall attempt to write a book in the ecmelic style.

"I like it," I said to the composer. "I really like it very much."

"I've already got a title for the piece," he said. "I'm going to call it 'Efraim's Visit.'"

He stood before me blond and gangling, there was a friendly, absent smile in his eyes behind their light tortoise-shell glasses. Of the many nice people I met in Berlin, Werner Hornbostel was the nicest. He escorted us—for Anna left with me—upstairs, and stood looking after us. We waved to him from the street corner before he vanished into the factory gate.

"Isn't he sad about your leaving?" I asked Anna.

"Not at all," she said. "He wants to work."

We took a wide street called Alt-Moabit, where there was some chance of coming across a cab at that late hour.

"We don't sleep together very often," said Anna, as though to justify herself for not staying with her friend. "Sex is rather important, but really not as important as most people think it is nowadays."

I couldn't help laughing: she was funny, although she was so right. Because she was so right.

"You're very detached for your age," I said.

"You mean enlightened." Enlightenment seemed to be her favourite word. I forgot that she had been enlightened "over there," as they say in West Berlin with a characteristic sweep of the hand, a gesture composed of resignation, pity and antipathy.

Her tone irritated me. I wondered if I could shake her self-assurance.

"Is this the first time you've heard that your boyfriend wants to leave Berlin?" I asked.

"He's told me a couple of times," she admitted without hesitation. Her voice gave no indication of how she felt about it. "But this is the first time I've had the impression that he really means it." After a pause she added: "Perhaps under your influence."

She dismissed my protest. "Oh, yes," she said. "You have a way of making it look as if it's perfectly simple to leave. When of course it's not simple at all, not even for you. But you're able to act as if it were. . . . You with your Italian directors!"

Because I liked her a good deal, because I had fallen in love with her, I decided to sound her out.

"Would you be sorry if Hornbostel went away?" I asked.

We were not walking as fast as earlier in the evening; we might almost have been said to be sauntering down the deserted street, through the grey night of the working-class quarter, and our steps were much better attuned to each other than before.

"You're just trying to find out if Werner has asked me to go with him," said Anna.

"You're right," I admitted. "That's probably what I want to know."

"No," she said, "he hasn't asked me."

"Does that make you sad?"

"A little."

"You mean you'd like to go with him?"

"No, I certainly wouldn't go with him. I don't even want him to ask me. But he might broach the subject. Then I could explain why I'd rather stay here." And to her candid complaint she appended an explanation: "You see, I believe I only like him here, in his jazz club and his cellar. Can you understand that?"

I nodded. I understood very well. Again we were caught up in

the mutual sympathy we had felt at Lampe's party at the sight of
the ponderous German novelist.

"Besides," Anna declared, "all the king's horses couldn't drag
me out of Berlin."

That was a profession of faith. When I think of the tone in
which she said that I am still amazed that I succeeded three days
later in persuading her to go on a jaunt to Rome. True, she broke it
off in Frankfurt and flew back to Berlin, but I wasn't to blame
for that, not directly at least. In that first night of our meeting I
learned something of her reasons for insisting on staying in Berlin,
and wanted very much to draw her into a conversation on the
subject, but just as she finished telling me, and quite convincingly,
that her relationship with Berlin was more important to her
than her relations with Werner Hornbostel, a taxi emerged
from a side street. We stopped it and got in. Anna didn't want to
be driven to Neukölln, she said she could catch a late Stadtbahn
train at the Zoo. I said that was out of the question. Accordingly
we first directed the driver to Neukölln, but we didn't get there
because, as we were passing a night-club in Uhlandstrasse which,
Anna declared, was very nice, she suddenly announced that she
felt like dancing. Though it was Saturday night the place, a small
discothèque, was almost empty at that hour; apart from ourselves
there were only two couples on the dance floor. I dance rather
well, and I was able to make up for the bad mark I had earned in
the taxi. Anna Krystek proved to be a magnificent dancer, concentrated, unsentimental, and after a time radiantly free. We did
both open and closed figures. In the open ones I could see how
effortlessly Anna shifted from the graceful and sprightly use of her
legs to a deliberate, and by no stretch of the imagination innocent, movement of her whole body; during a long bass solo she
shook it just enough to make her silver-green dress flow over it
as water flows over a willow branch. Through the glittering gesture that she projected into the golden-green pond of the room,
I looked for the transparent brown of her eyes; and when I had
found them, she did not look away. When I again put my arm

over her shoulders, her tall thin body was feather-light, and the skin of her face and arms felt dry. Meg's skin, too, is always dry, but dry and hot, it seems to crackle when one touches it; the dryness of Anna's skin is pale and cool, though without a marble quality; one can scarcely conceive of anything less classical than Anna; one is reminded rather of glass reflecting bright shadows, of a lake under a white watercolour sky, of something fragile. She did not recoil when I touched my lips to her cheek—in a spot beside her right ear, from which I first had to push away a wisp of all-too-soft ash-blond hair—one could hardly have called it a kiss. But neither did she respond; still, she did not seem displeased, a fact I now attribute to the effect of the dancing and of certain octaves of Charlie Byrd's guitar, which unfortunately stopped a moment later, so that there was nothing for us to do but go back to our whiskey glasses at the bar.

I told her that I had danced a good deal in London, described our—Meg's and mine—favourite dancing place, an enormous low-priced jazz barn in Oxford Street, frequented by people of all colours. They stand silently in the dark, smoking and drinking Coca-Cola, and then, when the music starts, transform themselves, against the light of the orchestra platform, into a welter of dancing shadows.

"That's where I always went with my wife," I said. I purposely clothed the sentence in the past tense—I might just as well have said: "That's where I always go with my wife." Anna, however, took no notice of the intransitive verb employed in the past tense, but asked me with candid curiosity whether my wife was with me in Rome. I told her it was a long time since I had seen Meg. "How long?" she asked, visibly interested, and I answered: "About a year."

"Well," she asked eagerly, "did you go to bed with her?"

To gain time, I said the Kinsey Report had already been published, but she might find employment on some other public opinion survey. She stuck to her guns and repeated her question.

When I said yes, she exclaimed: "Then you love your wife! Why don't you live with her?"

I had my reasons, I said, and changed the subject. Under other circumstances I wouldn't have had such a conversation. It was the typical two-o'clock-in-the-morning bar-room conversation one falls into with a random acquaintance. To tell the truth, I had the impression that Anna would already have been willing to go to bed with me if I had insisted. With the music, with my shadow of a kiss as we were dancing, and with my mention of Meg, I had carried the process of seduction a long way, almost to the point where a woman—women are much braver and more determined than men—wants consummation regardless of the consequences. This conviction has not been shaken by Anna's "There's no more in it, Georg" on the telephone Monday morning, though her words may apply to the time following that Saturday night. In view of my blunder in the cab, I can take a certain pride in having transformed Anna's attitude towards me into sympathy. Because that was why Anna broke off our ride in Uhlandstrasse—not because she was suddenly taken with a wild desire to dance. After getting into the cab in Moabit we stopped talking. I am unable to resist the effect that the back seat of a car, a closed lift, or a telephone booth has on the relations between a man and a woman. Who can? Perhaps Anna oughtn't to have retired into her corner as she did, all buttoned up in her grey coat, perhaps she should have gone on chatting easily about Hornbostel, about her feeling for Berlin, or heaven knows what. But she sat there in silence, she too gripped by the power of old cave memories which reduced us to being nothing more than a man and a woman. I could only see the strands of her hair flickering in the passing lights; she let me touch her neck. Then I behaved like a bull in a china shop—the expression Anna used in her cool but energetic protest. She pushed my hand away.

"Couldn't you have asked me if I want *that?*" she said in a furious whisper.

Against such a formulation of her resistance I was powerless.

I couldn't help laughing; the scene had lost all its violence and oppressiveness: true, why couldn't I have asked whether she wanted *that?* Then came Uhlandstrasse and her pretext of wanting to dance, so that she could get out, because now she really couldn't trust me to behave on the long ride to Neukölln. But at the bar she had sufficiently forgotten the incident to believe that in bringing me here she had anticipated pleasure.

Why didn't I take advantage of the situation? I had transformed an overhasty aggression into a flirtation, and the flirtation into a prelude to seduction, things were going nicely. True, I still hadn't asked Anna whether she wanted *that*; by demanding to be asked she had made me reflect that I myself wasn't sure I wanted it; it is possible that I wanted it at least at the moment when I thrust my hand into the soft silken bend of her knee. In the back seat of a car, in a lift or telephone booth, a man does that kind of thing in order to maintain his status: he presumes that his companion expects the assault and as a matter of fact she does, she would be secretly disappointed if there were not at least some hint of it; even the clumsiest importunity arouses more sympathy in her than cold neutrality. But before Anna pushed away my hand, the possibility that she would not do so and that consequently I should very soon be forced into her bed in Neukölln, because at that point I could not have retreated without sorely offending her, held no appeal for me. At the bar, while we were dancing and afterwards, the idea of possessing her, as they call it, had again struck me as possible; I was in love with her slender mobile mouth, with the skin of her arms. They looked anemic under ordinary circumstances but in that warm muted light her arms transformed into pale gold stems moving against the silver-green of her dress; I thought of flowing green-and-gold plants as I looked through my rimless glasses into her irises which I have described as very light in colour and clear as the morning. But even while savouring a complete and precious image of something I wished to possess, I knew that I should obtain nothing of the sort, but instead an overheated body, which would not necessarily be physically attractive to me, and that in her embrace I should be unlikely to capture anything more than what my short-sighted eyes, from which after a time I would remove my glasses, enabled me to see: a close-up of a certain number of pores. With worries of this sort you don't get to be a lady killer. Yet during my meditations in the night-club it didn't even occur to me that in all likelihood I should not even be able to acquit myself hon-ourably in bed with Anna without the help of Meg's image, which I had been obliged to invoke every time I attempted, since my separation from her, to find pleasure with other women. Anna seemed to me so charming, to offer a possibility so decidedly dif-ferent from Meg, that I might have been tempted to experiment, to see whether with her I might manage without recourse to the memory of Meg. However, I decided to carry the flirtation no further. The feelings Anna inspired were not exactly new to me—I said as much at the beginning of these notes, adding that the whole process of courtship struck me as absurd, that whenever I've got involved in it I've heard the mechanism creaking at the joints. That statement stands; even for Anna's sake I can't with-draw a jot of it, though she in particular seems to have a capacity for guessing my thoughts and turning them into thoughts we hold in common. Just as it became clear to me that I must make up my mind whether or not to ask the question she had invited, she announced that she wanted to go home. And, pressing out a ciga-rette with her gold-illuminated hand, she added: "When it's loveliest, that's the moment to stop."

I made a feeble attempt to change her mind, pointing to her infinitesimal cigarette butt that continued to smoulder for a mo-ment—Anna has the unwholesome habit of smoking her cigarettes down to the last quarter of an inch. "You don't stop smoking at the right moment," I said.

She only shook her head and stood up.

It was sweet of her to use the word lovely in reference to the time we had spent together. We really did have an hour of perfect harmony. But now that I think of it, brooding over my drawing

board at the Albergo Byron after my return from London, it seems
to me that her utterance of the commonplace that one should
stop when it's loveliest was merely a friendly, polite way of saying
the same thing as she said on the phone Monday morning:
"There's no more in it, Georg." Perhaps I shouldn't have been
able to exploit the situation even if I had wanted to. Perhaps, no,
unquestionably, my hesitations born of my misgivings about sexual intercourse were quite superfluous, because Anna Krystek, if
I had asked the question she prompted, would have turned me
down. I'm not really sure. On Tuesday when I went to see her
in Neukölln, and when we were saying good-bye to each other in
Frankfurt, there were moments of such tension that I was tempted
to believe that anything was possible. Even today—Monday, 26
November 1962, just four weeks since I met Anna—it seems quite
conceivable that the reception clerk will ring up from the desk to
say there is a young lady from Germany in the lounge (that windowless room, with its wobbly gilt chairs and its engraving of
"Painful Memories," which serves as a lounge at the Byron), a
"Signorina Krystek" who wishes to speak to me. Anna's name
would sound droll in this combination and in the pronunciation
of a Roman reception clerk. Perhaps she suspects as much and
that's why she hasn't come. No—that's a bit far-fetched. If she
hasn't come and probably won't, it's because of her reluctance to
leave Berlin, and, ultimately, for the same reason that led her,
after the door man of the night-club had hailed a cab, to reject
my offer to take her home to Neukölln. To wit: she must have
sensed the lack of intensity in my efforts to approach her. We
were standing in the cool night air and I was shivering because I
had brought only my rain-coat to Berlin. When I announced my
intention of taking her home, she smiled and said it was silly,
since my hotel was right around the corner. Then we made the
appointment for Sunday afternoon at the Bristol, which I failed
to keep. So it came about that I woke up at about four in the
morning in my hotel bed and not in Anna's bed in Neukölln.
There perhaps I would not have awakened, would not have heard

the whish of the rain coming down on Berlin, would not have
switched on the lamp or raised my wrist-watch to my short-sighted
eyes. Who knows? On the way to the hotel down the glittering
but deserted Kurfürstendamm, I reflected in a last access of cynicism that if I was not on my way to Neukölln it was because I
had already been to Wannsee and Moabit, to Grunewald and the
banks of the Spree, which was enough Berlin geography for one
day. I decided to sleep a few hours and when I woke up to stop
beating about the bush and go right out to Bismarckstrasse. But
today I know why I didn't take Anna Krystek home that night.
If I hadn't met her, I should not, that Sunday afternoon when I
forgot her and stood her up, have started on these notes, this
record. That much is certain. I know with equal certainty that I
should not yet have begun to write, but would have gone on living
from day to day like a lost journalist if I had spent the rest of the
night with her in the usual way. Sometime or other I should have
started, but not that Sunday four weeks ago, more than a year
ago—I can no longer tell exactly when I executed this or that
figure on the galvanic field in which I have been moving since
then.

No, that is not true! I know every detail of the text on which
I have been working so long, I remember very well how, during
the autumn after my return from London, I abandoned my plan
of first rushing through an account of my days in Berlin, and
turned to other reminiscences until I came to the point where I
was again able to concern myself with Anna—so that the material
thus far treated fell, almost of its own accord, into three chapters.
The use of words like "material" and "chapters" already makes me
feel like a novelist, that is, a man who creates a time continuum
with words. How difficult that is! And how loathsome! It almost
turns my stomach when, for example, I consider that in the last
paragraph I saw fit to claim that I had written a sentence on 26
November 1962, although in actual fact—I've looked it up in my
notes—I didn't write it until 3 December 1963. Why first the de-
ception and then the correction? Why this playing with time?

Obviously because the compulsion to transfer various grammatical tenses into a coherent segment of time left me no other choice in that passage than to use the present. A mirrored present, as it were, which I now retrieve from the mirror; now the image is right side up again. Incidentally, this difficult operation has reassured me: thank the Lord, I'm not a real novelist after all. I am able to describe nothing more than the truth of my existence.

I showed my hand some weeks ago when I admitted that I have been spending almost all my mornings for over a year on these papers. My second Roman Christmas has passed, this is January 1964, and I have begun to look seriously for a flat. In the afternoons I explore every conceivable area, I study the *affitto* signs and the *portieri* show me the flats. Most of those I have visited are too big, suites of enormous rooms, *ampi locali*, with resounding tile or even marble floors, Pantagruelian kitchens, and labyrinthine servants' quarters. They are bare, a glance at the radiators shows you you would freeze, but such palatial halls fire the imagination. I picture a life in the old style with manneristic furniture from Via dei Coronari (strangely enough, Uncle Basil's old Dutch pieces would be as much out of place in one of these flats as in an interior inhabited by Meg, they are too middle class for Rome on the one hand and for Meg on the other), with a cook versed in secret Bolognese recipes, and with a Neapolitan servant who swindles me, it goes without saying, but who knows his way amidst the intricate system of underground relationships that dominate the life of the quarter and who from time to time, when I so desire, brings a young courtesan to my door. I also furnish my exquisitely stylized solitude with two macaws, perched bright-coloured and screaming on brass bars to which they are attached by golden chains, and with an elderly, melancholy chimpanzee who, when I stand at the window, swings silently beside me or sets his black leather fingers on my shoulder and joins me in looking out at the cornelian light, muted by decay, of Via Funari—a contemplative, tubercular dwarf. I saw that light this afternoon; it would cost two hundred thousand lire a month, apart from the two thousand pounds or more it would take to furnish the place. I can't afford that much even if I sell the house in Bismarckstrasse; I shall need that bit of capital to live on for the next few years without taking a job, as befits a writer. With a shrug of the shoulders I left the Cinquecento Palace in Via Funari, which they have broken up into flats and hope to let. Of course I should like best to live in *Roma vecchia*, but I should also be willing to settle for the Aventine or Trastevere. The only modern quarter that might tempt me is the southern edge of Parioli, those houses on the hill-top above the old Valle Giulia, with windows from which one can look out over the tree-tops of Borghese Park. But the flats there are not only too expensive but also chic in a way I don't like—*scichissimo*, as the Romans say. I'm looking for something that may not exist in Rome: a simple quarter in which one can lead what in England is called a decent life, a respectable middle-class existence in a neighbourhood inhabited by doctors, lawyers, teachers, and the better class of office workers and civil servants. In Rome there seem to be only proletarian or aristocratic or *nouveau riche* districts; doctors and lawyers live in luxurious flats with maids and butlers, who serve at table—the sociology of Italy is beyond me. Of course this division into classes gives life a grandiose, unbourgeois quality, but it also seems frivolous and irresponsible; obviously these people live on credit and squander their capital.

One afternoon during Advent, I found myself in the proletarian district at the foot of the Aventine. Though an atheist, I had been to Mass at Santa Sabina, having heard good reports of the Gregorian chant at that church, and indeed it had proved to be excellent; I especially enjoyed the plain song antiphon, which moved like a solemn dance amidst the columns of the pure silvery basilica; afterwards I strolled past cloisters and gardens, into the filigree seclusion of Piazza Cavalieri di Malta, over whose garden walls Piranesi cast a fabric of mortuary monuments, which in the twilight reminded one of names and countries that will never return, a pale scroll of obelisks, steles and ghosts. I surrendered myself to aesthetic pleasures and historical reminiscences of the most precious description, and it was not until I descended the slope to the broad Via Marmorata with its torrent of cars and its clanging trams that I found my way back to so-called reality. I say so-called because a Gregorian antiphon and a Piranesi drawing seem to have as much right to be thought of as real as a cluster of two dozen honking Fiats. After having an *espresso* in a lively and rather dingy bar, gazing at glass cases full of cheap pastry consisting of custard, icing and thin chocolate, quantities of which were being sold, I roamed about amidst large boxlike houses in the style known in Rome as Emanuelesque, reddish blocks of flats teeming with life; I passed lighted shops and workshops, came to a covered market overflowing with fish, meat and vegetables, and stood listening to a market woman who was feeling the belly of a younger woman—pretty and pregnant—and paying her compliments: *che bella*, she said. In one house there was a flat to let. There are no *portieri* in that quarter and I inquired at the tailor's on the ground floor. The tailor himself had the key to the flat which was on the top level. A youngish man, he jumped down from the table on which he had been squatting, and went upstairs with me.

"You're a foreigner?" he asked, stopping on one of the landings. He seemed to stutter. I said I was.

"A German?" Apparently he had experience of the ways in which the different varieties of foreigner pronounced his language. He was a dark-haired man; he stared at me gloomily from under bushy brows.

I said I was English, at which he seemed to brighten a bit. We continued up the stairs, past doors behind which children screamed, people sang, and radios blared.

"This flat isn't for you," said the tailor. He didn't stutter, he merely had difficulty in bringing out the first word of each sentence. Once he had surmounted this obstacle, his sentence flowed on smoothly to the end.

"Why?" I asked.

"It's not a flat for a gentleman," he said. He didn't say *per un signore* but employed the adjective *signorile*. The flat, he said, was not *signorile*, so invoking the magic wishing formula of an Italian man who wishes he were a *signore*: not necessarily rich, but self-possessed, crisp, stern, sovereign—in short, a gentleman. He, this tailor, wasn't one; he was sombre but soft, a dark man with a speech defect.

The flat proved indeed to be anything but *signorile*: a few large rooms with cheap paper peeling off the walls (I'd have them whitewashed), no bathroom (I could have one installed; the whole house would follow the proceedings with amazement), in the kitchen an archaic gas stove and a single water tap, a Turkish lavatory and a bucket to flush it with. But the view from the windows was breath-taking. In the waning light I saw the pyramid of Cestius, travertine-white behind the trees of the Protestant cemetery, which I had once dutifully visited; but in the background two enormous gasometers, great iron balloons enclosed in rusty bars and surmounted by chimneys that gave off poisonous vitriol-green smoke. To the left a hill, wintry-dead, Mount Testaccio, Mountain of Shards, a mound built from the boulders dredged from the old Tiber harbour. I opened one of the windows. The world smelled of gas. Of gas and poison and rubbish and decay.

"Hideous," I said. "Hideously beautiful."

"Like the world," *come il mondo*, said the man who had brought me up there; it took him several starts before the word *come* would come out. And he added with resignation. "I knew it wasn't the right kind of flat for you."

Half-interested, I asked about the rent.

"Forty thousand," he said. That was cheap. He gave me the name and address of the owner, whom I should have to see, a *pezzo grosso* he called him, a big gun. He uttered the term with fierce contempt.

"I suppose everybody belongs to the Communist Party around here?"

"Almost everybody," he said. "I don't."

"What did you mean," I asked, "when you said the world was like that?"

Outside, the last light was dying away. It was almost dark in the flat where we were talking, on the top story of this Roman block of flats.

"You said the world was hideously beautiful. That's how it is."

"I only meant the view."

"The whole world is like that." After violent struggles, clutching like a drowning man at the timber of the first word, which kept slipping out of his grasp, he finally brought out the sentence: "And will be until the Messiah comes."

I was surprised. I proceeded very cautiously.

"But he's already come," I said.

"No," he answered violently. "If he had come, the world would be all beautiful. And you see the way it is." With a despairing gesture he pointed out the window.

"Are you a Jew?" I asked.

He nodded. I did not declare myself. He was a believer, and if I had made myself known as a Jew, a brief exchange would have made it clear to him that I am not a practising Jew, in fact, that I know next to nothing of the Jewish religion. That would have displeased him. I merely protested when he said: "You Christians are mistaken. He hasn't come yet."

"I'm not a Christian," I said. "Don't count me in with them." That wasn't quite true; I was baptized a Protestant.

"Don't you believe in God at all?" he asked intently.

How had I got into this conversation? But the words of that Italian Jewish tailor I fell in with some weeks ago have troubled me ever since. If one could make oneself believe that the Messiah has not yet come, the world would be explained. One could reconcile oneself to the world as it is now. Strange that Uncle Basil was never able to explain the Jewish faith to me so simply and convincingly. He probably had too much education. Undoubtedly he had sceptical misgivings, which is why he started me off where he had ended up: with Spinoza. Keir, on the other hand, the second great teacher in my life, would have been pleased with this stuttering Jew who made and mended clothes in a working-class Communist quarter of Rome. The idea of a still unredeemed world was closely related to his belief, which he had come across in his study of all manner of Scottish and English sects, that all created things were evil. His rejection of salvation—Creation, he held, was the work of the Devil, God was the Great Absent One who took no interest in it whatsoever—was the only thing that distinguished him from the usual sectarian preacher in Aberdeen or Hull. Apart from the fact that he had taken the Classical Tripos at Cambridge and been a member of the establishment ever since. On the strength of a thesis on Marcion he had obtained a lecture-ship in the history of ancient religions. A great Gnostic theology was called upon to justify Keir's conservative snobbery. He often expounded it to me, especially in those first few years, during the war and shortly afterwards when I picked him up almost every day at The Three Tuns on my way to work. At that time I was wholly under his influence, though I already suspected that his belief in the Devil had something to do with Esther; rather than blame himself that his child had been lost, he preferred to believe that she had been carried off by the Devil. This is a crass state-ment of what Keir expounded with learned circumlocutions, never of course mentioning Esther, but only the order of the world, which in his view is governed by a subtle, diabolical spirit who, among other things, made Keir first a college fellow at Cambridge and later a conservative newspaper editor and journalist. He fully understood the left, he assured me, when my reaction to some-thing in the headlines suggested a left-wing attitude on my part; he agreed with the Socialists that the world was badly ordered, but he found it impossible to believe it could be ordered well. The most one could do was to teach those in power that power was evil by nature. For this, long traditions were necessary, centuries-old laws and institutions, all revolving round a common core: the guilty conscience of Power. But the powers as such must not be done away with; they would only be replaced by other powers possessing no tradition of conscience but regarding themselves as good, and these fanatical pedagogues were the worst of all; the terror of the world-improvers was more frightful than the cruel, oppressive rule of a few outstanding individuals who, tortured by the dungeon of conscience in which they lived, tried to break out of it. Once arrived at this idea, Keir usually lost himself in bumblings about Shakespeare's plays. "What about Hitler?" I once asked, wishing to bring him back to the subject from Richard III and Lady Macbeth. "But don't you see," he cried out, "Hitler was one of those men who had a formula, a formula and no tradition, no education, no mature culture, no tutors to drum it into him from early childhood that power must be exercised with irony." With such words Keir reminded himself of what he loved most: his own ironical snob years at Trinity College. As a journalist Keir always yearned to return home to Cambridge, but some druid's foot prevented him from escaping the magic circle of editorial offices and printing presses. That is something which no one who has not sat at a copy desk can understand. "What about Marx? How does Marx fit into your picture?" I asked. "Oh," said Keir, "he of course was a cultivated man." He thought his answer out carefully, knowing I would not be satisfied with phrases. "Well educated, extremely cultivated. I believe he wanted to establish a new tradition. Yes, occasionally someone starts something new. Augustine, for instance. After a few centuries the new becomes part of the old. With Marx it may go faster." Even later, even today, I have not wholly thrown off the influence of Keir's opinions. To be sure, I side with the left in almost all current political questions and am consequently a troublesome contributor to the conservative paper run by Keir; but I have to admit that my left-wing colleagues failed me when I discussed Auschwitz with them. They wanted to *explain* Auschwitz: sociologically, historically, medically. Their rationalism stunned me, their left-wing banalities bored me. Undoubtedly Keir's subtle Hellenistic hypothesis—that Satan lived and ruled the world—

was on a higher level. But it was the naïve faith of that poor Jewish
tailor, his belief that the Messiah had not yet come into the world,
that really fired my imagination—miraculously! Why, when Uncle
Basil showed me a reproduction of a portrait of a rabbi by Rembrandt, hadn't he imparted the very simple idea behind that forehead which the painter's genius raised from darkness to light?
Obviously because he wasn't expecting a messiah; even when he
went to the synagogue, what interested him was not religion, but
only the humanity and spirituality of that head and of Rembrandt
himself. He passed on to me his deep-seated lack of faith; as for his
humanism, its only mark on me is a feeling of profound sadness
that I can no longer believe in anything but chance and chaos.

I did not go back to the poor stutterer, I did not take the flat
he had shown me. The quarter smacks too much of folklore; I
wouldn't fit in. That of course is not true. The quarter doesn't
smack of folklore at all, it's just enormously alive, perhaps a bit
garish, colourful in the sense that it would have forced me to show
my colours; apart from that, it would have accepted my ec-
centricity, I should surely have been respected; I'm a fool for not
taking that flat, for looking for a more neutral environment, a
middle-class quarter where everyone will ignore me and I can carry
on a shadow existence; I don't want to show my colours, to be
made to participate in other people's lives, I want peace and quiet.
I stare at the five words I have just written, it cost me no great
effort to put them down on paper, they put themselves down quite
as a matter of course. I want peace and quiet. For a man of my
age such a sentence is a declaration of bankruptcy. I began these
notes at the age of forty-two and now that, still working on them I
have turned forty-four, I find myself writing: I want peace and
quiet. I ought to chuck these papers. Why don't I give them up
and go back to journalism, where, come to think of it, I had the
peace and quiet that I lost when I started building this labyrinth
around myself—like a mole scraping crumbs of words and sentences
out of a dark firm mass and throwing them behind it?

But I can't stop now. I'm stubborn, *stur*, to use a word often heard in Berlin. "You are an obstinate person," Keir sometimes said to me when he was pleased with my work, whereas when Meg angrily, laughingly called me stubborn she was referring to the demand I persisted in making on her. And when I had finally persuaded Anna to fly to Rome with me, she said: "You're a *sturer Hund* (a stubborn dog)." Because I am stubborn by nature I was a tolerable journalist. I never contented myself with the surface of the things that come one's way in the course of a story, with the glib and apparently illuminating answers one obtains in so many interviews. Instead I tried to look under things and behind words, for I am short, dark, supple and stubborn. Similarly I shall go on looking for a flat in Rome, though I've begun to doubt whether I shall find anything suitable here. But I'm determined to keep on trying for a while. What deprives my search of the extreme resolution without which it can hardly succeed is a thought that I am unable to dispel: the thought that there are many very different places where I might live. That night at the end of October 1962, for instance, while walking along Kirchstrasse in Berlin-Moabit, I played with the idea of living—no, I sincerely wanted to live—in Kirchstrasse, Moabit. Or London— I can think of parts of London where I should gladly settle. Actually the only thing that keeps me away from London is that Meg lives there—London is too small for Meg and me—at least for the present; if I lived in Chelsea or Hampstead, I should be unable to deny myself the short trip that would take me past the grey light of eight or ten tube stations to Malet Street. No, London won't do. Perhaps what makes it so hard for me to decide is that I have visited—I prefer not to say "known"—so many countries and places in the world. True, I have never been in the Soviet Union or Australia, and all I know of Africa is the theatre of war on its northern fringe, but I have travelled through a large part of Asia, I was fast becoming a Southeast Asia specialist when Keir sent me to the Arab states and Israel, and once he even shipped me off for six months to the southern United States, but then brought me back to Europe because Meg wanted him to and

Keir never refused her anything. Meg gave me a long tether because she knew that was the only way to hold me, but she didn't
want me to lose the habit of her entirely and so, though by a cir-
cuitous route, I had to go back to Europe. I could have objected.
When a newspaperman has made as much of a name for himself as I had, he can choose his own territory; even so mighty an
editor-in-chief as Keir can't arbitrarily transfer an Asia specialist
out of Asia, but the truth of the matter is that I raised no objection; it was I who had left Meg but I couldn't repress a desire
that she pull in my tether now and then; it was pleasant to feel
that she was still interested in me. Now at last I believe that I
am independent enough to decide freely where I want to live—
perhaps even somewhere far away from Meg. But Israel is out of
the question; I have no intention of letting myself be shut up in
that super-ghetto that we are voluntarily building for ourselves.
We, I write, though I'm not so sure that I'm really one of us, for
all in all I feel quite comfortable in my role as a German-born,
naturalized Englishman, and member of a minority, but I should
feel rather ridiculous if I were suddenly transformed from a Jew
to an Israeli and possibly placed under obligation to think and
feel patriotically. Yet in the event of a war against Israel I would
take up arms; I was in the British army, I have adequate combat
experience, my health is good; I could make myself useful to Israel
—that war I would not observe as a journalist. But otherwise? In
so far as I am a Jew, I became one through the death of my parents and through Uncle Basil's upbringing, on the one hand in
the glaring light of a horror for which there is no explanation, and
on the other in a half-light of mystical tolerance, in the transparent shadow of Spinoza. What would I do in Israel with such a
heritage? Conceivably Israel would remove the burden of this
heritage from my shoulders; one goes there because one can't bear
it alone any longer and in order to embark on something utterly
new; but oddly enough, this prospect does not tempt me, I prefer
to keep my heritage, both the thoughts and images of an extinct
culture and the memory of how it ended in horror. If I am con-

demned to live in a ghetto, then at least let it be not a public, collective ghetto, but a private, closed one; then I prefer to build my own ghetto, a Jew alone among goyim, respected or despised, liked or disliked, it doesn't matter, I want neither to be loved nor hated, all I ask for is a safe-conduct, I can understand that they should be annoyed with me, for them I am one of those who are still waiting for the Messiah; that annoys them because they think they have already found their Messiah, it's perfectly possible that we Jews are mistaken in not believing that he was really the Messiah, but he's not the one I mean, I am referring to all the many other messiahs they still believe in because they are possessed by the desire to believe in something, whereas we are able to believe in nothing and no one, but prefer to go on waiting, each one of us critically and sceptically watching and waiting in his exile.

Where am I? I ought to be attending to my little problem of lodging and instead I trouble my head over big abstract theories. Before dropping the idea of Israel, I develop it in an entirely different direction. Though Meg and Anna Krystek are not Jews, it suddenly occurs to me, either one of them would follow me to Israel if I made up my mind to go there. In Meg's case a number of motives would converge: her distaste for old, overpopulated, civilized countries; for this mixture of Brighton and Canterbury, as she contemptuously calls England, for the domestication of England; she always envied me my trips to Asia. Israel would be to her, first and foremost, a part of the Near East, it would be the desert; she was fascinated when I described Beersheba or Sodom to her or the Negev, places where she and her camera would no longer have to struggle to disengage Hunnish colours and emblems of the steppes as she had from the plane trees of Terrace Gardens, places where there was an abundance of everything she had dreamed of at night as a child in a terrace house deep in the Potteries; that would appeal to her; but in addition there was the modern, progressive experimental element, the emancipation of women; in Israel she would become a part of all that, or so at least she imagined when we talked about Israel; there she would no longer belong to a minority as in England, but become one of those who shape the consciousness of the country. For this, for this amalgam of desert and exalted consciousness that Israel was to her, she would give up her successful life in London without a murmur and make a fresh start. And Anna? For her Israel would be an utterly unhoped-for escape from the situation she has fallen into in Berlin, the situation that presses her to choose, though any choice would betray her conscience and her convictions, so that she lives from day to day, paralyzed with indecision like a bird under the eyes of a cat. All at once it comes to me with certainty, though alas much too late, that she would not have turned back in Frankfurt on 1 November 1962, that she would not have flown back to Berlin, if we had then been on our way to Israel rather than to Rome. A country where she could become a member of a *kibbutz*, a land of youth, of the radically new, of rich poverty—to Anna that would have been an irresistible lure. Instead I was taking her to a city more cluttered with ancient bric-à-brac than any other. How stupid of me! I just didn't offer her the right thing. In taking her to Rome I was thinking only of myself, of this old red light which, as I have written, suggests that even the most intense, most senseless suffering might in the end fuse into a sum of grief, into a red twilight—so that Rome still strikes me as a possible place to live. It would have been absurd to expect Anna to understand this problem of a man almost twenty years older than herself. There really are generation gaps. Meg, on the other hand, understands very well why for some time now I have been slipping away from journalism and sitting about in Rome, doing next to nothing—since my visit to her she has known how important a very different kind of work has meanwhile become to me—but she doesn't accept it, she criticizes me for it. "Stop feeling sorry for yourself," she said to me in London, and in the margin of a recent letter, which had been all about Keir, she wrote quite irrelevantly: "You're too bottled up inside yourself." Going to Israel with me would also give her a chance to see how things really stood between us. But the pure air of the East

—I know that air, it exists—doesn't tempt me enough. I have admired the Negev and the Arabian deserts, and once on an island in the Gulf of Siam I actually shared Kipling's famous Mandalay feeling. But the dawn that *comes up like thunder, outer China 'crost the Bay* wasn't meant for me, no, not for me.

London then must be postponed; to Israel, to Asia I append a question mark. That leaves Rome or Berlin. Does it really leave Berlin? It's high time that I put myself back in Berlin, on that Monday morning when I rang Anna Krystek. The calendar I have hung up in my room at the Byron, whose pages I conscientiously tear off, says 11 May 1964. It can't go on like this, I write more and more slowly, when shall I ever get done if I keep losing myself in reflections, so that I spend several weeks on a few pages? (Get done—another of those expressions. Does beginning something necessarily imply getting done?) Almost exactly a year ago the Pope died, next Sunday is Whitsun and Pope John XXIII died on a Whitsun Monday. The evening when the Pope's death was announced was as grey and sultry as this evening, the end of a day of *scirocco*; the whole day had been old and sick, grief-stricken at having to lead up to that minute; the forty-ninth minute of the seventh hour after noon. I remember that point in time so well because with it I put an end to my time as a journalist. That evening I swore to stop. If occasionally I put through a story or an article, it is merely the gesture of the runner who after the thousand-meter run goes on for another few yards to avoid heart strain. And out of consideration for Keir. Often, to be sure, I am discouraged when after days of aimless brooding over this manuscript I have set down no more than two or three sentences. Then I wonder if I shouldn't keep on with journalism after all; I go to the Circolo della Stampa Estera, chat with my colleagues, and in the late afternoon put through a call to our news telephones. We're having another government crisis in Rome.

But now I pull myself together: I'm back in Berlin on Monday, 20 October 1962; I rang Anna Krystek at half-past seven, then I wrote all morning, continuing what I had begun on Sunday afternoon—later on in Rome I shall revise these first pages drastically, transpose them from the third to the first person; I had Königsberg meat balls for lunch at the Schultheiss Restaurant; in the afternoon I went to see Mother Ludmilla, the Carmelite nun, in Steglitz and talked with her about Esther. After that—it was already dark—I took the Stadtbahn to East Berlin, passed through the crossing point at Friedrichstrasse station and walked across the Spree to the Theater am Schiffbauerdamm to attend a performance of *The Days of the Commune* by Bertolt Brecht. I knew the mechanism of the crossing points and the way to the theatre as well, because on Friday morning, on the advice of my English fellow-newspapermen, I had gone to East Berlin to procure a ticket. On Friday everything had gone smoothly, but on Monday I reached the crossing point in the midst of a rush-hour bottleneck and had to wait a long time in the basement of Friedrichstrasse station. I sat there for an hour on a wooden bench amidst cold cigarette smoke with hundreds of people from West Germany, who spoke to one another seldom and cautiously and read no newspapers, but just sat there bathed in yellowish light. From time to time policemen and policewomen in dull green uniforms passed, they did not give the impression of concentration camp guards, they gave no impression at all, they were just there, doing something or other, but down there in that underground silence I no longer thought of the fine dust of puritanism as I had Friday morning on my walk through the streets of East Berlin; I thought only of cold cigarette smoke, slops and bureaucracy. Then we were called into another room and our passports were returned. The man who passed through the gate ahead of me was smoking; the policeman who was taking a last look at his passport said to him: "Take that cigarette out of your mouth, how do you expect me to check your passport if you've got a cigarette in your mouth?" His tone wasn't hostile or menacing, no, it was quite matter-of-fact. Both the man and I went white with rage, but we said nothing to one another, not even twenty steps past the gate; I merely watched him as he returned the cigarette to his mouth but after one drag spat it out again with revulsion. To me the policeman had said, while examining my English passport, that I should have gone to the foreigners' window, I'd have been taken care of more quickly. I was still mute with rage, otherwise I'd have replied that it was very interesting to me as an Englishman to see how Germans took care of Germans, but today I know those words would have been a lie, for at that moment I wasn't an Englishman but a German.

The beginning of Brecht's play was spoiled for me by the consciousness of being in a country where you have to take the cigarette out of your mouth to have your passport photo checked. I sat through the first and second scenes feeling disgruntled and far away, but then I was caught up in the old bird's-eye view of Paris which served as a backdrop, in the light-grey, almost colourless props suggesting Paris streets and interiors, and the dark deep blue or brown which was occasionally allowed to spread out in the costumes. Delicately and carefully the wearers etched the awakening of the masses to criticism, revolt and death into the dove-grey ground; certain scenes moved imperceptibly from Place Pigalle to Schilda, into a fine-spun German dream world; I couldn't help smiling—never have I seen a more lyrical revolution on the stage. Effects of misty vagueness had been aimed at, not only in the *piano* of the crowd scenes, but also in the *forte* of the debates in the Central Committee: the hubbub of voices speaking out of turn was played so artfully as to carry me away and make me forget that no one spoke out of turn, and certainly not artfully, in this country where the days of the Commune were being recalled to memory. Anna Krystek's remarks on points of detail were borne out: the portraits of Thiers and Bismarck contributed to this picture book by the pale, broad-shouldered, sinister-looking, but humorous actor Martin Flörchinger are still with me, and the youthful Hilmar Thate, of whom Anna had spoken, played the young worker Jean Cabet with true proletarian gusto. Such a Jean Cabet would be the right man for Anna, but I'm afraid that in Europe at least he exists only on the stage. What was Brecht's play—and the way in which it was produced!—but a requiem for the revolution?

But his Paris had what on Friday morning—after my first passage through the underground corridors of Friedrichstrasse station —had so attracted me in East Berlin: the bluish shimmer and the hardness of an old steel engraving. In the course of my walks through Rome, on which at present I often look at flats, I see myself time and again walking down Friedrichstrasse on a cold, dry October day: I have been at the box office; standing on Weidendamm Bridge, I have watched the skin of the Spree steaming in the frosty morning air, and now I am on the corner of Friedrichstrasse and Unter den Linden, looking at the wide, empty, grey-blue avenues with the sparse lines of pedestrians on the pavements and the few cars in the roadways. Even the sky seems emptier and harder than the sky on the other side of Brandenburg Gate, that of course is nonsense, it's exactly the same dry, light-blue sky as I saw this morning—my first morning in Berlin since 1935—from my room at the Hotel am Zoo. Charmed, I make my way into the steel engraving, down Unter den Linden in the direction of the Arsenal, the Castle isn't there any more, I know that in advance, so I turn off to the right, roam about on Opernplatz, which has been beautifully restored, and then on down to Gendarmenmarkt. I am pretty much alone. It's unbelievable: I am a lone, freakish wanderer in the centre of Berlin, through whose dense hubbub I often made my way as a child. I enter Hedwigs-Kathedrale, the interior has been renovated magnificently and in good taste, a few people have actually come here to pray, and at one of the side altars a Mass is being sung. When I come out, the square is as bare and solitary as ever, on Gendarmenmarkt not a living soul, not a single car, and this on a week-day morning. The cupolas of the French and German cathedrals tower over their ruins, the steps of the big stairway of the Schauspielhaus are cracked. I'd like to live here. This emptiness, this silence, would be even better than Kirchstrasse in Moabit. No advertisements, no one shouts at me urging me to buy something; instead, the smell of poverty and disinfectant, of fine grey dust and puritanism. I know I am basking in illusions, I am not going about in a puritanical city, but only in an impoverished, backward city; the people here long for wealth, for a flood of commodities, for herds of motor cars, they look with envy at the production gone wild, the fashions, the speed, the jokes, the books and naked flesh on the other side of the Wall. They are only too eager to rid themselves of what strikes me as their one and unique advantage. Unwittingly and unintentionally, they have set down a very old, impoverished, silvery Prussia at the edge of the great Slavic plain—it's too bad they don't seem to know it. I could live here. But then this business with the cigarette and the passport. At her home in Neukölln even Anna's eyes narrowed when I told her of the incident at the barrier on Tuesday, though later on she said I made too much of it, that there were cops with the souls of cops everywhere. On the other hand, she did not understand me when I tried to explain the motives that might induce me to live in the Gendarmenmarkt-Französische Strasse area, on Hausvogteiplatz or the southern Spree Island. My guess is that she wasn't really listening to me, that she regarded my talk about steel engravings and Brecht's lyricism as bourgeois aestheticism, or at best as private lunacy; the one thing that interested and aroused her was that I, a Western newspaperman, a British subject and German Jew of middle-class, almost conservative family, should think seriously of settling in East Berlin. My irresponsible chatter reminded her painfully of her own inability to make up her mind and consequently gave her the jim-jams—that was the turn of phrase she used when I suggested that perhaps I might find everything East Berlin had to offer in West Berlin, in Kirchstrasse, Moabit or right here in Neukölln. "Man," she said with an angry laugh, "you give me the jim-jams." And she added: "If you want to live in West Berlin, why don't you go back to your old house in Wannsee? Where could you be more comfortable?" I looked at her speechless; how, I wondered, could anyone think me capable of living there again? In writing just now that I should prefer to keep my heritage, I certainly didn't mean the house in Bismarckstrasse, not that tangible piece of horror. Then I remembered that Anna had been seven years old at the end of the war; there were certain things she could not understand. There really is a generation gap. Actually Anna's belonging to a generation which could no longer understand certain things might be one more reason for living with her. I wish I knew what has become of her. Perhaps I'll write to Sandberg one of these days and ask him for news of Anna Krystek. At the Frankfurt airport Anna and I agreed not to write—ever. We have kept our agreement. But I might, on the sly, ask Sandberg, who knows everyone in Berlin, for information. I ought to do it right now, a few lines would suffice, but at this moment, at noon on a grey, sultry day of *scirocco* in Rome, already tired and feeling cooped up in my room at the Byron, I am interrupted by the sound of Meg's key in the door of our Malet Street flat. I hear it distinctly as I did on that first night of my stay there, when I lay down in my clothes on our living-room couch and decided I'd pretend to be asleep when Meg came home. Why should she burst in on my comfortable Roman noonday fatigue with that jangling of keys? Why now of all times? I suppose she was getting impatient; she has never stopped to consider my moods and feelings when she was impatient with me. She probably wants to remind me that I've spent enough time weaving a net of memories and digressions just to kill the hours while she spent the evening in Chelsea with film director Cameron and kept me waiting. "You've taken a lot of time for this evening, my dear," she says. "From November 1962 to May 1964." And she tears my net to pieces. She is sitting on my bed at the Albergo Byron, I am standing at the window beside the drawing board at which I have been working all morning. Yes, she has entered this room in Rome while still on the landing of 31 Malet Street. I hear her turning the key in the lock. Hurriedly I switch on the little lamp over the couch. I raise my wristwatch to my short-sighted eyes. It is a quarter to one. Meg is here.

Four

I had intended to turn out the light at once and pretend to be asleep but by the way Meg opens the door, stops, and puts down an object in the corridor, I can tell she has brought my suitcase. So I get up after all—I had lain down in my clothes, removing only my shoes and jacket—to give her a hand. I put on my glasses and go out to her. She has closed the outer door and put my suitcase, which would be better described as a fat frayed bag, down beside the hat stand.

"Thank you," I say, "I didn't hear the car or I'd have gone down for the bag. I must have been asleep."

I'm quite certain that I was not asleep or I should not have heard the sound of her key so instantly. From my failure to hear Cameron's car I do not infer that I may have been asleep after all, but only that at Meg's request he stopped his Bentley as silky-softly and soundlessly as is possible only with a car of that class. Or Meg may have had him drop her off at the corner and walked the few steps to the house—my bag isn't heavy, I'm not planning to spend more than two or three days in London and have only brought the barest necessities, Meg is a strong girl, the heavy cameras she's always hauling about don't bother her in the least.

Meg smiles at me.

"Go back to sleep," she says. "But as long as you're awake, put your pyjamas on at least."

She points to my bag. She makes no attempt to explain how she came home. Since I myself have said I must have been asleep, she has no need to explain how she arrived so silently at the door of 31 Malet Street.

I'm being most illogical; I forget that she has no need to creep into our flat like a thief. She has no reason to use kid gloves with me.

I help her off with her coat, it's wet. We go into the living room. I look at her dark tweed suit, her stockings. Though I have no idea whether she has come from Cameron's flat or not, I picture her getting back into her skirt half an hour ago, slipping on her stockings, tidying up her lipstick and combing her hair. With a passing glance she registers the fact that I have made up my bed with blankets and cushions on the living-room couch.

"I'll get you some sheets," she says.

"It's not necessary."

"It's very necessary," she says. "You'll sleep much better with sheets." She goes to the bedroom and comes back with the sheets.

"How was it at the King's Head?" I ask.

"We didn't go to the King's Head. We picked up the suitcase, then we had a quick snack at the Musketeer, because it's round the corner from Cameron's. Then we went to his place and talked about the picture."

"Hm," I say, "that's a typical Meg report."

"What do you mean by that?" she asks in astonishment.

"Meg's patented mixture of carrot and whip."

"I really don't understand."

"It's not very hard to understand," I say. "First you stay away from the King's Head because I reminded you—you had forgotten—that the King's Head was *our* King's Head; that's your tender consideration for me, I ought to appreciate it and I do; really Meg, I'm grateful to you for at least not going to the King's Head with Cameron this evening. But you don't want to be too considerate, I might get ideas, so you slap me in the face by telling me you went to his flat. . . ."

"George," she says, "you're ill. There's no other word for it."

I ignore her interruption. "Actually," I go on, "your staying away from the King's Head is no mark of special consideration. I haven't forgotten the Musketeer, we used to have very pleasant evenings there, don't you remember? We discovered it together, the Musketeer was *our* Musketeer too," and I break off, overwhelmed by the memory of the tiny dark dining room of the smart old pub in Belgravia. The Musketeer is old and dark and sophisticated and cosy, a good place to take a girl because you can't sit at a table without touching the girl's knees with your own. But even as I am working myself up over Meg's going to the Musketeer with Cameron, I realize that in this moment the word Musketeer is nothing more to me than the name of a certain place in my imagination; I give this name to an infinitesimal point in my grey matter which I might—I've done it any number of times—equally well mark with some other word, because even if Cameron had dragged my wife to another pub, even one totally unknown to me, I should lose control just as I am doing now; the very unknownness of the place would serve to justify the hysteria whose by no means innocent victim I am tonight.

"You don't know Cameron," says Meg, laughing. "He's a Scotsman. He's six foot six and bony and looks like a ghost. And all he talks about is films. He's not interested in anything but films."

"You mean he's just your type," I say, "a man obsessed by his work." I trot out my trumps: "He must be a very fashionable ghost. I saw his Bentley. And his white cuffs. And the way his left hand stroked your legs after he'd closed the car door."

"He didn't stroke my legs," says Meg furiously, "that's pure imagination." She tries the calm, reasonable approach. "Now listen to me, George, listen to me quietly for a moment: the scene of Cameron's next film, the one he's engaged me for, is the Liverpool docks. I was in Liverpool a fortnight ago, I looked things over and took a few pictures. This evening after dinner we looked at the pictures, they're colour diapositives, you can see them if you like, I told him I wouldn't work on his film unless he accepted my conception of the colour and had his cameraman photograph the docks exactly as I've photographed them; we had quite an argument, but in the end he gave in. Then he took me home and now I'm here. That's all there is to it, George, really."

Her tone proves nothing. If Meg has made up her mind to lie

to me, she will do it as convincingly and intensely as if she were telling the truth. She will deceive me without a qualm, just as she'll tell me the truth without a qualm if for some reason she thinks it preferable. For instance, it may be that her sexual relations with Cameron have just begun, that they are still in the experimental stage, so to speak, or it may be that they are doing splendidly, with harmonious love play followed by great passion; in that case Meg will tell me nothing. Or perhaps she wishes for professional reasons to keep up the appearance of a mere business relation with Cameron, then again she'll conceal the truth, and with such conviction that her lie will become a substitute for the truth, will become identical with it, a kind of higher truth with its own intrinsic rightness, because if Meg and Cameron make love, whether still hesitantly or already in deep drafts, or if they work together and go to bed only in passing, because the occasion arises or because it improves their working relationship, they have a right to keep the matter secret, and the lie that safeguards such a secret is justified and therefore true. Meg has always been able to do that: to lie with integrity. On the other hand, it's conceivable that she isn't lying. Meg is capable of playing this sort of relationship straight and sober, possibly because she has taken it into her head to see if she can exert a good influence on Cameron's picture by her work and by her work alone. That too is "in" Meg as they would say in Berlin. Perhaps Cameron really is the Scottish ghost Meg describes. I'll ring up Baron Collaudi tomorrow and find out what the industry knows about Meg and Cameron. In any case it would be absurd to suppose that their relations are confined to business if Meg stays from ten or eleven to half-past twelve in the flat of a man who obviously lives alone; there has been no mention of a Mrs. Cameron. Once again a figure of speech picked up in Berlin occurs to me: *Ich bin doch nicht bekloppt,* "I haven't been hit over the head, I'm not stupid." I cast about for an English substitute for the German slang phrase—what cruel amusement I derive from these new German colloquialisms—and find nothing but the rather pallid question "What do you take me for?" which I fire at Meg, adding scornfully that I fail to see any of the boxes in which she carries her diapositives, she must have left them at Cameron's. She rummages for a moment in her handbag, takes out a soft leather case, opens it and shows me the photographs in it.

"There are only ten of them," she says. "Or did you think I gave Cameron an illustrated lecture?"

"No," I said. "I certainly don't think that."

"What an inquisition!" says Meg. Without raising her voice—if anything she lowers it somewhat—she asks: "Do you think you have the right to make such a scene?"

Almost any other woman would go on to explain exactly how I have forfeited the right to make a scene. Our separation was my doing, I haven't shown myself for a whole year, we're both free, and so on. Meg makes no use of this prerogative. She is highly skilled at cutting such dialogues short. She knows they do no good and that some logical demonstrations can be unfair. Meg is always fair. She makes it clear that I have no right to make a scene, but she doesn't press the point because she is well aware that she would be disappointed if I didn't behave as illogically as I have just done. I'm horrified at myself. I thought I'd got over this kind of thing. While Meg spreads the sheets and converts the couch into a bed, I stand at the window with my back to her, looking out into the dark rainy street because the sight of personal services is distasteful to me. I hear her going into the bedroom. She leaves the door open.

"You've been working," she cries out. Her voice sounds as though she were pleased.

I follow her into the bedroom. "I've got to put the stuff away," I say.

She sits down at the table where the typewriter is and looks at the spread-out papers.

"Good God," she says. "You're writing in German!"

I only nod. What should I say?

"Then you must be writing a book," she says. I say I'm only

jotting down a few things for myself, but she takes no notice.

"Keir told me you were writing," she says.

This sentence is interesting to me in two respects. First, it tells me that she sees Keir and that they talk about me, though I already guessed as much when it became clear that she knew of my trip to Berlin; second, it confirms me in the knowledge that when people say someone is writing they always mean he is writing a book. As long as I was a journalist, no one spoke of my writing as such; at the most they said I was writing an article or a news story.

"Keir has suspected you of literary ambitions for some time," Meg goes on. We both have to smile, because we know Keir and know that he speaks of literature in a tone of grim irony, although he himself is a connoisseur of literature with definite preferences, such as Trollope and Shakespeare.

"He says it's an occupational disease. Almost every journalist, he says, has a secret desire to write." Again she utters the word "write" as if it denoted something entirely different from the writing done by journalists, a mysterious occupation *per se*. Keir, too, used it in this sense.

"I told him not to delude himself," she says. "Once you start something, I said, it's serious."

"I don't take it all that seriously," I reply. On the night of 14 November 1962 it was still possible for me to claim that I didn't take *it* so seriously. After all, only a fortnight had elapsed since I had stumbled, as though by chance, into this way of keeping busy. Meanwhile nearly two years have passed. And even now, two years later, there are moments, hours, days, when I wonder if I haven't been wasting my time. When that happens, I sit around in a state of paralysis.

"What a pity I can't read it," says Meg. She bends over the papers, tries to decipher a sentence, but quickly gives up.

I'm glad she never studied German. If she had, I should now have to snatch away these pages, in which I recorded my fear that Cella might know by looking at me, *what I had been doing two hours before at the Circolo della Stampa Estera. Like all men who indulge in self-abuse, I have strong guilt feelings.* The thought of Meg reading such sentences brings a flush to my cheeks and at the same time suggests to me how preposterous it would be to try to work my notes into a book, into something that would *appear.* Nowadays any novel that's any good at all is translated into every conceivable language, sentences like this one, which I wrote a few hours ago on my old typewriter in our—Meg's and mine—flat, would come to Meg's eyes in the English edition—no, it's unthinkable!

Meg propped her chin on her hands. After a time she said: "You've been in England almost thirty years, you've become an English journalist and you've married an Englishwoman. You speak perfect English with hardly any accent. Then you spend a few days in Berlin, you start to write, and guess what! You write in German!" She breaks off and sits there for a moment speechless. Then she says: "Oh, George, I've suddenly realized that you're a stranger."

She rises, comes over, and throws her arm around me.

"You're a stranger, George," she says, "and I haven't always been good to you. I haven't always been as friendly and polite as one should be to a foreigner."

She smiles. By substituting the word "foreigner" for the word "stranger" and by taking her arm away she has forestalled any feeling of embarrassment that might have arisen. By now of course the question of whether we should sleep together has become acute. We both want to. But instead of doing anything about it I go to the table, arrange my papers and put the oilcloth cover on the typewriter, while Meg disappears into her darkroom. I lie down on the couch. I hear her rummaging about, then she puts out the light and goes to bed. She hasn't closed the door between us, but she doesn't come into me. When we lived together I sometimes slept on the living-room couch, and Meg often came in to me when she felt like it, but tonight she knows it would be a grave mistake not to leave me the initiative. I'm supposed to capitulate and the rules of warfare forbid her to anticipate my capitulation. The rooms are so small and close together that after a while I hear Meg's soft, regular breathing—she has fallen asleep. I ought to have gone to a hotel. I shall fall asleep myself soon, I'm tired, I had to get up rather early this morning in Rome to catch the plane for London: even with my fast little car the drive out to Fiumicino airport takes me almost an hour. I think of my car that is waiting for me in the Fiumicino car park, it belongs to me, I think of various other things I can count on because they're inanimate, then I fall asleep.

In the morning I can't indulge my habit of having breakfast alone with the newspaper, because Meg has got up first and made breakfast, but today I don't mind, I find it quite pleasant for a change not to have breakfast by myself, especially as I've already glanced through the paper which Meg has been kind enough to bring in and toss on my bed. We sit at our kitchen table, Meg in a tracksuit, she never wears dressing gowns and that kind of thing, but always makes her first morning appearance looking fresh and athletic; I'm still in my pyjamas and probably look rather unkempt because it's a principle with me not to wash until after breakfast. As a rule I shave, have breakfast, and then shower, today I am also obliged to put off shaving, Meg upsets my habits, the fact is that I often have to modify my habits under the influence of people and places, in Rome for instance I'm obliged not only to shave before breakfast but also to wash and dress, because there I never breakfast at home—in my room at the Byron, I mean—but in a bar, usually the bar of the Caffè Greco. These observations make me think of habits in general; somewhere in this record—I make a note of it—I shall have to describe my habits in detail, after all they take up the greater part of my time, but they are not only quantitatively significant, they also have an intrinsic quality, some-times pleasant, sometimes lugubrious, at all events a life-devouring force. Of course it's nonsense when I write that my breakfasting rules started me on this subject, my reflections about my dealings with Lidia are mostly to blame. I spent yesterday evening with her, and when just now at my drawing board at the Byron I put down the key word "habits," my thoughts strayed from my breakfast, washing and shaving problems to Lidia and the nature of my feeling for her. She too is a part of my "pattern of life." But for the present I suspend these reflections before even embarking on them —I want to go on breakfasting with Meg, there's bacon and eggs, buttered toast, jam, orange juice and tea, an unaccustomed treat after Rome with its cup of *cappuccino* and a dry croissant; I greet the emblems of England with gratitude, I must admit that I feel very much at home in England. Meg brings up the subject of Esther, asking what I've found out. She asked me the same question yesterday evening, but Cameron's arrival prevented me from answering. Now I tell her I'm going to see Keir later in the morning and that prompts her to ask what I have to say to him about his daughter. I tell her what I've heard from Frau Schlesinger— that Esther ran away from home in November 1938 and was never heard from again.

"Good God," says Meg, "then she may be alive! Have you any idea where she might be?"

Anna and I have worked out a theory, but to Meg I make no mention of Mother Ludmilla; what I learned from the nun concerns only Keir; it's bad enough for me to know things that concern only Keir. If I told Anna, it's only because the idea of going to Esther's old school was hers and I thought I owed her the satisfaction of hearing that her hunch hadn't been a bad one. Besides, she doesn't know Keir and there's little likelihood of her ever meeting him.

"But why, if Esther's still alive, didn't she get in touch with anybody after the war?" Meg asks. "She must have known her father was in England, she was already thirteen when she ran away; her mother must have told her about him."

Not wishing to mention Mother Ludmilla to Meg, not at least until I have seen Keir, I can only shrug in answer to her pertinent question. To put an end to the discussion I say Esther must be dead, though I feel sure she is not. Meg is visibly disappointed at the apparent indifference with which I dispose of the matter. Actually I cut off our speculations as to whether Esther is dead or alive, not only because they strike me as futile, but also because during our discussion my mind has been occupied by a very different thought. I have begun to ask myself whether I ought to tell Meg about Anna, to describe my relationship with this young girl in Berlin, and perhaps even own that I should like to try to live with her. At Frankfurt airport, to be sure, Anna couldn't bring herself to go on with me to Rome, but that was a fortnight ago, maybe she has changed her mind, maybe there's a wire from her at the Byron right now, telling me she's coming after all, maybe she arrived yesterday while I was on the plane to London—just like that, without wiring; in Frankfurt I expressly told her she could do that. As it has turned out in the meantime, she didn't come, but I couldn't know that when breakfasting almost two years ago with Meg in our Malet Street flat; at that time the problem of Anna still had urgency for me. It would interest me to see how Meg would react to hearing about Anna and what advice she would give me, for regardless of her feelings in the matter, I know she would give me good level-headed advice. Though Meg is capable of jealousy—a violent, primitive jealousy as I discovered several times in the course of our life together, though not of me to be sure, I never gave her any grounds—she can always be counted on to appraise a man's feeling for a woman correctly, to know or to sense whether it is genuine or not, and to give her opinion without regard to her own interests. Besides, since I've told Anna about Meg, it would only be fair to tell Meg about Anna. But for some reason that escapes me, probably cowardice or at least the fear of inconvenience, I abstain; instead of talking about Anna and myself, I do the exact opposite, I drift into a dialogue about Keir and Meg. Meg provides the cue by saying that it would mean a good deal to Keir to know that his daughter may be alive, especially if there were some prospect of finding her.

"How is Keir?" I ask. My purpose, I imagine at the time, is to divert Meg from Esther; in reality, I want to find out whether Meg knows how Keir is. Of course I know she knows, I've already found out that she sees him, that he keeps her posted on my whereabouts, but so far I haven't mentioned Keir's name, I haven't yet tried, through the direct question—"How is Keir?"—to determine the quality of Meg's interest in Keir's well-being. From the nuance of her tone in answering this seemingly so conventional question I hope to learn the nature of her relations with Keir. For the moment my hope is disappointed.

"Bad," says Meg in a tone of dismay. "I don't know what's wrong with him."

I wonder if she really doesn't know. But Meg's voice has that note of grey that it always takes on when she complains. It sounds almost as though she were complaining that Keir neglects to tell her what is wrong with him.

"Has he been drinking too much?" I ask.

"Yes, he's been drinking a good deal in the last few months. Even more than usual."

She's been seeing a lot of him, I conclude, if she knows he's drinking more than usual, seeing enough of him to be able to judge his drinking habits and their effects. Since she isn't intimate with any of Keir's associates—of course she knows everyone on our paper, but her acquaintance with the members of Keir's staff is limited to the usual formulae of greeting and an occasional chat about professional matters—she can't have got her information about Keir from the other editors or their secretaries. They all gossip about Meg, but since her relations with Keir and myself are an open secret, they don't gossip to her. No one helps her to read Keir's gin-and-beer gauge. Of course I keep these reflections to myself; in sharp contrast to my agitation over Cameron—a trifle put on, I must admit—I now say nothing about Keir; on the subject of Keir, there is nothing more to be said between Meg and me, we have been through it often enough. Compared to Keir, Cameron is nothing—it was silly of me to make a scene over Cameron.

"But it can't be that," she thinks out loud. "He's often had spells of heavy drinking and it hasn't hurt him. I mean it hasn't interfered with his work."

"Perhaps a time comes when one just can't carry on," I suggest. "Keir is in his middle sixties. . . ." I break off, sensing that at this point language has driven me into an ambiguity; the words "carry on" have carried me beyond the limits of a discussion on Keir's alcoholism. I think of the imaginary continuation of my telephone conversation with him a fortnight ago in Berlin when, against my better knowledge, I expected him to tell me that he was prepared to give up. *This whole imaginary dialogue*, I have written in the meantime, *stemmed from my wishful thinking; it is only because I had certain reasons for wanting Keir to give up, that in my imagination I made him express opinions that are not his.* In reality he doesn't dream of giving up, not at all, he carries right on.

Meg, too, realizes that my remark has led us onto dangerous ground. She takes up where she left off.

"The paper has been slipping," she says. "But I don't have to tell you that."

Yes, I know all about it; I didn't need Sandberg to tell me that Keir didn't seem to have his heart in it any more; I can read the paper myself, but now Meg brings up a point which has hitherto escaped me.

"Strange," she says, "that the two of you, you and Keir, should weaken at just about the same time. As if you'd arranged it in advance." She laughs and asks: "Did you?"

I shook my head. But it's true—as I think it over, it comes to me that she's right. About a year ago I lost interest in journalism, or more accurately, for roughly the past year I have been aware of my loss of interest. As long as my dissatisfaction was not conveyed to my consciousness, I worked hard at my job; only when it dawned on me that journalism had nothing more to offer me did I begin, as Collaudi put it, to be on the downgrade as a journalist. Yes, it is odd that Keir began to weaken—to use Meg's expression; no, if I remember right, her actual words were that we were no longer "up to the mark," I suppose she was being as tactful as possible—at the same time, but I don't know whether he too is fed up with journalism. At all events I'm sure he has entirely different reasons for a feeling which in my case runs the whole gamut from simple antipathy to the most complex disgust. But what reasons? Meg doesn't know either.

"In your case," she says, "it's obvious—you want to write. Your book means more to you than anything else. But what's wrong with Keir? I keep racking my brains but I can't figure it out."

Time and again in this conversation she comes back to the question: "What's wrong with Keir?" I am familiar with the fact that she often thinks about him; that Meg's thoughts and feelings busy themselves with Keir is the first premise of my relationship with her, I've accepted it once and for all, no comment is necessary. I only say: "You ought to ask him. Perhaps he'll tell you."

I was careful not to put a trace of irony, let alone hostility, into those two sentences, but Meg stiffens at once, a far-away look comes into her eyes; without her having to say a word, that look tells me she has been asking Keir all along but obtained no answer. I change my tack: I am still very curious to find out what's going on between Meg and Keir, but my curiosity is a little less urgent than before.

"It's pure chance," I say, "if we slumped at the same time."

"All the same," Meg remarks, "it's odd that you should turn into lame ducks together." She says nothing more. She knows my stubborn hostility to all attempts to find predestination, profound meanings, or fate in any events whatever, she knows I believe only in chance and stopped arguing with me about it long ago. She's a woman—she believes in fate, she believes in it so much that she instinctively sidesteps all philosophical considerations that might throw doubt on it. But she is also incredibly pigheaded, she just has to say something more about the coincidence between my behaviour and Keir's. She must have the last word, though she pronounces it not triumphantly but merely as a statement of fact.

"Anyway you're no longer shining lights of journalism," she says gloomily. "Are you aware, George, that you're no longer a shining light?" And when I reply that I'm well aware of it, she nods and says: "Forgive me. You see, I wasn't sure you knew it and I wanted to tell you before you go to the paper, so you won't be surprised if they make you feel it."

"Thank you, Meg," I say, "I'm prepared for anything."

"Oh, they won't be unkind," she says. "Besides, they all know you're writing now, and they respect that."

As now, almost two years later, in my writer's antrum at the Albergo Byron in Rome I put down this conversation, this record of my last meeting with Meg, I still remember keenly how horrified I was at those words of hers. We're sitting at the kitchen table beside the window which looks out on narrow gardens and the backs of the houses fronting on the street that runs parallel to Malet Street; the weather is grey but dry with just a slight haze, we've finished our breakfast and lighted cigarettes, but the friendly, almost homely atmosphere—if such a thing is possible between Meg and me—has suddenly evaporated because Meg has told me in passing, as though referring to some trifle, that they all—all!—knew I was writing. The moment she utters these words, I know I've seen a danger signal. I still can't make out what the danger is, but I've been alerted.

"How so?" I ask. "How do they know?"

Meg looks at me in surprise; I have stood up and am pressing out my half-smoked cigarette.

"From Keir, of course," she says. Perceiving my agitation she finds it necessary to clear him: "I put him up to it. He kept complaining of you to me; he said he wouldn't be able to keep you much longer. That's why I advised him to tell the staff you were writing; if he lets you go, that will give you an honourable exit. Isn't that better than being fired for incompetence?"

I look at her in consternation. "Damn it all, Meg," I bellow with gnashing, helpless rage, "why do you two half-wits keep harping on my writing? Always this talk about my writing, writing,

writing!" I really shout the word three times. Our kitchen is so
small that it swallows up my cry as water swallows a stone that is
thrown into it. Meg stops her ears and laughs at me, which
further increases my rage. But then I abruptly pull myself together
and say: "For months now Keir has been accusing me of writing,
he brings it up every time we talk on the phone. Actually I only
started a fortnight ago, I'm only jotting down a few notes for
myself, really just for myself and nobody else. My newspaper work
went bad long before I started to write."

"Nonsense," says Meg quite calmly. "The book has been in you
the whole time. And now it's coming out."

Again Meg is trying to arrange my life. I look at this masterful
woman to whom I am still married though we make no use of our
marriage; I wonder if she's right, of course she's right in a way,
the book is in me, but there's no proof that it will necessarily, as
Meg thinks, come out. Many, perhaps all people, have a book in
them, but they go right on with their lives and don't let it out.
Even today, in these weeks when the season has turned again to
autumn, autumn in Rome, the Sabine hills are again clear and
slate-blue after the white summer heat, the autumn of 1964
promises to be a fine season, soft and transparent—two years then
after I began to *write*, as Meg puts it, I am still unable to agree
with her. In a superficial sense she has proved right—my manuscript has grown to more than two hundred typewritten pages, I
have thrown a good many pages away, and those I have put into
the binder have been rewritten and corrected countless times—
and still I say that all this, this whole effort, need not necessarily
have been undertaken. There is still some truth in my reply to
Meg's remark, which strikes me as too pat, to her attempt to pin
me down once and for all.

"You're mistaken," I say. "If I really give up journalism, I may
do something entirely different from writing. I may go into business or advertising, or buy a little bookshop. Or, even at my age,
I may start to study again for a year or two. Philosophy or mathematics might tempt me."

Any number of occupations occur to me, all at once I see innumerable possibilities for a fresh start. On that subject Meg says nothing: her attitude as she sits at the kitchen table smoking her cigarette makes it clear that she has no intention of offering any suggestions.

I intensify my assault on her serene conviction. "Or perhaps," I say, "I'll stick to journalism," and for a moment I even believe it. "It's quite possible. In that case I'll go back to Asia." And already in my mind's eye, I picture a life in Singapore, Bangkok or Saigon.

"Keir would be delighted," I hear Meg saying. Startled out of my Far-Eastern fantasy, I catch just enough of her tone to tell me that she would not exactly share Keir's joy at the return of the Prodigal Son. Strange! But disregarding the tone, I take her words at their face value; their meaning is that Meg will put in a good word for me with Keir, whereas the tone in which they are spoken is trying to tell me that my giving Keir a chance to be delighted leaves her cold.

"If I start working for a paper again," I say, "it definitely won't be Keir's paper. I'm fed up." I try to compose a last, definitive statement, but even while making it I'm aware that it's nothing but a childish boast: "And now I'm going to see Keir and tender my resignation. He doesn't have to keep me. I've already told him more than once to throw me out."

"Stop feeling sorry for yourself," she says.

That remark is totally illogical, or at least so it seemed to me at the time.

"Anyway," I said furiously, "I can do without your pity. I want Keir to stop being considerate of me. And I want you to stop telling him how to camouflage his considerateness."

As usual when Meg comes to an impasse in a conversation with me, she has to do something with her hands, it's an old habit with her. She gets up and starts clearing away the breakfast things.

Suddenly I grasp her left arm and hold it fast.

"Stop playing housewife," I say. And she does indeed stop. I feel the play of her arm muscles under the cotton of her track suit. My assault comes unexpectedly, her attention was concentrated on our conversation, but she adjusts instantly, she knows my weakness for quick changes, the sudden effect that her body and its movements can have on me, she knows the whole nervous structure of a dark, short, thin man. I had to seize hold of her and Meg knows it. I draw her to me, release her arm and thrust my right hand under her jersey, flat against the skin of her back, I let it slide down her body to the rise of her buttocks. Meg feels as she has always felt: warm, firm and as smooth as silk. Her skin is dry and has a good smell that blends with a trace of perfume. I am an unsatisfied man, I have sunk so low that last Sunday afternoon in Rome I tried to satisfy myself, and this is the only body in the world with which I am wholly familiar, the only human being who can free me from a deep-seated aversion to sexual intercourse, the only woman I can always make love with and who is always glad to make love with me.

Not at this moment, though. With a quick, adroit movement she slips out of my embrace.

"Not now," she says. "I haven't got time now. I've got to be in Hyde Park at nine, I'm to photograph some models at Albert Gate. I'm late already."

And she quickly leaves the kitchen. She hasn't said that I'd had all night to think of that—that would have been too easy, Meg doesn't say such things. All she said was "not now," which in Meg's language simply means: "as soon as I have time." I look out the window into the light mist and wonder if I oughtn't to take my bag with me and leave town without a word after seeing Keir. This is exactly what I didn't want: to get into a situation in which Meg could say to me: "As soon as I have time." My resistance doesn't seem to be as strong as I had hoped. When Meg reappears, she gives me a key so I can come in whenever I please. When I ask her when she will be home, she says that of course she'll be free this evening. She is wearing black slacks and a black sweater under a light rain-coat; two cameras in leather bags are slung from her shoulders.

"George," she says, "please don't drop Keir now. I know you're eager to give it up, but if you possibly can, stay with him for a while."

"You'll be late," I say. I look at the alarm clock on the kitchen shelf. It's a quarter to nine.

"I meant what I said before," she says. "I'm thinking of you too; if you must go, I want you to make a graceful exit. But things are much worse for Keir."

She ignores my glance at the clock and even sits down again on a kitchen stool. She wouldn't be Meg if she didn't finish out a discussion to which she clearly attaches a great deal of importance. I interrupted her before by seizing her arm; she countenanced the interruption because she saw at once how important it was; it means as much to her as talking about Keir. But no more. To her way of thinking, here are two equally important undertakings, one of which can be postponed but not the other. She explains why she has given priority to Keir's interests.

"You have your book now, you can get along without the paper, but Keir! . . . He has to keep up his front. I'm afraid he doesn't even know that it's ceased to be anything but a front."

I shake my head and smile increduously because I'm still thinking of Meg's saying that I had my book and should like to shatter the naïve obstinacy of her faith in my new vocation. But Meg interprets my gesture as a rejection of her plea that I shouldn't leave Keir.

"In case it interests you," she says, "it no longer gives me pleasure to see Keir."

She utters this retraction of a statement which formerly played a crucial role in our marriage as calmly as she once uttered the sentence which differed from it only by the absence of "no longer."

"Oh," I ask frostily, "can't he do it any more? Is he feeling his age?"

Meg looks at me almost meditatively before she answers.

"No," she says, "he's still doing all right." Then after a silence:

"That's what you wanted to hear, isn't it, George? You wouldn't like it to be different."

For some reason I can't help thinking of Frau Heiss, of her indignation that I should be disappointed at not finding the people who had taken the house away from my parents. Frau Heiss saw through me. Meg, too, sees through me, though of course it's much easier for her.

"But that's not the point," she says. "The point is that I really don't want to any more." She falls silent, then goes on as though talking to herself. "If I only knew whether I don't want to just because I don't want to, or because something has gone wrong with Keir. There is something wrong with him, I don't know what."

She has risen and is already in the doorway.

"You'll notice it the moment you see him," she says. And then offhandedly, as though the question were without importance, she asks: "Will you go to his flat or straight to the office?"

"If I don't get sidetracked in town," I answer just as offhandedly, "I'll call for Keir in Chichester Rents."

We both know what the name of the street where Keir lives means to us. Keir's flat has been so important in our life that we utter the address with as little stress as possible.

Like last night when I looked after her as she was crossing the pavement to Cameron's Bentley, I look after her as she walks down Malet Street this morning, no, she doesn't walk, she runs as fast as her heavy bags permit, in the direction of the garage in Gower Street where she keeps her mini, which she will steer swiftly and skilfully through the London traffic to Albert Gate, Hyde Park, where some models and their agents are waiting for her; obstinately, in a tone that brooks no opposition, she will direct the movements of the marionettes under black leafless trees swathed in thin mist, she can afford to be domineering, today she is one of the most sought-after photographers in London, but even when she was quite unknown she brooked no opposition, and so became one of the most sought-after photographers in London;

now she will work hard for a few hours, just as hard as when she was quite unknown; as though possessed, she will peer into the viewfinders to establish the relations between colours or shades of grey in a picture, she will create relations between lines of flowing hair and the cut of a coat, between a smile and the sepia cloud of a fur piece, and decide whether to give maximum sharpness to a button or to an eye. She is in too much of a hurry to look up at the window where I am standing; it probably doesn't even occur to her that I am looking after her, I who now at last am touched and grateful to realize that she believes in something she has called *your book*; of course it's ridiculous, I'm not writing a book, I've merely become an incompetent journalist who spends his time, while casting about for something else to do, over some sort of notes: all the same I look after Meg almost tenderly until, at the end of Malet Street, she finally dissolves in the fine bright mist.

Then I rang up Collaudi at his hotel and arranged to meet him in an *espresso* bar in Soho; I don't know the place but he tells me exactly where it is, at the corner of Wardour and Broadwick streets, he tells me he has business nearby, and I remember that the film producers have their offices in Wardour Street. His hotel is in Bayswater, as I have just found out from the phone book, an area of low-priced hotels and dismal boarding houses, where you live if you can't afford a hotel in Mayfair or Kensington; the dusty, lifeless gloom of Bayswater is well known to me, for Clanricarde Gardens, the street where I grew up, is also in Bayswater, but with its diabolical colours it is an exception, a fact to which it lends emphasis by blocking itself off from the rest of Bayswater with the black tarred wall of a blind alley, so that one can only leave it by way of a wide road roaring with motor cars, along which the eye loses itself in the grey-green of Kensington Park. The baron can't be doing very well if he lives in a cheap hotel in Bayswater, if he looks out through curtains grown yellow from too much washing upon a lifeless street bordered by cream-coloured Regency houses. But his voice gives no indication of how he is doing. It remains impassive even when he tells me—because I ask him to give her my regards—that Lorenza is no longer with him. "You know," he says in a tone of Austrian nonchalance, "London was too much for her. Too dark and gloomy." Lorenza must have given up very quickly if she's already gone; Collaudi left Rome only three weeks ago—what can have happened? I mutter a few words of regret; Lorenza is a lovely girl but not my type, I always feel helpless in the presence of women who are nothing but rather tall and rather blatantly beautiful, but for the baron it must be depressing to have lost an attractive young lady and to be living in a hotel room in Bayswater. It seems to me that he is hiding his dejection behind the noblesse that makes him speak of the loss of Lorenza as he might of any other stroke of adversity.

I shower. The bath is still wet from Meg's shower. Why didn't I burst in on Meg's shower? I heard her going into the bathroom, there would still have been time, but my randiness didn't come over me until it was too late.

It was past nine when I found myself outside in Malet Street. I had plenty of time ahead of me, there's nothing doing at a newspaper office before two, especially on Thursday at a weekly. Of course they're all very busy, because the last articles have to be in print by tomorrow morning, but for that very reason it's rather quiet, we're not a daily after all, on Thursday Keir holds only a brief conference, the storm doesn't break until Friday when they make the paper up, it starts in the afternoon and goes on until midnight when the late news page is put to bed. I had purposely chosen a day when Keir would have time for me; I planned to turn up at his place at about noon when he'd had his sleep. In Rome it had been dry and sunny, here it was damp and grey, light-grey to be sure, transparently misty, my favourite kind of weather. On a November morning in 1962 I strode with delight through the London climate.

I went into Dillon's University Bookshop, situated in a house adorned with turrets at the corner of Malet Street; the flat that Meg and I moved to when we were married is in the university area; I can't quite remember why we picked Bloomsbury, I believe because Meg had a weakness at the time for the long, uniform, chocolate-brown street fronts and because I thought it would be convenient to be near the big libraries and the British Museum, though my newspaper work seldom left me time to make use of them. The bookshop, which occupied several floors, was empty so early in the day, the shelves and the books displayed on the tables exerted an immediate fascination on me; as usual when I go into a bookshop, I was in a state of high tension, determined to investigate the books systematically, an undertaking which always comes to grief, though not as disastrously as it did that morning at Dillon's. When I try to work out why I become so tensely eager at the sight of large collections of books, I can think of nothing else then electrophysical impulses. I sense the presence of thousands of impulses and know—or at least hope—that among them there will be one capable of responding to the impulses which my own nervous system never ceases to produce. The thing is to find it. At this point I must anticipate my projected account of my habits and mention at least one habit to which I devote a large part of my time: I am a reader. In my case I cannot think of any adjective to define the word "reader" more closely; none of the epithets I have examined with this in mind—words like "excessive," "intensive," "incessant," "indefatigable"—would be quite accurate for my kind of reading, they would all be misleading, because reading with me is not a dissipation and I don't lose myself in my reading (as the most consummate readers are thought to do), I welcome interruptions, I am easily diverted from my reading, and I tire quickly. Nevertheless, it is no exaggeration to say that I am always reading. Any room I live in soon becomes clogged with books and magazines—here I am not speaking of my newspaper reading, that mechanical absorption of news—they soon cover all the tables, fill the cupboards of my hotel rooms, and ultimately pile up on the floor; if I settle down for any length of time, I usually have to ask the concierge to put a couple of bookcases in my room. At the Byron where I have now been living for more than two years, the situation has become quite hopeless; my tiny attic room has long been what the French call a *cité de livres*, and I have had to turn over several large bundles of books to the management for safekeeping. Such bundles are being stored for me all over the world, perhaps the only memories I have left with friends in Hongkong, New Delhi, Tel Aviv and New York. The desire to gather all these dispersed books around me is possibly the strongest of all my motives for wishing to leave my hole-in-the-wall in Via Borgognona and set up house on my own. The sadness that came over me yesterday evening, that is, on a yesterday evening two years ago, while contemplating my books in Meg's flat, was grief at the loss of them; when a marriage breaks up, the rending of the joint library which follows the decision to separate, is almost unbearable—the thought of Meg some day having to pick out "my" books, to separate them from "hers" and ship them to me somewhere, strikes me as so inhuman, fills me with such horror, that I reject the whole idea out of hand. And so I shall leave my books at Meg's; after all they won't be the only pieces of my existence I've left behind at Meg's. Or perhaps I should say up front at Meg's, while I am left behind somewhere. But when I have a place of my own I will disinter Uncle Basil's books, his fine collection of Judaica and of old, probably priceless albums of engravings after Rembrandt paintings, which are still in storage with the London shipping firm.

I have said that I am always reading, by which of course I only mean to say that I read continually when I am not writing, taking walks or sleeping. Occasionally I go to the cinema or a concert, but mainly I read. If I had a wife, I should not read so exclusively, then I should have to occupy myself with her, talk to her, perform this or that action with her or for her; if children should come along, I should busy myself with their upbringing and so on. Instead of all that, I read. I read wherever I go, at meals, in cafés, on walks; I always have reading matter on me; yesterday, for instance, on a bench in the Pincio gardens, in mild windless weather with a pleasant overtone of coolness, I read one of V. S. Pritchett's short stories—a masterfully discreet, so it seems to me, portrait of a most unpleasant London society lady, a certain Mrs. Barclay. The most salient feature of my way of reading is that I don't forget the people about me as I read, no, I am very well aware of them. I watch them out of the corners of my eyes; yesterday, for instance, along with a paragraph of Pritchett's short story, I took in the halting steps of a well-dressed elderly gentleman, who with the help of a blind man's cane was feeling his way along the balustrade of the Pincio terrace. Recently the sad *Certo! Sicuro!* of a young girl listening to a man in a café I had happened into on Piazza Fiume slipped between the lines of a philosophico-sociological article in a Milanese periodical that I was reading at a metal table near the door. The girl, who was standing at the bar, was stirring the sugar in her cup of *espresso;* she interrupted the man's whispered stream of words with a clear and disconsolate *Certo! Sicuro!,* which hovered like uncertain music over the astonishing thought processes of Professor Mario Praz. Sometimes it seems to me that my books and magazines serve me as tarnhelms, they make me invisible and bring me stories, for it is my experience that people let themselves go in the presence of a reader: he's reading, he's not here.

But I am there, for though I read, I'm not fanatical about it. Nor do I devour printed matter promiscuously, nor ride steeplechase through world literature. I'm selective and I specialize; some day, I hope, my collection of early medieval texts and of books about the period will rub shoulders most congenially with Uncle Basil's Judaica, especially his works on the history of the Wandering Jew. I also buy almost all the experimental literature I lay eyes on, though I should be at a loss to say what so attracts me in these potterings; perhaps it is only the arrogant smile of the traditionalist critics that gives me a secret sympathy for them. More effectively than the experiments to which it is addressed, that bigoted philistine smile proves to me that there is a necessary relationship between the new and the extravagant. Among such novelties, I must own, I have seldom encountered anything that appeals to me as much as Werner Hornbostel's ecmelic music. My personal taste, I admit, is rather conservative—in fiction I am always on the lookout for stories in which human beings are put into relationships with human beings, and like them best when the narrator strives for extreme clarity, because the subject matter, to wit, these relationships, is in itself subtle and mysterious enough.

At Dillon's I first looked to see if there were anything new by Samuel Beckett, whom I had lost sight of in Rome because there he is spoken of only as though he were a legend. In England, too, he was for a long time no more than a rumour; this was still true in the years when I left England for more and more extensive travels; I knew nothing of his but his first play, a few early poems, and his novel *Molloy*, which I had read in the French version. I found that a large number of his works have now become available and that new ones are still appearing; the novel *How It Is* had come out that year, and I started leafing through it. I succumbed at once to the old magic.

> how it was before Pim how it was with Pim how it is
> present formulation
> how it was with Bom how it is how it will be with Pim
> how it is how it will be with Bom how it will be
> before Pim
> how it was my life still with Pim how it is how it will be with Bom

—such litanies of indifference out of a world of chaos and chance have an extraordinary appeal for me. Still, I had a slight feeling of queasiness, and casting about for an explanation found it in those deep reaches of the mind where one regrets that a legend has become reality. Somehow, while reading my first snatches of Beckett I had hoped—and of course such hopes are absurd—that this writer would escape from what is known as *literature*, that the marvellous formula which this man had found for the absolute absurdity of the world would ring out in a never-ending echo from a world beyond all literature. What world? I don't know. Instead, I found myself leafing through an *oeuvre*. Beckett had *appeared*, that is, he had become an author like any other. No, not like any other, of course not, each one is different, and quite conceivably Beckett is the greatest of them all, though I am not especially interested in the objective greatness of an author, but only in the question of whether I find in him impulses responding to the impulses of my own nervous system, and if I find such impulses in a crime novel and not in Goethe, then, I must admit, that crime novel is more important to me than Goethe. But I should like to dwell for another moment on Beckett, whose books I bought at Dillon's two years ago and which during the last two years in Rome I have been reading over and over again. I cannot dispel the impression that this writer came very close to . . . here my thoughts fail me, I am incapable of saying what Beckett came close to, and I prefer to abstain from the usual bilge about silence. The panegyrists of silence give me a pain. Literature isn't silent. It speaks.

How I feel in my fingers the weight of every word. Two years ago at Dillon's I also bought Virginia Woolf's *Diary*, but I didn't read it until recently, now I've been reading it every afternoon for a week at Babington's Tea Room near the Spanish Steps, where I occasionally go for a rest from Rome; I sit there in the early afternoon hours when the grey room is almost empty, at one of the wobbly tables that squeak against the floor no matter how carefully you move them, for you have to move them to get behind them and sit with your back to the wall where you can read in peace while drinking excellent strong tea, a beverage otherwise unknown in Rome; outside the windows you see the *flâneurs* on Piazza di Spagna, at first only their legs, for Babington's Tea Room is somewhat below street level; occasionally one of them bends over and, shading his eyes with his hand, looks down, but all he sees is me reading, and one or two ladies likewise reading, possibly two gentlemen, devotees of the Greek Eros, talking in bored whispers, and the haughty waitresses in old-fashioned green uniforms, English-speaking Italian women who are arranging the cake in the glass case beside the door. Here then I read the ex-

cellent Virginia Woolf, succumb to the spell of her telegraphic
style, look upward and see *all the marsh water: in the sun deep
blue: gulls caraway seeds: snowstorms: Atlantic floor: yellow islands: leafless trees: red cottage roofs,* the entire flood, and ponder whether I, like Mrs. Woolf, would conclude the passage with
the cry: *Oh may the flood last for ever.* I should be glad to read
an uncut version of this entry, one in which the traces of Virginia's
madness would be more easily discernible, for mad she was, at
least in the last years of her life, as I recently learned from the
Times Literary Supplement. Is one not doomed to go mad if in
writing one arrives at such perfection as to feel the weight of every
word in one's fingers? Could the word that I couldn't find just
now, the word I came very close to, to which I brought Beckett as
close as possible—could that word be *madness?*

I remember how, just before leaving the bookshop, I spied a
new edition of Henry James' *English Hours* and added it to the
pile of books I handed the cashier with the request that they be
sent to me in Rome. I paid and left the shop in haste, almost as
if I had been chased, though no one chased me, on the contrary,
I had two hours of undisturbed browsing and leafing behind me,
and I had scarcely scratched the surface of the stock, I had fairly
well covered the *belles-lettres,* and passed through the history and
humanities section, reading titles, nothing more, and merely
glanced at the art books and illustrated works spread out on tables.
All that was still ahead of me, I had been looking forward to it,
but then what always happens to me after I have spent a certain
length of time in a bookshop or library happened: suddenly stopping still and raising my eyes from the one book I have in my
hands, I perceive the masses of books that silently surround me.
No, they're not silent, they're dead, and their death crushes me,
they crowd in on me, I breathe in the musty smell of these walls
that are shutting me in, fear and disgust take possession of me,
and I have to get out.

That's how it ends almost every time I go to a bookshop. Which
is strange because at home, in my various hotel rooms which are

always brim-full of literature, the presence of books doesn't bother me, in fact life in those rooms would hardly be conceivable without them. Is it because they there become my familiars; because in my room I can at any time return to one of Henry James' fine sentences as though returning home, and ponder *whether I too should grow less weary of the rugged black front of Exeter than of the sweet perfection of Salisbury,* though I would not necessarily incline to Henry James' taste and might after all decide in favour of Salisbury which I once visited with Meg? Yes, that sentence, along with my memory of Meg's delight—for in Salisbury even Meg was for once delighted with a "sight," with the light grey of the cathedral in the midst of its greensward—might tempt me to pack my bags, leave Rome, and find lodgings in the sweet perfection of Salisbury.

But it was not only disgust with books that drove me out of Dillon's University Bookshop on 15 November 1962, a Thursday as I see by the calendar I acquired a long while ago. I left the shop, slipped round the corner in order to expel it as quickly as possible from my field of vision, and walked slowly in the direction of the City. Something had happened inside me amidst those bookshelves, and making my way between the rows of Georgian houses, I finally understood what it was. Looking up from the pages of a book I had been reading, becoming aware of the thousands of book spines that stared at me, I suddenly realized to my horror what Meg had meant with her *you're writing now* and her *they all know you're writing.* I was expected to turn into a book. In her eyes I had found my vocation: I had become a being with a title and an author. A dead being. As dead as any inanimate thing. As dead as the light-blue and black lamp-post in the mist of Russell Square which I was just passing.

I was writing a thing. In writing I became that thing. If I make a thing, I am that thing. What is the thing called?—a book. How it was before thing how it is present formulation how it was with ping how it is how it will be with thing how it is how it will be with ping how it is how it will be with ping how it will be before thing how it was my life still with thing how it is how it will be with ping that fellow too had other plans than to become a row of books thing ping like any other instead of remaining a legend a rumour a rumour of words a smell *certo sicuro* a passing breath in a stream of speech the tapping of a blind man's cane no view from the Pincio—and neither would I succeed in becoming something other than a book. I, who could conceive of being something other than a Jew, Englishman, German, for instance, an Italian or a Negro or a wolf, a motor car or perhaps Beckett or Agatha Christie, for it was pure chance that I didn't turn out to be Beckett or Agatha Christie or a travertine slab, a beer bottle or a lamp-post. . . .

At this thought I came to my senses, I recovered. It wouldn't be so bad to be a light-blue and black lamp-post in Russell Square.

And that was certainly not what Meg meant. If I held it up to her, she wouldn't even understand me, she would say: "But you're not a book, you're an author."

Of course. There was cause and there was effect. How could I have forgotten that? A cobbler wasn't the pair of shoes he made. Or was he? Can it be that when all's said and done the masons down through the ages are the travertine blocks which for these past two years have encased a window across the street from me? I don't know.

In any case I'll make my pair of shoes. My illusion of writing only for myself is gone for ever. In my years of writing this insight which hit me with such force in Russell Square that I stopped in my tracks, leaned against the above-mentioned lamp-post and lit a cigarette, has often slipped my mind, but I only repressed it, I didn't forget it. Today I know that I shall not escape from my book.

To the very end I clung to a ruse by which I hoped to outwit it. If I revealed the truth about Meg and myself, so I thought, the book would finally throw down its cards and rise from the table defeated. The truth about Meg and myself is indeed the winning card, but unfortunately it's not in my hand, the book holds it.

The book will play it without mercy and win. The truth is always in the hands of the book. The author can never play the truth against the book. If all manner of things exist, you must say that all manner of things exist.

Of course you can write an untrue book, just as you can play with marked cards. Or you can write nothing. But for me, I fear, it's too late to cheat or to stop. You get tired, the light hurts your eyes, and meanwhile, impassive and relentless, your opponent, who holds the card that will take the trick, watches you. You give up.

Five

Gain time, preferably with the help of Anna Krystek. Postpone the truth about Meg by remembering Anna. Ponder the question: was Anna my opportunity to win more than mere time in my game with Meg? For instance, if Anna had come to Rome. If I were writing a novel, I should even now, at this point in my notes, be free to give the book a happy ending with Anna. Redemption in the shadow of the young girl. Unfortunately I'm not a novelist. Anna hasn't turned up. I have no choice.

I made a fatal mistake in inviting her to Rome of all places. She would probably have followed me to Israel, or to London; politically London would have appealed to her, but London with both Meg and her in it, *quelle salade!* And I doubt whether even in a place better suited to Anna than Rome, things would have come to a happy end between us—that, I am inclined to think, just wasn't "in it."

I can say all this precisely because on the Tuesday morning when I saw Anna again I was absolutely determined to seduce her. Having stood her up on Sunday and, reluctantly, gone to the Theater am Schiffbauerdamm without her on Monday, I was rather impatient to see her. Impatient and horny. By this I don't mean that I had any intention of trying to get her to bed that day in her flat, but only that I wanted to speed things up a bit. On Saturday night, to use Anna's own words, I had behaved like a bull in a china shop; I wouldn't let that happen again. I had slept well, a steely dove-grey sleep after my return from the Prussian Paris, I had showered and once again observed that my body is thin, no longer young and not yet old, and covered with pale but not pasty skin, that I have copious dark hair on my chest and private parts, that my legs are firm and powerful. Then I put on my glasses, had breakfast and read the papers. While going out to Neukölln on the Stadtbahn by way of Papestrasse on that cool October morning—it had rained on Monday, but on Tuesday the air was again dry and transparent—I looked forward to my meeting with this tall, pale bird-girl. I looked forward to it in all simplicity, resolved to seduce her and free from my usual misgivings, my carefully nurtured reservations about sex. Consequently the atmosphere between us was good from the start, I showed no sign of Saturday night's brutal sensuality but courted Anna carefully and without exaggeration: I explained to her the extraordinary effect of her eyes, how they were the lightest-coloured thing in her face, lighter than her skin that was already very light, and at the market in Treptower Strasse I pointed out to her that her hair was almost the same colour as the fresh linseed oil in the large transparent bottles from the Neukölln Oil Press. Out in the open and by daylight the blondness of Anna's hair did not seem as spent as I remembered it at Lampe's party; it almost shone, though with a muted, refracted light, like the linseed oil in whose transparency the colours of the grey houses and of the October sky were mingled.

I arrived punctually at half-past eleven, but she was already waiting at the station gate, tall and slender and schoolgirl-like, her hands in the pockets of her grey coat, the coat with the wide collar in which I liked her so well, though it is not really becoming to her. We walked down a broad avenue and then turned right into a small irregularly shaped square, surrounded by old houses and bathed in an old violet-grey light. The street had been called Karl-Marx-Strasse and the square was called Karl-Marx-Platz; I remembered that my father had spoken of Neukölln as a Communist stronghold and that it would never have occurred to him to take me there.

"So Neukölln is still Red," I said, pointing to one of the street signs.

"It used to be Red," Anna corrected me. "But, you know, when it was Red this street was called Berliner Strasse. The square had a different name too. I'll have to ask my father." She pondered for a moment, trying to remember the name, then she gave up.

"It was only after Rixdorf stopped being Red that they put in all these Karl Marxes."

She uttered this assertion in a tone which reminded me that she was a girl who had read Marx *over there,* as they say in Berlin with a vague contemptuous sweep of the hand in the direction of the eastern, walled-off sector of the city, a gesture compounded of resignation, pity and antipathy. Before the Wall was built, Anna had lived *over there; over there* she had read Marx, and now she was cut off from *over there,* perhaps she still read Marx, but alone, and passed angrily through the streets that were named after him but where no one sat studying him any longer. Since I had met many women and girls in Asia who had read Marx, I was not struck with awe by Anna the Marxist. I myself have tried once or twice to read *Das Kapital,* but never got beyond the first few pages. Still, I believe I know more or less what's in it from reading about it. From reading about it and from certain experiences in countries where Marx is not jealously guarded behind a wall.

I now regret not having told Anna how I occasionally encountered Marx in tropical rain forests, in fever-ridden huts, in hungry faces, in the cold flame of the spirits that flitted over the Chau Tau Mountains. It would have pleased her, but I abstained for fear of provoking a discussion. The mere word discussion repels me. This blabbering between monads! This sound that convictions make! Yes, yes, I know there's got to be an exchange of views, authentic dialogue as they say nowadays in Germany, where apparently there are so many inauthentic dialogues that they have to single out the authentic ones, or declare the inauthentic ones authentic. The new German slang makes me laugh most when it's most pretentious. In Rome lately I've been reading German papers at breakfast to keep in touch with the language. Such reading is not without its rewards. Today, for instance, I read a story about a high government official who was dismissed for being homosexual: the man was held to be a *Geheimnisträger*, a bearer of secrets, and hence open to blackmail on the basis of his *Intimsphäre*, intimate sphere, that is, his private life. Two magnificent words which I quickly added to the neo-Gothic *vocabolario* I have been drawing up for some time now. As the journalist I still am, I can't help interrupting my story at this moment to knock together a headline: *Secretbearers in Authentic Dialogue on Intimatesphere*. No, better get back to Anna. I had no desire for authentic dialogue with her, not even about her *intimate sphere*, let alone about Karl Marx. True, I would have liked to penetrate her secrets, even at a pinch to become her *secretbearer*, but for the present I was satisfied to converse with her. I don't like to discuss, I prefer to converse. One learns more from conversations than from discussions. More about people, I mean.

"Rixdorf?" I therefore asked, by way of diverting her from Marx. "Why Rixdorf?"

"Anybody can see you're from Wannsee," she said. "Here in Neukölln we call Neukölln Rixdorf. Never heard it?"

I dimly remembered having heard the name years ago, but it never had any associations for me.

"Böhmisch-Rixdorf," Anna enlightened me. "That's what it used to be called. Look, look at this!"

She had stopped outside a wrought-iron gate that closed off the passage between two houses. A plate affixed to the top of it read: *Bohemian Graveyard*. I stepped up to the gate and looked through the bars. At the end of the passage I could see a few crosses and tombstones.

"Wait a second," said Anna. She disappeared into a tobacconist's beside the gate. I thought she had gone to buy cigarettes, but she came back holding a key with which she opened the gate.

"Come," she said. "I'll show you something."

At the end of the passage there was indeed a graveyard, lying still in the mild October light. It was surrounded by the dark-red walls of six-story working-class houses, by black fire walls and dingy-white back gardens. But the elm trees that grew amidst the graves seemed to rise even higher than the houses. As though drawn in charcoal, their verticals traversed the entire space from the ground to the sky.

The cemetery was well cared for, some of the tombs we passed were very old and others more recent; several bright-coloured watering cans were hanging on a wooden rack. I thought Anna merely wanted to show me this hidden necropolis, which had indeed come as a surprise; in amazement I contemplated this idyllic resting place of the foreign dead, in which we—my grey-blond guide and I—were quite alone; but apparently she had something more in mind, for she did not slacken her pace but proceeded deliberately; her goal proved to be a row of dark bronze plaques set in a brick wall. She said nothing, merely pointed at them, and I made out that they were Slavic memorial plates dating from the eighteenth century. *Ludmilla Bedlichowa*, I read, *1708–1768*, and then other names and similar dates in beautiful antique lettering; *Marya Pechakowa, Katerina Jirechowa, Anna Slawikowa, Maria Salome Krystkowa, Jane Tauffala*. Further on to the right the plates bore the names of men: *Johann Dani Prokesch, Jiri Prosk, Jan Vitman, Martin Mares*. And then at last: *Adam Krystek, 1721–1785*. So that was why Anna had brought me here. She watched me eagerly as I discovered the name.

"Well, well," I said. "Then I'll call you Anna Krystekowa from now on."

At that moment her eyes seemed to have taken on an even lighter hue than usual. "No," she said. "I'm only a Krystek. I don't know a word of Czech. But that's my ancestry." She pointed to the name. "He was a Bohemian weaver, a Protestant. When the Catholics drove them out of their country, the Bohemian weavers were given permission to settle in Rixdorf."

Yes, strange as it may seem, Prussia had once been a haven of religious freedom, and what's more this had happened under the Soldier King, who had his soldiers beaten with cudgels and executed the best friend of his brilliant son. But then my thoughts were diverted, for turning away from the old inscriptions, my eyes fell on a more recent grave. I seldom laugh aloud, but at the sight of Luise Zoufal's grave I was unable to restrain a loud laugh full of mockery and higher wisdom. Anna looked at me with astonished disapproval; she must have thought I was laughing at her for introducing me to her ancestors, so I made haste to point out the grave that had caught my eye. The name of the person buried here was Luise Zoufal, she had lived from 1878 to 1924, and under her name and the dates the words were incised: MINE HAS BEEN A GOODLY LOT.

Of course Anna failed to understand why I was still laughing. I tried to explain my unexpected merriment.

"She believed in her lot," I said. "She thought her life was goodly. And on top of that her name is Zoufal—'chance!'—Zoufal!"

Not knowing my philosophical quirk, Anna must have regarded my comment on this epitaph as pure foolishness. But as we made our way to the gate of the Bohemian Graveyard, past graves with Czech, Silesian and Huguenot names, past the eternal peace of *Daniel Friedrich Barta* and *Anna Niemetz, Marie Handwerk* and *Marthe Vincent, Emil Schidlack* and *Willi Munk,* through this Prussian haven for the persecuted of various countries, which sad to say was unknown to my father because to him Neukölln was nothing more than a Red district, she pondered my words, turned them over in her dialectically trained mind behind the pale skin of her forehead and understood them.

"I don't see it that way," she said hesitantly, when we had almost reached the gate. To me it's as if she meant to say: "I've drawn the winning ticket in the lottery." And pausing at the gate, she added thoughtfully: "I wish I knew why she thought her life was goodly. Funny word: goodly."

When we were back on Karl-Marx-Platz and had closed the gate behind us, I tried to prove to Anna that the inscription on Luise Zoufal's tombstone was a quotation from the Bible and that the word must therefore be interpreted as a synonym for the word "fate."

"Maybe," she said. "But she thought her fate was a ticket she'd drawn in the lottery of the God she believed in. That's certainly what she meant. She knew it was chance, but she thought this chance was her fate. To her they were one and the same thing."

In Berlin my great systematic intellectual edifice founded on chance and chaos suffered two hard blows. The first when Mother Ludmilla responded to my doubts as to God's omnipotence with the words: "Our Church believes that God is all-powerful and that He endowed men with free will." That was yesterday afternoon, and this morning a bright young lady tried to prove to me that I was worrying my head over a pseudoproblem: if Anna understood the idea underlying Luise Zoufal's goodly life better than I, then the two words out of which I had forged an irreconcilable opposition were identical.

After returning the key to the tobacconist, she voiced her reproachful critique: "Look, Georg. How can you bother with such a petit-bourgeois subjectivist problem?"

With these words she took my arm. I have already said that Anna uses certain words and combinations of words, such as *political consciousness* or *dialectical relationship* and now *petit-bourgeois subjectivist problem* quite naturally, that they don't give the impression of having been drummed into her, though of course they must have been drummed into her at one time. *Over there.* It was really high time I had a serious talk with her, it was after all an outrage that this little Berlin snotnose should dispose as she did of the questions of a man almost twenty years older than herself, but instead I decided to behave like a subjectivist petit-bourgeois and, unencumbered by any discussion, to enjoy the fact that this great-great-great-granddaughter of a Protestant Bohemian weaver had taken my arm. Arm in arm we sauntered on, and consequently our steps on that Tuesday morning were not as poorly synchronized as they had been on Saturday night in Moabit. I felt the material of her schoolgirl's coat against my arm, I knew without looking at her that her flat face— flat because of the high cheekbones—was next to mine, parallel to mine, because Anna is my height, actually a bit taller, and when I finally did turn my face towards her, I could see that the knot into which she had gathered her excessively fine hair, hair the color of weak tea, at the neck, was in danger of coming undone. Another reason why I refrained from discussion was my suspicion that in a discussion she wouldn't weave the name Georg into her conversation with me so often, it was pleasant to hear it not as a soft English palatal vowel, but at long last, after almost thirty years, as a sequence of two sharply delimited vowels embedded in three precise consonants and illumined by Anna's voice as by a magic lantern, while in the course of our walk she pointed out the brown sleepy village smithy and the whitewashed stone church in Richardplatz and the Neukölln—or should I say Rixdorf or Prussian-autumnal-proletarian—light seemed to set itself in gentle motion whenever Anna pronounced the name Georg, so that in retrospect Richardplatz in Rixdorf seems to me as beautiful as any of the illustrious squares of Rome, if not more beautiful.

I'm getting lyrical. The reason is that I was in love on that Tuesday morning, steadily in love, not vacillating as I had been on Saturday night when my feelings changed from one minute to the next. Had Anna's mood changed too, or did the *anyway, there's no more in it*, which she had spoken into the phone the day before, after telling me that she found me interesting and liked me, still hold good? I don't know.

"Anna," I said, "I like Rixdorf. I could live here."

"You certainly could live in a lot of places," she said disapprovingly. I had just told her about my experiences in East Berlin and how impressed I had been with Gendarmenmarkt and Hausvogteiplatz; I had told her that I could see myself settling in East Berlin if not for the episode of the passport and cigarette.

"Man," said Anna. "You give me the jim-jams. First you want to live in the East, then you want to live in the West." And then came the sentence that revealed the generation gap between us.

"If you want to live in the West," she asked in all seriousness, "why don't you move back to your old home in Wannsee? Where could you be more comfortable?"

I preferred not to discuss this suggestion. Instead I asked her a question.

"Anna," I asked, "why do you go on living here? You'd be much happier in East Berlin. Apart from everything else, you'd have much better professional opportunities."

Of course she understood what I meant by "everything else"; her ideology, which couldn't be shaken by such trifles as the passport and cigarette episode, though her eyes had narrowed for a moment when I related the incident at the barrier.

She didn't answer my question, perhaps because at that moment we reached the premises of Eduard Krystek, wood and coal merchant. After turning a few corners we had entered a rural looking area—board fences and gardens surmounted by the gables of frame houses. At the end of the street, under a clump of trees, there was a monument.

"Come," said Anna, "I'll introduce you to my father."

So Adam the Bohemian weaver had become Eduard a Berlin coal merchant. Again I felt reinforced in the theory of chance which only a little while before had suffered so severe a blow, but I withheld comment. Eduard Krystek, as I observed on entering the yard enclosed by a board fence and the fire wall of a block of flats fronting on Richardstrasse, dealt chiefly in briquettes. Walls of briquettes occupied one whole side of the yard, forming a façade of evenly piled units which in the decanted light of the dry pale-blue sky displayed every nuance of black from almost-violet to dull ebony, from carmine-dark glints to reminiscences of the dusty smalt-blue of the old soft-coal mines. I stood gazing with admiration at the gentle rhythm of those walls, which struck me as no less a work of art than the façade of the Palazzo Farnese; I was also fascinated by a tall, mysterious, verdigris-encrusted machine, presuming that it was this mechanism of tubes and gripping arms which turned out the black mass-produced music of the briquettes, but Anna, to whom of course there was nothing new in all this, drew me onward to a board shack where her father was sitting over bills and delivery slips.

When he stood up to be introduced, I understood why my bird-girl was so tall, for Eduard Krystek reached almost to the ceiling of his shack; a long, thin crane, over six foot six in height; he towered over me, who am rather short.

"Father," said Anna, "Herr Efraim is going to have lunch with us."

Oddly enough, I was not disappointed to learn that I would not be alone with Anna. Up until that moment I had expected to be taken to the usual, internationally standardized landlady-proof *garconnière* with kitchenette; I have already fled from such rooms as fast as my legs would carry me, acquiring with their occupants the deplorable reputation of a *séducteur jusqu'au bord du lit*, which I am not. I simply can't stand up to the sadness of such rooms; I'm a conservative man; in my opinion women, especially young ones, shouldn't live alone; they should be surrounded by families, they should stay with their parents until they marry. The discovery that Anna lived *at home* was in my eyes one more point in her favour. Besides, her invitation reminded me that I was in a country where a stranger is readily admitted to the family circle. I had forgotten this custom during my years in England and found it surprisingly attractive.

Anna's father looked down on me from the heights and in his face, hollowed with toil, I rediscovered his daughter's flat cheek-bones and light-coloured eyes. I guessed him to be in his early sixties, which Anna confirmed; Eduard Krystek was born in 1900; he was past forty when he begot his daughter, Anna was born shortly before the outbreak of the Second World War.

"Pleased to meet you," said the coal merchant with comical stiffness and an unmistakably Berlin intonation. And turning to Anna: "It's nice your bringing company for a change."

"But, Father," said Anna, "I bring Hornbostel all the time."

"Werner?" he said thoughtfully, looking back in my direction. "He's just a young pipsqueak."

Anna came to her friend's defence. "There's nothing childish about Werner Hornbostel," she said with a show of irritation, but I could see there was great sympathy between father and daughter. Actually she seemed rather pleased that when she brought someone home her father should draw a distinction between a *visitor* and a young pipsqueak.

"You're not looking well today," said Anna.

"I know. I'm as white as beer foam," he said. "But I feel better now. I've taken a pill. Make me a dish of *hackepeter* with plenty of onions and a light beer, and I'll be all right."

The tall thin man's face was hollowed out, not only by work but by illness as well. "He has angina pectoris," Anna told me when we had left him. We walked down the street between hoardings. "He got it in Oranienburg."

"What was he in a concentration camp for?" I asked.

"For being a Communist, of course." It sounded as if she could conceive of no other reason. "First in 1933 and 1934," she went on. "Then they let him out, but they put him in again towards the end of the war."

"How can he be a Communist," I asked, "if he has a coal business? The first thing the Communists would do is to take his business away."

She looked at me as if she found my ignorance almost pathetic. "You really don't know anything about Berlin but your Wannsee," she said. "My father would be the first to hand over his shop to the Communist state. That's the way it was here in Rixdorf, even the coal merchants were Red."

We had come to the monument that I had already seen in the distance. Under a clump of trees beside a countrified looking frame house, it was a statue of the Soldier King, as I could see by the inscription. From under his three-cornered hat the Soldier King gazed at the houses of the Herrnhut Brethren. Since I take an interest in forgotten lore, I have since acquired, through Herder's Bookshop in Rome, *Count Zinzendorff's Words of Wisdom* and *Rixdorf-Neukölln, the Historical Development of a Section of*

Berlin by Professor Johannes Schultze. The Herrnhut Brethren erected a monument to the otherwise obnoxious Frederick William I because he had saved them from persecution. Yes, once upon a time Prussia saved the Herrnhut Brethren and the Bohemian weavers and the Huguenots, and was one of the first countries to give the Jews the rights of citizenship. It hardly seems possible. I didn't want to ask Anna whether she also regarded the Herrnhut Brethren as Red, it wouldn't have done any good to argue with her about the range of the colour red, the Soldier King would have turned out to be a Red, a brother of Marshal Budënny, I am not of the opinion that there are only red secrets, there are also blue and black secrets, and above all white ones, or perhaps exclusively white ones, but as far as Rixdorf was concerned Anna would doubtless have been right: Rixdorf was a Red district. Or had been in any case as long as the place had any importance. Did it still? I doubted it as I walked with Anna past the pietist gardens to the market in Treptower Strasse.

"Is your mother dead?" I asked. "I mean because of your cooking lunch for your father."

"She died when I was three," she said. "Killed in an air raid."

On hearing this I asked myself whether Frau Krystek's death could be compared with my mother's death, but quickly dismissed the question. Frau Krystek's death must have been terrible, and there was no possible excuse for our dropping bombs on houses in which people were living, just living. But we didn't kill Frau Krystek as one exterminates vermin. We were brutal swine, we laid about us like madmen, only last Saturday I hit a man in the face because he was planning to do the night spots until he was gassed; I'm sorry, no, I'm not really sorry though I've created one more anti-Semite, with one blow revived the hatred that will one day put new gas chambers into operation; still, I have no regret about striking him, about increasing with a minimum of effort the world's awareness of how what happens in language can at any time become reality; I am not sorry, I say, because this man, as his language demonstrates, was not innocent. I am very sorry about

Frau Krystek, she was surely innocent, it's a pity that Anna should have grown up motherless, that she can't go to East Berlin where she belongs because she's tied to her father, this bird-girl alone in the world with her big crane-father. All the same we didn't kill Anna's mother in a gas chamber. There's a difference between Zyklon B and a bomb that falls from the sky.

In retrospect I am struck by the fact that apart from that fellow at Lampe's party I met only nice people in Berlin: Frau Heiss, who was unhappy about living in a house to which she couldn't invite certain people—me, for instance; Inspector Von Cantz who didn't believe in national characteristics; Werner Hornbostel who hated his father for having been an *enthusiastic fellow traveller* and who had wanted to smash one of my parents' murderers; Mother Ludmilla, who may have saved Esther; Anna's father, who had even been in a concentration camp; and Anna herself, Anna, who after my *gaffe* at Lampe's had taken my arm as a matter of course, who had ridiculed me with her *You don't seem to have all your marbles*, but hadn't for one moment hesitated to side with me. I can't say that as a Jew I should find Berlin unliveable. Perhaps I've been especially lucky, perhaps such people are only a small minority in Berlin, but where in the world aren't they a minority, these Herrnhut Brethren, Bohemian weavers, Huguenots and Jews?

My new girl-friend had again taken my arm and was showing me the bright local market, spread out under canvas awnings in the Prussian autumn. Forgotten were our mothers, who would have been so glad to live a little while longer to go marketing in it. There were green-red country apples, and pears that seemed to have just been picked from the tree of Herr Ribbeck at Ribbeck Farm in Havelland, stalls of asters and dahlias, stalls of cottons and rayons; and the large transparent bottles of linseed oil from the Neukölln Oil Press which shone like Anna's hair. "What would you like for lunch?" Anna asked, and I was already hungry for all sorts of things that I saw on display, fish and sausages, *mettwurst*, for instance, with sauerkraut out of a large clean oaken bucket, or perhaps I'd prefer fish after all, finger-thick eels, or one

of those smoked fishes with the funny names, mailed cheeks or
suck-stone. "What do you want 'em for? Fish balls?" asked the
market woman when I stopped and looked avidly at the eels.
I bought some but we didn't eat them because the words *hackepeter*, onions and light beer were still rattling round in my head,
the thought was irresistible, and when I admitted as much to Anna
she laughed and said she had all the ingredients at home.

We left the market and went to the house at Treptower Strasse
21, where we climbed to the fourth floor. I was in love with Anna,
in love and still determined to seduce her. Nevertheless I was very
glad she wasn't taking me to a landlady-proof *garconnière*, though
it turned out that here in her father's house she had her own room
where she could certainly do as she pleased, a so-called *Berliner
Zimmer*, one of those long rooms taking up the whole width of
the house, with dormer windows front and back. For a time we
stood at the windows, first looking out in front on the market
crowds, then at the back on a yard full of clothes lines, behind
which to the southeast the vista opened out on workshops and
car cemeteries. The landscape seemed wide and flat and open,
though in the distance barbed wire fences and the Wall were
clearly discernible.

"Look over there on the left," said Anna, pointing. "There's
a gap in the Wall. That's the Sonnenallee border crossing. I could
be over there in five minutes." But we didn't pursue the thought.

In her room there were photographs of actors in various roles,
but believe it or not the old Communist Eduard Krystek had the
pictures of Marx and Lenin hanging over the sideboard in his living room. Until he came in, we sat in the kitchen together, talking about everything under the sun as I watched Anna making
hackepeter. On our walk we had already talked a good deal; Anna
had asked if I had found out anything at Esther's school and listened eagerly when I told her about Mother Ludmilla. It was
Anna who had advised me to go there in the first place, and now
it was she who saw the possible significance of a particular to
which I had attached no importance; Mother Ludmilla had told

me that she herself and the other nuns at the school belonged to a Silesian chapter of the order and that Mother Klara, after exposing herself too much on Esther's account, had been transferred to the parent convent at Ratibor.

"They hid the child there too," Anna cried out. "I'm sure they took her there."

I'm not so sure, for the impression Mother Ludmilla made on me was one of guilt and hopelessness, though I realized it only after I had left her.

"Maybe Esther became a nun?" Anna suggested. And added regretfully, "That would be a shame."

It wouldn't seem a shame to me; strangely enough I can easily conceive of my childhood friend with the stiffly set hair and flushed face as a nun, provided she were allowed to keep a black spaniel at the convent, though he could hardly have borne the name of Devil; still the whole thing seems very unlikely. All the same, I ought to go to the Carmelite chapter house, which must be in Rome, one of these days, perhaps they would consent to give me some information; but since then I've settled down to my great Roman indifference; the grey and blond light of hope, which Anna cast for a moment on my life is extinguished; and indeed what would be the good of finding out that one of those millions of children who were killed is still alive? I am also deterred from making further inquiries by the memory of Keir's haughty Samuel Johnson face, by his indifference, for suddenly he seemed to content himself with the suspicion that I was aware of his guilt. Instead of asking me about his daughter, he told me about some commonplace dream and took a ceremonious pinch of snuff—that man of the baroque age, that fat British snob with the trembling hands, who on the Sunday morning of my stay in Berlin had wept into the phone but a fortnight later had no longer wanted to hear what he had sent me to Berlin to find out. Anna, on the other hand, who was in no way concerned, took a keen interest in Esther's fate—to use the meaningless word which designates nothing more than a bundle of chaotic events—so that on our walk through

Karl-Marx-Strasse and then in the Bohemian Graveyard I had to tell her of my visit to Steglitz the day before.

It wasn't until we reached Richardplatz that she questioned me about the theatre in East Berlin; she wanted to know all about it. I replied at length, dwelling in particular on young Thate, of whose success she was frankly envious. Quite offhandedly I related my experience at the Friedrichstrasse crossing point, and had the satisfaction of seeing her eyes narrow and darken; then after the bitter pill I gave her some more sugar, suggesting as though talking to myself, that I could live on Hausvogteiplatz. As we were looking at the old village smithy in Rixdorf, she finally brought forth her critique of my aimless, dilettantish style of house hunting. "You certainly could live in a lot of places," she said disapprovingly.

In the kitchen we talked some more about the theatre. In the meantime a significant change of scene had occurred, for on entering the house we had taken off our coats; under her coat Anna was wearing a white blouse and black skirt, rather conventional garments to be sure, but garments which quite divested her of any schoolgirlish quality. Her grey coat must have been a very old possession, perhaps a vestige of her teens. Especially her white blouse, which I had leisure to examine as she was putting the chopped pork into the pan and covering it with rings of onion, took on a certain significance for me because after lunch, when old man Krystek had left us alone again to go back to his briquettes, I tried to undo the buttons. I got no further than the topmost button, but even so the image of white Prussian linen still hovers like a cool promise over my Roman days and nights.

Anna put on an apron before starting to fry the meat. While it was cooking she made a salad.

"It's a fine thing," I said, "Lampe giving you that part in Shaw's play. When do you start rehearsing?"

"Next week," she said.

"You don't seem very enthusiastic," I said. And jumping from one idea to another in an attempt to sound her out: "Lampe seems to think the world of you."

"He stinks," she said. "A really rotten director."

"But influential. And you're in with him."

"Do you by any chance think," she asked, still quite calmly, "that I've gone to bed with Lampe?"

"What harm would there be in that?"

She put down the salad bowl, turned round and looked at me in consternation.

"That," she said, "would be . . ." and after a moment's search for the right word: "prostitution!"

At first I had to laugh. Then I realized that she was a puritan, a puritan from *over there*. She could talk nonchalantly of sleeping infrequently with Hornbostel and with Lampe not at all, the vocabulary of sexual enlightenment flowed easily from her lips, but she had been brought up very strictly, she had been taught that prostitution was the lowest form of human exploitation. Thinking of Anna, I am shamed by the fact that I have since then solved my sexual problem with the help of a Roman prostitute by the name of Lidia. I met Lidia last summer, the summer of 1963, one night when, unable to sleep because of the heat, I was driving my car down Viale Tiziano. There she stood in the light of a street lamp, not far from the Ponte Milvio, aflame in the red rag that served her as a dress, looking like the Babylonian harlot in person. In reality she is a nice sensible girl with whom I get on very well. Sometimes we spend the evening together without even doing it, just chatting about Rome, about her family and her childhood in Calabria. I had to do something to keep from relapsing —witness that time at the Circolo della Stampa Estera—into certain habits. Nevertheless, whenever I recall Anna's horrified *but that would be prostitution*, it comes to me that I am degrading and exploiting a human being, even if Lidia feels nothing of the kind and is patently glad to serve me. True, she doesn't suspect that the only reason for my steady patronage is that her silent sensible way of making love enables me to think of Meg while I am lying with her.

Apropos of Lidia, I now abandon my project of giving a comprehensive account of my habits. Leafing back through what I have written thus far, I see that I have already mentioned not only my reading, but also most of the periodic recurrences that form the ding-dong and tick-tock of my life, including my sexual practices. In the most divergent contexts I have made it clear that I like to eat, but drink only moderately. It is a habit with me to read at meals, I nap after lunch, smoke a packet of cigarettes a day, enjoy dancing and drive a car. I have also pointed out that I have no family, that I am careful almost to the point of niggardliness about money, like to take walks and sometimes go to the cinema or a concert. Ought I to add that my bowel movements are regular and that my physical condition is in general excellent? My project of treating this entire routine in detail was prompted by the fact that the reader of these pages—assuming that such a being will exist—might come to the conclusion that I am to be pitied. Not at all! I am enviably independent and quite capable of enjoying life. I am anything but a Roquentin, a sufferer from existential nausea. I like to eat, I love art, and my feeling for purity is a Platonic tic, nothing more. Am I not, objectively considered, rather a fortunate than an unfortunate man?

I had still another motive for wanting to throw full light on these ornaments of my everyday life—a question of literary métier, so to speak. For instance, I am a wearer of spectacles, and I should have liked to perform the feat of being a spectacle-wearer throughout my book. I am obliged to wear glasses with the considerable correction of minus ten diopters, which causes me to see the world very sharply, or, when I take off my glasses, in very much of a blur, dissolved in vague islands of colour. An author, it seems to me, ought to be able to keep so important a feature of a character constantly present in the reader's mind. In this, I fear, I have failed, and there's certainly no point in trying to make good my failure with a separate little essay.

Our lunch was calm at first, later it became agitated because Eduard Krystek didn't content himself with light conversation; when the conversation came to revolve round his daughter, he really opened up. Even sitting down he was still a head taller than I. Anna's *hackepeter* was excellent, grainy and finely seasoned, and the light beer tasted cool and bitter. Anna told her father about me, my Berlin origins, my British development, and my international profession.

"Herr Efraim is a Jew," she said, and again it gave me pleasure to hear how naturally she uttered the word Jew, without the slightest catch in her voice or trace of the obscene note it took on in the mouths of most Germans.

"Yes, I can see that," said Eduard Krystek. "Big deal for you coming to this wonderful country, ain't it?"

At the beginning of my notes I spoke harshly of the Berlin jargon, I said I was allergic to the famous *Berliner Schnauze*, but with old man Krystek I didn't mind being cut off sharp by a pithy remark. It really was a big deal for me to be here again, and there was no more to be said about it. I only nodded.

"Sure," he went on. "But you can take a powder. We got to stay here."

With each of his sentences the coal merchant hit a nail on the head. I suddenly realized what it meant for some people having to live in post-Auschwitz Germany. And that I was the kind who could take a powder. My homelessness has advantages for me, but it gave me rather a powdery look in the eyes of people who had a country, an abject country, but still a country they were condemned to live in.

"Herr Efraim is thinking of staying on here," said Anna in a tone of mockery.

Krystek looked at me incredulously. "Don't be a fool," he said. "You've only had a sniff of it."

And he expatiated on the political condition of Germany as he saw it. From a journalistic point of view it was interesting to me to meet in Eduard Krystek a Communist who had no hope in

East Germany either. Marx and Lenin looked down on us from over the sideboard. There seems to be in the Communist Party an underground of old revolutionaries, the Bohemian weavers of many centuries. They are Communists as I am a Jew or a Negro a Negro. A Negro's colour doesn't wash off. Accordingly, I didn't believe old Krystek when he concluded his speech with the words: "To tell you the truth, I only keep on being a Communist for the hell of it. It doesn't mean anything any more."

Something in his voice seemed to worry Anna. "Father," she said, "you mustn't get worked up."

"All right," he said. It was evident that the mere sound of Anna's voice soothed him. But at the same time her interruption gave the conversation a turn which embarrassed her in the extreme, for it put him onto an idea, and when old man Krystek had an idea he came right out with it.

"And you, young man," he asked with apparent affability, "what are your intentions towards my daughter?"

"Father!" Anna cried out. She had already stood up to clear the table, I had lit a cigarette. Now she stopped still and looked at her father with indignation.

"Don't get excited," he said. "I can ask, can't I?"

The shift from the political to the personal had come rather suddenly, but the brief battle of words and feelings between father and daughter gave me time for a lightning decision.

"I've asked Anna to go to Rome with me," I said, looking at Anna. "It would please me to show her around Rome." Then I turned back to her father. "But of course not if you have any objection, Herr Krystek."

That had been an inspiration. It had come to me in an instant that it was better to make Anna my proposition now, in her father's presence, than later when I should be alone with her. For all its impudence, my application to her father made me look serious. And another point in my favour was that he had put her into the situation of having to resist his authority.

"See?" she said to him, still furious. "That's what you get with your questions."

Then she laughed. She was sharp enough to sense that I had carried off a parody of a proposal. It was as though I had asked her father for her hand. Only the bouquet was missing.

Eduard Krystek had risen. "What objection can I have?" he grumbled. "Anna's not a minor." Long, thin and visibly ailing, he paced the room.

"Yes," he thought out loud. "But Rome? I don't know if Rome's the right thing for you, Anna. What's Rome? A landscape."

"I'd only go for a few days," said Anna. "That is, if I decide to go."

"You never can tell," he said, and pursued his thoughts as though alone with his daughter. "He ain't wet behind the ears like Werner Hornbostel," he said, and at that moment I existed only through his gesture in my direction. "He's kind of short for you, Anna, but at least he's not a sawed-off giant."

"Father!" said Anna, embarrassed. "Don't be getting ideas."

He went to the door.

"Got to get back to the shop," he said. "Don't stay away too long, Anna, if you go. I get gloomy all alone."

He was so tall he had to bend down in the doorway. I watched Anna look after him with an anxious expression that persisted for some time after he had disappeared.

Quite possibly it was then and not Thursday afternoon in Frankfurt that I lost Anna. Come to think of it, it was astonishing that she consented to fly to Rome with me in the first place, that at the end of the half hour we spent after lunch in her *Berliner Zimmer* she finally said: "All right. I'll go and take a look at Rome." I certainly didn't owe this decision to my attempt to unbutton her blouse. We had gone to her room with its photographs of actors, Anna had made coffee, she was lying on her couch while I sat on a chair; that was where she must have been lying when I rang her up early the previous morning and pictured her fine-spun hair lying loose and ash-blond on the pillow, and

now the memory of my imagining made me bend down and kiss
her. She let me, she didn't seem to find the contact unpleasant,
but then when as cautiously as possible I undid the topmost button of her blouse, she asked me in a clear voice and for once not
in her stage German but in the purest Berlinisch: "D'you always
do that?"

For emergencies she apparently had a little stock of Berlinisms,
linguistic cold showers, in readiness. On Saturday night when I
offered to introduce her to some Italian film directors, she had
reacted with: "Boy, oh boy, you're certainly a fast worker," though
then her pronunciation hadn't yet been so clearly tinged with
dialect as in her present "D'you always do that?" In the cab she
had successfully put me in my place by telling me coolly that I
behaved like a bull in a china shop. Yes, my new Berlin girl-
friend could certainly be bumptious, no doubt about it. Still, her
third formula of resistance had not been brought forth with the
same accent of finality as the first two, it had more of a gay,
friendly ring, I was able to withdraw with the feeling that at least
my defeat had not been definitive. She had given me to understand that it was still too soon.

"Besides, Georg," she said when the intermezzo was at an end,
"besides, you love your wife. We've agreed about that, haven't
we?"

"You've agreed," I said with irritation. "I haven't."

I don't know why I then proceeded to tell her about Meg. Not
everything, not the ultimate secrets, but enough to give her an
idea. She lay in the half-light of her corner, and something about
that tall, pale, rather shadowy girl made me tell her what had happened to me in my marriage with Meg. Originally I must have
thought my motive had been to prove that I could no longer love
Meg, that it was all over between Meg and me, that it had to be
all over. Later I realized that something entirely different had
moved me to speak, to wit, that to me inexplicable component
of Anna's nature which—of this I am absolutely certain though I

can't prove it—made me start writing these notes the day after I met her. Anna started me speaking. Speaking and writing.

I told her nothing more than the scene I had with Meg on the third day of our marriage. I didn't describe the soft London light, the grey drizzly day waning into a rainy night, that night which marked itself so terribly on my memory, when Meg came into the room where I was reading the paper after dinner. She had on her light-coloured trench-coat. "I'm going out," she said. "I have a date with Keir."

"With Keir?" I said and let the paper drop. "At this hour? You're not going to sell him pictures at this hour?"

"No," she replied. "I'm not going to sell him pictures. I'm going to his flat."

I felt my body shrinking with fear.

"Meg," I said, "you can't do that. Meg!"

"Why can't I?" she asked. Her tone wasn't harsh. No, it was friendly, friendly and detached. "It gives me pleasure, George."

All I told Anna was that exchange, not the black rainy hours I spent roaming the streets of London that night. She could imagine that for herself.

She questioned me. I had to describe Keir—whose name she had heard in connection with Esther—Keir and Meg's relations with him.

"Did your wife tell you before you were married that she meant to keep on with this man?" she asked.

I was obliged to admit that she had. "But I didn't believe it," I said. "I somehow didn't think it possible."

"But did she like to do it with you too?" she asked. "Or did she go to Keir because she didn't like it with you? Forgive me," she said, "but it's important."

"I had the impression she enjoyed it with me too."

"Then she's a wonderful woman," said Anna. "She was perfectly honest with you. She's a woman who's able to live with two or more men, and wants to, and she told you so quite openly. I'm sure she loves you, or she wouldn't jump into bed with you every

time you go to London. That has nothing to do with the love
she feels for Keir or anyone else. Why didn't you accept it? You've
got to take a woman like that the way she is."

That was exactly what Meg herself had once said to me in a
single, more succinct English sentence: "You must learn to live
with it." What schoolmistresses women are!

"I wish you'd stop using the word 'love' that way," I said impatiently to Anna.

"You're right," she conceded, "it's outmoded." Then after thinking it over: "I probably couldn't live like your wife. I'd rather do
it with one man."

I know there was nothing contradictory in this allegation
despite her relations with Werner Hornbostel and her sudden ac-
ceptance, after I had told my story about Meg, of my invitation
to Rome. In the first place Hornbostel—quite unlike me in my
feeling for Meg—wouldn't care in the least whether she went to
Rome with me or not, because his thoughts are far away in the
realm of music, though in his own way, the way of a child immersed in his games, he loves Anna dearly, and in the second
place because he had dismissed her on Saturday night with his
announcement that he was leaving Berlin soon. I witnessed the
end of a children's love affair. Moreover, Anna hadn't accepted
my invitation with any great enthusiasm; she had merely said "all
right" in the tone of one ceding to tiresome insistence, adding:
"Though I don't quite see what I'm supposed to do in Rome."
But despite her misgivings she laughed in the end and said:
"You're a stubborn dog, Georg."

Back at my hotel, the first thing I did was to stand at the mirror to see what Eduard Krystek could have meant by saying I
wasn't a sawed-off giant. I came to the conclusion that he had
been referring to the harmoniousness of my rather small dark
frame, to the medallion-like impression that we Semites, scions of
a Mediterranean culture, make on Nordics. Though I am the son
of a Berlin Jew who was a short, stout, solidly-built man, I look
like a Latin; possibly I get that from my mother, who was also short,

but small-boned. In any case I am not one of those excessively slender, nervous scholars or musicians, the product of centuries of religious speculation in the ghettos of Cordoba and Kiev, who have assimilated themselves so perfectly to the Teutons and Slavs as to invite the hatred of a loathsome hybrid, a pale human toad. I'm not a Jewish aristocrat like my Uncle Basil. But I don't believe Anna's father recognized me for exactly what I am. Behind the complete, self-contained impression I make, hidden by my quick smooth journalist's gestures and the angularity of my rimless glasses that stamp me as an intellectual, there is something open, aimless, and immature, in short, an inferiority complex. With his Berlin idiom old Krystek recognized my problem, but the conclusion he drew is incorrect, too flattering; perhaps something gigantic did want to grow in me, but then one fine day the giant within me was sawn off. No sooner have I launched on this outburst of self-pity than my English upbringing makes me turn it off.

My return to my hotel was depressing because alone in my room I was suddenly unable to summon up a feeling of being in love with Anna. What in heaven's name had I let myself in for with this invitation to Rome? For a moment I thought of sending a telegram saying I had been called away unexpectedly and would write. I overcame my panic by going out, booking two plane tickets to Rome via Frankfurt for Thursday morning, and ringing Anna to tell her when and where to meet me. In the course of our telephone conversation neither she nor I suggested a meeting on Wednesday; as though by a secret accord we coolly arranged to meet at Tempelhof at ten-thirty on Thursday. This gave me time to recapture at least part of my feelings, so that when the time came I did not entirely regret having set in motion the mechanism of courtship, which I find absurd, and let myself in for something which might in a short time become irksome to me, the necessity of looking after a girl whom I probably did not love.

What may also have contributed to my depression on Tuesday is that towards evening, on my return from the airline office, an attempt to work on my notes proved a total failure. Finding that I was empty, that my machine had run down, I put the blame on my visit to Anna and wondered anxiously whether her presence in Rome mightn't seriously interfere with my work. On Wednesday morning, however, I worked well and decided that from then on I should never work at any other time of day. My spirits revived, perhaps I should be able to divide my times of day in Rome between Anna and the book. By an effort of reason I came to the conclusion that it was only a sign of being in love, if from the heights of in-loveness I had fallen into a feeling of listless defensiveness, and at length by a process of auto-suggestion I even came to envisage something resembling pleasure in my impending adventure. My sense of pleasure did indeed return to me on Thursday, because when we met, Anna seemed sullen and distrustful, making it quite clear that she would have preferred to drop the whole undertaking. Like myself she had stuck to our agreement only out of a sense of duty. She was sitting huddled and shivering in the gloomy airport waiting room; she scarcely held out her hand, but insisted on paying me for her ticket. "Father wants it that way," she said obstinately. No discussion was possible.

Some evenings when I sit alone over a glass of wine at the Rosati or at Alfredo alla Scrofa's, or even with Lidia in a *trattoria* across the Ponte Milvio where she lives, I wish Anna had come. In Frankfurt, to be sure, nothing I could possibly have said would have prevented her from taking the plane back to Berlin, but a little later she might have given herself a jolt and repacked the bedraggled leather suitcase she had had with her at Tempelhof. I can see her arriving at Fiumicino. I'm looking down from the terrace as she appears in the door of the plane and descends the stairs; unfamiliar with the Roman climate, she's wearing her grey coat; she's taller than the other women getting off the plane. It's a fine windy day, an east wind, the *levantina*, is blowing over the Roman Campagna, etching the Alban Hills clear and blue into the horizon. I run down to the waiting room, we wave at each other as I wait for her to go through customs; and now she's

coming towards me through a cross-fire of Italian men's glances.
She's crazy about flying, as enthusiastic as she was on the plane
from Berlin to Frankfurt, when she was flying for the first time
in her life. We go to my little dark-green sports car, an aged but
still lively contrivance, which I can count on because it's inanimate, and drive into the city. To the right of the long curve after
the Tiber Bridge the ruins of Ostia Antica appear, in the middle
of the field there's a new excavation, three small Corinthian
columns set on brickwork. I explain nothing to Anna, I've resolved not to play the guide, I'm certain that Anna cares no more
for sights than Meg. She gazes in silence at the reddish light over
the ruins. She's delighted with the big umbrella pines along Via
del Mare. We drive past factories and barracks and then—late in
the afternoon—into the tumult of traffic, the concerts of horns,
amidst the palaces of the inner city. I've reserved a room for Anna
at the Byron on the same corridor as mine. It's anything but
luxurious, but she seems to like it. She goes right out, just as I
would, on the narrow balcony, looks out over the rooftops, a few
deep-purple bougainvillaeas are still in bloom on the roof terrace,
and for the first time Anna hears the melodious cries from the
chasm of Via Borgognona.

We become a familiar couple in Rome, sometimes we sit with
theatre and film directors at the Capriccio; then Anna wears her
silver-green dress from Lampe's party; in that dress she can bear
to be seen in Rome or anywhere else. We've got her a new coat,
though; after some resistance Anna has let me give her a be-
witchingly cut black gabardine with a fur lining, that we discovered in Via Condotti. She wears her schoolgirl coat from
Rixdorf only in the daytime, on walks and errands. My hunch has
been a good one: fanatical Brechtians, the Italian directors take a
keen interest in this young actress trained at the Schiffbauerdamm.
Besides, her light eyes and long legs make her an unusual type
for Rome. Cella has already arranged to give her a test. He has
spent a whole evening at the Rosati studying her shadowiness
from behind his dark glasses. She can't get over it that men like

him should be card-carrying members of the Communist Party.

No, I don't show her any sights. Of course we go everywhere and sometimes I drop a remark, a hint. I've bought her the Reclam *Rome Art Guide*, just in case. Once after we have passed Trajan's market she comes to my room, indignantly brandishing the book.

"How do you like this?" she says. And she reads in a loud, clear voice: "The transformative power of the Greek agora, where man met man in freedom, made itself felt in the portrait which the Roman Empire painted of itself at this centre of its action and tradition."

"But the place was a slave market," she cries out. "You showed me where the slave market was." Furiously she throws down the book on the table. "I can't take any more of this bourgeois crap," she declares.

I'm careful not to say that I have no fundamental objection to slave markets. I love the deep colour that slavery gave the ancient world. To Anna such a statement would undoubtedly be bourgeois crap. She has no feeling for the aesthetics of slavery.

I'm unable to infect her with the heavy sensuous sound of Rome. But she reacts to entirely different things which I've never noticed. Once we go into San Clemente; I'm curious to see how she'll respond to the temple of Mithras under the church. The church appeals to her instantly, she is delighted with the Cosmato mosaics and with the way Masolino makes St. Catherine look out one of the windows. "It's beautiful," she says. And she also feels the sacred awe that comes over one on descending into the underworld of San Clemente, from floor to floor, into the lower strata of Rome.

"What's that?" she asks suddenly. She stops to listen; she has heard the sound of water.

"It's the rivers," I say.

"What rivers?"

We go down deeper and deeper and for the first time I pay attention to that sound of water. It starts in the Basilica Inferiore with a thin tinkling note, grows louder though still unseen, subterranean and remote in the Navata Mediana, and then at last, in the bottommost passages, the rivers emerge from openings in the rock and flow swift and foaming into a millennial darkness faintly illumined by an electric light bulb or two.

Anna kneels down and puts one hand into the torrent.

"Where do they come from?" she shouts to make herself heard over the sound of the water.

"Nobody knows," I shout back.

People used to think these rivers came from the Esquiline Hill. But even now, two thousand years later, no one knows for certain.

"The water's cold," Anna shouts. She stands up, so overcome with emotion that she hugs me. Then we enter the Mithraeum, but she scarcely looks at it, takes no interest in the bull or the serpent, the phallic symbols of the Oriental god, or any of the orgiastic bric-à-brac. She's in a hurry to get out again to the flowing waters.

All that is fancy, scenes as I've said that I sometimes dream up late at night sitting in a café after I've been to the cinema or a concert or nowhere. The summer of 1964 was hot, even after *ferragosto*. Now as I write this at the beginning of 1965, it seems to me that last summer was long, hot and tedious, a season of thirst during which I lost sight of *your book*—oh, Meg!—neglected it, or at the very most reworked some of the more involute sentences in my account of my journey to Chichester Rents, and waited, waited, waited. For what? Certainly no longer for Anna. It's too bad we didn't love each other, Anna and I.

And yet it started out very well. Her bad humour fell away from her when she felt the four jet engines driving the plane forward and lifting it into the air. I had given her the seat by the window and she saw the city down below, then the lakes and then only the evergreen forests, while I read the paper. I had no consciousness that I was leaving Berlin, that I'd been in Berlin for a week, that I'd gone back after an interval of twenty-seven years and was now leaving it behind, and would probably never see it again. For the last time in my life I had entered my old home, and

it had no longer meant anything to me. At one point Anna remarked that she couldn't see the border—she meant the border
between East and West Germany—and shortly before Frankfurt
she tugged at my sleeve to show me that we were flying over the
clouds. Deeply moved she looked down at the great glacier of
water vapour gleaming in the sun, that white illusion of eternity.

When, as I recorded at the beginning of these notes, I tried
to explain to Anna that I should sometimes have to leave her alone
in Rome because I had work to do, she hardly listened, she was
too preoccupied with the fact that she was flying.

At Tempelhof the weather had still been clear, but the sky over
the Frankfurt airport was grey. The plane for Rome wouldn't be
leaving until afternoon and I persuaded Anna to drive into town
with me, though she really didn't feel like it.

"I'd rather get my first glimpse of the West in Rome," she said.

"You see it every day in Berlin," I argued, but even as I spoke
I knew there was truth in her words. West Berlin is not yet the
West.

We took a cab into the centre of Frankfurt. There we fell in
with a student demonstration. Some fifty students were standing
or sitting on a traffic island in the middle of a square while trams,
cars and pedestrians streamed past. The placards they were holding showed they were protesting against the police assault on the
offices of *Die Revue*. Even in Berlin there had been more of a stir
about *Die Revue* than about the island off the American coast.
The possibility that Germany might become an arena of atomic
warfare if the poker game between K. and the President of the
United States got out of hand interested people much less than
the arrest of the publisher and some of the editors of *Die Revue*.
To tell the truth, I find it perfectly normal that people should react with a shrug to the possibility of being hit by an atom bomb
but become aroused when journalists are thrown into jail. Anyway,
here were fifty students taking an interest in the matter. The
pedestrians and motorists turned their heads to look at them.
Anna said she wanted to watch. The students were well-dressed.

None of them seemed excited. But on Anna's face there was a look of exaltation such as I had seen on the faces of student demonstrators in Asia. I might just as well say a look of hysteria.

The students formed a procession which moved along the right-hand pavement of a broad avenue in Frankfurt, past shops, and through the crowds of shoppers. We followed it. This was obviously an *authorized* demonstration, authorized on condition that it keep out of the roadway and not interfere with traffic. To lengthen the line and appear more numerous than they were, the boys and girls went only two or three abreast. Some of them were visibly ill at ease. It might have been better if they had formed a compact group, a small fist that would have parted the flow of pedestrians. This thin line only made a trifling change in the street scene. Unpolitical passers-by looked on for a brief puzzled moment, but there were also gawkers, fellow-travellers and sympathizers like Anna and myself who joined the march. There must have been about a hundred of us on that grey cloudy day marching down Bahnhofstrasse. The street was much too wide, the people on the opposite pavement could scarcely have seen what it was all about. A police patrol car drove slowly at some distance behind the procession, stopped from time to time and started up again. Anna forged ahead, trying to get to the head of the march, though I'm sure she had no intention of becoming active; I believe she just wanted to study the tactics of West German student demonstrators.

We hadn't reached the head yet when the leaders began to shout. Their shouts were taken up by those round us, but since they started after the leaders, the shouting wasn't in unison but sounded more like a spoken canon. The substance of their message was that the publisher of *Die Revue* should be released, and that the cabinet minister who had sent him to jail should be locked up. Here I must depart for a moment from my principle of coding (*Revue, Island*), which I have explained at length, and use the names of the two men in question, because there is no other way of reproducing the phonetics of the shouts, which un-

fortunately, in this very wide street, seeped away without reso-
nance. The students shouted: *"Strauss rein—Augstein raus!"*
(Strauss in—Augstein out), a rhythmic sequence made up of the
classical cries of pain *au, ei, au, ei au,* and punctuated by the sharp
consonants *s, t* and *r,* which might perfectly well have been
whipped into a howl as inflammatory and full of hate as the
hundred-times repeated *"assassini—assassini—assassini"* I once
heard outside the Spanish Embassy in Rome after Julian Grimau
was executed by the garrote in Madrid. But the German students
had nothing comparable to offer; the quality of the outcry with
which murderers are hunted down, the lust for vengeance didn't
enter into their voices; calmly they formulated a canon of moderate indignation, a prearranged vocal protest. Augstein, to be sure,
wasn't facing the garrote, but at most a few years in prison if
Strauss had his way, nor was Strauss a murderer, no, he was only
a sly and jocular bar-fly, who would drop in on his prisoners
now and then to drink with them in his jovial, malicious way. Or
maybe he wouldn't. Maybe the whole affair wasn't very important.

At the edge of Bahnhofsplatz the students stopped because the
traffic signals for pedestrians were red. I heard Anna say to the
students near us: "Keep going. What are you stopping for?" Her
advice fell on the wrong ears. A chorus of voices informed her that
the police must be given no pretext for disbanding the demonstration. Anna, as I could see by the look on her face, was aghast.
I shrugged my shoulders and told her in an undertone to keep
quiet or she'd be taken for a provocateur. Only when the signals
turned green did the students enter the square in front of the
railway station. Their respect for law and order almost broke up
the demonstration, for the light changed twice again between
the head and tail of the procession; they rounded the square in
dispersed order and were almost lost in the crowds outside the
station; but doubling back along their prescribed route, a street
parallel to Bahnhofstrasse, they all managed to get together
again.

This street was narrower, a ravine between sinister-looking blocks of flats built at the turn of the century, at night undoubtedly haunted by streetwalkers. The dingy underside of the cloud ceiling, which, as Anna and I knew, was in reality the glacier of eternity, cast a mouldy light. The demonstrators had grown tired, their shouts sounded even thinner than before, they ambled along with the indifference of a tired school outing. But suddenly a deep rumbling was heard and when we turned round, there was the police. Reinforcements waiting in the side streets off Bahnhofsplatz must have been set in motion; I counted five patrol cars and ten troop carriers; three companies of police had been mobilized to follow this sparse procession of gentle protesters. It was laughable but no one laughed and I saw Anna thrust her balled fists into her coat pockets. The throttled-down motors clanked, the policemen sat upright and motionless in the cars. The ghetto, I thought, I never knew the ghetto, I'd never been in the ghetto, but that's how they must have driven into the ghettos twenty years ago, rumbling past the rows of bleak houses and pale faces, the exterminators of vermin, the murderers by iron and gas. I'm exaggerating. The police officer in charge in this Social Democratic governed city must soon have recognized the absurdity of the picture, for at the end of the street he ordered the greater part of the escort to turn off; the reinforcements vanished as suddenly as they had come, and after that only two patrol cars kept watch on the students, almost politely. Then the demonstration had its big moment: passing a building site—a new theatre—they were hailed by the construction workers; standing amidst the lattice work of iron piping that served them as scaffolds, the workers waved down at the students. But not even this scene out of an Eisenstein film could brighten the face of my taciturn Anna, on the contrary it seemed to grow darker than ever, for my Berlin girl-friend is a realist, you can't fool her, it didn't escape her for one moment that the workers were only waving, that they weren't coming down from their scaffolds to join the students, to occupy the streets of Frankfurt and overthrow the minister—who actually

was overthrown in the end, but not by them, not by them! All
they got from Anna was a look of contempt and not the glow of
enthusiasm that must have come to her face when for the first
time she saw the sailors of Odessa refusing to eat soup with mag-
goty meat in it.

The end of the demonstration was rather a success. When they
got back to the wide business street in the middle of the city, the
students began to amble along with their natural youthful ease.
They moved in a straggling line shouting their slogan, "*Strauss
rein—Augstein raus!*" The nature of their success was that people
stopped, shop assistants and customers stepped out of the com-
modity-clogged shops. Assistants and customers crowded into the
doorways and asked what was going on. And when the students
reached their final destination, a patrol car stopped, a police officer, tall and handsome, though perhaps somewhat overfed, got
out; immaculate and resplendent with leather harness, he went
over to them and thanked them for their excellent discipline; not
a trace of indignation or menace in his manner, he was merely
a tall, engaging military man and Social Democrat who thanked
them, requested them to disperse, and only smiled when the students stayed on a little while longer talking things over. He had
his instructions.

We took a cab back to the airport. On the way Anna didn't say
one word, but as we entered the airport building she stopped still
and said: "I want to go back to Berlin."

There was something so irrevocable in her tone that I didn't
argue; I could only help her to book a flight. My plane to Rome
left two hours earlier than hers; we shook hands and as I went to
the passport window, Anna looked after me unsmilingly. Before
that we had agreed never to write. "Please, no letters from the
front," she insisted. "But I'd be glad if you decided to come one
of these days," I said, and I suppose she didn't have the strength
to say anything that would wholly stifle my hope. At Fiumicino
I had some trouble getting hold of her bedraggled leather suitcase, which we had been unable to have removed from the plane

in Frankfurt, and shipping it back to her. When I finally had it
in my hands, I'd have liked to open it, but I had no key, and the
customs officers didn't need one because they weren't interested
in a bag that wasn't going to enter Italy. I'd have liked to know
what a girl from Berlin puts in her bag when she flies to Rome. I
didn't even have a piece of chalk or crayon to scribble something
gay or sad on the suitcase, just one word, perhaps nothing more
than the word *Anna*. Then I went to my car and drove into town
through the darkness, not in the *levantina* but in a sultry *scirocco*
that gave me a headache.

At this point I could ride my pseudoproblem; I could assume
that Anna would have continued on to Rome with me if we hadn't
fallen in with that demonstration, and draw pertinent conclusions.
For one thing, a problem can be petit-bourgeois and subjectivist
without necessarily being a pseudoproblem. Even the petit bour-
geoisie can be right once in a while. But I have no desire to. No
desire and no time. Since Anna didn't come and a happy ending
with her is out of the question, I have no alternative but to take
out the pages on which I began last summer to relate my visit to
Keir. After all, I've got to put things in the right order. I polish
them a little, it's not real work, I dawdle over it, already wondering what I'm going to do when the whole thing is finished. So the
spring of 1965 passes. I still take a look at a flat now and then.
But Rome is beginning to bore me.

Six

So I continue on my way, leave Bloomsbury, cross High Holborn, slip into a lane that takes me away from that vast thoroughfare and its flow of traffic, and suddenly find myself in the morning quietness of Lincoln's Inn Fields. Still the same transparent mist over the wintry elms, the deserted tennis and netball courts, and the sonorous-brown three-storied houses, behind whose square white-framed windows lawyers have their chambers. I consider dropping in on Spencer to tell him about my visit to Bismarckstrasse, but immediately abandon the idea, first because it would be improper to call on the old gentleman, Uncle Basil's solicitor and executor, unannounced, and second because I've postponed my meeting with Keir long enough. Instead, I wrote to Spencer from Rome, asking him to go ahead with the restitution proceedings, and informing him of the further decisions about the house that I had arrived at after my conversation with Collaudi. Collaudi's advice, he wrote back, struck him as sensible; he would have given me the same.

I linger a while under the squat Gothic arches of the chapel, because here I am already in one of Keir's haunts. Often at noon, when the students and professors of the old law school strolled about the open cloisters, he brought me here to talk shop in the academic atmosphere to which he was so much attached. On such occasions, I believe, he would think himself back to his beloved Cambridge. Now, so early in the day, this corner of the Middle Ages is deserted. I too desert it, contemplate for a moment the distinguished silence of the plane trees in New Square, stop outside a stationer's window where registers with marbled edges and legal forms on parchment or deckle-edged handmade paper are on display, silver-grey or slightly yellowish sheets on which marriages, property sales or death sentences will be recorded over water-marks. But at length I turn away, slip through the open door in a high wooden gate and find myself in another world, a tiny slum between Chancery Lane and the high wall of New Square, in which the black wooden gate through which I have just passed is inserted. This is Keir's corner of the city, he has been living here for many years, it consists of a few alleys squeezed in between courthouses and the backs of the Fleet Street newspaper buildings; I haven't been here for ages and it seems a miracle that everything is just as it was, for the whole area was supposed to be torn down long ago. I firmly believe it has been saved by the curses and prayers with which Keir has responded to every attempt to destroy it and so drive him out of his cave, that obscure retreat he has made for himself, where he is very hard to find though within a few steps of the paper. What I have just said is not a literary conceit, I really do hold a superstitious belief in the magic effect of curses and prayers.

Perhaps it was the sight of the scratched frosted-glass panes of the Rogers Artists Agency that deterred me from going straight to Keir's. Those shabby opaque windows reminded me that there behind them, in a room I have never entered—I picture a few worn wicker chairs and a dark-brown counter under a forlorn white light —Meg heard Keir's name for the first time. Fourteen years ago Rogers, who makes his living selling pictures—photographs, comic strips, drawings of all kinds—to the newspapers, promised to show her work to Keir whom he knew personally as well as professionally and sometimes joined in a glass of beer at the bar of The Three Tuns. It must have been at The Three Tuns that he showed Keir Meg's photographs. Keir had been impressed, perhaps Rogers had intimated that Meg was attractive; in any case Keir had told Rogers to send her to see him. Keir had first received Meg at his flat, it was only later that Meg gained leave to call at his office when she wished to see him on business. Yes, that's how it started; at that time, in the mid-fifties, Meg was twenty, Keir fifty-one, and I thirty; a year later I married Meg, two years after that, in 1955,

I left her; at that time I was still doing home news and not making much; it was only after my separation from Meg, when Keir, for reasons of soul hygiene so to speak, sent me abroad that my professional ascent began; after the purgative winter in Dalarne I went to Paris, discovered the secret mission of the Vietminh, and was sent to Hanoi where I arrived just in time for the battle of Dien Bien Phu; I knocked around for a while amidst Far Eastern developments and Arab rivalries, reported the 1956 Suez crisis from Israel, and then went back to India; in the late fifties my interest in high journalistic achievement waned; Keir offered me New York as a shot in the arm, but after Asia the U.S. wasn't what I needed (I believe that I now know which way the cat of history is going to jump, which is no great distinction, practically everyone knows), I was soon bored with the U.S., and since 1962 I've been stagnating in Rome. In between I've returned to London at intervals, seen Keir and Meg, and invariably gone to bed with Meg, the last time on my visit a year ago. All this happened because someone gave a certain Margaret Ellis from Stoke-on-Trent, who, having come to London at the age of sixteen to learn photography at the studio of some distant relative, was photographing with talent, eating irregularly and determined to make a career, a tip to the effect that Rogers & Co., Artists Agents, could help her place her photographs with the press. Because the name of that still extant firm in faded so-called Egyptienne lettering on scratched frosted-glass windows has led me to recapitulate the years since 1950 and to bring new grist to the mill of my theory of chance, I wander about for a while longer, postponing my visit to Keir. I crossed Chancery Lane quite some time ago. Here everything looks the way Keir's street is bound to look soon: new functional-style buildings have replaced the ramshackle old houses. I look about me with curiosity, the modernizers have proceeded with piety, between two new office buildings, part of a graveyard dating back to the times of Samuel Johnson has been preserved, a rectangle of black, weathered tombstones, round which a new era has begun, a new Fleet Street in which I shall have no part. I have retired. But something old has remained: a sound. In Fetter Lane I walk along the back of my conservative paper; through the walls I hear the muffled sound of our big rotary press printing our daily, a strong steady hum accentuated by a sharp beat that comes from the end of the machine where the roll of paper is cut, the sheet folded, and the finished newspaper thrown on the conveyor belt, a newspaper appearing in four and a half million copies. We have a circulation of four and a half million. I stop and listen for a while. Did I really think *we* and *my* and *our?* I go my way.

I must make a correction. When I started on this walk to Keir's, fourteen years hadn't, as I have just written, passed since Meg turned up at the Rogers agency, but only twelve. Unintentionally I included in the past of that London morning the two years I have spent over my manuscript, as though I were starting on my visit to Keir's now, in the midst of this sweltering Roman summer of 1964, and not in the pearling cool mist of a London November two years ago. Since I have been living in Rome since the spring of 1962, this is my third summer up there in the fiery furnace under the roof of the Albergo Byron. I still go looking at flats, now and then I find one that would suit me perfectly, but at the last minute I shrink back from the bother of moving and setting up house, picture to myself the paper war I should have to wage with the Roman authorities, for since last spring I am no longer an accredited journalist and would consequently have to apply for a residence permit as a private citizen; once I actually went to the Anagrafe, the municipal registration office in Via del Teatro Marcello, dived into the hot dust of the crowds, listened to the discreet or turbulent application-form crises that broke out amidst the knots of humanity at the windows, and went away discouraged; with a sigh of relief I sat down in the shade of the arcades of the ancient theatre where the cats were having their siesta. I am assured, it is true, by people in the know that it's all very simple; all I have to do is slip a couple of ten-thousand lire notes to some clerk in the foreign residents section and in a few days I'll have my *domicilio* without the slightest difficulty, but I can't screw up the courage to face it. I still remember how while admiring the cats at the theatre of Marcellus I longed once more for a dog, one of those beings whose genius resides in their loyalty. But as long as I'm staying at the Byron I can't have a dog. To give myself an illusion of permanence I've had Uncle Basil's desk sent from London, an unwieldy fumed-oak thing in the art-nouveau style, which was already out of place at Clanricarde Gardens, where it clashed with the Dutch pieces. What with my books and now this desk my little room is exceedingly cramped; when I want to move about, the only possibilities are the space behind the balcony and of course the balcony itself, where I still stand at frequent intervals, always alone, looking down into Via Borgognona or over the rooftops. But now, when I write, I sit at a real desk, though I've set up my drawing board beside it; it gives me more room for my dictionaries and all my little slips of paper. Now I'm a real writer. It's not just the desk that makes me a writer, but also a circumstance that wrings a crooked smile, a sheepish grin, from me whenever I think of it: I have a publisher. It's the fault of John, that German journalist who once disturbed me in a secret, obscene occupation and possibly saved me from letting it continue to the bitter end. Here's what happened: some time last spring, when word had got round at the Circolo della Stampa Estera that I was definitely going to retire, this brisk little man came up to me and asked me what I was planning to do in place of journalism. Just to get rid of him, for I had no desire to be drawn into a discussion about my life, I said curtly that I was writing a book. But I still wasn't rid of him, for the man is a journalist born; without a moment's hesitation he asked me in his cold Rhenish intonation: "Have you got a publisher?" I was so taken aback that the only sound I could produce was a bewildered "No." Heedless of my embarrassment, he followed through: Was I writing in English or in German? When I said I was writing in German, he informed me without mincing words that in that case I needed a German publisher. At this point in our conversation I

recovered my composure and, almost as rudely as when he had
wanted to tell me one of Conte B.'s delightful Hitler anecdotes,
sent John about his business. But a few days later his suggestion,
which he had made as though it had been the most obvious thing
in the world, began to rattle round in my head; I remembered
that John himself had once been obliged to withdraw from journalism and to live as a free-lance writer, though under very different circumstances; it occurred to me that he had only wanted to
be helpful, assuming no doubt that my retirement from journalism would confront me with an economic problem. The upshot of
it was that I rang him up, apologized for my rudeness, and asked
him to tell me what he knew about German publishers, which he
most obligingly did over a dinner to which I invited him. He even
offered to put me in touch with his own publisher, one of the best
in Germany, he assured me. After some hesitation I accepted his
offer. I find it hard to say what made me do so. Probably a kind of
play instinct, I tell myself today; thus far I had been keeping my
manuscript a secret, but why, I reflected, shouldn't I let someone
see it? And mightn't a total stranger be better than someone I
knew? I was extremely curious to find out how a publisher would
resolve the question I keep asking myself in my manuscript: are
these papers I am working on private notes or are they what Meg
with such fine assurance has called *your book*? After all, I said to
myself, it's just an experiment, it won't commit me in any way;
I'm under no obligation to let this joke get out of hand. Consequently, the publisher, a distinguished, rather elderly gentleman,
who actually turned up in Rome at the beginning of June, found
me in a facetious frame of mind which, I'm afraid, I didn't conceal
very well.

What I hadn't counted on was that he had brought with him a
certain Dr. Heckmann, his top editor, a young man in his thirties
with a doctorate in German philology and himself the author of a
book on Kafka. Dr. Heckmann was blond, lean, devastatingly
humourless and very German. My facetious mood deserted me
completely when the two gentlemen, after retiring to their hotel

for two days with my manuscript, reappeared in a state of extraordinary tension and suffering visibly from loss of sleep. The young editor did almost all the talking. He reeled off a whole list of criticisms, he took my book apart like a machine. I have seldom lived through a more depressing hour. As he spoke, the luxurious, comfortably air-conditioned lobby of the Hotel Excelsior where we were sitting transformed itself gradually into a grimy grey repair shop. To my central question he had a simple answer: "Your hero keeps saying that he's writing just for himself; that must be deleted. No reader would believe him. He conceived the book as a novel from the very start."

I was speechless. I had been prepared for anything, but not to be spoken of as my own hero. Then I summoned up the courage to talk back.

"I started writing that Sunday afternoon in Berlin," I said in a furious undertone. "I can assure you that I had no idea what would come of it." I paused and withdrew the anger from my voice. "Later, to be sure," I owned, "I set up a kind of framework, but at the present moment, for instance, I don't know what's coming next or whether I'll be able to finish it altogether."

Dr. Heckmann looked imploringly at his boss, who now at last intervened.

"Don't you see, Herr Efraim," he said, "that we have no choice but to speak of your book as a novel. Unless you expressly wish to call it an autobiography. But surely you wouldn't want to do that?" He thought for a moment, then he said: "Perhaps you ought to change your hero's name, to give him some name other than your own."

That opened up amazing new perspectives. So they wanted me to break with myself!

"The word novel would protect you in a way," I heard the publisher say, "though not very much."

All three of us sat in our shirtsleeves in the air-conditioned hotel lobby, smoking. In a different tone, the publisher asked: "But

we're going to publish the book all the same; aren't we, Dr. Heckmann?"

"Definitely," said the editor, still without the slightest suggestion of a smile. He was really very German. An English editorial
adviser would surely have mixed a little humour into his criticism,
wrapped it in familiar or unfamiliar Oxbridge jokes that would have
made it clear to a connoisseur of academic life—which I am not
—whether the speaker sprang from the Leavis or anti-Leavis camp.
Dr. Heckmann gave no inkling of any school except the school of
German thoroughness and efficiency. I admired him but he also
frightened me. We Jews are not the only people who associate
German thoroughness and efficiency with the memory of Auschwitz. I can't help it, that's how it is. Of course it's absurd. Heckmann, as I quickly calculated, must have been ten years old at
the time of the war. He has nothing to do with Auschwitz. Besides there's no such thing as national characteristics; I still lean
towards this opinion of Inspector von Cantz. Surely, English editors are also thorough and efficient.

The publisher then steered the conversation to the question
of terms. He seemed disappointed when I declined the advance
which he offered me to enable me, as he said, to complete my
work—I must admit that for a moment I was delighted to hear my
protracted scribblings referred to for the first time as a *work*; but
a moment later my self-critical mechanism began to function again.
I found the man congenial; when he promised to send me a contract from Germany, I gave him reason to believe that I would
sign it; he sent it at once, but it's still lying without my signature
in one of the numerous drawers of Uncle Basil's hideous but
practical desk. All the same—I'm almost a writer now: I have a
publisher, if I say the word, and I'm producing a *work*. But I
haven't accepted the earnest money yet, so I'm still entitled to regard myself as an amateur.

Before we parted, the publisher referred again to my attitude towards my book.

"Doesn't it seem strange to you," he asked, "that when your

book appears it will be a German book appearing in Germany?"
And without waiting for an answer he went on: "Doesn't that
conflict with your theory that everything is chance?"

"I won't deny," I replied, "that an accident can have consequences. I consider it an accident that I was born a German. And
I refuse to regard the consequences of that accident as fate."

A harmless quirk, he must have thought. He hadn't really meant
to involve himself in a philosophical argument.

"Besides," I said, none too politely, "this thing we've been talking about is a book. And what's a book? A piece of work like any
other, a pair of shoes or . . ."

"Or the travertine block whose history you've given us to read,"
he said, requiting my rudeness with affability. "I understand. In
your opinion work is exempted from chance. Building houses, making shoes, writing books—those are necessities, the only necessities.
Very good. I like that idea."

At this point, Dr. Heckmann and I exchanged a quick glance.
For the space of that glance we were fellow conspirators, connoisseurs, specialists, amused at someone *liking* an idea, as if it
had been a kind of cheese or a bunch of flowers. But this escaped
the liker of my idea.

"It doesn't matter," he said. "I merely wanted to ask you not
to regard the fact that you write in German and are going to publish in Germany as totally absurd."

The man had courage insisting on that point with me; moreover, he was cultivated enough not to strike a false note. I might
have fallen in with someone tactless enough to speak of my *homecoming* or, worse, to drop the word *reconciliation*. That was spared
me. Still, it was high time for me to take my leave of these visitors
who had come from Germany to Rome for the sole purpose of
reading my private notes and transforming them into public ones,
that is, publishing them should the venture strike them as profitable.

They gave me back my manuscript; they had treated it with
care as I convinced myself when I got back to my room; the pages

are merely a little less tight in the binder, now it is a read manuscript, and sometimes when I look at it I have the impression that the eyes which read my words and sentences have left traces. Still, I couldn't have hoped for more discreet readers. With what consummate tact and delicacy of feeling they relieved me of any possible embarrassment by pretending to have read a novel, one more narrative written in the first person singular. With the utmost detachment they discussed *my hero* with me, as though he were not myself. And a strange thing has happened: since hearing those two first readers of my book speak of it as *fiction*, I sometimes succeed in looking upon the George alias Georg Efraim who is writing it as though he were really no longer myself but someone else: my hero. That might beguile me into treating him as such: that is, I might invent his story. My problem would be solved—instead of writing the truth about *myself*, I should only have to write a novel about *him*. What a relief it would be not only for me but for my hypothetical readers as well, if from now on I were to use not the first but the third person singular. I thought of providing an interesting and relevant plot; I dream up variant solutions, whole clusters of them, with the help of which I could have this Efraim—or whatever his name would turn out to be—escape from the constraint of his ego. Some of these developments are perfectly credible, more so perhaps than what I shall have to relate if I stick to the truth and its ego. But, as I have already said at the end of the previous chapter, it's too late for that. I can no longer summon up the strength to impose a 180-degree turn on my *work*. I shall end it as I have begun it.

I did not, as Dr. Heckmann maintained, conceive it as a novel. When I stepped out of the air-conditioned coolness of the Excelsior, the heat of Via Veneto gripped me like an incandescent mass of bitterness. I took refuge on the shady side, passed along the café tables to Porta Pinciana, and plunged into the park, but the cover of pines was not impermeable to the sun and offered little coolness. That Sunday afternoon in Berlin I began to write almost unconsciously, not knowing what course my adventure with

Anna would take on the following day. Perhaps my past with Meg, my memories of my parents, Uncle Basil, Esther and Keir did form a conception—I am a journalist after all, not a naïve writer, I've learned that one has to organize one's material—but when I described my room at the Byron I had no idea how long I'd be living here. Naturally the longer I sat over these pages the more I remembered—I wrote afterwards, not before—but even at the present moment, almost three years after those days in Berlin and London, I don't know whether Esther is dead or alive, what has become of Anna, whether my relations with Meg will end well, badly or not at all. And as at last I resume my journey to Keir's on the morning of 15 November 1962, I swear that even now as I tell of it I don't know where it will lead me. Of course I know what has happened since; but where I shall be when I have concluded these notes, I don't know. And consequently, as I gaze at the lamp-post beside The Three Tuns, the lamp-post which closes the alley known as Chichester Rents to motor traffic, I have no idea what's to come next. Can that be called plotting a novel?

In any case the lamp-post, which is not to one side of the alley but in the middle of it, didn't help me to look into the future, didn't give me second sight. But it did remind me of something, of certain slum streets in Naples closed off to traffic by stone posts. In those side streets leading off Via Tribunali as here amidst the Inns of Court, one is in an area of law courts. Which is strange. I enter Chichester Rents and pass The Three Tuns, that showpiece of a pub in the City Tavern style which is Keir's second home; the opaque window panes are set in a fine tracery of wooden columns in bas relief, painted brown below and white on top, with black bands in between; the doors are blue-grey: all the colors are dry and subdued, yet they shine in the foggy smouldering lamp-light which is one of the secrets of the English masters; when they tear these buildings down, they will have to preserve The Three Tuns. Right beside it, across from the house where Keir lives, there is a cheap restaurant with red-checked table-cloths, where

you can get steak with chips and tomatoes for four and six; I look
in, a waitress is setting the tables, but there are still no customers.
It is half-past eleven. The ground floor of Keir's house is occupied
by a cardboard wholesaler, the shop is piled high with brown boxes,
it smells of fresh cardboard and cold. The entrance to 4, Chichester Rents is a gateway, but it no longer leads anywhere, it may once
have opened into a large loading yard, now it ends in a tiny open
court full of old newspapers, broken brick, chips of wood, and overflowing slop buckets.

I can't help laughing when I recognize Keir's handwriting on
a cardboard sign nailed to one wall. "This is not a rubbish dump,"
he has written in Indian ink, in large furious letters, much in the
manner of the dreaded or welcomed notes in which he distributes
praise or blame round the office. His protest seems to have been
in vain, for though the little sign is already worn and grubby,
the yard is still a filthy hole. There is a red motor-bike leaning
against one of the walls of almost black brick. I enter the stairwell,
which is clean but old and shabby. Once again, as I did years ago
—when was I here for the last time? certainly not a year ago on my
last trip to London, it must have been before that—I read the
signs on the doors. Keir is the last remaining resident, the rest of
the place is devoted to cheap offices or workshops. On the first
floor are *E. Smith, Photo Lithographers,* and *Stevenson, Wilson
& Co., Chartered Accountants.* Messrs. Stevenson and Wilson are
representatives of a firm of provincial house agents. The wooden
stairs and banisters are a discoloured brown, the walls are painted
green to a height of some five feet. Down below it is rather dark,
on the second floor I still have to bend over the name plates to
read them. *Finnemore & Field, Ltd.* is a new name, I must ask
Keir who they are; the other two are old acquaintances: *Paul
Trummel & Associates, Design & Print,* and the mysterious *Allan
G. Barness Esq.,* who identifies himself as a member of the International Press Istanbul. In all these years Keir hasn't been able
to find out what Mr. Barness of Istanbul is actually up to. Behind
Paul Trummel's door I hear voices; they must be conferring about

design or print. Between floors there are lavatories, alternating ladies and gents. The smell of fresh cardboard and cold rising from the first floor fills the entire stairwell. All these miscellaneous existences have some connection with the newspaper world; life has cast them up on this back shore of Fleet Street where they have collected like a colony of insects: Smith, Stevenson, Wilson, Finnemore, Field, Trummel, Barness or whatever, I could be one of them; just as well as I'm Efraim, I could be Smith or the mysterious Mr. Barness, who has some connection with Turkey. Some idiotic chance has brought it about that I know this house better than any other house in the world. I know it at least as well as my parents' villa or as Uncle Basil's house in Clanricarde Gardens. Of course there are reasons for my familiarity with 4, Chichester Rents. It's not because Keir lives here that I've studied the place so thoroughly. If it were merely the house where Keir lived, I might perhaps have come here just as often, but I'd surely not have observed it so closely, not have memorized it so desperately—this I've done because it's the house where Meg met Keir and still meets him, where she came to see him for the first time in 1950 when Rogers sent her, and kept on coming until last week when, to be sure, as she has just told me, it ceased to give her pleasure. Especially in the period immediately after our marriage I literally digested 4, Chichester Rents. I am referring less to those hours of primitive tracking and watching that I spent at the steak and chips restaurant across the street, waiting for Meg to appear in the gateway and quickly vanish, usually in the direction of Chancery Lane where she would take the 171 bus which set her down not far from our flat. Those hours taught me no more about the house than that the lower part of it is painted dark-green, that the entrance to Briggs' cardboard establishment is framed in dark and cream-coloured glazed tiles, and that the whole place looks dismal, especially as night descends on the alley. Once Meg found me there, for she stepped out of Keir's house just as the lights went on in the restaurant where I was sitting at a table with a red-and-white checked cloth. I started up in a fright and averted my head but she had already seen me and came in without a moment's hesitation. "George," she said, "have you taken leave of your senses? Come along." She seized my hand and holding it fast in hers led me to the bus; we rode home without exchanging a word. After that I stopped going to the restaurant and chose an entirely different tactic; I went to the house only when I knew Keir would not be home. In his and Meg's absence I was able to investigate undisturbed; I imprinted on my mind the names on the shabby office doors, I studied the sound of my steps on the wood of the faded grey-brown stairs and imagined by comparison the clatter of Meg's shoes; I heard voices from the offices of Paul Trummel or E. Smith and, steeped in the smell of cold cardboard, tried with my eyes and sometimes even with my nails to scratch the riddle of this thing between Keir and Meg out of a small area of green wall paint. Of course I solved nothing. When I say riddle, I am not referring to the all too patent fact that Keir and Meg were doing it together, but to underlying motivations. I wanted to know what made them tick. Often in the stillness and dust of the stairwell I listened, hoping to hear the clockwork of the affair between Keir and Meg ticking. I heard nothing, but I came to know the house at 4, Chichester Rents very well.

Here I am at the third floor, where only Keir lives. I wonder if, like me, Meg stops here and looks out the window before knocking at Keir's door? Surely she does not; surely she steps straight up to the door and knocks. But I always stop for a while to gaze at the jumble of old brick walls, the backs of the squat tenement houses and tall commercial buildings behind them which are today lost in fog, the rows of chimneys on the slightly inclined roofs, the fire escapes and water pipes along the house walls, the little panes of the sash windows, some with geraniums behind them. Meg probably never stopped to look at all this, Keir enjoys it though, this view is one of his reasons for living here, Keir's love of a Dickensian view and Meg's indifference to it are two possible reactions to the same landscape, whereas I embody a third attitude: to me the house and the area in which it is located are a scene of action, the scene which has played a greater part in my life than any other. I can ask myself quite dispassionately whether I might not be mistaken, whether certain other places may not in the last analysis have been more important, Bismarckstrasse, for instance, or Clanricarde Gardens, or a battlefield in Sicily, or Vietnam, or the extermination camps where my parents were killed. But I come obstinately back to Chichester Rents, I persist in believing that my life was decided here; it's a mania with me, I know it, a manic fixation on an utterly unworthy place; moreover, when I stop to think, it's preposterous that all this should have happened merely because one day a shabby agent sent an ambitious young woman to call on some old swine, but that's how it is, the name of the place is Chichester Rents, I can't help it.

Keir isn't an old swine, hatred made me say that; in the first place he wasn't old when he met Meg, he was only fifty-one, and in the second place he's not a swine, but only lecherous in a natural, free and easy way, he has something that makes it easy for a woman to let herself go, he is infectiously uninhibited, which makes me envious because I am inhibited. I am the typical prod-uct of a Jewish bourgeois family from old Prussia: a pure-bred puritan. My father was a businessman, he wasn't quite as cultivated as Uncle Basil, but the supreme and self-evident values governing the home of my childhood were idealism and monogamy. Uncle Basil, who wrote poems in which he sublimated his love for a blond lady by the name of Cora, did the rest. The upshot is that I'm afraid of women. I'm afraid of women and I'm envious of a chap like Keir who can carry off a seduction as easily as he can un-cork a bottle. Yet his origins are far more puritanical than mine, a clan of Scottish Presbyterian parsons from Argyllshire; in his flat, which I am about to enter, there are pictures of gaunt, grim-faced ancestors, stiff as pokers, but Keir, though tall, is not at all gaunt; on the contrary, he is a stout man and in him the stiffness of the Scottish Hornes has transformed itself into the placid cor-pulence of the habitual drinker; of their religious gloom little more has remained than the sceptical coldness in the blue of his eyes,

a blue that always seems to have a thin film of dust on it. Which
shows that a man can also develop in opposition to his origins
and makes me still more envious of Keir. When I once called his
attention to the difference between himself and his ancestors, he
explained wryly, with one of his usual far-fetched appeals to philosophy, that he embodied the dialectical swing from quality to
quantity. The quantity of women he consumes is indeed enormous, perhaps exceeded only by his consumption of beer—strange
that his alcoholism has impaired neither his sexual powers nor his
intelligence—that is, until recently, as I gather from Meg's remarks. I don't mean to say that Keir is promiscuous, he's much too
particular for that, he has taste and shows great discrimination.
Still, he helps himself to every pretty woman he can get. To draw
on one of my recent Berlin acquisitions, Keir has rolled almost
every remotely attractive female reporter and secretary on our conservative paper on the hearth-rug. I picked that up from the group
of men at Lampe's party whose congenial merriment I punctured
with an uppercut when, from speculations about whether ladies
should be rolled on the hearth-rug, or on some other variety of bed-
ding, they proceeded to talk about being gassed. That's how I am,
a puritan, a spoil-sport, a disrupter of innocent enjoyment. Once
in the same vein I advised Keir to draw the line between office
and bedchamber, but he only laughed. "You don't understand
women," he said. "They work better for having had a tumble. And
not even because they're hoping for another; no, just like that." I
pointed out that some of our female employees had left us for
that very reason and had made names for themselves on other
papers. "That's just it," he said. "That proves I have no cause to
reproach myself. It didn't do them any harm. It spurred them on
to higher things." Not only I, myself, but most of my colleagues
detest Keir when he puts on this pasha act. But he is a pasha.
He has developed into a father figure, the office patriarch. He
helps himself to the women who, we dimly sense, were meant
for us. Accordingly, he is hated or loved or both. He created un-
businesslike but productive tensions in the office. Occasionally,

to be sure, one of his women lasted. He married twice. Of his first
wife I know nothing, she died before the war; by that marriage
he has two grown-up daughters whom he rarely sees. I met his
second wife. He lived with her after the war in Wimbledon in a
ramshackle bungalow with a wooden veranda, she was some sort
of leftist aristocrat, a hard-drinking beanpole of a woman, but interesting and handsome, who derided him for his political opinions; the atmosphere in their home was sort of English Chekhov.
It must always have been winter when I called on them for I
don't remember ever having seen Keir's wife except in a rather
empty room, warming her hands over a little paraffin stove, surrounded by three or four setters. As far as I know, they were never
divorced, but in 1948 or thereabouts he moved away from Wimbledon and set up house by himself in Chichester Rents. At any
rate some time before he met Meg. Meg wasn't to blame for
breaking up Keir's second marriage.

Keir has no name plate. The grey paint on his door is peeling
in places; I've never seen it in any other condition, one would think
the paint would be all gone, to my knowledge Keir has never
had it renewed; at some moment or other the door must have decided to stop deteriorating, outwardly at least; now it merely looks
hard and desiccated like an old biscuit. There is a brass plate bearing the arms of the City of London, then further down, a slit
for letters and a brass knob. No bell, not even a knocker. I give
three quick knocks with the knuckle of my right forefinger; my
old familiar knock: if Keir hasn't forgotten, he already knows who
is at his door. Behind the door there is a tiny windowless corridor;
the flat consists of a living room, a bedroom, this corridor and a
boxroom containing all sorts of rubbish in addition to a tin bath
and a lavatory—so that Keir is not obliged to use the lavatory on
the stairs. No sound. I wait, expecting to hear the door between
the living room and the corridor open, a development which will
be accompanied by the creaking of the rocking chair where Keir
has been sitting, which always continues to rock and creak a
little more when Keir gets up. Today this sound—that has played

so important a part in my life—I must have heard it a hundred times—does not produce itself. I knock again but nothing stirs. I look at my wrist-watch, it's not quite twelve; Keir must have gone out earlier than usual. Today of all days! Here I've flown from Rome to London to tell him what I've learned about Esther from Mother Ludmilla and he's gone. For this I wasn't prepared. I wait a while, alone with my irritation. Keir has put one over on me. This story I have to tell him—I can only tell it in the dusty silence of Chichester Rents, under the pictures of his ancestors who will look down gloomily as he sits in his rocking chair listening to me. It's not a bar-room story, and it's not the right kind of story to tell in his office, not even if he switches off the phone and instructs his secretary not to disturb us. I catch myself thinking—in my newly acquired German argot—that I won't tell him this story, no, I'll hit him with it. If anything can stop the creaking of that Victorian article of furniture, it's my story. But I am obliged to withdraw, my business undone. Slowly I descend the stairs, past the name plates, past the conversation that is still going on behind the door of Paul Trummel & Associates, amidst the cold smell of cardboard and November.

Somehow I had expected a convent when I rode out to Steglitz on that Monday afternoon to meet Mother Ludmilla; but the house in Steglitz proved instead to be a large Berlin villa dating back to the eighteen seventies and remodelled as a school. A nun serving as attendant or secretary led me to a room with dark brown panelling and a resplendent parquet floor, where I waited at least fifteen minutes for Mother Ludmilla. In this room there was nothing but the high panelling, a desk, chairs, and a large Madonna in rather poor taste. Since the afternoon was declining into dusk, the ceiling lamp had already been lit, but its light made scant impact on the darkness of all that wood, which strenuous cleaning had raised to a high polish. Not a grain of dust sparkled, and throughout the time I spent waiting I heard not the slightest sound except once the striking of a clock. Then Mother Ludmilla entered, held out her hand affably but did not press mine, bade me resume my seat, and sat down at the desk across from me. She is a rather large, stout woman, but she did not strike me as heavy because she moved easily and her handsome aged face was pale and transparent. With such adjectives I am drawing the conventional picture of what one expects of an elderly dignified nun; but since Mother Ludmilla's face had indeed the beauty of old age and was also pale and transparent, I have no choice. Her habit consisted of a brown gown and a white mantle. During our conversation she seldom looked at me directly; she sat with her profile turned towards me, but she did not pose or take an unctuous tone; her manner of speaking was quite unpretentious and not devoid of sympathy. I had planned to open the interview with a little trap, by asking if she had been at the school in 1938, but such was the impression she made on me that I immediately abandoned any idea of sounding her out and stated my mission directly. I described my own origins, the circumstances of my acquaintance with Esther and her mother, and finally explained that Keir desired news of his daughter, should there be any. At first she seemed quite willing to speak.

"I remember Esther Bloch very well," she said. "A delightful child. She had trouble with mathematics, but she was very good at languages. I wasn't the principal at that time, I taught English and French—I haven't time for that any more—and Esther was one of my best pupils."

I waited, to give her time to search her memory. That is inaccurate: actually I watched her pretend to be searching her memory; in this she was not very successful, for it was plain that she had remembered Esther instantly. She saw it all quite clearly and I had the impression that like Frau Heiss she had been expecting such a visit as mine for a long while. Expecting it, yes, but not dreading it like Frau Heiss. Unlike Frau Heiss, Mother Ludmilla seemed very much at her ease.

"Of course," she said, "Esther was often downcast. She was our only Jewish pupil." And with a sigh: "It wasn't easy for us."

"You mean it wasn't easy for you to dismiss Esther from your school?" In making this remark I was unable to repress a slightly aggressive tone, but Mother Ludmilla remained unruffled.

"Oh," she said, almost disdainfully, "that wasn't until the end. Long before that, Esther had ceased to understand the world. When I say it wasn't easy for us, I mean that it wasn't easy for us to communicate with her. It was our duty to explain the world she lived in, and that we were unable to do. We ourselves were utterly bewildered."

"Bewildered?" I said. "You?"

This time she looked at me only briefly, then again she turned aside, and in the long silence following my question I heard the clock that had struck before striking outside somewhere.

"What could we have told the child?" she asked. "That God was putting her to the test? We talked it over among ourselves and came to the conclusion that God couldn't be so cruel. The only other explanation would have been that men had become so evil that now the Devil ruled the world. We didn't feel we had the right to instil so terrible a truth in the heart of a child."

"And besides, if God can't prevent people from being wicked, you'd have had to admit that He's not as all-powerful as you claim."

"Our Church," she said, "believes that God is all-powerful and that He has given men free will."

This last sentence sounded as though, even in speaking, she had begun to doubt it.

"Then what did you do?" I asked, my impatience getting the better of my manners. I hadn't come here to listen to theological arguments. "After all you had something more important to do than explain the world to Esther."

"You wish to know whether we helped her? Of course we tried."

I am a journalist, or at least I was. In our trade there are moments when we hold our breath in expectation, when we suddenly feel that a story is about to break. This is a truly instinctive reaction; a feeling in the lungs and belly, not in the head, tells us there's something in the air, a new possibility, a news item that will change the situation. How rare such moments are in our work! Even in the most thorough investigations we seldom come across a news item that really changes anything. It seems possible that in my entire career as a newspaperman I only once had the privilege of sending out a really big story—when I discovered, and was in a position to prove, that while the fighting was still going on in Indochina a Vietminh delegation was holding peace talks in Paris with the French government. Of course the private news I obtained from Mother Ludmilla can hardly be compared with such a break; the story I phoned to London at that time, in 1953, long before the battle of Dien Bien Phu, materially influenced international reactions to the war; beside it, quite apart from the absurdity of comparing public and private affairs, what the Carmelite nun had to tell me about Esther was not great, but, at the most, interesting news; and yet oddly enough, I waited for Mother Ludmilla to tell me what she had done to help Esther with the same eagerness as I waited in that house with the re-sounding iron doors in rue de Nevers—I dreamed of it that after-noon in Berlin when I embarked on these notes—for the hints, proffered in a slow, hissing French by three small lean men in European dress, three small lean men with high cheekbones and topaz-coloured skin, who, because they wished to influence inter-national reactions to the war, had decided to reveal a secret to me. Was Mother Ludmilla going to disclose a secret in a moment? In any case she was thinking of things she was reluctant to speak of, for she showed no consideration for my silent expectation; per-haps she wasn't even aware of my eagerness; it was a long while before she withdrew her eyes from the dark panelling in which her thoughts seemed to have been immersed.

"We knew that Esther's father lived in England," she said finally. "We knew he was an Englishman. And when the situa-tion became really critical, we got in touch with the British Em-bassy in Berlin after a talk with Esther's mother. I remember it all clearly; one morning Mother Klara, our mother superior at the time, drove to Wilhelmstrasse where your embassy was then situated."

Your embassy, she said, although I had told her that I had been Esther's childhood friend. She fully acknowledged my transformation into an English journalist.

"Mother Klara," she went on, "spoke to one of the ambassador's secretaries, an intelligent and influential man, so she said. He promised to take the case in hand, to communicate with Esther's father, Herr . . . what's his name again?"

"Horne," I said.

". . . to get in touch with this Herr Horne, at whose behest you have come here today, and to discuss with him what might be done. Actually I don't believe there was much possibility of doing anything. Herr Horne, to be sure, was registered here as Esther's natural father, but Frau Bloch had sole custody of the child, she had never sued for support. The only thing Herr Horne could have done was, with Frau Bloch's consent, to initiate adoption proceedings, which as you know are very complicated and long drawn out, and even if he had succeeded in adopting the child, it is doubtful whether Esther would have been allowed to leave the country."

"That is not true," I said. "Up to the beginning of the war all Jews were allowed to emigrate. They merely had to renounce their property. The problem was not whether Esther would have been allowed to leave Germany, but whether she would have been admitted to England. And for that a simple affadavit from her father would have sufficed."

"Really?" she muttered. "You must know." But she seemed to regard my remark as a diversion. "I believe we waited too long. We sisters should have taken steps in Esther's behalf years before."

She went into further details, lost herself in legal subtleties and political considerations, circumnavigating some dark truth that lurked behind her words, waiting to be released. At length I interrupted her.

"What did Mr. Horne do?" I asked.

She kept her eyes averted. "Nothing," she replied. "When she went back to the embassy a fortnight later, Mother Klara was told that Esther's father wished no steps to be taken in the matter."

During our conversation it had grown dark outside. The lamp made little impact on the polished panelling of the room and merely cast a circle of drab light on the desk between the nun and myself. It was so quiet; impossible that this room should be in Berlin. Where was it then? I don't know. I stumbled over Keir's secret in a place beyond space. Since I've known Keir's secret, I've come to understand why even at that lunch in Rome during the war, in the course of which Keir told me he was Esther's father, I seemed to see more in his eyes than a father's fear for his child. Even then, as I have written, I saw a shadow of guilt in them when he told me with a shrug that he had last corresponded with Marion Bloch in May 1936, and now I understand the urgent, hectic tone that always came into his voice when he asked me, and not only me but all sorts of other people, to get him news of his child. Now I know why he wept during our telephone call that Sunday morning in Berlin.

Mother Ludmilla talked fast to get the embarrassing part of the story over with. "The people at your embassy were distressed at having to give Mother Klara such news. They wanted to help her, they offered to engage an English lawyer to exert pressure on Herr Horne, but we were obliged to let the matter drop because the Gestapo began to question Mother Klara about her visits to the British Embassy, they always had their spies watching the entrance; she spoke of school business, the transfer of books and other materials from our English schools, but of course they didn't believe her, and in the end we thought it would be safer to send her to our parent convent at Ratibor. We're Silesian nuns, you see."

I didn't listen very attentively, because my thoughts were still with Keir. The moment Mother Ludmilla informed me of Keir's behaviour, I began to understand what it means to share the secret of another man's guilt. Consequently the important hint she gave me in speaking of Silesian nuns and the convent at Ratibor made no impression on me at first. My attention revived only when she began to speak of Keir, trying to find excuses for him.

"I presume," she said, "that Esther's father just didn't know what was at stake. Frau Bloch was also partly to blame. She should have insisted on Herr Horne's adopting Esther before it was too late. If Esther had been adopted, the German authorities would have regarded her as a half-Jew, she could even have stayed on at our school, quite possibly she would have had no trouble at all."

"Except," I said, "that one day they'd have taken her mother away and killed her with poison gas."

We spoke a little more of the legal possibilities, until we realized that all our sentences began with the little word "if." The conversation had run aground, but I was nevertheless surprised when Mother Ludmilla rose to conclude it. I had no choice but to get up myself, but I was determined not to let her off so easily.

"You've told me," I said, "what Mr. Horne failed to do. But you haven't told me yet what you yourself did."

She had thrust her hands into the pockets of her brown gown; she had ceased to be anything more than a brown and ivory-white habit with a pale, transparent, elderly face. She was taller than I. Almost everyone is taller than I, in Germany and in England at least. That's one reason why I feel more at my ease in Rome. In Rome most people are about my size. Still, I can't say that Mother Ludmilla was looking down at me, for she wasn't looking at me at all.

"What do you think we should have done?" she asked.

I shrugged my shoulders. "Save the child, for instance," I said. "Your Church is very powerful. It has often saved people when it wanted to."

"We were not very powerful at that time."

Each of her answers had a purpose, the purpose of withholding the one answer I anticipated. If I had only known during that interview whether nuns are permitted to lie! I still don't know. Though I have been living in Rome all this time, I know almost nothing about the ways of the Catholic Church. I decided to stake everything on one card. Then I should see whether or not nuns lie.

"Mother Ludmilla," I said, looking her straight in the face, "you are concealing something from me."

Now that I had addressed her for the first time by her name and title, she at last gave me a friendly, attentive, expectant look.

I appealed to her. "I bet," I said quickly, "that when Esther ran away that morning she came to you. Tell me now, that's true, isn't it? She came to you or to Mother Klara, and you saved her?"

Her look was still friendly, but her eyes, which were blue—blue and old—had lost their shadow of a smile.

"You must remember how it was when Esther came to you," I urged her. "She had a little grey-black dog with her, a cocker spaniel, don't you remember, Mother Ludmilla? It's not possible that you didn't help a thirteen-year-old child who came to you with her little dog."

"We ordered her to go straight back to her mother."

At last it was out. Anna Krystek's hunch had been right. Esther had gone to the nuns. And now I'd get the rest of the story out of Mother Ludmilla.

"But she didn't go home," I said.

"How can you know that?"

Now she seemed tortured, I felt sorry for her but I didn't stop. Feeling that I was on the brink of the truth, I repeated what Frau Schlesinger had told me on Friday afternoon at the Jewish Old People's Home in Iranische Strasse.

"Frau Bloch told Frau Schlesinger she never saw Esther again. You don't keep secrets in a cattle waggon on the way to Auschwitz."

To this she had nothing to say. She had averted her eyes from me long before.

"We ordered Esther to go straight back home," she said. "I can't tell you any more."

The reception room of that villa disguised as a convent surrounded us with its meticulous cleanliness, its unbearable stillness. I went to the window and looked out on the broad drive, the tall, almost leafless trees in the garden, the iron railings, and behind it a lifeless street lighted by a street lamp.

"That morning when Esther came to you," I asked, "was it in this room that you spoke with her?"

"I believe so," she said.

"And when she went away, you and Mother Klara looked after her as she went out the gate and along the railings with her little dog. She must have spoken to her dog, she must have told him not to run out into the road. You did look after her, didn't you, Mother Ludmilla, you didn't just go back to your classroom to give an English or French lesson? You looked on as a child in tears, a child you knew well, walked along talking to her dog."

I tortured Mother Ludmilla. Slowly she took her hands out of her pockets and raised them to her cheeks. She turned round to me and the movement withdrew her face from the grey circle of lamplight. In the shadow I could not make out what expression it took on, whether it became an image of guilt or of indignation, neither perhaps, perhaps only an image of darkness. She did not confess. When she lowered her hands, she had regained her composure. She went to the door.

"But you'll admit," I said, "that Mother Klara said to you: 'Quick, quick, run after the child.' Or she told you to take her home? That's what happened, isn't it? You left the villa with Esther, meaning to take her home, and on the way you changed your mind and you didn't take her back to her mother, but saved her. Won't you tell me that's how it was?"

She had already put her hand on the door handle. When she spoke, her tone was quite official.

"Herr Horne has no right to ask us such questions," she said.

She gave me a brief nod and left the room. A moment later the

attendant came and took me to the front door, which she bolted
behind me.

Keir didn't give me a chance to tell him this story—to hit him
with it—although I found him in Chichester Rents after all that
November noonday, not at his flat but at The Three Tuns. Knowing his habits, I look in at the pub. I push the door of the
luncheon bar, and there he is, standing at the mahogany bar with
his usual pint of mild and bitter. He always orders full pints, he
would never, like a common mortal, content himself with a half
pint. How many he already has under his belt I can't make out;
in the course of the half hour we spent together he drained three
pints; it's beyond me how a man can pour such quantities of beer
into himself, but Keir's capacity seems unlimited. I don't care
for this lukewarm English draught beer, I order a bottle of lager.
Keir gives it a look of derision. Our greeting has been a casual
hello, as if we had met the day before. Very briefly Keir showed
that he was glad to see me: for an instant his eyes, which always
seemed to be coated with a film of dust, were clear blue. He is
dressed as usual: pin-striped trousers and black jacket; dirty trench-
coat open at the top, revealing the flowered silk waistcoat from a
shop in the Burlington Arcade. As he drinks, the waistcoat
tightens over his belly and slips upward, showing me that as usual
his trousers are held up not by a belt or braces but by two ties
knotted together. He is shod in the extraordinary wide pumps
which he has made to order. This get-up brings him as close to his
ideal—an English gentleman of the days of Bishop Berkeley and
Edmund Burke—as is possible in the twentieth century. Another
advantage of it is that there is no need to change when his work
permits him to go straight from the office to Covent Garden,
the place, I believe, which he loves best in all the world. He hasn't
always dressed like this; he adopted this costume in 1948 when
he became editor-in-chief of our conservative paper; up until then
he had played all manner of roles; I have described, for example,
how on the day I met him he played first the military man and

then the Cambridge don. In those days he relished those parts; today all costumes have become indifferent to him; in the end, to be sure, he kept one of them, but it has ceased to be a masquerade and become a mere eccentric habit; all Fleet Street knows his manias, Keir is a Fleet Street original, nothing more, and seldom does Keir's habit of holding his trousers up with ties provoke so much as a smile.

I'm not satisfied with this description of Keir. Reading the previous paragraph over at Uncle Basil's art-nouveau desk at the Byron in Rome, I feel that I have not succeeded in bringing him to life. Innumerable drafts of a portrait have found their way to my Roman waste-paper basket, but what I have finally retained and here inserted still doesn't suit me, it strikes me as incomplete, fragmentary. Yet Keir is so conspicuous a type, a man with such striking features, that I long thought I could portray him with their help. While speaking of my telephone conversation with him in Berlin, for instance, I still believed I could show the man by listing his salient characteristics; I spoke of his fat face, bloated with drink, of the mop of white hair over it, the bushy white brows and dusty eyes; later I described Keir at the age of forty-five as I first met him during the war in Rome, a man already fat but still nimble; I called his mouth at that stage *arched* and *full of character*, his nose *prominent, rather broad* and *well shaped*. Goodness! What a man must learn, what bad habits he must get rid of if he wants to become a novelist, that is, someone whose trade it is to bring people to life. (I hope Dr. Heckmann doesn't take this sentence—should he ever see it—at face value. Since the man is utterly devoid of humour, I wish here to state explicitly that I have no ambition whatsoever to write a novel. These, my dear Herr Doktor, are private notes, though your boss has my permission to call them a novel if I ever finish them and decide to let him have them. The magic word *novel* boosts sales, so I am told, and I shall have to think about such things if I finally set myself up as a professional writer. I haven't been drawing a salary since last spring, I can no longer list my meals and hotel bill as expenses, my small savings are running out, and I shall have to decide what to do about the house in Wannsee, whether to accept the advance the German publisher has offered me, return contritely to journalism, or take up some other trade. The mere thought that I may some day be compelled to wonder what to write *next*, sends the shivers down my spine. Well, for the present I'll wait and see.)

Keir's fingernails are as dirty as ever. When a man has such dirty fingernails, he ought to know better than to produce six little silver-edged tortoise-shell boxes, to set them up on the counter under the eyes of the barkeeper and of several gentlemen who are having their morning beer, and perform his snuff-taking ritual. But Keir is not the least bit embarrassed. At once fascinated and repelled, his audience looks on as his thick, strong and none too clean fingers toy with the delicate boxes. His hands are the hands of a sensitive colossus; with his right hand he carefully selects a few grains from each box and piles them on his left wrist; critically the dust-blue eyes under the mop of white hair that has fallen over his forehead look down across his belly, examine the mixture of light and dark grains, until at length his nose, which is of the same caliber as everything else in Keir—heavy, voluminous, pendulous—draws them in. The inadequately washed fingers rub the nose. During the whole procedure Keir has talked shop with me, we have struck up a conversation about the paper, Keir has begun to expatiate on make-up and type sizes, as though the crisis into which he has steered our paper were a typographical problem. And I have gone along with him. Now Keir is silent, we are all waiting, not only the gentlemen in the luncheon bar— where no one ever has lunch—but also the workers standing at the public bar across from us. The private bar to the right is deserted, it is intended for ladies, but I have never seen any ladies at The Three Tuns. An atmosphere of high suspense sets in— framed in mahogany, plush and mirrors, for the interior of The Three Tuns is not in City Tavern but in Gin Palace style, a prime example of the great Victorian contribution to bar-room architecture. As Victorian as Keir's rocking chair. Incredible that Meg should do it with this filthy colossus. At length he is shaken by a mighty sneeze, a vast release; he takes out his snuff-browned handkerchief and blows his nose copiously; after that he feels freer, he talks more fluently and coherently; the whole pub goes back to its conversations and glasses.

"Good job," I said to Keir a moment ago, pointing to *The Observer* that is protruding from his coat pocket. He took my allusion to our chief competitor for what it was meant to be, an indirect criticism of our own product. We got to talking shop. Keir takes refuge in technical and aesthetic considerations. I find no opening in which to slip my resignation, let alone my Mother Ludmilla story. Here in this ancient pub Keir is fighting on his own ground, he is unconquerable. But in the midst of our conversation I notice that his hand trembles when he picks up his beer glass. It trembles only while he is raising his glass from the counter and holding it up in front of him, before he sets it to his lips; Keir knows this, and he is also aware that I have stared at his hand for a moment and seen it trembling; consequently he makes a visible effort to abbreviate the interval between the seizing of the glass and the drinking, although it has always been one of his drinker's pleasures to prolong this moment—Keir holding forth with beer glass in hand has always been one of the local sights. I am surprised. All the more so because I noticed no trembling during the snuff-taking ceremony.

Here I must insert a digression about the British weekly press, because Keir's existence cannot be understood without a knowledge of his professional problem. Such a sentence shows, incidentally, to what extent I am already thinking of my publisher and his public, before whom I am to "appear"; if I were merely writing personal reminiscences for private consumption, I could spare myself the trouble of such an explanation, for then I should be alone with Keir; two masons setting a travertine block in place can communicate by means of an occasional cry unintelligible to outsiders. But a prospective reader has buttonholed me and wants me to explain what I mean when I point to *The Observer* and

say: "Good job," and what it means when Keir begrudgingly
agrees. Very well, I'll make it as short as possible: We have in
England Sunday papers which knowingly and ruthlessly purvey
sex and crime and run into millions of copies; then there are the
Sunday editions of the daily papers, which affect a more serious
attitude, one of these is our weekly which is the Sunday edition
of a moderate conservative daily; and finally there are the weeklies
in folio format, which provide serious analyses and are not, strictly
speaking, newspapers but reviews. Keir's problem is that he would
like to put out a popular, mass-circulation paper, but that for this
the usual Sunday paper is not equipped; papers like ours are
staffed, not like the daily papers, with professional journalists, but
with university men, writers and intellectuals; Keir himself is a
university man; true, he has hard years of journalism behind him,
but Cambridge sticks to him, he is far too cultivated a man to hit
on the tone that would be needed to transform our middle-class
Sunday paper into a mass organ. Nevertheless he pursues this
phantom, despises the highbrow members of his staff and is sometimes furious with me, because I, who am not an academic but
one of the few professional journalists on his team, am always
trying to raise the level of his publication. For a few years he had
some success with his policy, he made inroads on the masses,
though of course he lost quite a few regular subscribers in the
process. But for some time his system has ceased to work, because
he refuses to take account of the effect of the technological revolution on the lower classes; the lower classes are not as low as they
used to be, they are inexorably rising, developing into a new in-
telligentsia who wish to be provided with information and adult
entertainment; this doesn't fit in with Keir's conservative outlook,
in which society is eternally divided into sharply delimited classes,
a working class, a lower middle class, an upper middle class, and a
leisure class; the mixture that is taking place goes against his grain,
he can't adjust to it; this man, who wanted to put out a paper for
the little man in Finchley or West Bromwich and who is well
equipped to edit an academic review, has succeeded in doing

neither; he gapes in bewilderment at a faceless new world, with
the result that his paper is either too boring or not boring enough;
the headlines are poor, the subjects of the articles ill chosen, and
the presentation inept; the whole tone is wrong. I have no intention of asking him about the circulation; Simmons, our circulation
manager, will tell me later. (I never did find out, because I didn't
set foot in the office on that visit to London.)

Professional problems—I'm sick to death of them. Keir seems
to sense my indifference, for our conversation gradually dries up.
Silent, undoubtedly weighed down with beer, Keir Horne, gentleman, stares across at the public bar framed in engraved mirrors
which transform his colossal figure into a shadow. He has always
planned our conservative paper in this pub, with an eye to the
order which he holds to be eternal: for gentlemen, for workers, for
ladies.

To bring him back to earth, I take advantage of this moment
of silence to bring up my visit to Mother Ludmilla. We've been
beating about the bush long enough.

"Keir," I say, "I've been to Esther's school. I've spoken to
Esther's old teacher. Esther really did run away in 1938. . . ."

Am I mistaken, or has Keir raised his hand? Is he really signal-
ling me with his raised and slightly trembling hand to say no
more? Has he really started to talk about something else, something entirely different, just as I'm on the point of giving him
the news for which he supposedly sent me to Berlin? I stare at
him aghast as he begins to tell me about a dream he had last night,
or so he says; since he doesn't sleep at night but in the morning—
he certainly hasn't been up for more than an hour—the memory of
this dream must be fresh.

"In my dream," he tells me, "I had a picture, a colour photograph or something of the sort, of a beautiful Italian villa. Over
the picture there was a sheet of transparent paper, and when I
moved the paper the villa appeared either by day in the sunshine
or at night in a wonderfully blue Italian light."

I've already caught the meaning. Indifferently I enter into the new subject. "Splendid," I say. "You've finally decided to take a holiday. It's high time you got away from Chichester Rents for a while."

He shakes his head irritably. "It must be a memory of some stage set I've seen at Covent Garden. In *Norma*, if I remember rightly, there was a villa of that sort, or in *L'Elisir d'Amore*." He forgets himself and hums a Donizetti aria. Keir's real love is music. He's a passionate operagoer, he spends almost all his free evenings at Covent Garden, they've often sent for him at the opera when a crisis arose at the paper. Unfortunately his musical taste is very British: he listens raptly to romantic operas, Rossini, Bellini, Weber, or worse, Lortzing, Meyerbeer, Massenet's *Manon*. He has no use for Bach, but for César Franck, as he once assured me, he could die. He breaks off the aria and with trembling hand takes a sip of beer.

"The funny part of it was," he goes on, "that this trick with the transparent paper, the change of night and day in the picture, only worked when I was alone. I tried to show it to someone but it just wouldn't come off."

"To whom?" I ask quickly. "Anyone in particular?"

I notice his hesitation at once. He's wondering whether to tell me, finally he decides to lie.

"I don't remember who it was. I've forgotten."

So it was Meg. But perhaps it's only my jealousy that makes me suspect that—my jealousy which died long ago but still twitches like a dead eel. Actually it's all the same to me whether the sleeping Keir wanted to show his magic picture to Meg or to someone else. But of course the key to his dream lay in this person's identity.

"Come on, concentrate," I said. "Who was it?"

His antennae are still functioning perfectly, he decides to tell me the name.

"Now I remember," he says. "It was Goodman."

Mark Goodman is our sports editor, a wiry little man of fifty, a Jew. Keir likes him but there is no great intimacy between

them. I'm ashamed of having thought of Meg; I should have
known that dreams never feature the character one would expect.

"What, Goodman?" I ask in amazement. "He's certainly not
interested in Italian landscapes."

"Yes, isn't it odd?" says Keir. Then he breaks down and tells
me all about it. "Imagine. We were lying on a bed together, a very
neatly made bed, the cover was turned down. Mark lay at the head,
I at the foot, and he kept talking; he was saying weird things on
some mystical subject, I don't remember what, only that he was
talking very profoundly about something very obscure."

Both of us have to laugh. "Mark, of all people!" I say. Mark
Goodman is extremely sensible and down-to-earth, just about
the sanest man on the staff.

"And all the time he was talking," Keir went on, "I wanted to
show him my picture. But the paper wouldn't move. Earlier, when
I was alone, I could move it back and forth and produce day and
night at will, but I couldn't make it perform for Mark. After a
while I discovered that the paper was fastened to the picture with
an iron clamp, but when I tried to loosen it, I woke up."

At the time, at The Three Tuns, I was unable to interpret the
dream. Today in Rome I presume that it reflected Keir's desire to
be a normal man. In his sleep he had power over day and night,
but his gift horrified him, so he haled it before the court of common sense; he tried to show it and explain it to a sound sensible
man, but he couldn't; under the eyes of our sports editor the
mysterious picture shut itself up tight. Keir's masochism has in-
vaded his unconscious: in his dream he transforms the affable,
sensible Mark into a great teacher of mysticism, Mark lies at the
head, Keir at the foot of the bed; Keir longs for normality,
he wants to submit to it. Because Keir isn't only a pasha, a father
figure; at least half of him is the exact opposite, and that is the
source of his success with women; women sense that they will
be able to dominate Keir, at least in certain moments, that he
will surrender to them, and the prospect attracts them irresistibly.
This isn't mere guesswork on my part or something I've inferred

from a dream that I may have analyzed all wrong. No, Meg herself has told me as much in her sometimes rather brutal way.

Why does Keir talk about type sizes and dreams—while ingurgitating vast quantities of beer—instead of asking me impatiently what I've found out about Esther as he did on the phone three weeks ago when he rang me at my Berlin hotel? Granted, my story about Mother Ludmilla isn't a bar-room story; but still he might arrange to meet me for a quiet talk, or ask me to his flat that afternoon. But he does nothing of the sort. Perhaps he's expecting me to go to the office with him later and stay on for hours, in the course of which a conversation would spring up of its own accord, an informal chat in which understatement, the tutelary deity of British conversation, would gloss over all unpleasantness? But I don't believe so. I am convinced that the moment I pushed the door of The Three Tuns he knew why I had come.

I suddenly realize that the man before me is done for. It was absurd to fly from Rome to London to tell Keir what I had learned about Esther from Mother Ludmilla—he has no desire to know. For he knows it already, he's bound to know it if the nun told the truth. If the nun told the truth, Keir knows that he was once asked to save his child. And that he declined to do so. Though in the course of my conversation with Mother Ludmilla I already knew that Keir had forsaken his daughter, that he had not responded to her cry for help, I still thought, quite absurdly, when taking the plane in Rome that I was doing him a favour; I would bring him hope, the hope that Esther had survived and might still be found. He must have known that this would be the outcome if I had any luck with my inquiries. Nevertheless when I boarded the plane at Fiumicino I imagined that I should be a messenger of hope, and it didn't dawn on me until this morning at The Three Tuns that I am first and foremost a man who shares the knowledge of Keir's guilt. I, Georg Efraim, am the sole witness to his shame. That's why he talks about dreams and type sizes.

Then why did he send me to Berlin if he doesn't want to hear

what I have found out? I don't know. But I dimly suspect that
it's enough for him to know that I now have my ear to the wall
behind which he committed his crime. There is no need for me to
say that I have listened: Keir knows that I know the whole story.

Crime! What a word! Contritely I go back to the technique of
understatement—what Keir has on his conscience is a sin of omission, nothing more.

Can he have wanted me to share the knowledge of his guilt?
Is it so heavy a burden to him that he needs someone to confess it to? Possibly. Yes, it's possible, but not very likely.

Or did he wish at this late date to even old scores, to make
amends to me for the fact that he has long been aware of the
taint on my life? Now that his hands have begun to tremble when
they hold a beer glass, now that he has become editor-in-chief
of a paper whose circulation has been steadily falling off and that
Meg has probably stopped coming to see him, has he decided to
leave me a legacy: the knowledge that he and I are quits? Are
my journeys to Chichester Rents, is the creaking of a rocking chair
to be made good by the tears of a child who was betrayed by her
father? Is Keir trying to tell me that there is a curse, a scandal, a
secret shame at the bottom of every life, that no life is complete
unless it bears the secret brand mark of a crime? Has he wished,
at the end of our relationship, to give me a lesson in tolerance?

To tell the truth, I drew a different conclusion from his lack
of curiosity. Before leaving The Three Tuns I reviewed the main
events of Keir's life. He was born in 1899, which made him sixty-
three—I am speaking of that day three years ago. He barely escaped the First World War and in the second he was too old for
combat duty—lucky bastard! His forbears were sombre men from a
rainy country. From 1918 to 1928 he was at Cambridge; a brilliant
undergraduate, he took the Classical Tripos with a first. Because he went in for philosophy, he studied German; learning
German had been child's play for him, just as it is child's play for
him to do the *Times* crossword while dictating an editorial. He
learned German in Berlin, where he seems to have attended the

university for a term or two in the middle of his Cambridge period. He must have begotten Esther in 1925 after helping himself to Marion Bloch, one of the most beautiful women in Berlin. He must have been one of those who left the bars in the early morning hours and walked down the deserted Tauentzienstrasse in the cool light of dawn. The women who walked with him were charmingly daring. Marion Bloch was surely something else; she was beautiful and nothing more, which is why he dropped her. He was quite unaware that she was a Jewess from old West Berlin. He listened to the German professors and students, and learned a good deal. What he heard amused him; he listened with amusement to this strange race of men, and it never occurred to him as he listened that everything he heard might end in the tears of a child, of his child. Then he went back to England, wrote a little book about Gnosis and obtained a lectureship. In 1929 he threw up his academic career and went into journalism. He grew fat. Fat and wearing a succession of masks, he made a career in journalism; he married twice. In 1938 he disowned Esther, a year later the war broke out. Now after thirty-five years of journalism he is done for. To understand this life I should have to start a new book. This is the man I have known best, yet I understand his life no more than I understand . . . Sandberg's, for instance. If I got to the bottom of it, I should—of this I have no doubt—discover that it is composed of an infinite number of accidents. It was an accident that Keir met Marion Bloch at a party given by a Berlin physician, an accident that he gave her a child, an accident that he ignored the child's cry for help. Free will may have had something to do with all these events—but not much. The dominant factor was chance, playful chance; almost unawares, he was captivated by Frau Bloch's beauty and distinction, surely he had no intention of pouring his sperm into her, and no doubt when the letter came asking him to take Esther under his wing he was suffering from a momentary psychological disorder, or perhaps was merely immersed in other interests. No, a destiny cannot be forged from such trifles, and they give me no explanation of Keir's trembling hands. He himself, it is true, seems to regard his guilt as his destiny. But if he asks me no questions about Esther, if he is satisfied to know that I know and lets the matter rest there, this merely proves to me that there is nothing more to explain. That morning at The Three Tuns he showed no sign of interest even when I spoke of my stay in Berlin. Later on I saw his features harden. His arched upper lip lay contemptuously on his heavy straight lower lip, and his eyes looked at me as though he were the judge and not I, who with my untold story had questioned him on the darkest point in his life. More than ever in that moment he had a baroque face, it positively clamoured to be framed in a full-bottomed wig, so as to be able to survey me with the encyclo-pedic disapproval of a Samuel Johnson. Unlike Keir I care nothing for Dr. Johnson and his times, I am no friend of the baroque age, it must have been a bombastic, hypocritical period, I respect only its music, but that is the one aspect of it Keir has no use for.

Seven

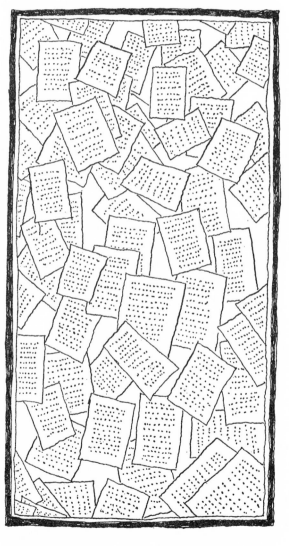

I am coming to the end. Now that it has become clear that this book is just going to peter out, I shall cease to impose on the patience of my presumptive readers and conclude my work—alas! —as quickly as possible. No, not really conclude it, just let it stop. Observe that the manner in which I now speak of readers—in the plural—is a far cry from the disparaging tone in which I referred in Chapter Three to that other being—singular!—who allegedly watched me with a sneer as I wrote. Disgusting! my pen cried out at the time, and even that contrasted strikingly with my statement in Chapter One to the effect that I was not only writing for myself. Dr. Heckmann has been begging me to delete all these contradictions from my manuscript; my repeated allusions to the private character of my notes, he writes, are pure coquetry—he's very hard on me!—but some sort of obstinacy prevents me from obliging him. In one of his letters he calls my attention—I can hear his scornful laughter—to the way in which I reeled off the names on the tombstones in the Bohemian Graveyard; "Your hero," he writes—he's always bringing in this hero who is allegedly not me!—"didn't see those names when he visited the graveyard with Anna Krystek; no, you, Georg Efraim, dug up those names in order to give your novel local colour and, still more, precision. In other words," he cries out triumphantly, "you proceeded like a novelist. And what's more, a realistic novelist: you collected material." All right, I can't deny my journalistic past, I did procure those names afterwards in order to document Anna's Slavic origins, and also because it amused me to cite them. Does injecting a few *facts* into a sheaf of purely subjective notes make me a novelist? Or organizing my *material* into *chapters?* That I am unprepared to believe. In my opinion one thing alone makes a man an author: the decision to publish what he has written. An author is a man who has signed a contract with a publisher. The crucial event between my parting from Keir in the late autumn of 1962, or rather between the account I wrote of that parting in the summer of 1965 and the writing of the final chapter of my book, has been my decision to publish. One day I fished the contract, which the publisher, that grave, elderly, well-groomed man, had sent me a year before, out of the bottom drawer of Uncle Basil's desk and signed it. After that I packed up the first six chapters and sent them *raccomandato* to Germany. Since then I have been corresponding with Dr. Heckmann. They want to publish the book next autumn. The whole idea gives me the creeps.

To avoid going to the office with Keir, I left him on pretext of having something else to attend to first. It was with a sense of relief that I closed the door of The Three Tuns behind me. I dislike having to lie to Keir. He definitely expected to see me that afternoon, for he spoke of my doing a piece about the Pope, more bad news concerning his health had come in during the night. Though I had just come from Rome, I had less information than Keir in London; I inwardly cursed our informant at the Vatican who had obviously let me down, but I pretended to know what was going on and Keir said he wanted to discuss the content of my article at the editorial conference before I wrote it. So as not to disappoint him entirely, I dashed off something about the Pope before taking my plane and posted it at Heathrow; unfortunately it couldn't be used. I crept away from Chichester Rents, did not go down the broad Strand, but slipped away westward. In the jumble of lanes round Covent Garden I breathed in the aroma of fruits and vegetables with relief. Though I did not fully realize what it meant that in order to escape from view I had dived into the densest tangle of streets in all of London, I already knew that I should never see my dear old conservative paper again. And indeed I have never since set foot on the premises, though there have been days in Rome when I've yearned for the place. I feel a kind of nostalgia for the lobby of the building, the reddish cream-colour stairway, the brass banisters that I liked to touch on my way upstairs to the editorial rooms with their light-oak panelling. After all, this piece of characterless, worn and outmoded architecture was my home for many years. Yes, I'd gladly be sitting in the library, in amongst the rows of iron filing cabinets, digging out material for some article, or rush into the telex room for a sheaf of the latest tapes that I would work over in the sub-editors' room. The years I've spent in that room! Some thirty of us, young men and women, sat at the long tables in the thin white glow of the skylights, surrounded by dark walls, practising the art of rewriting, rustling papers and pounding our tired Remingtons and Underwoods; and into this nerve centre of a network of information, shot through with personal friendships and enmities, Keir would irrupt once a day to tell us what the lead story was going to be. That was before he persuaded the owners to publish a weekly and took me with him as his assistant, allegedly because he needed at least one experienced journalist amidst all those literati, short-circuited professors, retired army officers and literary-minded M.P.'s with whom he surrounded himself; but in reality because he had to have me near him. I was the man who had known Esther, and later the man who had married Meg but couldn't prevent him from having her whenever he wanted her—reason enough for Keir to keep me with him. And so my memory of his office where I spent so many hours of my life is not so pure as my image of the sub-editors' room, for when I sat in one of the leather armchairs during the editorial conference or at smaller meetings, contemplating Keir's desk, the oak panelling, the frayed carpet, the table on which lay copies of our paper and of our competitors, the fireplace in which a few burned-out coals were crumbling away, I often recalled to mind how sometimes in this same office, in the silent latter half of the night when everyone else had gone home, Keir would reach out for Meg, and I'd rack my brains trying to work out where and in what position they would do it when desire overcame them. Enough of this! Today I've stopped—except now as I write this—thinking about Keir's office, whereas the large

composition rooms come readily to my mind as I walk the streets
of Rome or sit in some bar; my nostalgia for the newspaper feeds
on the rattling of the linotype machines, on the system of black
pipes and ladders along the white walls. I have always loved that
smell of lead. And I remember moments at night when on my
way home I would stop in the yard and look on as the millions of
newspapers, illumined by floodlights, would appear on the conveyor belt, as the bundles fell into the open maws of the lorries,
which would drive off as the next in line moved up and more
papers fell with a thud, from eight in the evening until two in
the morning, four and a half million papers full of news that
O'Connor had taken down on the telephone and I had rewritten.
I kept on for a while after my desertion that morning at The Three
Tuns, because I felt sorry for Keir and because it was convenient;
because working as Roman correspondent for a weekly provided
a relatively effortless income, I continued to communicate occasionally with the news telephones until the end of last year,
although even before I reached Soho on that foggy November
day in 1962 I knew I would never see O'Connor again. Never
again would I see him turn off his cool light-blue eyes as he took
down a story. I had been guilty of desertion, if only from a desk
and a telephone line, and sometimes at the Byron as I sat over
this bundle of notes, watching them grow steadily bulkier and
more complex, as I sat over this orgy of subjectivity that I've
been perpetrating for the last three years, I have been sorely
tempted to chuck the whole thing and go back to clean newspaper
work.

Soho reminded me that I had arranged to meet Baron Collaudi
at five o'clock in Wardour Street, and strange to say I kept this
unimportant appointment, whereas I let my far more important
call at the newspaper office ride and even stood Meg up that evening. I had already decided to take a cab to Malet Street to pick
up my bag when I found myself in the vicinity of Charing Cross
Road and idled away an hour looking into the windows of book-
shops. What kept me there was not, like that morning at Dillon's,

my love of literature, but the gruesome attraction of the jackets of pornographic books and of the obscene magazines so liberally displayed by some of the booksellers in that area that their windows are a tourist attraction not mentioned in any guide book. I was totally unprepared, and when I passed one of those shops in a narrow passage behind Wyndham's Theatre the photograph of a girl jabbed me like a hypodermic needle. The poison that flowed into my consciousness paralyzed me instantaneously and completely. Seemingly unruffled, I went my way, inspecting one shop window after another; outwardly calm, I proceeded quite methodically all the way to St. Giles Circus, but there I turned round and hurried back through side streets to the first picture. It seemed to me more provocative than the hundreds of pictures of naked or half-naked bodies that I had seen in the meantime. Twice more I returned to that picture, examined it so thoroughly that every detail, every line imprinted itself on my mind with a terrifying sharpness. I don't know whether that girl's diabolical beauty had its source in her actual body or in the retoucher's art; I must say to Meg's credit that she never did nude photographs, that she rejected that way of making money; consequently I had no knowledge of the art of retouching nude photographs. I am at a loss to say whether the rounded buttocks of this girl kneeling beside a divan, whether her firm, not too large and not too small breasts barely touching a cushion with their tips, whether her long legs, slightly parted at the knees, reflected the living reality of the girl who had lent herself to this photograph, or whether she had been stylized to produce so demonic an effect. It doesn't really matter; I only wonder why no woman of flesh and blood can arouse me as such paper women do. I who am conscious of a definite distaste for sexual intercourse, who dislike the heat and sweat of the embrace and in particular fear the ensuing sadness, emptiness, acedia—only with Meg was I able to forget it, I lay beside her in contentment, chatting of this and that—I surrender every time to paper replicas. What had driven me a few days before to my dismal occupation at the Circolo della Stampa Estera was not the

women in the streets of Rome but a film poster and the covers of
Le Ore and *L'Europeo*. It's absurd! I am aware that these pictures
show me beings who don't exist, that if this girl of printer's ink
and rotogravure paper in the window of a London bookshop were
really kneeling before me, even in a brothel, she would not be the
perfect two-dimensional commodity here on display, but something else: a body that lives, moves, smells in a certain way, has
a certain colour, says words, breathes, and would vanish in the
end because I would come so close that I could no longer see it.
Even in its vanishing it would be a living body, something that
would offer me resistance, that would compel me to busy myself
with it. I should be compelled to come out of myself, to be no
longer exclusively with myself, but with someone else. Such reflections, however, are of little help to me—the pictures are stronger.
What makes obscene pictures so obscene is that they gave one
the illusion of being able to dispose of a human body as of a dead
object while remaining by oneself. We are alone as we bend over
these seductive corpses. They are corpses, but they are seductive.
The provocativeness of this photograph of a girl was proportional
to its lifelessness. I could have bought it, but I can never bring
myself to go into a shop and buy pornographic pictures or books;
I have barely the courage it takes to buy an occasional illustrated
magazine; too cowardly to fight down my inhibitions, I can only
stare at shop windows. I am a puritan, my reflections on this subject are undoubtedly puritanical, puritanical is my fear of women,
even paper women, and at the same time I am perishing with
sensuality, it drives me to newsstands and to certain films, I feel
dirty, no, I am dirty; in my paralysis I gaze at obscenities and shun
sexual intercourse. Consequently, now that I have lost Meg, all I
can hope for is salvation, redemption, although Keir has warned
me against such notions. He's right—how can I utter such words,
I of all people, a puritan to be sure, but a puritan without God!

I calmed down. On my third visit the tension between the picture and myself relaxed, I had worn the picture out by staring at
it and now I could throw it away; bored, I left the shop window

and went, not by cab but on foot, to Malet Street which was not far away. For about an hour, until four in the afternoon, I stayed in the empty flat. In waiting an hour for Meg, I staged a kind of medieval ordeal: if, I said to myself, she comes home within this hour, I'll stay with her; if not, I'll go away for ever. She didn't come home. As everyone knows, these ordeals by fire or water didn't give women suspected of witchcraft much chance of clearing themselves. And I didn't give Meg much chance. She had said she would be back by evening—why then should I expect her in the middle of the afternoon? Of course an accident might have happened, some accidental change in her timetable, or a sudden tuning in of her highly developed sixth sense. If she was a witch, she could surely guess that I was waiting for her in Malet Street. One difference between my ordeal and those of the Middle Ages was that I wanted Meg to be proved a witch. She would have withstood her ordeal if she had demonstrated that she was in league with supernatural powers. But that afternoon the old serpent whispered nothing to her.

Collaudi seemed unchanged, and behind the green vegetation-smothered window panes of the *espresso* café, which made me feel as if I were in an aquarium swimming in a green liquid and looking out into the darkness of Wardour Street, it seemed to me that I was still talking with the baron at the Caffè Greco or in the muted windowless lounge of the Albergo Byron. But in contrast to the atmosphere of hopelessness in the airless, ill-lighted rooms where I have always met him, he himself is invariably full of plans, business ventures, and practical suggestions. He's an operator; he listened attentively to my account of my meeting with Cella, but not a word about the fee he had promised me; oh, well, I didn't mention it, because I felt sorry for him, probably because of my father I feel sorry for all businessmen, even the successful ones breathe a kind of sadness, they drift this way and that, coming from nowhere and going nowhere, they buy something and sell it, the money and merchandise pile up or slip through their fingers, I like to watch them in their aimlessness—these melancholy clowns.

Again Collaudi wanted to talk me into some deal, I think he suspects me of having money, he wanted me to invest in some production; as a diversion I told him about my parents' house which I had revisited a few weeks before in Berlin.

"All of a sudden I own a house," I said, in a tone calculated to make it clear that I owned nothing else.

"Not bad," he said with a knowing air. "A house like the one you describe, a villa in good condition in that part of Berlin, is worth several hundred thousand marks. What are you going to do with it, Herr Efraim?"

Not wishing to encourage any business propositions, I told him I was planning to sell it so as to be able to write for a few years in peace. He caught my meaning at once and made no further attempt to draw me into his deal. But he was very much opposed to my plan.

"You're out of your mind," he cried. "That's no reason for selling a house nowadays when money isn't worth anything. Let it. You can get at least a thousand marks a month for a house like that. That's enough for you to live on, a man like you. You don't need much, you're not even married. . . ."

I must have looked at him with something close to consternation. Why hadn't I hit on so obvious an idea? I had been obsessed with the desire to sell the house as quickly as possible, to cut this last tie with my childhood. Instead I took Collaudi's advice and held on to it. Some time in 1963 it was awarded to me. The linguistic sensibility of the Berlin authorities came as a complete surprise to me: the papers they sent me said nothing about making amends, but spoke only of restoring my property. Since then Frau Heiss has paid the rent into my account at the Banco di Roma punctually on the first of every month. I wrote that charming lady a long letter imploring her to go on living in Bismarckstrasse and assuring her that our relations were radically changed by my becoming her landlord, that there would be nothing to prevent her from inviting me to the house—if I ever came back to Berlin.

True, my use of if and the conditional shows that I have no intention of setting eyes on Berlin again.

It wasn't until last summer that I was obliged to dip into my receipts from the rental of the house; up to the end of 1964 I continued to draw a salary and expenses from the paper, so that I was able to build up a small capital reserve which now, along with the rent checks, enables me to live as an independent writer. John, with whom I once discussed the economic aspect of the profession, told me bluntly that I couldn't expect to live even frugally by writing, unless my books sold at least 20,000 copies and I turned them out regularly and at short intervals. By the way he looked at me, I could see that he doubted my ability to carry out such a program. "If you're lucky," he said, "and if your publisher knows what he's doing you'll get small grants, but it's mostly the radio stations that will keep you going. Don't expect anything of translations, of so-called international success—it brings in very little. Well," he added with his cold Rhenish intonation, "at least you and I aren't married men, that's a help." He doesn't know I'm married. And I haven't told him that I'm a house owner and therefore independent. I often wonder what attitude I should take towards the economic system in which I am hoping to ply the writer's trade. Strictly speaking, there is no such trade in our economic system; if you're not unusually successful, you've got to support yourself by all sorts of expedients while at the same time keeping up a front, giving the public the illusion that you live exclusively for your work. Consequently I ought to fight capitalism. On the other hand, chance, the totally planless, chaotic and therefore to me congenial principle which governs the capitalist system, has thrown a piece of private property my way, just enough so that the income I derive from it enables me to write what and how I please. I'm a lucky man. Like few of my colleagues, I enjoy a measure of freedom. John, who knew nothing of my good fortune, felt called upon to show me a way out. "Find yourself a patron," he said. "Don't laugh. They still exist." Since then I have given thanks to the small Berlin dealer in leather and hides who bequeathed me his house. He was my first patron and will be my last. I have no need to beg wealthy humanists for alms. Nor would I. I'd rather go back to journalism.

Of course Meg would always be willing to support me. She makes enough for two. But now I have the house. That deprives me of my last pretext for going back to her.

"Good God, man," writes Dr. Heckmann apropos of this passage in my concluding chapter. "Enough of your delaying tactics." I sent it to him separately and he shipped it back by return post, apparently after spending a bad night over it. In the margin I read remarks such as *Come to the point* or *Unnecessary loss of pace*. Over my discussion of my economic situation he really seems to have split a gut. *Delaying tactics* is good. Didn't I, at the end of Chapter Four, point out expressly that I must play slowly and cautiously if I hope to win my game against the book. I must prevent the book from playing its trump card. But that's not what Dr. Heckmann wants. He sides with the book. "Lose!" he writes. "Lose like a man, quickly and resolutely!"

It's easy for him to talk. Oh well, if that's what he wants. You get tired, the light hurts your eyes, and meanwhile, impassive and relentless, your opponent, who holds the card that will take the trick, watches you. You give up. Lorenza, the baron tells me with an airy wave of the hand when I inquire sympathetically after his girl-friend, has run off. Yes, with an Englishman, to whom she was a Roman revelation.

"I expected her to get on in London," he tells me. "That's why I brought her here. To tell you the truth, I wanted to get rid of her. Too messy; she was getting on my nerves."

He's not joking, no, he means it. He's the melancholy type of operator. He complains about Lorenza's messiness as though his own life weren't messy. A life full of senseless business deals strewn about cheap and messy hotel rooms. Cautiously I steal up on my quarry.

"Have you any connection with Cameron's new film?" I ask offhandedly.

His manner becomes subdued. Up until now he has always spoken of financing, fund raising and that kind of thing, as if he were about to become a producer; now it becomes clear that his position is on a much lower level. From his incoherent grumblings I gather that his work is in public relations, that he is doing the German-language publicity for the picture. But that's enough for my purposes, it means that he knows what's going on.

"Is that photographer girl in on it?" I ask in a conversational tone. I manage to bring out her name as if it had just occurred to me. "Meg Ellis."

"Oh, yes," he says. "And if the picture's a flop it'll be her fault. That girl wants everything her own way, you can't imagine." And he shakes his head in indignation over Meg's inordinate demands.

"There's a difference between wanting your own way and getting it," I object.

"You don't know her," says Collaudi. "She's a shrewd customer."

"You mean she sleeps with Cameron?" I ask.

He shakes his head and gives me the information for the sake of which I kept my appointment with him.

"Not with Cameron," he says. "She's much smarter than that. They say she's having an affair with the producer."

He gives the name of the man with whom Meg is supposed to be having an affair. Miller, Mitchell or something of the sort. An American.

"She's my wife," I say.

"Oh," says Collaudi horrified, "I *am* sorry." And he adds reproachfully: "How can I be expected to know that somebody by the name of Ellis is your wife?"

That's just it. The baron can't possibly know that in reality Meg was never a Mrs. Efraim. Meg has never been anything but Meg. Even her maiden name doesn't mean a thing. Margaret Ellis from Stoke-on-Trent, daughter of a family of potters, descended from at least six generations of "working-class nobility"—all that is nonsense. Meg is Meg.

"Oh, well," I heard the baron say. "You know how film people talk. Maybe it's not true."

On the one hand he sounds sincerely concerned over my feelings, but on the other hand he sounds as if he were already in divorce court, under pressure from me to testify that he has surprised Meg *in flagrante*. But at this moment I am no longer in this aquarium, this *espresso* café in Soho, where the baron and I are swimming about like elderly fishes, old inhabitants of the place, who from time to time bump their mouths softly against the glass walls. It's dark outside. Night in Wardour Street, whereas in Malet Street just now when I went to get my bag and waited an hour for Meg it was still light, a misty light fading into dusk. The baron has no way of knowing that his information has upset me very little. It doesn't interest me much to know that I'm a cuckold. What matters to me is not my wife's infidelity. She can go to bed with anyone she pleases for all I care. I'm well aware that no one can own a body. Or a soul. Not permanently at least, not lastingly, without deviations. The one thing that interests me is that rocking chair. In Malet Street just now I spent a whole hour thinking about it, that piece of Victorian bentwood furniture in Chichester Rents. I lied when I wrote that I didn't know what mechanism made Keir and Meg tick. They always did it in this rocking chair. The chair creaked. How do I know? Meg told me. Not voluntarily; I forced it out of her. At first. Later on she spoke of it voluntarily and repeatedly. In the end we couldn't even make love without talking about that rocking chair. That's why I took my bag an hour ago and left, as I did a year ago and two years ago, and the time I went off to Dalarne. I'm an ass. I ought to accept that rocking chair. Meg would love me for it; it's not as if she despised me when she made it creak; not at all, she admired the courage with which I faced up to it. Perhaps she despises me a little since I've been running away from it. "You should learn to live with it," she said once. She's a strange woman.

I look at the card which has at last been thrown down on the table, and suddenly I'm filled with unspeakable horror. The game is over. I feel sick, I step out on the balcony on the fifth floor of the Albergo Byron to catch a breath of air, the air of an October night in Rome. Today for the first time since that Sunday in Berlin three years ago I worked not in the morning but from late afternoon until far into the night. The air refreshes me. And sobers me. My malaise is gone. I am simply cold stone sober. I light a cigarette and lean against the wall. I smoke. Smoking, I recognize that I've spent the mornings of three years on a banal *ménage à trois*. A plain ordinary triangle story, one among millions. The book's trump card, which I have been waiting for all this time, is an insignificant sick joke, nothing more. My cigarette tastes like cotton, I press it out against the iron rail and throw the butt down into the silent chasm of Via Borgognona. Can that have been it?

Dr. Heckmann will be able to tell me what it was. He's one of those people who can explain everything, even Auschwitz. Sociologically. Historically. Medically. He knows the mechanism, he understands the gears which connect cruelty and subjection in the machine of love and death. He even knows why babies are tossed into the air and shot to pieces like clay pigeons, and that will make it easy for him to explain my case. Here in all fairness I must add, at a later date, that I underestimated the man. He hasn't said a word about all this but merely done his job: he has confined himself to formal criticism of my book.

On leaving Collaudi, I took a cab to Heathrow. Of course the last plane for Rome had left; I was obliged to spend the night in the airport lounge. The chairs are comfortable. Until about midnight I waited for Meg. She was to be in Malet Street by dinner time; she must have noticed at once that my bag was gone and could easily have worked out that there was a chance of catching me at Heathrow. But I waited in vain. Perhaps she thought I had moved to a hotel as I had the year before. And probably she decided, as she had last night, that I must come to her of my own free will. It was up to me to choose. The declaration of unconditional surrender must come from the defeated. But she could have met me half or quarter way. If she had stepped through one of the big glass doors at Heathrow that night, I'd have capitulated once and for all. I'd be living with her in London and not be here in Rome, which is beginning to bore me.

To kill time after midnight when I stopped waiting for Meg, I wrote the article on the Pope for Keir on the thick, lined octavo pad which I had bought the day before on my arrival in London, at Barker's in Kensington High Street. I folded back the light-blue cover and wrote: The Pope is very small and very broad. He has himself driven about Rome in a black car. In front sit the chauffeur and a priest. In back sits the Pope alone, a short truncated cone. The Pope has the biggest ears I have ever seen on a man. Enormous ears. The Pope is a small elephant. Deep within him the Pope has a cancer. But he doesn't mind because he is so old. Except that he is sometimes in pain. The Pope remembers: *We saw an enormous fire and men were throwing things into it. I saw a man who was holding something that moved its head. I said: "For the love of God, Marusha, he's throwing a live dog into it." But my companion said: "That's not a dog, it's a baby."* He was able to look on. He did nothing to stop it. And He claims to be God. It's high time we found ourselves another. That's what the Pope is thinking. And then his car is gone. I tear off the paper, slip it into an envelope and send it to Keir. He didn't use my Pope story. He fumed over the phone. And yet I adhered strictly to the rules of journalism: nothing but *facts*, every sentence a fact.

That day and night, the day and night of Thursday, 15 November 1962, the devil got into me. It all happened at once: my break with Meg and my good-bye to journalism.

For a time I went on writing for the paper, with my left hand so to speak, because I had seen Keir's hands trembling and because it was financially convenient for me. I didn't give up for good until Keir ceased to be editor-in-chief. He retired to Cambridge, where, as he wrote me a few months ago, he is holding a seminar on Marcion.

I can't find a proper ending for this book. It's finished, that's

all. How strange! I had expected it to end differently. I don't
know how, but differently.

I meant to conclude with an account of my literary plans for
the future, I wrote it too, but Dr. Heckmann said no, this time so
firmly that I gave in. He said nobody would be interested. Well,
he ought to know.

Now I'm going over the manuscript again in accordance with
his instructions. On his boss's advice, I've decided to change my
name, which obliges me to change the names of the other characters. A back-breaking job. "And all this hocus-pocus doesn't
help me in the least," I wrote to Dr. Heckmann, "because it
won't prevent my wife from reading the book."

"Your character Meg," he wrote back, cold as ice, "can congrat-
ulate herself on her role. Your hero is an idiot not to have stayed
with that woman."

That was the first and last time Dr. Heckmann indulged in an
opinion on the content of my book. Otherwise his criticism has
been purely formal.

He's even more obstinate than I. With unswerving obstinacy
he took me out of myself and transformed this Efraim into my own
hero. One night not long ago, on my way home to the Byron, it
dawned on me what an opportunity I had missed. I was free to
make something else out of Meg than an English photographer,
to make Anna a girl from somewhere else, Orléans or Solothurn
for instance, and Keir . . . hm, whom could I have turned Keir
into? Just about anyone. In Via Sistina I suddenly stopped in my
tracks for it came to me that I might have changed myself from
the German Jew and English journalist that I am into someone
entirely different. As I continued on my way, I considered all sorts
of masks I could have adopted. When I came to the square outside the church of Trinità dei Monti, I stood for a long while
leaning against the stone parapet. I looked down the stairs, wondering whether I shouldn't rewrite my book from start to finish.
My thoughts turned to my little philosophical quirk: if chance is
the great underlying principle, if, as I have insisted so tediously

throughout my book, I might just as well have been an Italian, a Negro, a wolf, or a motor car as a Jew, Englishman, and German, then there was no need to unmask myself as I have done.

But the same train of thought helped me to evade a task which had lost its appeal for me. If it makes no difference who I am, I said to myself: I might as well go on being myself. Among all the masks one has to choose from, perhaps oneself is the best. Perhaps, it finally occurred to me—though I dismissed this thought, first as illogical and later as mere sleight-of-hand—perhaps it doesn't even make any difference whether I have written or been written.

And yet, immersed in the problem presented by the possibility of transforming an intransitive into a transitive verb, I made my way down the Spanish Steps through the impressive illumination which the municipal government of Rome projects upon its monuments, and vanished round the corner past the newspaper stand which was already closed at that time of night, and after a few steps in the darkness of Via Borgognona entered my hotel.